THE KING

by

Ivy Fox

After Hours

To
Hope you enjoy this
one.
wink wink
love, Ivy Fox

Copyright

The King – After Hours Series Copyright © 2018 Ivy Fox

All rights reserved. No part of this publication may be reproduced, distributed, or transmitted in any form or by any means, including photocopying, recording, or other electronic or mechanical methods, without the prior written permission of the author, except in the case of brief quotations embodied in critical reviews and certain other noncommercial uses permitted by copyright law.

This is a work of fiction. The names, characters, places, and incidents are a product of the author's imagination or have been used fictitiously. Any resemblance to actual persons, living or dead is entirely coincidental. The author acknowledges the copyrighted or trademarked status and trademark owners of all word marks, products, brands, TV shows, movies, music, bands and celebrities mentioned in this work of fiction.

Editing by Sandra Nguyen Editing: A Fresh Set of Eyes

Cover image, formatting, and edit courtesy of X-Factory Designs

https://www.facebook.com/pg/X.Factory.Designs/shop

For more information, visit:

https://www.facebook.com/IvyFoxAuthor/

https://ivyfoxauthor.wixsite.com/ivyfox

ISBN: 9781726618984

Dedication

To my King
For making me feel like a Queen every day since
the moment you came into my life.
I love you, Baby.

Prologue

EDIE

You're probably wondering who I am.

Me?

I'm no one.

No one of importance, at least. I'm not rich or beautiful, as are most of the women I find running around this office. And there are many since I work for one of the most illustrious fashion magazines in the country.

No, not that one.

The other one.

Royal Magazine. This one. The one that everybody who is anybody would sell their grandmother off to, just to be on the cover. You see, fashion magazines aren't only for the wafer-thin, drop-dead gorgeous model types. Now actors, actresses, musicians, socialites—hell, even politicians, get a crack at being plastered on the Royal pages. The only thing they have in common? Money and charisma. They need to have that *it* factor to even be a contender on any of the pages of this high-end fashion magazine.

Now, I don't want to sound bitter. I'm not. Truly. It's just… coming to work every day and living amongst the beautiful people, when I am anything but, kind of sucks sometimes.

So why do I stay, you ask?

Two reasons.

First, I work for my best friend whom I've known since kindergarten. My mom was her in-house nanny, and when my dad left, I became a permanent fixture to the Richardson House. Devina was just a bit older than me, but right from the get-go, she and I became each other's confidants—almost sisters, even. The only time we ever parted was when she went to an Ivy League school down in Boston—yeah that one—and I stayed put to go to NYU, thanks to my big brains and maybe even a few strings pulled by Devina's mom. Both of us studied business, but while Devina is fully focused on numbers and figures, I'm more of a people's person. So when she came back to New York to take a seat at Royal, I wasn't surprised when she called up asking me to be her personal assistant once I graduated. Thanks to her, I know everybody that has any weight in this town, and they come to me directly if they want anything from Devina. So I get a lot of people kissing my ass on a constant basis, but I also have to translate her blowing them off as diplomatically as possible. Not always easy. So, yeah, I love working with Dev behind closed doors. It's when I open said doors do I get to see the other reason I love working here.

The King

Dean Knox.

My Achilles' heel in every way it counts. Always immaculate in his Gucci suit, the man oozes confidence and apathy. I have seen half-naked models making absurd figures of themselves to get his attention, and yet the man is stone cold. He enters the office each morning without even hinting a smile to anyone. Unless he is talking to his sidekicks—his best friends from college who also work at Royal—he rarely says much of anything, really.

But he watches. God, does he watch. He is one of those people who lies back and takes everything in until he's made a judgment of you before you've even said a word to him. How do I know he does this? Well, while Dean watches his adversaries, I watch him. Pathetic? Maybe. Can a day pass by without me doing it? Hell to the no! Being a no one has its advantages, after all. A man like him doesn't even know I exist, and I've been working for Dev—who, I might add, is his fifty-fifty partner in Royal—for the past two years. Been in the same office with him numerous times. Been to staff meetings, boardroom assemblies, and social gatherings—with him at every one—more times than I can count. Yet he's never once spoken to me more than a few odd words here and there. Still, I live for these moments.

Okay, now I sound pathetic, but believe me, if you ever crossed Dean Knox's path in your life, you would probably not be too proud of your antics, either. Think of the hottest guy you ever came into contact with. Yeah, you got that picture in your head?

Good. Now double that hotness by a thousand, and even then I'm not sure you're in the same ballpark. You see my dilemma now?

I live day in and day out amongst the beautiful people, yet I only have eyes for one.

And he's the reason I both love coming to work and hate it.

Because being reminded you are a no one kinda sucks when you desperately want to be someone's someone.

Chapter 1

EDIE

"Edie, are you really wearing that to work?" my roommate Lexi asks, eyeing me up and down in distaste.

"What's wrong with what I'm wearing?" I ask, unaware of why she's giving my ensemble the thumbs down.

"I think my grandmother wore the same thing last weekend to our family dinner. On her, it looked sharp. On you, though, it just looks so wrong in so many ways."

"Oh, shut up. It's conservative. Perfectly acceptable for a day at the office," I tell her, walking over to the counter and pouring myself a good, hot, steaming mug of delicious coffee. Coffee is life, people. Anyone telling you otherwise is absolutely bonkers.

"White blouse with a brown skirt can be considered okay for where I work, which is not the high-end fashion magazine where you spend every moment of every freaking day," she huffs out dramatically.

"You're exaggerating, Lex. I don't spend *all* my time there. It's just that Dev really needs me right now. The magazine is doing so well, but to stay on top, you have to work your ass off."

"Yeah, whatever. Still, it wouldn't hurt you to look hot doing it," Lexi sing-songs, wiggling her eyebrows at me.

"Did you miss the part when I told you I'm surrounded by gorgeous models every day? I could spruce up all I want and still not look even half as good as those girls. So there is no point in waking up an hour earlier just to look my best. Conservative and proficient works just fine for me, thank you very much. With the added bonus that I get to click the snooze button at least three times before I have to get out of bed," I brag, knowing how Lexi usually is up at the crack of dawn to look like a million bucks. While I'm still snoring up a storm, my roommate has already done a full hour of cardio, showered, blow-dried her hair, put on her warrior makeup to accentuate her wardrobe of choice of the day, with still plenty of time to spare to make us both breakfast. I envy her morning drive, but I wouldn't trade my two extra hours of blissful slumber for anything in this world. Especially if my dreams contain a certain sexy billionaire CEO—but I digress.

"Not if you still want to get in Dean's pants. How is the guy supposed to notice you when you hide that bombish of a figure in granny wear every day?"

I sigh in defeat because this conversation with Lexi

is as old as time. She thinks that putting on some red lipstick and a short mini would be enough to turn any head, even that of the most eligible bachelor in New York City. She just doesn't realize that no set of wardrobe or makeup would get his attention. I've never seen a man more immune to female seduction than Dean. I have seen models, and even actresses trying to get his attention to no avail. He's never had a girlfriend that I can attest to, nor do I see him in the society pages going out with numerous women. That task is left to his best friend and marketing director of Royal Magazine, Connor Walsh. He's infamous for his sexcapades, while Dean is known for his no-nonsense attitude and workaholic ways. I don't think the man thinks of anything but work. Honorable as that may be, it kind of saddens me how he has no time for real human affection. His circle of friends includes playboy Connor and the quietly intense Sebastian Kelley, who also works at Royal as finance director. The three men are tighter than the skinny black jeans Lexi's showing off.

"At least take your hair down. Give them something to look at, for crying out loud," Lexi goes on as she rummages through her bag, making space for her beloved laptop.

"The bun is fine. Having my hair out will only get in my way," I say, pushing my black-rimmed glasses up the bridge of my nose. "And anyway, I refuse to take the advice of a woman who dyes her hair every color of the rainbow once a month," I tease.

This month, Lexi is sporting a vibrant pink, which

looks amazing on her but would look ridiculous on me. Prim and proper is the way to go in my case. I'm paid to be invisible anyway, so wearing vibrant colors would only be a distraction to the purpose of my job. Devina likes my discretion as well as my ability to be in a room, hearing and seeing things most people wouldn't realize I was privy to. It pays to be a fly on the wall, and to most people who work at Royal, that is exactly what I am.

"Yeah, yeah, yeah. One day, Edie Vanderwalt, you'll want more in life, and then I'm positive your freak will show, too." She grins a pearly white smile at me, and I laugh at her for even thinking I have any 'freak,' as she calls it, in me. I think boring is more my style. I'm fine with boring; I'm comfortable like this—even though from time to time, I do wish I was a little bit more adventurous. Maybe if I were, I'd finally get a certain someone to take notice of me. But I'm so off his radar, it's not even funny. More like depressing.

"Oh, I forgot to tell you. That movie studio called again. They sure are persistent, aren't they?" Lexi remarks, halfway out of the door of the box we call an apartment.

"Same message, I gather?" I exhale.

"Yep, same one. They said they could have a plane ticket ready for you whenever you change your mind," Lexi states, and I see the tension in her eyes, concerned I may take them up on their offer and leave her to venture out to California.

"Cali is too sunny for my liking, so they can keep their plane ticket. They'll tire of the chase sooner or later," I say, trying to ease her worry.

"It's a great opportunity, you know. I'm sure Devina would be okay with you ditching her to become the go-to PA of one of the biggest movie studios in the world. I bet the pay is also more than what she's shelling out," she continues, biting her lower lip.

The pay is almost five times what I'm getting now. Mind you, Dev pays me well enough, but if I were in this business for the money, then California would be a no-brainer. One of the executives saw how I dealt with their most high-maintenance actresses and was so impressed he offered me a job on the spot a month ago. I, of course, refused politely, but it seems the studio can't take no for an answer. They have plenty of problematic cases, where a person like me— who likes to solve problems before they arise, or effectively clean up the mess when they do—is a hot commodity to have on the West Coast.

The thing is, I like my job at Royal. I love working for my best friend. Sure, it's long hours, and it's grueling at times, but I usually have fun doing it. Going off to California, where I don't know anybody, would be ideal if I wanted a fresh start, but life is good as it is. And of course, there is the other issue at hand. There's no Dean Knox in California. And even though he doesn't know I exist, I live and breathe that man. No way am I going to sever the only line I have to be in contact with him, even if only from afar. Yep, my crush, as well as my loyalty to Devina, were the only things keeping me in New York. Sure, Lexi and my mom living on the East Coast doesn't help matters in persuading me to uproot my life to Hollywood, either. I couldn't leave either of them in good conscience. They are the only family I have, so it doesn't matter how many calls I get, or how many perks they offer, my answer will always be no.

"Lex, I've made up my mind, so don't sweat it, okay? Now get going before you're late for a big scoop or something," I tell her as I throw the kitchen towel her way to hurry her along. Lexi's genuine smile springs up, taking up her whole face, with the reassurance that she won't be losing me to La La Land.

"It's not a scoop, unfortunately. It's investigative reporting of some labor law that didn't pass, Edie. It's boring as fuck, and I wish Tom had given this story to someone else who could stand being cooped up in a room reading a bunch of boring legal jargon, instead of praying for a natural disaster to happen to shake things up," she replies, rolling her eyes.

"Jesus, Lex, please tell me you're kidding? You don't actually pray for bad shit to happen just so you can get a better story for your newspaper, do you?" I ask, my eyes wide in disbelief, and a bit worried that my friend is a little psychotic when it comes to her job.

Lexi just gives me a wink and a smile, throwing the

kitchen towel back into my hands and strolling out the door without giving me an answer. If Lexi thinks I'm obsessed with work, then she needs to take a long, hard look in the mirror. She lives for that newspaper, just as much as I live for Royal. We were roomies back in NYU and recognized the drive and ambition we each had in our respective fields. It was probably the first thing we connected over, but while my life is now a predictable occurrence, Lexi is still driven by adrenaline and craves it on a constant basis. Being locked up in any room is not her style. I shouldn't be surprised she gets down on both knees praying for that one story that will distinguish her as a proper established journalist. But still, wishing for bad stuff to happen has bad karma written all over it.

With Lexi now gone, I grab my purse, put on my jacket, and take one quick look at the silver-framed mirror in our hallway. I slump my shoulders when I confirm that I do look like an old maid. Maybe Lexi's right. Perhaps if I shook things up a bit, my boring routine would get some life into it.

Guys, again, I'm okay with my life as it is.

Really!

But lately, I have been feeling lonely, which is weird since I enjoy being alone whenever I can. I'm usually around so many people, most of them loud, arrogant, and obnoxious, that when I get home and pour myself a glass of chardonnay, I instantly relax, feeling gratitude for the silence.

But lately at night, I find myself missing something, craving something I don't yet have. I'm not sure where these feelings come from, but they are there, right at the surface, whispering how there must be more to life than this. Am I really happy with my life, or have I just accommodated to it? Am I confusing happiness with mere contentment?

I'm not unsatisfied with my life enough to do something as drastic as moving all the way to California, but maybe I'm just no longer happy going through life as I have been. The fact I haven't had a boyfriend since college might be a factor. I've had little human intimacy in the last three years, and I think it's finally catching up with me. I'm twenty-four years old and in my prime, and yet I live like an old woman with five cats as companions. I don't actually have five cats, but you get the idea.

I'm in a rut. That's it.

A rut of my making, and it's caught up with me. Sparkling green eyes come to mind, and I shiver in place. Dean is my rut. He's the reason I don't even look at other men. But it's so hard to, when perfection prances around in his sleek suits, rubbing it in my face Monday through Friday.

Okay, enough of that!

I shake my head, trying to remove all thoughts of the Adonis, and tell myself to have this pity party another time. Right now, I have to pull myself together and get my ass out of the apartment before I arrive late for work. Of course, no amount of skill is enough to prevent myself from thinking about Dean when, in an hour or so, I'll be going to the first of various meetings taking place throughout the day, where he will also be present.

It's hard not to obsess on someone when you have to be attentive to their every word.

Who am I kidding? I'd obsess over him even if he said nothing at all.

Chapter 2

DEAN

Devina waltzes into my office like she owns it and shows little regard for my personal space. I ignore her like I do most days, and continue to read the latest report of this trimester's numbers. I'm happy to see we are trailblazing light-years ahead of our competition. I'm in too good of a mood to let Devina's little demonstration of power affect me in any way, but I still hope that whatever has brought her here will not dampen it. As always, her demure sidekick is at her heels with her trusty iPad and in-ear phone, waiting on Devina hand and foot. Devina places both hands on my desk, staring daggers at me. Whatever has got the blonde Ice Queen's panties in a twist, I bet a million dollars it has something to do with our marketing director, which also happens to be one of the closest friends I have in the world.

"You said you were going to keep him in line, yet I just found out he used our company plane to go to Milan this weekend," she grunts through gritted teeth, and it's a miracle my office doesn't burn to the ground with the fire her eyes contain.

"This is a fashion magazine, Devina. Milan is one of the top high-fashion cities in the world. Why is Connor's trip so upsetting?" I say coolly, going back to the reports in front of me, unintimidated by her temper.

"If the trip were on the books for business, I wouldn't object. But him flying across the world to get foreign pussy cannot be deducted on our tax return, now can it?" she trails on. I notice her PA stifle a laugh, and when she sees I've caught her snicker, she immediately turns crimson and lowers her eyes back to the device in her hands. I turn my gaze onto Devina yet again, who is still fuming, and cross my arms over my chest, still unfazed.

"The trip wasn't on the books because it was last-minute. And I doubt very much that him meeting with Donatella Versace herself—so we can get the inside track of her next launch—needs to be scheduled beforehand. After the deal was made, Con could have fucked the whole of Italy, for all I care. And that is no concern of mine—or yours."

Devina goes red in the face from both anger and humiliation, but she is nothing if not consistent in her comeback.

"And it took him the whole weekend, did it? What if another unexpected opportunity arose and the plane was needed?"

"Yes, Devina. It took all weekend, and no emergency that you speak of happened, so your point is moot. Now if you'll excuse me, I have more pressing matters to attend to, than to continue debating a futile what-if scenario that will only waste my precious time and yours," I state, finished with this conversation.

I don't look up from my reports, but I can hear her grinding her teeth, enraged that I'm immune to her tantrum. Devina, taking the hint that I'm done with her unscheduled visit, leaves like the hurricane that she is. I then look up to see her assistant still fixed in place, though, her eyes glued to my scowling face.

"Is there anything you need, Miss Vanderwalt?" I ask the woman who is dressed more like a dull librarian, bun and all, than the fashion assistant to one of the world's most prestigious magazine's managing directors. She shakes her head and starts to make her way out the door, only to stop on its threshold.

"Mr. Knox?"

"Yes, Miss Vanderwalt, what is it?" I ask, annoyed, since my previous cheerful disposition is no longer present and accounted for, and I doubt will make a reappearance anytime soon.

"If you wish to maintain Mr. Walsh's alibi that he was meeting Ms. Versace over the weekend, then maybe it's best if you change the dates on the agreement Royal had done with the Versace house last Thursday. I know for a fact you did this deal personally, and, well, Ms. Versace was also photographed over the weekend by the paparazzi in Paris, not Milan."

I feel the corner of my lip wanting to lift in a grin, but I school my features enough for the woman before me not to think her quick reasoning and astute knowledge of all the Royal dealings has impressed me—although it has, and it is a rare thing to have gained such a sentiment from me.

"I'll see to it," is my only reply.

She nods and leaves my office without saying a further word. I fall back on the chair and place my palms over my eyes. It is barely noon on a Monday, and I already feel a migraine coming on. So much for the good mood I had been enjoying. Of course, anything that pertains to Devina and Connor's feud has this annoying effect. These two have been on each other's nerves since we attended Harvard together. Worst of all, they don't limit their war to only themselves. No, they had to bring innocent civilians and bystanders into the equation.

I push a button and tell my secretary to summon Con to my office, and Bash, my finance director, as I'm sure he was the one to give the green light to the unexpected expenses that Con's weekend partying accumulated. They both need a little talking to, and just like children, I doubt my scolding will be heard.

Twenty minutes later, both are seated at their preferred places—Bash on the couch looking at the New York skyline, and Con in front of me, cocky as ever, wearing a satisfied grin.

"I'm growing weary of these games you continue

to play with Devina. You promised that if we all took over Royal, we would do it in a professional manner. Yet both you and she act like infants at every turn." I scowl, wanting to inflict my headache on his cocky ass.

"What did the witch accuse me of now?" Con asks smugly, knowing damned well what my next words would be.

"Using company resources for your own benefit," I deadpan, sitting on the edge of my desk, tapping my fingers repeatedly on the smooth surface.

"I think Dean is referring to your joyride this weekend—mainly using the company plane for your own benefit and not Royal's," Sebastian adds in, rolling his eyes at my friend, confirming how Con's little antics are also wearing his patience thin.

"I was just giving a ride back home to some of the models from Friday's shoot. It's not my fault they live in Milan and not the Bronx." He laughs out loud like this is all a game.

His carefree attitude was always something I admired in Con back at school, but not so much now that we are all heading a multi-million-dollar business. Con needs to be taken down a notch. He needs restrictions to be set in place, especially when it comes to tormenting Devina.

"Next time you feel the need to be so chivalrous, pay out of your own pocket. Or at least be smart, and buy them seats on coach out of the modeling expenses. I couldn't give a rat's ass. Just don't do stupid shit like this just because you know Devina will get wind of it. She's been even more insufferable the past couple of months, and you, instigating her at every turn, is making my life hell. I like my life, Con. What I don't like is Devina's screeching howls first thing on a Monday morning because of the elaborate stunts you think will get a rise out of her. Understood?" I raise my brow, daring him to defy me.

He nods, defeated, even though I know for a fact I'll be having this goddamned conversation with him again in a couple of weeks. It's a vicious circle with these two—if it's not Devina bitching about Connor, it's Con about her.

"Both of you should just hate-fuck each other and get it over with," Bash states, and I'm in total agreement with his observation. A good fucking would do wonders for both of them, in my opinion. But Con just shuffles in his seat, acting as if Bash had just told him to screw his grandmother.

"If I want my dick to shrivel and die, I might consider it. Until then, it's going nowhere near Devina's ironclad pussy," Con spits out, rising from his seat. "We done here?" he asks, apparently not liking the way our conversation is going.

"Yeah, we're done," I tell him, lifting my arm and showing him the door. Worse than a cocky, arrogant Con, is a pissed off, pouting one. And Bash's suggestion did the trick in getting him to sulk like a five-year-old; he can't help but chuckle at our friend's hasty retreat from my office.

"You know how sensitive he gets when you say shit like that. Devina is the guy's kryptonite," I remark, walking back to my chair.

"The day he realizes why she is, it's the day he will no longer protest the idea of screwing her pretty brains out," Bash states somberly, rolling his shirt sleeves up to the elbows. I'm inclined to agree with Bash, but Con's business is his alone. It's only when it messes with Royal business do I give a shit.

"I'll make it up to him tonight. I was thinking of having a little nightcap at After Hours once we were done for the day. Care to join us?" Bash asks, with a hint of mischief in his dark gray eyes.

"Unfortunately, I'll have to pass tonight," I answer him, even though the idea of going to our private club does appeal to me—and would end this crappy day on a better note than the one it started in.

"Are you sure? The three of us haven't had some fun in a while," Bash coaxes, throwing in his idea of the type of diversion he's expecting to have tonight. I rub my chin, contemplating how a little amusement might be just what this day needs.

"Come get me before you leave," I relent.

Bash's smirk is branded on his face when he leaves

my office, knowing full well that our playtime is always the way I like to end the day. However lately, I've become hungrier for a little more than what the club is able to offer. I keep my eye out for any new talent, but it's been slim pickings as far as any diversity goes. Everyone seems to lack the certain fire and innocence I crave, but still, I go thinking maybe tonight is the night such a creature will land at my feet. New York tends to hold the jaded and apathetic, but at the club, their truest desires come out, and I love to watch it unfold. My cock starts to stir at the thought of having a pretty little thing at my mercy. I still haven't found what I'm looking for, but it hasn't stopped me from taking pleasure from the runners-up.

Maybe tonight will prove different. Even if it doesn't, my visit won't be in vain.

It never is.

Chapter 3

EDIE

Another grueling day catering to models who think they are the next Naomi Campbell or Gisele Bündchen when in reality no one will even remember their names come this time next year. Still, overseeing that every photo shoot goes without a hitch and report back to Devina, it's one of my daily tasks. Everyone knows I'm her eyes and ears, so they play nice for my benefit, at least.

I'm starving since we've been at this shindig for hours, and these girls' idea of food is sparkling water and cigarettes, so of course the buffet table is less than stellar. Since everything looks like it's dying down, I make up my mind that there's really no need to stay a minute longer. My jacket and purse are in the changing area, and I'm already daydreaming about going to Joe's Pizza and grabbing a slice or two as a reward to this tiring day. I'll probably end up eating a whole pie and feeling lousy in the morning but screw it. That greasy pepperoni is already calling my name.

I'm halfway dressed, and my skin starts to prickle when I overhear the name Knox on one of the model's lips behind a big-ass hanger of designer dresses. See, this is when I should acknowledge that I have a real problem when it comes to Dean since the mere mention of his name makes my whole body take notice. But being trapped in this stupid photo shoot means that I've gone without seeing him all day, forgoing my daily Dean dose, so just hearing his name does stupid things to my stomach. We're talking about a whole other type of hunger, people. Something that not even a slice of Joe's pepperoni-gooey deliciousness can fix. My feet have a mind of their own when I close the distance between me and the hanger rack to hear what the two girls on the other side of it are saying.

"I heard you can get all three at After Hours," one of them whispers, but even though there is techno nonsense blasting away in this room, it still isn't loud enough to tamper with my hearing.

"That place is an urban legend. So is the possibility of getting into one of their pants, let alone all three at the same time," the other one scoffs, applying some gloss while looking in the mirror, obviously more in love with her reflection than with her friend's conversational skills.

"I'm telling you, it's true. One of the runway models I worked with in Madrid swears she got all three of them, and it so happened to be at one of the soirees at the After Hours club," the platinum blonde whines.

"Really? Well, if we're paying attention to idle gossip, someone also told me that even if the place does exist, it has a strict policy of making their guests completely anonymous. Like, they wear masks or some BDSM crap like that. How could this girl even know it was them in the first place? Hmm? She just probably said it to impress you. Or better yet, to show off," the ebony diva answers, pleased with the image the mirror is giving her, even when scowling.

"Now don't you be stupid enough to tell this lie of a story to anyone else. If people in this place heard those types of rumors and traced it back to you, they'd fire you in a heartbeat. Your ass will be escorted out onto the street by security faster than you can say the words After Hours."

The blonde continues to bite her nails in contemplation of her friend's advice and nods once she realizes the raven goddess may have a point. I, on the other hand, wish she hadn't ended the blonde's conversation so quickly. I wanted to find out more about what the hell this After Hours club was, and if one of the men she was referring to was, in fact, Dean Knox.

My Dean Knox.

Pizza already forgotten, I take the elevator to the last floor to locate someone who might know if this story is true. I mean, if I'm going to gossip about something, it's going to be with my best friend. Of course, it doesn't hurt she knows everything about anything that is happening in this city. It's well past eight, and of course, I'm not surprised to see Devina still working hard as ever and looking immaculate doing it.

"I really don't know how you do it," I grumble, wanting her magic potion, and to look as impeccable as she does after ten hours on the job. I'm wrecked and look it. My hair is a mess, I have a run in my stockings, and there is a blotch of coffee on my skirt, which I spilled after one of the crew accidentally bumped into me downstairs. I look ready for a bath and a twenty-four-hour stay in bed. But not my best friend. She looks like she just stepped out of the shower, totally rejuvenated and ready to take on another ten hours.

Devina is my total opposite in the looks department, too. While I try to hide my curvy body, she flaunts hers in any man's face, unapologetic in appearance and attitude. I know what the rest of the magazine thinks of her. She is brash and quick to judge, but to me, Devina is the sweetest friend I have. Loyal to a fault, she would put herself in the line of fire to save the people she loves. She's a fighter. Always has been, always will be. Me? Not so much. Confrontation is not my thing. Devina, on the other hand, seems to live for it.

"Caffeine, Edie—and lots of it," she jokes, raking over, one last time, the article written by one of the magazine's favorite journalists. Her frown speaks volumes of what she thinks about it.

"What's wrong?" I ask, walking behind her desk, leaning in to take a peek at the article in question.

"Nothing. It's fine. The article is fine," she mumbles while leaning back in her leather chair.

"Fine, but not amazing, is what you're saying," I add, knowing Devina only wants greatness to be printed out in her magazine's pages. "What does the editor-in-chief have to say about it?" I query, knowing that if it's reached Devina's hands, then it would need to have had her approval.

"Sam is fine with it," she spits out, and I know the word fine is irking her to no end.

"But you want more," I conclude. She nods, defeated.

"I do, but it seems all I'm getting is the same old recycled shit every other magazine in the world is printing out."

"Well, that can't be right if you looked at the numbers I showed you this morning," I tell her, knowing full well that Royal is high above the rest, and the figures for this trimester alone are solid proof.

"I saw the numbers, Edie. I did. It's just… this magazine could be so much more, and it drives me up the wall when I see it doesn't. I wanted something fresh, innovative, maybe even taboo, but yet, they continue to send me the same old drivel." Devina exhales, placing the palms of her hands over her eyes.

"It's a fashion magazine, Devina. Don't expect a Pulitzer," I tease, trying to bring my dear friend's expectations down a notch.

"Anything is possible, Edie," she counters with her wicked grin in plain view.

I laugh at her arrogance, since I know full well, if anyone can pull something like that, it will definitely be Devina. I have never met a person so driven to succeed in all things than the friend at my side.

"What are you doing here so late, anyway? I thought you'd ditch the photo shoot long before now," she asks.

"It took longer than expected, but the photos look hot. Better than fine, at least." I sit my ass on her desk and place my hands on each side of the table, so I don't fall off."I heard something tonight, and I was wondering what your take on it was," I tell her, and Devina's brow raises.

"Oh, gossip! I feel like we're in high school all over again," she says sarcastically, but I know she's just as curious to what I've overheard.

In one quick breath, I tell her everything the two models were bickering about downstairs, and while I do it, I carefully study Devina to see if the name After Hours rings any bells. Of course, it's the sex part which grabs her attention.

"All three, you say?" she asks, looking at her perfectly manicured nails. "Lucky girl," she adds, smiling, not concealing for a minute that she's imagining such a scenario.

"Yep. Lucky girl," I repeat sullenly.

I move away from the desk and walk to the white leather couch next to the high glass windows. Dean has the same view from his corner office, and I wonder if he lies back on his couch to enjoy the scenery. Maybe he does, with some flawless model straddling him, while his best friends watch. Since the two girls downstairs put the possibility of some stranger enjoying not only my Dean—I know he's not mine, people, but my heart won't listen to reason right now, so deal with it—but also his two sidekicks at the same time, I'm both intrigued and gutted.

"I have to say, it surprises me. I mean, Connor seems the type to like those sorts of things, but Sebastian and Dean seem too level-headed to go to some underground sex club to get their kicks."

"Devina, don't do that. Don't judge something without even knowing what it is. And stop always making Connor into some sort of deviant. He's a nice enough guy, and you're always tormenting him."

"Edie, *you're* nice, not that douche out there. Trust me, he is not *nice*. He doesn't have one *nice* bone in his body. He's a womanizer and a cocky, arrogant jerk to boot. His friendship with Dean and Sebastian is his only redeeming quality.. If a club like After Hours does exist, believe me, Con has a full day pass to it."

"Fine, I won't say another word about Connor Walsh. But do you think this story is true, or just some made-up gossip?" I ask, biting my nails nervously. Devina looks up at the ceiling in thought, and I see the wheels turning in her head.

"The name isn't strange to me, that's for sure. I'm positive I've heard the name After Hours before, I just can't remember when and by whom. I'm almost inclined to say it was at the Met Gala a couple of months ago."

Yes! Jackpot! If Devina's heard of it at that party, then all she has to do is put out feelers to the guests who attended and see if anyone bites.

"Please, please, let's check this out," I beg, sitting up straight, giving her my puppy-eyed look.

"Why?" she asks suspiciously.

"Just because. Aren't you a tad curious?" I say, trying to downplay my excitement.

"Not one bit. Why would I be curious about a place that probably looks like a dungeon and has women wearing too little leather to cover the parts which should always be covered?"

"Well, when you put it that way, it's not much different than coming to the office," I joke, nervous that Devina won't let me investigate this further.

"Funny, Edie. Very Funny. I'm not curious at all. And neither should you be. Especially you," she deadpans, pointing the finger at me.

"Why especially me?" I ask surprised.

"First of all, you're still a virgin," she whispers as if the walls have ears when we are the only two at the office at this hour, still this work-obsessed. "A club like that is no place for a young woman who has been guarding her virginity for all this time."

"I haven't been guarding it," I reply softly, hating that she had to go there, of all places.

"You haven't, huh? Then why are you probably the only twenty-four-year-old New Yorker who still has her hymen intact?" Devina continues making her point.

"I just haven't gotten around to it, that's all. Between trying to graduate with high grades from college, and then coming here, I've been too busy." And if I'm being honest, I've been too much into Dean for the past couple of years to even think about sex with anyone else but him.

"No one's too busy for sex, Edie! After Hours is a case in point. A place where people make the time to hook up with total strangers just because it feels good. If you're not guarding it, then for the love of God, let's go out this Friday night, get our drink on, and pick the lucky winner who will finally see the color of your underwear," Devina chants out, excited with the prospect of me giving away my V card.

"Now who's the funny one?" I answer, rolling my eyes. "I'm not picking up a stranger from some bar to lose my virginity," I tell her, making it clear her suggestion doesn't thrill me.

"Exactly my point. If you're not going to do something that millions of women do every day, how the hell are you going to be comfortable enough to go to a hardcore club like After Hours?"

"So you're not going to help me?"

"Yeah, I am. I'm helping you by telling you to let this go. No good can come out of your curiosity. Trust me. Been there, done that," she replies softly.

I know Dev doesn't like telling me no, but she hates it even more when I get hurt. I should have thought this through better. Crestfallen, I stand up, feeling dead on my feet, and now hurt. She hasn't said it outright, but I know the real reason behind her lack of enthusiasm for not supporting me on this new whim of mine. It all comes down to Dean. Being my best friend, well, my sister, really, she knows me inside and out, and feeding my obsession with a man who barely makes eye contact with me, is what Devina considers as dangerous territory—unhealthy for my mental state, and more importantly, my inexperienced heart.

"Please don't be angry at me, E," Devina pleads, concern tattooed on her face.

"I'm not. Just tired. I think I'll head out," I reply.

"You want to grab something to eat? A slice at

Joe's, maybe? My treat," Devina adds, wanting the smile back on my face.

"Rain check, okay? I'm really tired, and tomorrow is going to be another mad day," I explain, and my justification seems to appease Devina's logical side—even though saying no to pizza is one of the first signs of the apocalypse to me. As long as work is the reason to turn things down, Devina doesn't find it odd at all. I can always count on that to mask sullenness.

"Okay. Good night, then, E. Love you."

"Love you, too," I repeat, and walk out the door. Sure, I'm disappointed my best friend won't help me learn whether the rumors are true or not, and I understand her reasoning and love her for trying to protect me, but something in me needs to know if such a place is real. Dean is such a reserved man that it seems improbable that this place, if it even exists, holds any appeal to him.

But still… What if it's true?

If such a place does exist and he engages in sex with total strangers, then I need to know. Most importantly, I need to get in. This might be the only way he sees me without actually seeing me. Before I've even reached the elevator door, my melancholy mood is nowhere in sight, and in its place, is a trace of hope—that maybe I can get close enough to the man who holds me captivated and will somehow share my bed, and as Devina pointed out, end my virgin status once and for all.

Yes, please!

And maybe, just maybe, this might be the way I can also get close to his heart like he's embedded in mine.

Devina may have closed the door at getting answers, but I'm excellent at breaking and entering.

Chapter 4

DEAN

"I think you're having a midlife crisis," Connor belts out of nowhere, looking intently at me as if he's trying to solve some metaphysical problem. The lighting around the club is dark, setting the mood for the usual lascivious activities, but I can still see his brows furrowing from where I'm seated.

"What the hell are you on about now?" I ask, shrugging off his unwanted concern.

"I think what our little Prince is trying to say is that we're not used to our King not enjoying the spoils the land provides," Bash adds, his smug grin in place, sitting by my side.

Bash and his damned theatrics. It's not like anyone is within earshot and can hear us or anything, but still, there was a time where I enjoyed playing my part in our little games, so I can't fault him for continuing the charade. But the past couple of months my heart hasn't been in it as much. Every time I hold 'court' I'm reminded of how shallow I've become. I truly am king of everything and yet of nothing of actual value. It's depressing. Maybe Connor is right. Maybe I am having some form of crisis, even though it feels it's more of an awakening instead. Still, saying out loud to the two men sitting next to me that meaningless, no-strings-attached sex has lost its appeal, will have them calling New York's finest psychiatrist team in a heartbeat. Con and Bash love the game too much to lose their taste for it. So I scoff and take another big gulp of my whiskey and ignore the two best friends I have in the whole world, as well as their lingering stares.

"What's wrong, Dean?" Con asks outright this time.

"Nothing," I state, my boardroom expression in place.

"Well, something is. Come on. Out with it."

"Why do you think anything is wrong, little Prince?" I taunt, leaning back on the velvet couch, playing with the chalice in my hands.

"Well, because you've been acting like a monk for the past few months now, and it's starting to freak me out," he hushes this time, even though no one in our midst can hear our conversation.

"Didn't know you kept tabs on my dick, Con. You switching sides now?" I mock him further.

"Fuck you and your ten inches, Dean!"

"Measuring my cock doesn't look good for your argument either, little Prince," I chuckle, feeling a little bit lighter for the first time since we entered the club. Con just flips me off and sits back in his love seat, disgruntled that I'm not taking him seriously.

"I have to say I agree with Con though, Dean. You have been a little bit off lately. Haven't been playing as much," Bash adds, stealing my light mood away with his somber statement.

"Nothing new there. You know I'm fonder of watching, anyway," I deadpan.

"Freak," Con coughs, with a knowing gleam in his eyes, while Bash smirks at my response.

"Fair enough. Still, it's not like you not to partake once in a while,"Bash continues.

"Haven't seen anything I like recently."

"That's it? Is that the only reason?" he asks, not fully convinced.

Between the three of us, Bash has always been the one with the most inquisitive nature, and can usually smell bullshit a mile away. But after a curt nod as my only response, he has the good sense to let it go. Hell, it's not like we're going to braid each other's hair and talk about our feelings and shit. They sense something is up, and even if I can't pinpoint the root to why I've lost my taste for this type of diversion, that doesn't mean I'm going to rain on their parade. It just means I've got to find something else to lighten me up—and the damn of it all, I can't fathom what that is.

Here's the thing. I have everything I ever wanted. I worked my ass off all my life to get to where I am now. All the aspirations I set up for myself when I was younger, I achieved before the age of thirty.

Graduating Cum Laude from Harvard—check.

Running the number one fashion magazine in the world—check.

Kickass penthouse with a view of Central Park—check.

Made it to Forbes Magazine as one of the most influential people under thirty—check.

Check.

Check.

I did it all. Everything I'd strived to do, and then some. I should be smiling twenty-four-seven and letting every fucker know I'm the *luckiest* asshole there is in this city. Because I got it all!

I *am* the fucking King in this city.

So please explain to me—why the hell do I feel so hollow?

See, this is why I can't tell my friends what's rummaging through my head. They've known me since college, and know how hard I've worked to get where I am today. They wouldn't understand me now if I told them that everything I've achieved isn't what I expected. I thought I'd feel something different. I thought I would feel accomplished somehow. And yet, all I feel is empty, like a big void inside me. I mean, I love my life, I do. And I'm grateful for it, I am. But it still feels lacking somehow. It's the oddest sensation.

And here in After Hours, where the faceless people pass by, the void is that much more persistent. As if it's screaming out at me at every turn, suffocating me with jaded smiles and shallow kisses. My breath is ripped from my lungs each time I feel yet another lukewarm hand touch my thigh with their usual advances. These bored, rich housewives and socialites looking for their next thrill feel like death to me, and yet, not so long ago they were exactly what I sought out to give me life. But I've done my time, and I've seen enough to know that the search for more can never walk through the doors of the After Hours club.

Whatever I'm searching for, whatever I need, I guess I'll know it when I see it.

Until then, I got Bash and Con, and apparently wingman duties to perform in a better fashion if I want to get them off my back.

Putting a pin in my inner turmoil isn't new anyway.

And being King means never letting them see you falter.

Chapter 5

EDIE

"Edie Vanderwalt?" asks the man on the other end of the line.

"Yes, this is she," I answer while continuing to type my notes of Devina's last meeting.

"You have recently queried about getting a pass to the After Hours club downtown, for Ms. Devina Richardson, is this accurate?"

I bite my lower lip hard, not only excited for someone to finally be giving me a callback, but also because I don't want the person on the line to hear the blatant lie I'm about to tell. Yes, it's true, I sure as hell have been going around asking for more info on the club, using Devina as my way in, for the past few of weeks and the worst part is she has no clue what I have been up to. She would lose it if she ever found out I was dropping her name in places she wouldn't be caught dead in, and to people she wouldn't even make eye contact with, let alone speak to them. Going behind her back has been torture, and doing it with a straight face has been a true testament of my flawed character.

I have sunk to a whole new low, people. Using

connections and Devina's influential name to open doors—that I know for a fact she would never want me to even think of knocking on—is beyond shitty. So as a reply to the British voice on the phone, I mumble something incoherent. I mumble and hope the man on the other side of the phone takes it as my confirmation. I'm pretty sure I'll be lying my way through this phone call as it is, so let's see if I can minimize how many fibs I lay on the chap. I mean, I should at least get brownie points for that, right?

Yeah, I didn't think so.

"Please, tell Ms. Richardson the After Hours club would be delighted to have her in attendance. This afternoon, we will drop an envelope with instructions and a key pass, as well as the address of the club. Shall we address this envelope to Ms. Richardson, or to you, Miss Vanderwalt?"

"To me!" I yell, grabbing the attention of everyone in the open office area. I scrunch down in my seat and put my hand over the receiver, attempting to act cool the second time around with my response. "I mean… to me. For discretionary purposes, you understand. It's best any correspondence between the club and Ms. Richardson should pass through me, her personal assistant," I state, more in control of my voice.

"Of course. We will have a messenger drop by no later than three. Please, also have Ms. Richardson's last physical report ready, as this is required from our guests."

Shit! I should have expected the club to have such policies in place. If everyone was having sex willy-nilly, then everyone must have a clean bill of health. Who wants to go to a place to rock their socks off and leave with a nifty STD? No one. I'm being dishonest with both Devina and this British guy, but I refuse to be so unscrupulous as to not sending my own medical records.

"As a forethought, Ms. Richardson has this documentation also in her possession. However, it has been altered to bear my name instead. Will this be an issue?"

"None whatsoever, Miss. Many of our guests also use pseudonyms as a way of not having a paper trail. Again, as a precaution, a medical appointment will be scheduled with our own in-house doctor to verify any and all reports. The day and location of the medical exam will also be delivered with the documentation you'll receive this afternoon."

Jeez, these guys don't play around.

"Very well, thank you, Mister… I'm sorry, I didn't get your name," I ask, realizing the posh voice on the other end of the line didn't introduce himself.

"My name is of no importance, as Ms. Richardson will soon establish. Good day, Miss Vanderwalt."

"Good day," I repeat.

Holy mother of God! This is happening! And I thought that after all these weeks, all my pesky little inquiries were leading nowhere, but apparently, someone must have big connections and wants Devina to show up in a bad way.

Only she's not the one showing up—I am. If Devina even suspected I was going through all this trouble, lying through my teeth just to get in through the front door of such an establishment, she would be both proud of my audacity and terribly disappointed about how low I stooped to get my hands on Dean.

But I'm not like her. Men can't help but notice my best friend and crave her attention. They hardly even look at me twice. You guys are getting the picture of who's the DUFF between us, right? Yeah, I came to that sad realization eons ago. The thing is, while men tend to throw themselves at her feet, she would rather walk on top of them than give them the time of day. She's become a real man-hater since college and over the years it's only gotten worse. It's so uncharacteristic of the girl I grew up with and I wish she would confide in me.

But since I'm keeping this little whopper a secret, it's a bit hypocritical of me to want her to share what's in her heart, when I deny her what mine wants. I mean, as far as she knows, she thinks I'm over my little office crush. It took forever for her to believe me, too, but it had to be done. Her knowing the truth was worse than my little white lie. Devina is, for the most part, like my big sister. She would do anything in her power to protect me, and getting my heart broken from a silly little office crush wasn't high on her list of things she wanted me to experience.

Her exact words.

So aside from Lexi, I haven't told a single soul of my crush on Dean. It's so damn cliché, having the hots for your sexy billionaire boss, isn't it? I would rather eat dirt than have anyone find out. That's why going to After Hours is so appealing. I'll be able to get close enough to him, without him knowing I'm the trusty assistant of his business partner. I mean, how awkward would it be for the poor guy to learn of my crush? Yep, staff meetings would definitely feel tense if he ever found out. But being in a different environment, where only the elite and beautiful are in attendance, he wouldn't expect me to be there in a gazillion years!

I'm so giddy, I feel like I'm in high school waiting for my prom date all over again. He was a dud, by the way. Dean, I highly doubt it.

The next couple of hours feel like torture. Not only do I have to make sure to be available when the messenger arrives and discreetly pocket the damned envelope he's bringing, but I also have to make sure no one—and when I say no one, I mean Devina— sees the exchange. Otherwise, she might get curious herself and ask me what it is.

When the mystery man on the phone said a messenger was coming, I assumed he meant a bike messenger, like the ones the magazine is used to receiving. Very laid back, usually wearing jeans, raggedy-ass t-shirt, and the aura of a guy who's smoked too many blunts the night before. The person who arrives, though, is anything but. This messenger looks like he just stepped out of the magazine pages himself. Wearing a tailored black suit, fitted perfectly to his well-built frame, he looks more like he was here for a photo shoot instead of handing over the details of New York's clandestine sex club. Still, even though his stature isn't one bit discrete, his way of knowing just whom he should approach is. Without even making eye contact with any other person in the office, he walks straight to my cubicle and hand delivers those precious papers that I've been dying to get my hands on. I thank him graciously, and he leaves me to my business. Carefully making sure no one saw the exchange, I put the big-ass brown envelope in my purse and leave a post-it on my computer, explaining I had to take off early. Devina will be too busy to notice my absence anyway, and if she needs me, she usually texts me.

By the time I get home, my skin is prickling with excitement. I run to my bedroom, not even making sure whether Lexi is home or not, and sprawl out on top of my bed. The first pages are all rules I must abide by. It feels a little like the intro to Fight Club.

The first rule of After Hours: do not talk about After Hours.

The second rule of After Hours: DO NOT TALK ABOUT AFTER HOURS. Jeez, I get it.

The third rule: Never divulge your name to anyone, not even staff. No personal details such as place of work, residence, or family should be discussed.

The fourth rule: Always wear a mask. It can be painted on or worn, as long as it disguises you enough from being recognizable.

The fifth rule: You must freely hand over medical reports of the last physical and meet the After Hours physician before participating in any intimate acts as well as monthly check ups thereon after once becoming a member of the club.

The list went on and on, and the gist was the same—anonymity above everything else; both of the premises and of the people who attended. If any rule were broken, I would be blacklisted and most likely sued.

A non-disclosure agreement is also amongst all the paperwork, with the request to be signed and delivered before visiting the said establishment. They also provided an email account for me, as well as their email address for all future correspondence, and a drop box so I can send those documents they want signed—in blood, apparently; I'm kidding. But after ten pages of rules to follow, I almost expected to read that demand in the fine print or something.

My doctor's appointment is scheduled for this Friday, which means I could engage in anything I want in only two days' time. Still, it's not fast enough.

In the folder, there is also a number I could call to set up my first visit. Tonight, I think, is as good as any night to get some answers. All I had to do is text the time I would arrive, and someone would be there to accompany me and show me the ropes. My curiosity would be fed sooner than I thought. All I need now is to look the part of being Devina, and for that, I'm going to need the appropriate wardrobe. Not thinking twice, I call the woman herself.

"Devina here," she answers without checking her phone ID.

"Hey, Dev. Do you mind if I go over to your house and borrow that little silver Chanel dress you bought in Paris last year? You know, the one you never wear? It breaks my heart every time I see it on the hanger."

"Of course. What mine is yours," I hear the smile in her voice. "But I do have a condition."

"And what's that?"

"You have to tell me why you want my over-the-top, lean-me-over-the-counter-and-take-me-right-here dress. Change your mind on what we talked about? Or did the guy I saw you talking with this afternoon have anything to do with the sudden urge of looking fuckable?" She laughs.

Jesus, Devina never misses a thing. I thought this afternoon's encounter with the tall, dark, sexy messenger didn't make it onto anyone's radar, but apparently, I was wrong. Might as well use it to my advantage.

"Something like that."

"So is it a date, or are you just going cruising? Because if it's the latter, you know I'm a great wingman." Devina continues chuckling.

"You suck at being a wingman. You scrutinize every poor guy who even tries to talk to me, and then list each flaw you can find as to why they aren't good enough."

"What can I say? I have high expectations for any guy who's going to whisk my Edie off her feet. He has to have it all. Otherwise, he's not the one."

"You know that's ridiculous, don't you? *I* don't have it all, Dev. I barely have half of it all," I affirm.

"Don't be silly. You have what every man should want," Devina deadpans like I'm missing the plot.

"You mean my virginity?" I ask since I really don't have anything else I can come up with that is at all alluring.

"No, dufus. A heart of gold," Devina confesses, and if it weren't the dorkiest thing she'd ever said to me, I would have been flattered she thought so highly of me.

"Now you're the one being silly."

"Just saying, I don't want you to settle for less than a man who is worthy of you, that's all."

"This from the one woman who, just a few weeks ago, wanted me to sleep with a total stranger to get my virginity out of the way," I spat, wishing she could see my eye roll.

"That is totally a different thing. Sex is sex. It doesn't have to be with the perfect guy. Just the right dick. ."

"Always the romantic, Dev," I huff out, exasperated with how my friend has done a one-eighty these past few years. I still remember our slumber parties in her room, watching *The Princess Bride*, how she used to fawn over Westley and wish for a love like that. Now instead of the girl with stars in her eyes dreaming of her own prince charming, I have this watered-down version instead—a bestie who doesn't mind hooking up with a stranger, as long as he doesn't want to cuddle afterward.

"So, do you know where he's taking you, at least?"

"Dinner. Dancing, maybe." I lie.

"Gotcha! So it is a date with that hunk who came over this afternoon? I want all the juicy details on how you two kids met, but it's already late, and you gotta get cracking if you want to go over to my house and grab my dress," she squeals in an excitement I no longer feel.

Yeah, lying to Devina is not my favorite pastime. Actually, it's probably the shittiest thing I've done, and her happiness for my fake date only makes me feel even crappier as her supposed best friend. I'm going to hell, guys. The small corner in that inferno destined for lousy friends is exactly where I belong right now.

"Okay. Talk to you soon, then," I meekly reply, hoping she doesn't ask me anything else.

"Sure, babe. Have fun tonight. Love you, E," she sing-songs, genuinely excited for me.

"I love you, too, Dev." I really do. And if one day I man up and tell her what I've been up to, I hope she finds it in her heart to forgive me.

I look back to the bedspread and see the taunting documents looking back at me—the same ones that apparently made me become the world's biggest liar.

"Well, if this is what I've sold my soul for, might as well see it through. I'm going to hell anyway, so let's see if this ride is worth it."

I grab my phone and use the number given, requesting my first visit.

Tonight, we'll see if After Hours is worth all this shadiness.

Because, God help me, I know it in my heart that

Dean is.

Chapter 6

EDIE

"You are not Devina Richardson."

Fuck!

I look wide-eyed at the Englishman in front of me, in his blue suede Tom Ford suit, looking more annoyed every minute of me being here in his office in my get-up and war paint.

"Hmm, I'm sorry?"

"I was expecting Devina Richardson this evening, and you, Miss, are not her," he states matter-of-factly.

Well, he does have a point. I am definitely no Devina, but the way he's scrutinizing me in this spectacular ensemble that I've got going on, I should at least get a thumbs-up for being in the same league tonight.

Man, I was so close, too. I mean, I got my foot inside the building and everything—which is kind of weird, by the way. I was expecting the address of this illicit night-slash-sex club to be some warehouse or an underground establishment of some sort, but instead, it is a swanky building on the Upper East Side. So not what I was expecting. I mean, how the hell is a club supposed to be here anyway?

When I walked through those doors, the doorman immediately showed me into the elevator and pressed the third-floor button, like he knew exactly where I was headed. Lo and behold, this guy was there waiting for me and ushered me into this apartment, which looks more like the office space we have back at Royal headquarters, cubicles and all. And now, here I am, sitting pretty, sweating bullets under his watchful stare, feeling as if I've committed some sort of major crime and been caught red-handed doing it in his personal corner office.

"So who are you, Miss?" he finally asks, looking as if he's bored of this charade already.

Damn it all to hell.

"I thought we weren't supposed to say our real names," I say, hoping my deflection helps me, even though I know I've been busted and now there is no way I'll know where the real After Hours club is.

"Miss, I won't ask again. Who are you?" he repeats, his British accent coming out more crisp, probably a sign that he's coming to his wits' end.

"My name is Edie. Edie Vanderwalt," I relent, sullenly.

"Ha. I see," he says, slumping back in his leather chair as if this makes all the sense in the world. It probably does to him. He probably sees this type of scenario every day. The low-level employee, using their boss' name as their way in to mingle with the high and mighty. God, I feel like such a loser. Those types of people are usually gold-diggers and leeches. All I wanted was to get closer to the guy I've been pining over for years, but I guess I'm no better than they are.

"Yes," I say, my shoulders deflating, as well as my hopes of ever getting close to Dean. It's a pity we're only on the third floor, 'cause I'm pretty sure my withered hopes would jump out the window and say something along the lines of *Sorry kid; you tried. See ya!*

"Alright, then. So, will this arrangement be for the whole experimental month?" he questions while fixing his bow tie.

"Excuse me?" I ask, not knowing what to call him since I still don't know his name and he hasn't offered me one at all, even though he's demanded mine and, well, I'm still too busy throwing myself a pity party to be paying real attention to him anymore. "I'm sorry, I didn't get that?"

"I'm referring with the arrangement Ms. Richardson has put in place with you, Miss Vanderwalt. It isn't unusual for members to send their personal assistants or discreet staff to get better acquainted with our establishment before entering our fine establishment themselves. That is why we always offer the one month free trial as a precaution," he explains, using perfect enunciation.

"Oh… Oh!"

"Yes, so again, will this arrangement of yours be for the full month?"

"Yes!" I yell, which gets me my first scowl from the prim and proper gentleman in front of me.

Take it down a notch, Edie. Don't spook the man with the keys to the castle now.

"I mean, yes. After Ms. Richardson has received a detailed report, then she'll consider membership," I explain, making sure each word is perfectly pronounced, mimicking the man himself. When his whole face lights up in approval, I see I did well.

Win!

"Very well, I'll make a note of it. Please make sure to advise me if this changes in the meantime. All alterations to the contract with After Hours should be done beforehand, you understand," he explains, his features far more welcoming and relaxed now that he's given me his seal of approval.

"Of course," I add politely, biting my inner cheek to keep a cool façade instead of jumping up and down like I want to.

"I see you have already submitted everything today, and that Ms. Richardson will be doing the physical this Friday, is that correct?" my nameless host asks, looking down at the tablet on his desk, swiping left to right, zooming in on the documents I sent earlier this evening.

"Yes." I nod, keeping to my one-word replies as my own safety precaution.

"Brilliant. Am I to assume that you will not be taking any hands-on activities and will be just a spectator?" he asks, still focused on his screen.

I place my hands over my bouncing knee on that little note.

Yeah, I am definitely not going to abide by that rule, buddy!

"Of course not. I will only observe what your fine establishment has to offer and report back. However, I will need to engage with guests and so forth to get the real feel of the area. You understand?" I state with my no-nonsense tone; the one I've mastered working at Royal these past few years.

"By all means, do what you must to give Ms. Richardson the most detailed and *satisfying* report at the end of your visit," he counters, and I don't miss his not-so-subtle hint on how he expects Devina to be a member this time next month, with the glowing report I'm supposedly going to hand in. Again, all I do is give him a tight grin and nod, and it seems to appease him greatly.

"Splendid. Well then, let me accompany you to the lift so you can meet your hostess and start your evening," he says, standing from his seat, and it dawns on me that he's ready for me to get this show on the road, but I still have a few questions of my own.

"Oh, but before I go, I do have some questions. I promise I won't take much of your time. Do you mind?" I ask politely, seeing as this stranger has shown his hand in responding well to such efforts.

I see it does the trick when he sits back down, no longer in such a hurry to kick me out of his office. Since he doesn't look as menacing, I have to say he does have that whole Clive Owen thing going for him. Very elegant and poised, black wavy hair with streaks of gray, and fit for a fifty-year-old. If he didn't work for a clandestine sex club, I would totally hit him up for his number.

Not for me, you guys! For my mother. Jeez!

Have you not been paying any attention? I'm a one-man type of girl, remember?

"Alright. Please, Miss Vanderwalt, how can I be of assistance?"

"Well, first of all, your name would be lovely. Since you know mine, I believe it is only fair I know yours. I feel awfully silly talking with someone for the past half hour and not even knowing their name, don't you think?" I remark, with a bit of amusement.

And for the first time in the thirty minutes I've been in his presence, a small smile graces his lips.

"Pardon me for my rudeness. You're absolutely right. I'm so used to not offering it, I forget that some people take issue with not knowing who they are conversing with. My name is Slevin."

"Slevin?" I repeat, intrigued at the peculiar name. Not the posh English name I expected at all.

"Yes, Miss. I am your handler and the only one who knows both your and Ms. Richardson's true identities. No one else will have this information, as I've said. We take discretion to be one of our key elements of running our business. I alone will be privy to this information. You have my word."

"I see. So if I have any questions, and I email After Hours by using the address that came in my package this afternoon, you're the one who will reply to it, no one else?"

"Correct." He smiles again like a proud teacher would.

I suddenly feel like I'm in a warped version of a spy movie, and Slevin here is about to hand me my kill papers. Is this really how rich people get their rocks off? I'm sure this whole secret-agent vibe Slevin has got going is part of the appeal, if not the entrée to the main course of the After Hours menu. I mean, it's almost as if I'm talking to 007 himself, with how sleek and cool he looks right now. He really is quite dashing, if you like the silver fox thing. My mom would go nuts for him. Still, no digits for her. I would never be able to set her up with a man who runs such a shady business. I'm all good with entering such a world. No matter what Devina thinks, I'm not that naïve. My mom, though, is a whole different story. This guy right here has trouble written on his forehead. Even if it is written in great penmanship.

"So another question, Slevin. How much will Devina, I mean, Ms. Richardson be shelling out to pay to be a member, anyway?"

"Miss Vanderwalt, those details are all included in the member's handbook," he points out.

"Hmm, handbook?" I shrug, having no clue what handbook he's referring to.

"Correct. The one we sent with the paperwork," he adds.

Come to think about it, I did hear something crash to the floor when I opened the envelope on my bed this afternoon. When I went to check, though, I thought it was the latest of Lexi's romance novels that she keeps insisting I read. But since it looked like a damned encyclopedia, I put it on my nightstand instead, completely ignoring it, so I could get cracking on the ten-page document that needed my real attention. Was that the handbook Slevin is on about? What the hell was in those pages? The Kama Sutra or something? It was massive!

"Hmm, sorry. Ms. Richardson must still be reading it," I lie. It's not like I'm going to read that whole thing.

"Fair enough. She should be getting acquainted with it herself, though I do strongly suggest that you read it as well. I will forward a digital copy this evening to your email address. However, to answer your question, the monthly membership is twenty-five—"

"Hundred? Well, that's a little steep, don't you think?" I say, outraged that anyone would pay two thousand and five hundred dollars just to be a member of an elite club to get their freak on.

"No, Miss Vanderwalt, I meant twenty-five thousand dollars," he chuckles, seemingly amused that I thought twenty-five hundred was even a possibility.

"But that's over a quarter million a year," I stutter, shocked.

"I know that to you, or even me, it seems like an exaggerated amount, but believe me, for the experience After Hours provides, it is worth every penny, and its members can well afford it."

Three hundred thousand a year to get laid seems excessive, if you ask me. I mean, what the hell am I going to find in this place? Genitalia laced in gold and diamonds or something? Suddenly my waxed hoochy rubbing against my silk panties doesn't seem all that special.

"Hmm," I reply, not wanting to say more on the subject.

I have to say, knowing that Dean shells out this type of cash to meet women, and maybe even sleep with them, doesn't sit so well with me. I mean, with that type of money, he could be doing so many other things—things that could actually help this city, not just his libido.

"Are there any other questions you would like to clarify now?" Slevin inquires.

"Yes. Just one more, Slevin. Is the club very far from here? Will I still be able to visit tonight?"

"Of course, Miss Vanderwalt. I will bring you up in a minute and introduce you to your hostess, as I informed earlier on. She'll stay with you for the next couple of nights until you're fully settled in."

"So it's here, you mean? In this building? The club?"

"Yes." He offers yet again an almighty grin.

"But how is that possible? How can a club even be here? I mean, what about the neighbors? Don't they suspect that something isn't right, with so many visitors arriving in masks and all?"

"I see you are a very inquisitive woman, Miss Vanderwalt." He smirks, not hiding how pleased he is with my incredulity.

"Just trying to understand, that's all. I don't mean to offend, Slevin," I remark, not wanting him to think I'm putting holes into his boss' business.

"You haven't. It all means you're taking your job seriously. I admire that. I'm a perfectionist myself," he puffs out proudly, and I almost slap myself in the head.

Great. Even Slevin has totally bought my cover-up story. I'm getting better and better at this lying thing, and I don't know if I should be thanking my lucky stars or worrying that I'm becoming pathological.

"This whole building belongs to us, Miss Vanderwalt, which means the neighbor issue is a moot point. And in regards to the club itself, you'll see soon enough. However, I strongly advise you to read the handbook, so you'll understand how the whole process works. Agreed?"

I smile and nod, which gets me another bright grin from the no-longer-stern man I was greeted by earlier.

"Well, enough dilly-dallying, as they say. Let me take you to Poppy. She'll give you the grand tour and answer any other questions you may have tonight."

"Poppy? I thought we weren't supposed to know each other's names?"

"We're not. Poppy is the name she goes by here. Have you picked out yours while you're with us?"

"No, not yet," I confess. If Slevin knew the trouble I went to get myself through the door in the first place, I bet he would understand how a made-up alias was the least of my concerns for the night.

"Well, you have time. For now, just introduce yourself as Lady. It's generic enough until you pick your own, and the members are accustomed to the introduction as a temporary one, should you offer it to them. It is understandable not to have a name prepared, but we will need one to update our records with, once you've made up your mind. So, are you ready?" He stands up from his seat, and I imitate the motion.

"As I'll ever be, I guess?"

"Did you bring your mask?" he queries.

"Oh yes, of course. Do you have a mirror?"

Slevin points to a door in the corner of his office. I stand up on wobbly feet and find, for the first time since I left the apartment, how nervous I am. After such an interrogation, and Slevin's hefty price tag, suddenly my excitement has dimmed, and my nerves have taken over my whole body.

Once inside the pristine, lemony-scented bathroom, I remove the black lace mask from my clutch bag and place it carefully over my eyes, making sure it's fastened tightly. The last thing I need to happen tonight is to come all this way and get outed on my true identity because of a faulty accessory.

I take one quick look in the mirror, and if I do say so myself, there is no way anyone back at Royal would even dare think the woman behind this mask was Edie Vanderwalt. Long gone are my black-rimmed glasses and usual bun. Tonight, my dark blond hair is a curtain of full long curls that took me decades to tame. Okay, not decades, but for a low maintenance kind of girl like me, it sure did feel like it. With contacts, my eyes showcase my natural ocean-blue, which tonight seem bigger, thanks to Lexi's trusty black mascara and liner.

Some helpful YouTube videos showed yours truly how to get the perfect shade and tone to keep me glowing, with just a hint of blush on my cheeks. Even my lips look like they are ready to get some action, with the vixen red lipstick they're wearing. And the whole thing comes together with Devina's silver backless sequined dress and high heels to match. How could anyone who works with me on a daily basis ever think the woman I'm staring at right now in the mirror is me? I don't think even my own mother would recognize me tonight.

Okay, just breathe. You can do this.

I open the bathroom door and see Slevin nod in my direction as he talks into his phone.

"She'll see you in a bit, then," he says before hanging up. "I apologize for not having said this to you sooner, but you do look marvelous this evening,

Miss Vanderwalt. I believe you will be the talk of the night." He offers a cheeky smile.

"Please call me Edie."

"You mean Lady." He lowers his brow.

"Oh yes, sorry. Force of habit."

"Make sure you curb that habit before you make it upstairs."

"Noted, Slevin. Won't happen again."

"Good. Shall we?" he says, offering his arm. I loop mine in his, and we walk out of his office the same way we came in.

"The first few floors are for staff only. After you read the handbook, you will understand which floors are destined for members and which are not. Rule of thumb is that after the fifth floor, members can partake in all activities in each floor after they have had their respective clearance. Any doubts, just come back to me, and I'll help you and Ms. Richardson accordingly."

"Thank you, Slevin," I reply, not having heard most of what he's on about since my belly is in knots as we get closer and closer to the elevator. I try to steady my shaky legs and pray he doesn't feel me leaning on him for support. What good does it do looking like a million bucks if I can't act the part?

The King

Get a grip, Edie. Just a few floors and you will finally see what all the fuss is about.

Slevin clicks on the elevator door, and once its doors open, he ushers me inside and pushes the button for the twenty-seventh floor, followed by a swipe of his card on a panel to the right.

"Tomorrow, when you come on your own, remember to always swipe the card on this panel. It will open every floor you have clearance on. At this time, those are the last four, which are the communal areas. Since it's a Wednesday night, Poppy will meet you on this floor. It's our most popular one, but tonight it shouldn't be too crowded. I hope you enjoy your evening, and that your report to Ms. Richardson will be a favorable one."

"You're not coming up with me?" I ask, and I don't miss the panic in my voice at the thought of being left to my own devices.

"No, Lady. As a handler, it is not my place to mingle with the members in their safe haven. Should you need me, you know how to reach me. Have a good evening, my dear," he says and kisses the back of my palm like a true gentleman.

"Good evening, Slevin, and thank you," I say as the elevator doors shut between us.

Shit.

Shit.

Double Shit!

"Okay, I can still back out if I want to," I say out loud, looking at the numbers on the panel blink from six to seven, eight to nine, and so on.

No, no. I came this far. Can't chicken out now.

Oh my lord, am I really doing this?

Have I completely lost it?

What am I going to find when those doors open up?

I mean, for a bit over a quarter of a million dollars a year, I'm expecting a whole lot of debauchery, and maybe my inexperienced little sex life isn't ready for what I'm about to see. I'm scared that the minute those doors open, I'm going to find myself surrounded by sweaty bodies in an all-out orgy, and I'm going to see things that will burn my retinas right off.

This is insane. I am insane.

And with the mental picture of ballsacks and hairy butts from overzealous fat men—who make a killing on Wall Street and can easily afford the After Hours price tag—I don't even realize the elevator doors have opened until the thumping of music hits my ears, and two tender hands pull me out from inside the elevator.

The King

"Lady, right?" a petite Asian beauty asks me.

"Huh?" I mumble ever so ineloquentlyas I gaze from side to side, not really understanding what's going on. Instead of the naked flesh I was expecting to see, I'm confronted by your run-of-the-mill New York nightclub. Bar on both sides of the open area, dance floor full of people shaking their asses to the beats the DJ is playing on stage, and dark red and black décor that gives the whole place a lustful vibe to it. Apart from that, I see nothing screaming sex to me, aside from the grinding bodies dancing away, and I've seen far worse done on a normal night out with Lexi and her crew.

"Not what you were expecting, huh?"

I shake my head, still stunned silent at my hostess, who is grinning ear to ear at me and ushering me closer to one of the bars to the right. One thing's for sure, Slevin was wrong on one account—if he thought this place wouldn't be crowded tonight, he was sorely mistaken. It's packed. Poppy has to nudge our own corner at the overpopulated bar, and I'm pretty sure this isn't the first time she's had to make room just to get a drink tonight.

"Let me guess, Lady. You were expecting a lot of leather, a ball gag or two and a bunch of whips, is that right?" she jokes as she summons the bartender over.

Crap. Hearing Poppy saying it like that means I must have looked like a deer in headlights when those elevator doors opened. Was I being judgmental?

Maybe for these people, this whole thing with dropping so much cash on an elite club wasn't about sex after all. And most importantly, it wasn't about sex for Dean. Maybe it had to do more about preserving their privacy? I mean, it makes so much more sense, doesn't it? To shell out that kind of dough, you must be a high roller, with paparazzi and everyone knowing your business. How else are you going to blow off steam without making it on TMZ or something? They're paying for their own privacy. Their freedom. You can't put a price tag on that. And here I was thinking less of him. Of all of them.

I suck, you guys.

"Sorry, I guess my imagination ran away from me."

"No worries. I get it. Although if that's your cup of tea, there is a floor which caters to that brand of kink, just FYI. Personally, I never had the guts to go there. Some things can never be unseen, you know?"

"I'm fine right here, thanks," I reply shyly, not wanting to learn any more details of such a place or its whereabouts. Hey, I swear, no judgment here. But from the mini freak-out I had in the elevator, I guess I realized I'm not as courageous as I pumped my ego into being tonight.

"Two glasses of champagne, please," Poppy asks the bartender once she's gotten his attention, and I take advantage of her distraction to inspect my hostess more fully. In a whimsical black lace Yves

Saint Laurent dress, paired with ruby slippers and all, Poppy looks like any man's wet dream, both sweet yet seductive. Yet, what I love about the raven beauty is the painted mask she has on. Red crystal beads cover her upper face to perfection, and I wonder how long it took her to glue each one on her porcelain skin just to maintain the illusion she's created.

As I look around the crowd, I see that everyone has taken very careful measures to ensure their anonymity, and still look fierce and beautiful while doing it. Some women sport gorgeous gowns like my own, while others went all out and decided a full-blown costume was the way for them. The men look sharp and elegant in their attire as well, and from a distance, it is impossible to distinguish age or race, let alone even guess who is in attendance.

Yep, I'm definitely starting to get the idea now why this place is so popular, even on a Wednesday night.

"Here you go, Lady," Poppy says, handing over my drink. "You want to take a seat and talk? Or do you want to have some fun tonight?"

"Define fun?" I ask warily. I thought Slevin said Poppy was supposed to show me the ropes, not throw me in the lion's den right from the start.

"Easy there, Lady," she laughs. "I meant if you wanted to dance. I'm going to stick by you the whole week, girlfriend. We'll visit the common areas together, one floor at a time, and by this time next week, you'll be good to go. Until then, we'll only have the fun you want to have, okay? Anyway, it's one of After Hours rules."

"What is?"

"What is what?" she repeats, not paying attention to me as her eyes are locked with one of the most intimidating, and largest man I have ever cast my eyes on—who is standing at one of the balconies above, looking down at her. His mask resembles that of a leopard somewhat, and even though he's at a great distance from us, I swear I can hear him growl. Poppy snickers beside me.

"I asked what is the After Hours rule you were talking about, but you were too caught up looking at the tall, dark, and handsome over there," I goad, and the little twinkle in her eyes tells me he's no stranger.

"Oh, pay no mind to Panther. He's in one of his moods." She giggles. "Come. Let's sit down, and I'll explain what I mean," she says, walking over to one of the long corner couches, where Panther can still keep his eyes on her, and she can pretend she isn't enjoying every second of it.

What did I tell you? The strong sense of déjà vu is overwhelming. It honestly feels like just another typical night out with Lexi and her crew. Jeez!

Only now I'm all dolled up, and I never try that hard for our girl's night.

What??

Come on, guys? Don't look at me like that.

It's not like I was ever going to bump into Dean in a club down in Queens. And if you've been paying attention, he's the only one I would make an effort to go all out for.

Keep up, you guys!

"If you're asking me about the rules, I take it you haven't read the Bible?"

"The Bible?"

"Yeah. The ginormous monstrosity they make us read, with all their rules and regulations. I know it's a bore, but trust me, if you want to learn the ropes to this place, you have to read it," she explains, taking a quick sip of champagne, as if to sweeten the memory of having had the displeasure of completing such a distasteful task herself.

"Can't you just give me the cliff-notes version?" I prompt.

"No, young Lady," she chuckles. "You have to do your time like we all did. But I'll do you a solid." She laughs and then leans in, beckoning me to follow her lead like two friends about to share a secret over coffee.

"The women here are the ones who really own this

place. The guys think they own the joint, but at the end of the day, we're the ones who have the last say," Poppy whispers proudly.

"How so?"

"Well," she hushes and leans in further, still making sure no one is in earshot. "It all comes down to the rules. After Hours lives by them. Stick around, and you'll see that soon enough. And the best rule this place has is its pleasure policy. Wink, wink," she says, nudging my shoulder.

"Huh? I don't get it?" I shrug, not really getting what she's hinting at.

"When I first saw you, I knew you were green, but I didn't think you were *this* green. Okay, no worries. I'm going to be as blunt as possible, so forgive me if it comes out cruder than what you're used to. But given the circumstances, I think it's best nothing is lost in translation, okay, sweetie? The pleasure policy means that the guys can only cum once the lady has, understand?" she explains in a soothing a tone.

"Oh. Oh!"

"Yep, pretty great, huh? Guaranteed satisfaction every time. The guys can stipulate their wants and their rules, but if we say no to any, they are shit out of luck. This whole joint is our playing field. They're the ones we let in for us to have our fun, not the other way around. This place isn't looking too bad to you now, am I right?"

"I'm surprised, actually. I didn't know what to expect, but I was sure I was going to find some sort of gentlemen's club," I admit.

"As opposed to a women's club? Welcome to the twenty-first century, Lady. So thrilled to be giving you the tour to your new kingdom." She laughs with a wide grin in place.

I see her eyes look up yet again to the balcony, searching for her favorite plaything, and suddenly that's when I see *him*. The reason I'm here, and why I spent four gruesome hours getting ready tonight, weeks lying to my best friend, and… Oh, you guys get the picture.

In all his splendor, wearing a gold mask that covers his face from the nose up, but does a poor job at hiding his sparkling emerald eyes—I'm transfixed with one look. A rare smile takes form on his lips, and I shit you not, ladies and gentleman, my heart stops right then and there, since this is only something I have seen on a rare occasion, and never once directed at me. I want to do the batshit-crazy thing and look left and right, just to make sure he really is looking at me, but thankfully, there must be some gray matter still functioning in my brain, confirming he *is* looking at me since the only thing behind me is a cold stone wall.

"Oh dear," I hear Poppy faintly say next to me, but it's difficult to say for sure since my heart is pumping harder than the drum and bass the DJ is turning in this place.

"Lady, sweetie, nuh-uh. That one is not for you, okay honey? Trust me," she continues on more insistently, trying to grab my attention. I want to play it cool, but the smirk he's got on now tells me he likes my full attention on him just as much as I do.

"Lady!" Poppy shouts, snapping her fingers in front of me for good measure.

"What?" I scowl.

"I said that one right there is not for you, okay?"

"Why the hell not?" I yell out, a bit more aggressively than I intended, but damn! I was not expecting this hoochy block tonight.

Her eyes go wide in disbelief at my sudden outburst, and it hits me how rude I'm being. Not to mention certifiable.

"Sorry, Poppy. I didn't mean to yell at you. I don't know what came over me."

Yeah, I do. Dean looking at me like I was good enough to eat. That's what came over me. But like hell I'm going to say something to Poppy after I pretty much yelled in her face because of it.

"Lady, don't take me the wrong way, honey. I'm sure you're a lovely girl. The thing is, for the past hour you've been here, I could tell straight away that some things this place offers just won't be for you. You're what I call a good girl, wanting to just peek under the curtain of this side of bad, but really never intending on taking a full step inside, which is fine. You'll have plenty of fun here without having to truly fall into darker temptations."

"Poppy, you're talking in riddles. What do you mean he's not for me?" I say, nudging my head to the balcony, making it perfectly clear who I'm referring to, but not wanting to make any eye contact for the sake of continuing this conversation.

"The man who has grabbed your attention is known as The King, and the cocky fucker holds his own brand of court," she exhales, defeated.

"Huh?"

"He's alone now, but trust me, he won't be for long. He's usually accompanied by his two sidekicks, aptly named The Prince and The Duke. They're a trio, Lady," Poppy explains, her tone disgusted.

"You mean…"

"I mean to get to the King, you have to pass his lackeys first. They're a package deal, and I sincerely doubt a good girl like you would find that scenario anything but appalling."

I'm glad I didn't have any champagne in my mouth when she added that last remark because I'm certain I would have sprayed the walls of this fine establishment with the expensive pink bubbly.

And for the second time tonight, my heart stops. Only this time, I'm not sure if it will ever come back to life because I'm pretty sure it's broken.

Chapter 7

DEAN

"Why are we always on the 27th now? I mean, didn't we do this like three times already this week and four last week?" Connor asks, slumping into his chair dejectedly.

"Our King seems to have an itch for dancing lately," Bash replies, lighting up his cigarette. Even though he knows he can't smoke inside the nightclub, he continues to light one up every time he has a beer on hand.

"I call bullshit! Dean doesn't even dance," Con goads while stretching his legs and placing his feet on the table. My little Prince is a true aristocrat at heart—never giving a fuck to anyone or anything.

I can't help but chuckle at the idea of actually dancing in this place. He's not wrong. I wouldn't be caught dead dancing to this techno drivel. But this floor seems to be where *she* feels most comfortable since it seems to be her preferred place to hang out. Therefore, my ass has been dragging itself to this particular floor just to get the best view of her I can get.

"I heard there's an auction going on tonight. That

should be fun," Con instigates, trying to change our current surroundings.

"We're staying," I deadpan, making my final say.

"Fine. Just so you know, you've become a real sourpuss in your old age," he teases.

I flip him off and go back to my entertainment for the night. The real reason why I'm keeping my friends put.

"I know that look," Duke states, sprawled out on the couch.

"Do you now?" I ask, with my engrossed stare not dismayed by my friend's curious nature.

"Yes. It's the look you get when you see something you like. So tell me, what little *pet* has caught your eye this time?"

I smirk at my friend for knowing me so well and let my eyes travel up and down the woman who has captivated my sight since the night she stepped into the room in that little silver number she had on. Tonight, though, she is glorious in a dark green, skin-tight dress with a side split up to her thigh, giving every man in here a hard-on just by imagining themselves running their hands up and down her legs.

"Nuh-uh, not a chance. No blondes," Prince says, slamming his glass of whiskey on the round table in front of us.

"She is quite fetching. Poor thing is trying very hard not to look scared of being here," Duke grins, loving her unsettlement. I, however, don't find it as amusing.

"Hmm," I murmur in reply.

The little pet is trying desperately to go unnoticed. If that was her intention, she should have worn something else. The dress she has on just screams out for every male here to drink her in. Actually, for the past two weeks since she's been coming here, she's been a hot commodity, rarely left alone for more than two seconds. Always some masked douche attempting to woo her to his bed. But I've kept my eyes on this new prize, and have seen her turn down each and every one. Odd, if you think about it. Anyone joining After Hours is looking for a good time, but this little pet seems to be terribly picky in her choices.

"Dean," Connor hushes next to me, fire in his voice. "I'm serious. No fucking blondes."

I've really had enough of his bullshit.

"If I want her, my little Prince, I'll have her—and you'll man the fuck up and go along with it," I tell him bluntly.

Like hell am I going to have his hang-ups hinder me from getting anything I want. It's been ages since anything has grabbed my attention in any way, and I for one, will not let Connor or anyone get in my way of keeping this feeling alive in me. It's bound to run its course, like all the others, but while the adrenaline is pumping in my veins, I want to feed it, not cool it down with Connor's self-imposed restraints.

"I've seen her around Poppy. That won't bode well for you," Duke adds.

"You disapprove of her, too?" I ask dead-on.

"No, just stating a fact. Poppy isn't exactly our number one fan." He winks.

"That's because Poppy is vanilla pretending to be rocky-mother-fucking-road," Con belts out.

"It doesn't matter what Poppy did or did not say. The only thing that matters is if she'll play along," I announce, making my wishes clear.

"So, when will this summons take place? Thinking about holding court tonight?" Bash asks, looking at the woman in question while taking another pull of his beer. My prize excuses herself from her present company, and by the direction she's going, I see that tonight might not be a bad idea at all.

"I'll tell you when I come back." I stand up from my seat and make my way down the long, dark corridor with one sole intent—getting to my new pet before any other asshole in this place gets in my way.

The moment I reach the outside balcony, I'm hit

with the November chill, reminding me of the upcoming family holidays I won't have. My previous momentum is somewhat stifled, and it's only a low sneeze in the far corner from the beauty herself that brings me back to the here and now, making me refocus on the mission at hand. I take off my coat, hating the feel of the cold air running across my back, but not wanting the woman in front of me to get sick, just because she needed space from all the vultures surrounding her inside the club. Her mind must be miles away, because she doesn't hear me approaching, and by the little yelp she lets out when I place my coat on her shoulders, her surprise of my presence is more than evident.

"Jesus, you startled me," she says, grasping her chest and my coat.

"I see that," I grin at her, loving how the sudden alarm got a soft hue to rose her cheeks a pretty shade of pink.

"Sorry, I'm usually not that skittish, but you really shouldn't sneak up on people like that. I mean, I could have clocked you just now."

"Clocked me?" I ask, intrigued.

"Yeah, you know? Knocked you out? As a reflex, mind you. It wouldn't be anything personal. But it could have happened! I used to do it all the time when I was a kid. Someone scared me like that, and I'd be decking that person with my best punch in the nose. You, mister, got very lucky just now," she says passionately, and I do everything in my power to keep a straight face.

"I apologize and vow to be more cautious in the future, so as not to surprise you," I remark, my tone as monotone as I can make it, which is an incredible feat since I have to control myself not to laugh at her cute remark of knocking me out with a single punch with her dainty hand.

"Thank you," she says and goes back to looking at the New York skyline.

"Lovely night, isn't it?" I say after a pregnant pause since it's obvious my pet isn't going to make this easy for me.

"Hmm."

I lean into the rail and watch her discomfort grow. It's apparent the woman at my side isn't one for small talk, and fuck if I am either. I didn't come for the view. I'm here for her, and idle conversation has never been my strong suit.

"My name is King," I tell her; at least making a formal introduction should appease her some and restore my decorum.

"I know who you are," she answers, never once making eye contact with me, but I see her pull my coat to her body tighter. I'm betting the shiver running down her spine isn't caused by the wind alone, but also from my unwavering stare.

"Then you have me at a disadvantage since I still do not know your name," I remark, taking a step closer to her, only to be rewarded by another shiver.

"It's Lady," she consents.

"Lady, huh? Does that mean you haven't decided on a name yet, or whether you intend to stay on after your trial month?" I question, my own hackles going up at this new piece of information.

"Correct," she states firmly, this time daring to look me dead on.

"On which account?" I cock my brow.

"Both." She shrugs, and turns away yet again, depriving me of the crystal blue waters I want to dive into.

"Pity," I let out, and I grasp the rail with both hands, this time looking at the same view she is insistent on watching. I decide not to say anything else, and let her make the next move. If she's remotely curious, she'll say something. If not, she'll return my coat and be on her way. In the meantime, I'm perfectly content listening to the noises my city makes at night, while her jasmine perfume teases me.

"How so?" I hear her whisper finally. My lip starts to lift on its own accord, pleased this beauty has made the right decision.

"Well, you've already spent half of your trial period, and you have yet to experience anything of true value this club has to offer. It's a shame you're wasting such an opportunity," I tell her, not moving once from my statue state.

"You're very observant."

"I observe everything that is of my interest," I confess, this time turning to face her. I want her to see how true my words are. She mimics me, and we are now just a hair's breadth away from each other. So close, all I'd have to do is to wrap my arm behind her lower back to remove the remaining space there is, and kiss this woman like I've imagined for the past two weeks since I first laid eyes on her.

"Am I to assume that I am of interest to you?" she asks in wary anticipation, looking up at me with wide, clear blue eyes. I place my thumb under her chin, and it kick-starts the blood pumping in my veins and the hardening in my pants. Smooth and silky skin touches my thumb, and as the tip of her pink tongue peeks out to wet her lips, I almost groan at how much I want a feel of it, too.

"Very much so," I answer her, my voice a little huskier than I prefer to reveal on a first encounter.

I'm almost tempted to go for the kill—lean in and steal a quick kiss from the temptress herself. But my thieving notions are quickly set aside when she takes one step back away from me, creating distance between us which shouldn't exist in my book.

"Hmm," she murmurs and crosses her arms over her chest. Like that's playing fair. Even with my coat on her shoulders, I still have an ample view of her voluptuous breasts from where I'm standing, and crossing her arms like that only magnifies their suppleness.

When I register she's wearing a frown on her pretty little face, I start to worry that maybe this pet might not be interested in After Hours, and worse yet, in me, either. I've seen her turn down men left and right since she got here, but my gut told me she wouldn't turn me down. Was I wrong?

"You don't seem to like my answer," I say, not wanting to ask the dreaded yes or no question outright yet.

"It all depends. You've made it clear I interest you. But you have yet to interest me."

"Are you saying you're not attracted to me in the least? Not one bit curious?" I probe, wanting like hell to be wrong with what I was hearing.

"I didn't say that. If there is anyone in this place I *am* attracted to, then it's you," she exhales, and I think I almost catch her rolling her eyes at me. "But as I've recently found out, attraction may not be enough to keep me interested."

"Ah, I see. So tell me, what doesn't interest you, precisely?" I ask, already knowing what her answer will be. Poppy and her judgmental ass have planted the seed of doubt in my pet's head apparently.

"I've heard you hold a certain type of *court,* which I'm not sure I'm comfortable with attending," she says confirming my suspicions.

"Hmm," I reply, giving back to her the same non-verbal cue she gave me not a minute ago.

"Does that mean I'm no longer of interest to you?" she asks, jumping to unwarranted conclusions.

"No, pet, you are. But After Hours has rules. At the end of the day, you say yes or no to the stipulation I have in place. I stipulate that I share with my friends. In my life, I've shared everything I've had with them. Money. Status. Power. Everything. After Hours isn't any different for me. If this is something you are uncomfortable with, I understand, and will bow out regretfully."

"Oh. I see," she says, and her voice almost breaks in the end. I see disappointment fill the sea in her eyes, and although for me this was just another fuck, another adrenaline rush, I have to admit, these last two weeks, waiting to see her, watching her every night, has been the most alive I've felt in a long time.

Before I know why I'm doing it, I lean over to her and bring her toward me. I feel her drape her arms around my neck, cradling her head gracefully on my shoulder. Her warm body hits me like a furnace—so invitingly—and the mixture of her soft curves fitting me perfectly, and her sweet jasmine scent enveloping me, makes me want to grab onto her tighter and bask in this new, unexpected find. I weave my fingers through her golden hair, only to confirm it's just as silky as I suspected. The fucking woman really is a dream come true. Why did she have to turn me down? We could have been so good together. Even if only for a moment.

"I won't lie and say I'm not disappointed, because I am," I whisper in her ear, and I see a trail of goosebumps rise on her neck.

Oh, what fun this creature is denying me.

"I really wanted to know what you tasted like. I've been imagining it since the moment I saw you walk into this place," I whisper and am rewarded with her lifting her head to look up at me, a soft crimson color filling her cheeks to perfection.

"Maybe you won't deny me one quick taste, will you, pet? Just so I know what I'll be missing? One kiss?" I ask—or am I begging? At this point it could be either one because I'm too caught up in those crystal blue eyes of hers, which are far too big and glorious to hold any secrets, and yet, they hold the mystery I'm being denied answers to.

"One kiss?" she asks breathlessly.

"Just one, pet," I promise.

When she gives me a small nod and closes her

eyes, it takes me a minute to pull the trigger. If this is all she's going to give me, I want to savor it. I pull her closer to me, eliciting a gasp from her lips, and her full breasts are firmly pressed against my dress shirt. It's fucking freezing out here, yet I wish I had given her my shirt as well so I could feel all of her on my bare skin. My hands roam her back ever so leisurely, gaining a wanton moan from her this time, and when my hands finally meet her round ass, I swear I hear her sigh.

I take just another quick look at this stunning creature wearing my coat, eyes closed, and trusting a stranger in a cold, golden mask to give her the one kiss she will never forget.

I lean down and join my lips with hers, delivering what I've promised. Only what I find isn't just sweet, but fucking fire, and I feel she should have warned me. Succulent lips have never before greeted me with such fervor, such adulterated need, and soon enough I'm not sure who is kissing who. It knocks the wind out of my sails since I was expecting to give her a magical moment to remember this evening by, not the other way around, and I've yet to breach open her lips.

What the fuck?

She doesn't even give me an opportunity to wrestle her tongue with mine, as she ends our kiss far too quickly for my liking.

"Wow," she sighs, running her fingers over her

lips.

Wow?

Wow?

What the fuck?

I'm still out of it and, frankly, speechless when she hands me my coat and starts to make her way back inside.

Hold on!

Hold on!

Hold on one goddamned second!

"Lady?" I yell.

Jesus, I hate that name. It's like I'm calling a dog or something, and yes, I'm aware how hypocritical that sounds on my part.

"Yes?" she answers me, barely turning around to let me look at her face entirely.

"Think about my offer. Don't say no until you at least consider it. Sleep on it, at least." I hear myself plea.

Shit! That kiss must have really packed some kind of punch because this is so unlike me. I'm a take-it-or-leave-it kind of guy, and I've never once made this much of an effort to get a woman to reconsider my peculiarities.

She offers me a shy smile and a small nod. I guess I can construe that in any way I want. It wasn't an outright no, so I'll take that for what it's worth.

"Tomorrow, then," I say.

"Goodnight, my King," she whispers back to me before leaving me out in the cold altogether.

"Goodnight, my pet."

Chapter 8

EDIE

So I know what you're thinking.

You're thinking that if I'm truly that shallow and hung up on looks, I'd really consider hooking up with three guys just to get close to the one I really want.

And you're right. I'm not that shallow.

But if you're asking me this question, it also means you probably think it's only his looks I'm attracted to, and that there is no man good-looking enough who is worth all this craziness that I'm subjecting myself to.

And if that were the case, then yes, I would agree with you. Dean is, in fact, a God amongst men, but still, looks should not be the only factor for any woman to jump through the hoops I have been plummeting through recently just to get close to him.

Nuh-uh. No way.

But see, here lies the kicker, ladies. Dean isn't just a pretty face. And believe me, I wish he was just a delicious piece of eye candy I wanted to lick up and down, and not think twice about after I had my fill.

Dean Knox is the whole package.

Don't believe me?

Yeah, well, I wish I was as skeptical.

In the past two years, for me to get rid of this stupid antagonizing office crush, I've kept a close visual on Mr. Knox himself to find the one fatal flaw to loathe and put me off. And to this day, I have found nothing. Yep. You heard me. Not a thing.

Zilch.

Nada.

Niente.

Not a goddamned thing, and trust me, I was thorough in my search for flaws.

Hey, I hear you. Yes, he's no angel, and I don't want you to think that's what I'm saying. He can be a real prick when he wants to be—believe me, I know. I've seen him in boardroom meetings, tearing people apart and not batting an eye while doing it. Still, that's not a fatal flaw for me. Hell, that's being a New Yorker. Between him and Devina, I'm not sure who could make a person cry faster, but it comes with the job of running the number-one fashion magazine in the world.

Aside from the fact the man is a workaholic, and that he rarely smiles, in my search for the eternal flaw,

I found something completely unexpected. And well, something which made it ten times harder to get over my office crush. I found goodness in him. Pure, genuine goodness—which is, if we're honest, guys, a rarity to find nowadays.

Don't believe me?

Okay, smarty pants, let me throw some examples down for you all.

Example number one: While most successful CEOs have drop-dead gorgeous secretaries to bring them their coffee, Dean gets his own. He would never ask any employee to bring any beverage to him, even though it's a well-accepted job duty for most of us low-level admin workers. Hell, I'm Devina's best friend, and I get her lattes all the fucking time. Of course, I get one for me too, but that's not the point I'm making, people. Let's continue, shall we?

Example number two: Still on the secretary bandwagon issue. Like I said, most CEOs like their eye candy just like most hot-blooded men, so if they are efficient in their jobs, nine times out of ten in the interview process, the looker will get it. And if she's in her twenties, well then, she's definitely getting the position. It's a harsh reality. You have to have brains and look good while doing it. Young, too, if you can swing it, especially if you work in the fashion industry. My Dean—yeah, I know he's not mine, but for the sake of argument, I want you to not confuse him with any other Dean out there. And besides, I like the way it sounds. Anyway—*My Dean's* secretary is a fifty-five-year-old black woman from Queens named Athena, mother of three and grandmother of two. And believe me when I tell you, she does not sit in her chair looking pretty for anyone's eye. The woman is fierce, and just like her boss, doesn't take shit from anyone. She's one of the most professional secretaries that Royal has. I might be harboring a small crush on her, too, but that's beside the point.

Example number three: When Athena's daughter drops her twin girls on her mom because she's got yet another unexpected dance audition, Dean lets the girls play in his office and then takes the three of them out for lunch, usually giving Athena the rest of the day off so she can take the girls to the park. I swear, when these days happen, I hear my ovaries sing sweet lullabies, and I'm not even the type of girl who thinks about babies and all that jazz.

See, I don't even have to go any further, do I? Are you starting to see his appeal now?

These little things he does go unnoticed by everyone but not by me. Because just like him, I pay attention, too. And last night, when he kissed me, boy, did I pay attention. You ever see those kisses in the movies and think, yeah no way would that ever happen in real life! Well, that was what it felt like—a real, honest-to-God, movie kiss. Only someone must have messed up the scene and got the lead hunk actor to kiss the awkward understudy. Still, I didn't care. If last night was going to be the only time I was ever to kiss Dean Knox in my life, then I was going to milk it for all I could. Hey, I kept it PG. Didn't go all R-rated or anything like that, since I didn't want to get too over my head, but yeah… What a kiss. I'm sure he's kissed thousands of girls before, and my little kiss will be just a bleep in a crowd of faceless women, but for me, I kind of pity the next guy who's going up against that performance.

I could leave this whole After Hours fiasco at a kiss—a great, magical kiss. I don't have to go back tonight and let him down again. I can just move on and be happy I fulfilled part of my fantasy. I really could.

Right?

I mean, After Hours served one purpose at least. It gave me the flaw I had been searching for so long to find in Dean. This thing he has going with Connor and Sebastian is all sorts of wrong, and knowing he openly shares his conquests with them leaves a bad taste in my mouth. Not to mention the deep cut it did to my insides. If I wanted him dethroned from his pedestal, learning they all shared the same women sure got the job done.

So, I won't be going back. I'll send an email to Slevin, informing him Devina is no longer interested in said membership, and hope Poppy will understand my sudden disappearing act.

I will just have to be content with the memory of how I kissed a king once, and it was just as enchanted as every fairytale book described it to be.

Ivy Fox

That memory should last me a lifetime, right?

Chapter 9

DEAN

It was one kiss.

One prepubescent, measly little harmless kiss.

How in hell am I so twisted inside out by one simple lock of lips with a total stranger, whom I will probably never see again in my life? I spent all night thinking about that wretched kiss. Tossed and turned, dreaming about it. I woke up, brushed my teeth, hopped in the shower, and jerked myself into oblivion fantasizing about it. Got dressed and went to work like any other day, but instead of being focused on Royal as I should be, I'm obsessing over that one fire-breathing-down-to-my-very-soul kiss, the entire time.

What the fuck?

Am I losing it?

Am I so out of it that one simple, innocent twelve-year-old peck has been able to knock me on my ass so completely?

All day, I've been too consumed with the memory of it to pay attention to anyone around me. Like a fool, my head has been in the clouds the whole day, ignoring important conversations I should be taking note of. And when those moments of lucidity did arrive, I found myself barking orders at the poor sods who have no business taking on my sudden juvenile frustrations. Although, if they grabbed my attention from my adolescent daydreams, then chances are they did shit to deserve my wrath anyways.

Bash, being the ever-perceptive one of our trio, had made sure to stay clear of my path the whole day. And even Con, who is usually the narcissist of our lot, was also in tune to my lousy mood today and made sure not to piss me off with any of his usual antics.

They didn't seem surprised, either, when I asked them to accompany me here tonight. Nor did they contest my request that they should stay put at our suite, while I checked to see if a particular new member had arrived at her preferred after-hours nightclub.

I guess I should be thankful for small miracles, at least. Last time, Connor wasn't thrilled with whom I had my eye set on, but tonight, he had the good sense to keep his opinions to himself. Maybe he thinks it's because I won't be able to get near her in the first place. But last night I did, didn't I?

Fuck.

One kiss.

One fucking kiss.

But it wasn't just the kiss that got to me, was it? For the past two weeks that I've been watching her every move like a hunter does his prey, I could sense there was something in her which appealed to me. I know it wasn't the one kiss that got under my skin so easily, but more the woman whose lips delivered such a powerful punch. I thought it was the chase that thrilled me, but she's the one who truly intrigues me. And last night, alone on that balcony, the moment I got a closer view into her eyes, I knew exactly why that was.

It was fucking innocence I had smelled a mile away on her.

Purity.

With all the glamorous dresses she wore, looking regal and elegant every night, making every man look at her in awe; it was the look of pure innocence they could feel crackling around her, and to wolves like us, we feed on that shit. It's our fucking breakfast, lunch, and dinner. Best dessert there is, too.

Of course, her kiss was hellfire. More delicious with each second that passed by. Her lips were still learning, still untainted, and inexperienced. Still thirsty to gain knowledge of what the world could offer, and fuck me if I didn't want to eat her up right then and there. Was it any wonder I almost begged her to reconsider my offer? Was it that hard for me to conceive how I had spent my whole day wondering if she would show up tonight and grace me with those delicious sweet lips again? And am I at all surprised that the clock keeps ticking, and my eyes are glued to those elevator doors? Which I know, deep down, she will not be walking through tonight.

No. Not at all.

I'm not surprised because, after twenty-four hours of obsessing and fantasizing, logic and reasoning have always been my faithful companions.

Purity and innocence have no business coming through those doors. Isn't this the appeal of After Hours anyway? Wasn't that one of the best sales gimmicks they had? I wouldn't be responsible for anyone's heart since everyone in attendance knew the game. Every person here knew the score and was in here for the enjoyment, not the complicated heartstrings.

My pet, though? One look into her eyes told me all I needed to know. She had no clue what she was getting herself into by joining this club. She was the very definition of the aforementioned heart complications.

Why would she be here in the first place, I wonder? Was it some sort of dare? Did someone put her up to it? Was it just an unfortunate mistake on her part? Or was she lost and trying to find herself in a place with no mirrors?

Whatever the reason, I understand now why she kept to this floor and didn't stray to any other. It resembles a regular nightclub, and to her, it's probably the most acceptable scenario she could fathom participating in.

And last night, I proposed what constitutes in her mind, as an orgy.

Yeah, she won't be coming.

Am I such a glutton for punishment that I'm actually relieved she stood me up and kept to her virtuous ways? I guess I am, in a way. Of course, I'm disappointed I'll never see her, sure, but some things should stay far from places like this.

I pick up my phone and start texting Bash, to tell both him and Con that court will not be taking place this evening, when, like a reverse spin on a Cinderella's tale, at the exact stroke of midnight, the lady of the hour strolls through those doors, and I immediately establish two things.

The first one is, I'm a fucking liar. When I see her waltz in, my heart leaps into my throat, and that's when I know I'm more than thrilled to put my eyes on her again. Telling myself I was okay with not seeing her ever again was just a bullshit lie, one that I was clinging on to make the unfamiliar ache—caused by her apparent rebuttal to my offer with her no-show—go away.

The second thing, which is clear as day, is the poor attire my pet has decided to wear this evening. Glowing in a translucent white gown, it's almost laughable how she resembles the innocent sacrificial lamb, seconds away from her slaughter. If she thought looking virginally sweet would make me think twice before corrupting her, she has another think coming. Her get-up has officially swollen me into painful dimensions at just the idea of how beautiful it will be to tarnish and deflower such a sweet, tender thing. When she locks eyes with me, my cocky grin is as evident as her nerves, but she still finds the courage to walk toward me, head held high.

"Good evening, my Lady. I was starting to think you'd forgotten about me," I tease, leaning back on the black leather couch, both arms sprawled wide on the back headrest.

"I fear that is impossible, my King," she replies.

"*My King.* That is the second time you've referred to me this way, my pet. I have to say, I like hearing the words fall from your lips," I confess.

Every time she's said those two little words, I feel my blood start to boil up and create a spark inside me. And now that she's here, I might have a chance to make her scream those words out before the night is through, and see just what type of thunder I can create.

"Hmm," she replies, not feeding my ego any more than what she already has, with her slip of the tongue. "I see you're alone," she says, her eyes now searching for the men she has yet to meet.

"I am. However, if you have reconsidered my

offer, I won't be for long," I deadpan. I won't elude her into believing otherwise. Con and Bash may not be here with me now, but that was more of a tactical move on my part, just in case my pet did show up. If she was skittish, as she obviously is, I didn't want their presence to scare her away entirely.

"Is your offer still the only one on the table?" she asks, her face schooled not to show any emotion, looking down dispassionately at my seated form. It's only the twitch on her lower lip that gives her away. She's nervous and anxious all at once, and I fear the answer to her question will make all of those feelings disappear.

"It is, pet," I state softly, and if I didn't know any better, I'd think I detect a small tinge of disappointment in my own tone.

This is as far as she will go this night. She came to see if I would back down and reconsider, but I am a man of my word, and though this creature is more fetching than most, she isn't enough of one to break a vow shared with the only two people I consider family.

"I suspected as much," she hushes in one breath, breaking our eye contact to focus on the ceiling above us as if the heavens had any answers for our dilemma.

She'd have better luck looking at the ground since I hardly think the pearly gates are paying much attention to the activities being held here. After Hours is more of a devil's playground and angels have no place here. I see her rub her lip raw in further contemplation, and something tells me this angelic beauty has just come to the same disappointing conclusion.

"Very well, then. I have conditions of my own," she announces, her new resolve knocking my world off its axis.

"Come again?" I ask because I need to make sure I'm hearing this right and it's not my imagination running away with me as it's been doing all day. "Did you say you have conditions?"

"Yes."

"Did you come here tonight to bargain with me, pet? Was this your intention all along?" I smirk, surprised at her bravado, and to be honest, I'm also impressed.

"Correct," she quips back.

"Alright. I'll play along. Let's hear it, then."

"You say you share everything with your friends. I can understand that to some extent, even though for me, sharing the same lover seems extreme, but since this is your only offer, my conditions are quite simple. If I allow myself to be shared, it will be what *I* allow to share. Nothing will be taken from me which I don't offer willingly."

"That goes without question and would never be

an issue, pet. Frankly, I'm a little insulted you'd think we'd take such liberties with you," I answer sternly.

"I won't apologize for making it clear beforehand what I'm comfortable with in this little game you want me to play. If my need to stipulate rules to make me feel safe offends you, *my King*, well frankly, tough shit," she answers me sweetly, accompanied by the most endearing fake smile.

It takes everything in me not to bark in laughter at her spitfire response.

"Your safety, as well as your pleasure, will always be our rule number one, pet. I give you my word on both accounts."

"Good to hear," she replies, trying to hide her own devilish smile.

"Well, if that was your only concern…" I start getting up from my seat, eager to get this show on the road.

"I'm not finished," she exclaims, placing her hands on my chest to keep me at bay.

I look at the small, fragile things so fiercely intent on keeping me from my prize. I take two steps toward her so she can see how pointless it is, from here on out, to prevent me collecting what's been promised. I hear her breath catch, and it feeds my pride knowing I affect her, too. The hands which so valiantly try to keep us apart are now firmly in my hands, and I place a soft kiss on each inner wrist as their reward.

"Please, my Lady. Do proceed."

"If this sharing business is of such importance to you, then I will concede it to you on one condition," she whispers, looking me dead in the eye, her resolve screaming at me that this is the one thing she will not negotiate.

"Which is?" I query, intrigued.

"I will only sleep with one man, *my King*. Only one. Not three. Not two. Only one," she affirms steadfastly, her shoulders locked straight and back stiff as a board to heighten her only rule.

"And you will choose the lucky man in question, I would assume?" I ask.

"Yes." She nods.

"Hmm, and that would be…"

"You, my King. If I concede to your proposal, it is only because I wish to have you. No one else."

"Hmm."

"These are my conditions. You have yours, and I have mine."

I bring her clasped hands to my lips again, and she

takes a startled step back to look up at me.

"Ah pet, I really thought you wouldn't show up tonight," I say as I take her hand in mine, giving her palm another delicate kiss.

I feel her relax, and the rigid persona she had taken on to list those silly demands starts to vanish before my eyes. I have no idea who this woman is, but if I were to venture a guess, I'd say she must be some sort of lawyer or power agent and is used to dealing with eager men and their far-fetched demands. No stranger to tough negotiations, my pet must be used to building her guard up, shielding herself in any way she can so no one can see her natural soft interior. But isn't that the basis of her appeal and what drew me to her in the first place? How I had this sneaking suspicion that hidden beneath this elegant package lay a treasure the world had no idea had been so well-hidden amongst the ruthless and the powerful? I'd had a little taste of it on the balcony, and I wanted to drink it until I was drunk from her. I wanted my fill, and here she was negotiating it with me, terms that I would have laughed at had they been offered by any other.

"You have yourself a deal, my Lady," I state affirmingly. "Is it still Lady?" I ask.

"What?" she asks, sounding a bit shocked at my willingness to concede to her terms.

"Your name, pet? Have you chosen one?"

"No. Not yet," she replies, biting her lower lip, suddenly seeming more nervous than before our little chit-chat.

"Hmm," I murmur, not really comfortable with the idea of her reluctance in not picking a name for herself. It shows just how undecided she still is about After Hours, and perhaps about its members as well, present company included. I take her hand and place it on my arm, and walk her away from our current surroundings.

"So, hmm… I just want to make sure I heard you correctly. You said yes to my terms just now, right? You agreed?" she whispers conspiringly, trying to continue our conversation discreetly, while I maneuver us through the crowd.

"I said I did, didn't I?" I smirk, cocking my brow at her for good measure.

"Okay… So where are we going?" she stutters.

"To my suite," I deadpan, finally reaching the elevator doors.

"What??? But I thought we couldn't know each other's identities?" she asks, and I see a cast of fear reach her eyes.

"Easy now, pet. I'm not taking you away from the building. Each one of us gets a private room to use in the building. It's part of the club's membership plan. The three of us have a combined suite. You should have one, too. Did your handler not tell you about this? It is in the handbook, you know?"

"Yeah, the handbook… Right. I've been meaning to read it," she says, rubbing her lower lip almost raw. I grasp her chin, ending her self-mutilation, and pin her blue eyes on mine.

"No more of that. Tonight, those lips no longer belong to you and are not to be mishandled in such a way. Understood?" But her blank, shocked stare is just as endearing as her nervous tic of biting her lip so viciously.

"Nod once if you understand, pet," I tease.

She nods as ordered, and then shakes her head out of her stupor.

"I'm perfectly able to construct full sentences, you know," she snarks, turning sideways to me and facing the elevator doors, depriving me of the blush which is creeping up her entire captivating face.

"I'm aware." I grin, following suit.

"Is that why you're taking me to your suite? So we can talk?" she asks hopefully.

"Oh, my sweet pet, no. We've talked enough for tonight. You've made me wait all night for you. I think it's about time I see what I've been pining for, don't you?"

All night? How about all damned day! The past two weeks, even. Or even longer than that. But let's not scare my little pet further.

I click again on the elevator button and the doors finally open. I usher my jittery pet inside and follow right along. I press my floor number, followed by a pass of my ID card, and make sure the elevator is set for no interruption; a lovely setting that After Hours has in place for the more adventurous types, and I for one am feeling very daring this evening.

"Now, pet, I only have one more thing to clear up before I take you back to my suite," I inform her, taking the necessary steps I need to diminish the distance between us.

"Oh? And what's that?" she asks, her apprehension far too transparent to be mistaken.

"This," I tell her, and grab her flawless face with both hands and bring those lips to mine as I've imagined all fucking day.

Now I could have done a repeat performance of last night's balcony kiss.

Of course, I could have, since it was perfection in my book. But last night, I had felt cheated. Cheated out of passing that little barrier which separates pure bliss right onto hot fucking passion. This kiss was now a no-holds-barred scenario. Yesterday, she was the one who took the reins and left me breathless. Tonight, this was going to be my show—my rules. I was going to make sure her knees would be left as weak as she had left mine. Grabbing a damned rail for support, watching her leave and being powerless to stop her was not how I intended to end this kiss. She was the one who was going to feel it in every crevice of her being. Her knees would buckle down so hard she would need to lean on me for support just so she could walk out of this elevator afterward.

But just like last night, she steals my thunder yet again.

The moment my tongue meets hers, an electric current vibrates through me. I never thought electricity would taste like sweet honeyed cherry wine. She wrestles me at every turn, her timid kiss long forgotten, and this new one overpowering her senses just as it's overpowering mine. We're clawing at each other, and all we are is teeth, tongues, and swollen lips. Driven to a corner in this elevator, we take every chance we can to get as close as possible, without actually devouring each other. It's as if she can't get enough of me, either, wanting to dive into my very inner soul and grab all that I can give her. And I do want to give it all to her, especially the part of me which is currently in agony, feeling her soft core rub itself on me.

"Oh, God," she moans, and her husky cry ignites me further, making me want nothing more than to rip off the buttons on her dress to suck on the voluptuous pair of breasts she's concealing, and give my cock the reprieve he deserves by thrusting into her tight pussy.

Fuck!

I'm dangerously close to forgetting any plans I've set up with Con and Bash and fucking her right here in this elevator.

Shit!

But this woman sure does give as good as she gets.

"Pet, slow down," I order, trying to get a grip on the situation.

But she's not having any of it and goes for another mind-blowing kiss, so I have to grab her hair and pull her away from me. I look into the lust-filled eyes staring back at me as if I'm the only one who has ever been able to give her this much pleasure with a single kiss, a sentiment I understand too perfectly.

We are saved by the ding of the doors opening, so I take her hand and step into the corridor, quickly making my way to where the fun can really start. As much as I enjoyed this appetizer, I have no doubt the full meal will be far more fulfilling.

I swipe the key card to my suite, my pet still lightheaded beside me, and soon discover that the living room has already been set up for our nocturnal activities. The grand chandelier above, offering a dim light, emphasizes the presence of candles around the room. Duke, in his usual black attire, rises from his seat and stands nonchalantly as I bring our guest inside. I catch the sulk of my little Prince from the corner of my eye as he pours himself a shot at the bar. In one take, he wolfs it down and marches toward us, his scowl no longer visible.

With my *court* in place, and my blood already heated just from getting my pet into this suite, I think it's about time I make my first royal command.

I've waited long enough.

Chapter 10

EDIE

"On your knees, pet," he orders, and my belly does a quick flip at his dominant tone.

I take a sharp breath and do as he says, slowly lowering myself one knee at a time, keeping my stare to the floor. It should intimidate me that I'm no longer at eye level with either of the three men and that their eyes are focused solely on me. Yet, I'm not daunted at all. I probably should be, given the circumstances and the fact that I have no idea of what I'm getting myself into, but there is a certain thrill of diving into the unknown. Call me crazy, but I'm excited to see what these three get up to together. But most importantly, I'm excited to hear what Dean will order me to do next.

"You're new here." It's not a question, just an observation. He takes a small step closer to me and pulls a thread of my hair through his fingers. That little caress has me breathless. "So there are still plenty of things you need to know before we begin."

"She hasn't been initiated yet?" I hear the Duke—aka Sebastian Kelley—ask and to this, I shake my head, too nervous to say the word no. He senses my anxiety and chuckles.

"Are you sure you want to be, pet? I won't think any less of you if you go back to your original answer from last night," Dean whispers beside me, and it feels awfully like he's giving me a way out. Maybe I'm not the only one who second-guessed the whole day through by tallying the pros versus the cons on what a stupendous mistake I'm making by going through with this. But I would rather live a life with one regret than live a life full of what-ifs. Dean will not be my what-if. He made his stipulation last night; I've made mine. I'm brave enough to follow through on my word as long as he follows on his, and Dean Knox always keeps his word.

"I'm ready," I say softly but still with the conviction I feel. I want Dean to take me tonight, and I'll do anything he asks to make that happen.

"So you do want to play. Good to hear," Duke's voice carries a timber of satisfaction to my confession as I feel him and Con approach closer behind me. Dean continues to play with my hair, and even though the act is innocent enough, being on my knees and having his body so close to my own, is making the ache in my lower belly increase with each caress. Of course, feeling the heat from the other two bodies at my back isn't helping to lower my libido either.

"I'm sure you've already been told the rules by Poppy, but if you're going to play with us, we have to make sure you know what they are. This is a safe place, where we can be who we want to be, without judgment or guilt or any of the petty outside moralities society dictates. As long as it is consensual, anything goes. One of the rules is that we don't use our real names, and we never take off our masks. Discretion and anonymity should always be upheld. Do you understand these rules?" Dean's tone is all business-like, and it takes me back to Monday morning's boardroom meeting. I nod again like the fool I am because apparently speech is too difficult a task right now.

"Good. As we don't have names, we've each chosen our own. You already know mine. The man behind you in the silver mask is my Prince, and in the black mask is the Duke. We hold court here in this suite, and only here. Any pet who comes requesting an audience gets a shot at becoming our queen for the night. However, she must earn it first. Are you ready, pet, to earn your crown?"

I nod again, desperate to start the initiation process. Dean closes in on me further still and places his hand on the nape of my neck, urging me to look up at his face. It's too dark to see clearly, but I can almost make out the excitement mixed with a pinch of amusement in his eyes, even if he's trying to hold it in. I wet my lips involuntarily, as the sight before me is too good not to gawk at.

"Everyone here will get a taste tonight, but only one will have the privilege of getting into your tight pussy, pet, as you so requested. Do you have any preferences?" My knees buckle together at his crude words, and at the idea that I'm finally going to get what I've been fantasizing about for years now. I'm sure if my panties weren't on, I'd be leaving a small puddle on this floor, just staring into Dean's eyes alone.

Yep, I'm a basket case. It's official. I have totally lost all sense of logic and morality.

"You, I want you," I tell him, and God help me, I wouldn't have set foot in this club tonight if I didn't want him so badly. Common sense has no place in my head, whenever the mere idea of Dean touching me in any way is so palpable. I'll be his toy, his plaything, his fucking entertainment, as long as he takes me like I'm the queen he's promised to make me.

The naughty grin he gives his friends shows me he likes my answer, yet, with a quick jerk, he twists my head to face Bash. I'm taken off guard at the sudden move, but immediately start to tingle in anticipation when I feel Dean's breath on my neck.

"Alright, pet. If it's me you want, it's me you'll get. But first things first. Like I said, everyone gets a taste. You'll start with Duke first," he whispers in my ear and bites my lobe before retreating to his previous stance. I look back at Dean, and his expression becomes stoic as he focuses on Bash's face instead of my kneeling form, so I take that as my cue to do the same. Duke's demeanor is already predatory. It's almost as if Dean has given permission to play to his heart's content. Bash's silver eyes are darker than ever in this shadowed room, but every time the light hits his face, there is no hiding that he loves looking down at me on my hands and knees. The bulge in his pants is another excellent indicator, and increasingly identifiable with each step he takes closer to me.

Oh shit! Maybe I can't do this!

"I don't think your new friend likes me very much, King," I hear him say above my shaking form, as I squint my eyes, trying to black out the room around me and the men in it.

"Only means she's a good judge of character," Con jokes at his side. "I hated your guts when I first met you, too."

"I'm an acquired taste," Bash continues.

They continue their banter, but all I hear is ringing in my ears.

Fuck! I've gotten so fucking close, and I can't do it. After all the trouble I went through to get me here, I'm going to chicken out at the eleventh hour. Maybe I am just what Poppy said I was—a good girl pretending to be bad. Oh, sure, I'll act like I'm brave enough to look under the wizard's curtain, but in reality, my scared ass will be running a mile in the other direction. And why is that, you ask? Because I don't know what the hell I'm doing, and these three will see right through me in two seconds flat. It will be too embarrassing of a scenario to live through, and such humiliation cannot be disguised by any mask I wear from this point on.

"Give me your hands," Dean orders beside me, and I timidly hold them in front of me, too out of it to do more. He grabs them both abruptly and places them on a man's hips, who is now standing right in front of me. The last bout of bravery takes hold to see who they belong to, and I establish that I am now eye level with Duke's engorged crotch, which seems to want to make its own introduction.

"Have you ever touched a man before, love?" Bash asks unashamedly. "Your eyes look too innocent to ever have taken cock into that pretty little mouth, so I'm just wondering if you've seen one up close, at least. Touched one, perhaps?" His words should offend me, yet I can't fault him for his spot-on perception of me. Although I'm not entirely innocent, as per his assumptions of me, and had some boyfriends in college, I can't say they ever crossed the dry-humping stages. So apart from my alone time, I have little to no experience in actually performing any of these acts. If this place really is a judgment-free environment, then my honesty shouldn't affect either of the three men nor prevent them taking their pleasure and giving me mine in return. I shake my head, showing not only Bash how naïve I am in the ways of pleasure but also Dean and Connor.

"Fuck! This night just got a whole lot more interesting," Con whistles, and as much as I want to see Dean's expression, I stay focused on the man before me, intent on Duke being my main concern.

"It's alright, love. I'll teach you every step of the way, and I promise I'll make this as enjoyable for you as it will be for me." I give him a shy smile, wondering how me giving him head will be equivalent to the same pleasure as receiving it. Bash removes my hands from his hips and starts to unbuckle his belt, slowly undressing, and I feel my heart thump in my chest. Yes, Bash is extremely hot and sexy, and never in a million years did it ever occur to me that I would have this man in front of me telling me he's going to teach me how to give a blow job. Still, I'm both nervous and terribly aroused at the idea. I know for a fact that Dean is the man I want in my bed, and let's face it, probably in my heart, too, but Bash stripping in front of me, one piece of clothing at a time, is pretty mouthwatering as well. My previous worry is diminished some, and it's partially due to my core becoming a complete mess when he finally throws to the side his dress pants and shirt, leaving nothing but black designer boxers sporting what I now see is one impressive ten-inch cock.

Sweet baby Jesus. Bash is packing some serious heat. Who would have thought that under those conservative designer suits he wears were defined, tattooed abs which would spar against any prison inmate on cell block eight, and a male anatomy that makes most porn actors weep.

"Okay, love, I'm going to introduce you to my best friend. We're very attached, and he's dying to meet that pretty pink tongue of yours. First, I need you to put your hands on me. Feel me first, love," he tells me sweetly, and I slowly do as he instructs. I'm not sure if he wanted me to touch him over his boxers first, but my curiosity has taken over my logic, so I grip his waistband and lower his briefs to the floor. What springs free is too impressive for words. Silky smooth skin with beads of moisture on top of its head greets my sight. My palm goes directly to the base of his cock and my fingers to the moisture above, smoothing that beautiful head of his.

"That's it, love, yeah, just like that. Feel your way," Bash coos, and my eyes are too engrossed at the scene before me to look away. I always thought a woman's form was so much more attractive and seductive than a man's could ever be. We are all curves and soft mounds, but having this majestic cock in my hand that shifts and hardens with my touch is just as seductive.

"That feels so good, love—you're a fucking natural. Try pumping me now. With your hand like this in a fist, pump my fucking cock to the base and back... Fuck, yeah, like that, love, like that!" Bash keeps growing longer and wider, and I have to admit, his moans and his shaft growing harder in my hands is getting me slick in between my thighs. I start to squirm a bit to get some friction of my own but to no avail.

"Shit, King, a little help here. I don't think I'm going to make it if she puts her mouth on me," Bash says, and it's the first time I look up at his face and see that he looks like he's in pain.

"Should I stop?" I ask mid-pump, my voice just as husky as Sebastian's.

"Fuck no!" Bash yells out, this time gripping my shoulders and making sure I don't move an inch. But at that moment, I feel Dean's breath behind me again.

"Open your legs, pet. Duke is being a lightweight tonight, but he can't cum until you cum. House rules. Ladies first, so open those gorgeous legs for me so I can get you where you need to go." I don't have to be told twice. I open my legs, but keep my hands on Bash, stroking and pumping him with all my focus; well at least with all the focus I can muster as Dean's breath is on my neck and his hands are skimming my legs, thighs, and then finally reach my panties.

"Why, pet, we've barely even started, and you're drenched already. This pussy is just begging to cum. Or is it the idea that you'll be riding my cock before the night is over that made you so wet?" Dean continues to whisper in my ear, and I want to say yes to all of it, but I'm too mesmerized at the feel of him parting my panties to the side and finding my soft tissue hidden beneath. Dean takes no prisoners, as he goes straight to my clit with his thumb and inserts two fingers into me right from the get-go. If I wasn't so embarrassingly wet, it might have hurt, but instead, all I felt was the ache being finally replaced with a smoldering heat. I rock my hips on his hands, and Dean's breathing starts to pick tempo with each thrust I make of my own. It's as if I'm the one in control of both men now, and it's one of the hottest things I have ever experienced.

"That's it, baby, fuck King's hand. God, you look so good!" I hear Con say beside me, and it's when I realize he's fisting his own dick, already stark naked. I look to my right to see if Dean is also in the same attire, and I'm confronted by his bare chest and broad shoulders flexing, as his arm pushes beneath my skirt, mercilessly thrusting another digit in my tight cunt, making me cum with a moan on my lips.

"Fuck, yes!" Bash yells out, and I suddenly feel his shaft shooting jet after jet of warm white liquid all over my fingers and hands. I'm still lightheaded with the earth-shattering orgasm, but the semen on my fingers is too tantalizing of an aspect for me to not inspect further. But before I can take each slippery finger into my mouth to see what all the fuss is about, Dean grabs my chin and shakes his head, silently ordering me not to. I feel my whole face burn red, only for the heat to travel further south with his next move. A swarm of butterflies crawls back up my belly with the gentlest kiss Dean places on my forehead, as a sign of his most profound approval.

"Shit, that's hot! My turn," Con shouts, and before I know it, he's picking me off the floor and sitting me open-legged on the sofa.

"I have no idea where you came from, baby, and frankly, I don't give a rat's ass. But right now, you've given me one hell of a hard-on just by watching you cum, as you rode King's hand and jerked off Duke at the same time like a pro. You, dear girl, deserve a reward, and I know just the one I want to give you," Con grunts as he raises my dress to my waist. From here, I can see my panties still pushed to the side, and my inner thighs are slick with my own juices. I don't know why, but suddenly I feel very shy, being so exposed like this. And if it weren't for the fact that Con was holding my ankles in place, opening me even further, I would have probably locked my knees together already.

"Such a pretty pink pussy we have here, boys. I wonder if it tastes as good as it looks?" Con jokes with his friends, but his eyes are locked on my wet folds. I clench involuntarily, and he wets his lips as if he's famished and the maître d' has just brought his steak dinner.

"I guess I'll just have to kiss it and see for myself," he says and lowers his head to my most treasured and secret of places.

He takes one long, soft lick from crack to clit, and it's the most excruciatingly wonderful feeling I have ever had in my life. I mean, I've heard Lexi and her girls go on and on about how they loved their respective partners to go down on them. Some even complained this type of foreplay was nearly nonexistent in their sex lives, and they hated it, since getting someone to eat you out was probably one of the best orgasms a woman could have. I still don't have much to compare it with. I know I preferred cumming on Dean's fingers rather than my own or with my trusty vibrator, any day of the week. But I have to admit, the moment Con put his lips and tongue on me, the previous orgasm quickly evaporated from my system, only to be replaced with something ten times more explosive. Con doesn't let up once. He licks, and tugs, and kisses, and I'm almost positive he's reciting fucking Shakespeare into my labia and clitoris. I'm seeing stars. I'm seeing fireworks. I'm seeing all sorts of bright colors in a previously dark shadowy room. I'm moaning like I'm in heat, and maybe, just maybe, I actually am, since I want to beg the man in front of me to fuck me with his cock, which is currently humping the sofa in search of its own release.

Which really doesn't make any sense, since I don't even like Connor Walsh. Okay, don't get me wrong. I don't hate him like Devina does. But he's not the type of guy I would bring home to my mother, either. Here's the thing with Con, or the so-called Prince, as he goes by here. Connor Walsh is a player, ladies. He's got the blond, blue-eyed, all-American bad boy thing going for him, and from what I've heard, he really is a true blueblood, rivaling even the Kennedys back in Massachusetts. His constant companions, aside from my Dean and Bash, are his panty-melting fake smiles and the numerous hearts he's publicly broken over the years, which consistently shadows him like a bad breakup song that won't stop playing on the radio. Women know he's bad news. Yet, they flock to him like moths to a flame. I have never been attracted to such a man in my life, but having Con recite the alphabet on my sensitive flesh, is evaporating such preconceived notions apparently. I'm no longer thinking of anything but this bomb that is on the brink of detonation.

"Please," I moan, but Con is too wrapped up in my inner walls to even hear my pleas. Oh, God, if I don't cum now, I think I might lose my mind.

"Please," I insist louder, and this time my savior hears my plea and comes to sit at my side.

"Please what, pet? What do you want?" Dean asks, patiently stroking my wet hair from my forehead. The mask itself is burning my already feverish skin, and this breeze is welcomed, but still not enough to pull me out of my current misery.

"Make me cum, my king. I need to cum. Please," I whine on the brink of insanity. Con's tongue is hot and eager on me, and I don't know how much more I can take his obsessive devouring.

"Does it hurt, pet? Tell me how much you ache," Dean says as he starts to unbutton my dress, one button at a time, as if the task before him was a typical day-to-day occurrence; completely banal, and not the first time he's undressed me in any way. The moment I feel the cool air hit my chest, I arch my back. It's when I realize that my nipples are hard buds, and my breasts feel so heavy and full. While Con has been going down on me like a fiend, my breasts seem to need the same attention. When Dean lowers his head to my chest, my heart freezes. My whole body is sweating, and I can see sweat pooling in between my two swollen breasts. Dean licks this centered spot, and my moans intensify tenfold.

"Oh, God," I breath out, and although I still feel my pussy demanding to own the show, Dean's attentiveness to my chest sets my blood on fire. He raises his head, and behind the mask, there is a sparkle of mischief in his eye. Suddenly, I feel my left nipple being bitten and sucked into his warm mouth as the right is being groped firmly by his fingers. And just like that, ladies and gentleman, I cum and cum and cum. Incoherent words come out of my mouth, but I'm pretty sure I've been to heaven's gates and back.

"Such a good girl," Dean coos, and his smoldering manner tells me he is anxious to have his turn. I, of course, am limb and bones—too out of it to even think straight anymore. I don't even register whether Con came or not, and the only thing I remember is being pulled into Dean's lap, and me cradling my head to his neck.

I remember another tender kiss placed on my forehead by the King himself before I do the elegant thing and black the fuck out.

Nighty night.

Peace out.

Edie has officially left the building.

Chapter 11

DEAN

"I wasn't done yet," Con grumbles, getting up from his knees.

"Well, you're done now," I deadpan, softly stroking my pet's hair away from her face as she snuggles closer to me.

Such an obedient little thing.

"We could just wake her, you know?" Connor exhales, putting on his shirt.

"Don't be a dick, dude. The girl is out like a light," Bash scolds my best friend, saving me the trouble.

"You sure got what you wanted—came like a fucking teenager. Lightweight," Con jokes while putting on his belt.

"What can I say? Virgin pussy turns me on," Bash smirks mischievously.

"So, are you going to wake sleeping beauty up or what, King? I've seen a lot of eager ladies wanting to join us this week, and for me, this little show was only a brief warm-up for what I have in mind," Con continues, but my mind is still on Bash's words.

"You think she's a virgin?" I ask quietly, not wanting the woman in my arms to neither hear my question nor wake her from her little nap. She's going to need her energy in a little while.

"Bet my life on it," Bash replies, eyeing the girl up and down. "Think Prince is right on one account, though. She really is quite the fetching sleeping beauty."

"Might explain why she was sweeter than most. Girl is all honey down there," Con interrupts Bash's praise, also eyeing her like he wants another go at her. But the boys have played already. I played a little, too, if I want to split hairs about it, but not enough with this pet. The boys can entertain themselves out on the floor. This little Beauty, as my friends have coined her, is going to be devoured by one mouth and one body alone tonight.

"Didn't you say the night is full of possibilities? Well then, I'll keep Beauty, while both of you get your own fairytale ending this evening. This one right here is going to find out how kings rule in the bedroom," I inform, continuing to lace my fingers through her golden locks.

"Maybe your Beauty should have a bit more experience first. Perhaps a Prince Charming to mold her until she's ready for you," Con says, licking his lips, eyes still fixed on her bare legs and breasts.

"Not when the only Prince we have here is still hung up on the Wicked Witch," I state coldly, knowing my words would put the image of a particular woman in his head, while I fix my pet's dress in place, preventing his leering from going any further.

"You're a fucking cocksucker, you know that?" he grunts, his eyes no longer holding the lustful stare. "Keep her, then. I'm getting my own. Duke, you coming?" Con asks, already making his way to the door.

"Give me a sec," Bash replies, walking to the leather couch where he left his coat and tie. Con doesn't wait, though, and fumes his way out the door. I should feel a small tinge of guilt for the woman he finds tonight because he will fuck her until she can't walk just so he can get Devina out of his mind. Angry revenge sex won't do it for him, but it will give the woman endless orgasms until he starts hearing her voice instead of Devina's ringing in his ears.

"That wasn't cool, King. You know how he still feels about her, even if he doesn't want to admit it," Bash states while fixing his cufflinks.

By looking at him, you wouldn't have guessed he just had a girl on her knees at his complete mercy. Back to his cool and collected form, he gives me a small scowl, showing me how I should go easy on Con. Frankly, I'm sick to death of this little dance he does with Devina, especially when our company's business is in the mix. But my little Prince and I go way back, and just like the man before me, he is my brother in all ways—if not by blood. I vowed to protect them both against all demons. And when it came to my younger brother, there was no greater demon than the self-sabotaging one who stares back at him in the mirror every day.

"I'll take that under advisement," I affirm. Bash gives me a small nod, and I know this is all he'll say about the issue.

"You staying the night?"

"I'm considering it," I tell him, even though I haven't made up my mind yet.

"You felt it too, didn't you?" Bash asks, tilting his head toward my slumbering pet. "The girl is too clean and innocent to even be here. If you keep her, be careful, King. We have it good here. I don't want you to do anything that may jeopardize it."

"You think I would hurt her?" I ask, a little insulted that one of my best friends would think so little of me.

"No, I think she's young and impressionable. She might be a clinger if you pop her cherry." A small smile tugs on his lips.

"I'll do my best to make things clear to her. That is, if I keep her," I reply with my own devilish smile.

"Oh, you're keeping her. Beauty looks too good

not to snack on the whole night through. Have to say, I'm a little disappointed she chose you," Bash taunts, making his way to the door. He gives my sleepy pet and me one quick look and shakes his head. "Something tells me that after tonight, you won't be too inclined to share her again. Pity I only got a damned hand job out of it. Live and learn, I guess," he quips, offering another sly smile before closing our suite's door behind him.

Even though I am enjoying the view and her warmth on my lap, I know I'll enjoy her much more the moment this woman awakes.

I pick her up and stand. "Where are we going?" she whispers on my neck, awakening from her little power nap.

"You'll see soon enough, pet," I answer, eager to show her what I have in store.

I walk us to the back of the suite and into my own room. My king-sized bed awaits us right at the center of the room. Fitting, I know, but I have always been a true believer that a man deserves the very best if he works and aims high enough for it. And I sure did aim for the prize I have in my arms , haven't I?

So now it's time to reap my spoils.

I place her on the bed, and she cuddles into the middle, still in a daze, probably from all the endorphins of the two orgasms she had in the living room, or maybe the little dream she had in my arms.

But my patience is running thin, and my body humming with how eager it is to claim her. However, despite popular opinion, I'm not the bastard most people believe me to be, and therefore, I won't touch another golden hair on her pretty head until she wills it so.

"Pet?" I hush.

"Hmm," she purrs.

"Are you tired, pet? Do you want me to leave you here so you can rest?" I offer sincerely, but to my utter contentment, her eyes fly wide open at my chivalrous suggestion.

"No! I'm not tired," she yelps.

Her enthusiasm is just another one of her enticing features I find myself smiling inwardly about, and it does my ego good to know the little performance she underwent in the living room wasn't what she truly yearned for. She went through all that to get her king, this beauty of mine. And I, for one, am more than ready to give her what she so valiantly bargained for.

But first things first.

"Pet, I'm happy to hear it, but I have a question for you first. I need you to answer me truthfully now. Remember, there is no judgment within these walls, so I want you to tell it to me straight. Alright?" I explain, using my most soothing tone, so as not to alarm her.

Regardless of my attempts to ease her into this conversation, she worries her bottom lip again, a tic I have learned is her nervous go-to move when she is stressed or unsure of herself.

"What we are about to do, pet, what you have bargained so fearlessly for this evening… is it your first time, pet? Honesty above all, Beauty. I need to know."

"And if it is, would that make you go back on your word to me?" she asks, unable to conceal the small stain of shyness and embarrassment from her voice.

"No, Beauty. My word is my bond. I gave you mine as you gave me yours. You honored your commitment to me, and I shall honor mine to you, no matter what your answer. But I would like to know. It will also make it easier on me to understand how I should treat you, if it is your first time," I try to explain.

"What do you mean?" Her brow suddenly raises, curiosity overcoming her shyness. Something tells me this trait might have been the culprit that got her through the After Hours' doors in the first place.

My curious pet.

"A woman's first time… requires certain attention. If you were experienced, I would do sundry things with your body; take certain liberties that I wouldn't if you were a virgin. With someone who is about to embark on a sexual experience for the first time, it should be done with care. It needs a special type of attention, pet. Roughness and other creative playing should be left for other opportunities down the line, but not for a first time. Understand?"

"Oh. I see," she replies, slumping her shoulders, her eyes no longer fixed on mine, but on the dark navy bedspread to her side. There is a soft pain in my gut in seeing her look so defeated. I much prefer seeing her brave me head-on, even if inside she's fighting every shy bone she has and nerves alike. Seeing her like this, torn and crushed, unsettles me somewhat.

"So what is it, pet? Is this your first time?" I ask, after giving her enough time to think about what I've explained. But if I'm honest, it could have also matched up with the limit of time I could bear her shielding herself from me.

She turns her head to face me, once again summoning her inner valiance and gives me a simple nod, accompanied by a soft blush she's unable to conceal with her answer. Her eyes close soon after, as if too embarrassed to keep their hold on mine when they shouldn't be closed at all. It took bravery for her to come into this suite in the first place, so I'm in awe of her gumption and her fortitude—a sentiment that people can rarely summon, and this mesmeric woman has been able to surprise me and leave me bewildered in each of our encounters.

It's time.

"Lay back for me, Beauty," I order.

"That's the third time you've called me that, my King," she whispers, but I see the small grin playing on her lips, letting me know she likes the nickname just fine. Probably just as much as I like her calling me her king.

"Since you haven't given yourself a name, as *your ruler* for the evening, I've taken it upon myself to give you one. And what name does you more justice than Beauty?" I remark, cocking my brow, daring her to defy my conclusion.

"You think I'm beautiful?" she queries, her elbows now on the bed, back slightly up, looking at me with a mixture of shock and thrill.

"Yes, pet. I think you are an exquisite creature. Too alluring to run around without a name for me to call on," I tease, letting myself run my thumb up and down her cheek. A pity her mask only lets me caress her face to a certain extent. The appeal of anonymity dims somewhat when it prevents me from having full access to all of her.

"Oh," she sighs, her eyes wide as saucers, marking my own facial features to memory.

"Now, like I said, lie back," I order, but this time I place a small kiss on the tip of her precious nose, and like an obedient, spoiled pet, she lies down, looking up at her master, eager for his next tender touch.

I take my time, just watching her sprawled on my bed. Her fixed stare on me suggests that this offering is so much more than just her body for my eager exploration. Her crystal eyes behind her mask are just too intense, and I feel them search mine for my next move or instructions, but while above her, I keep my standing form still. I then tell her to unbutton the rest of her dress, which is merely but a few buttons since I was so eager back on the couch to do the job myself. Soon enough she is left only in a matching lacy white bra and panty set—virginal to the very end.

"Can you stand for me, pet?"

She nods and gets onto her wobbly legs and feet. I remove her gown from the bed and place it on the side chair. Walking behind her shaking back, I sit down on the corner of the bed and put my palms down on each knee.

"Take off the rest, pet."

"All of it?" she breathes softly.

"Yes, pet."

She nods, visibly trembling, but does as instructed, going to the back of her bra and unsnapping it accordingly. When it falls off, I'm rewarded yet again with the view of two voluptuous globes and pink nipples, ripe for my teeth to pull and play with. But patience is a virtue, and delayed gratification has its merits, after all. This evening's unexpected turn of events has amped up my already peculiar interest in *my* Beauty.

I wasn't lying when I told her that taking one's virginity meant special care needed to be taken, but I can't remember ever being with a virgin aside from the time I was one myself, and that was back in high school. At the time, I was a fumbling fool who didn't know what I was doing, and the only precaution I took was to make sure I had a condom and that the back seat of my car didn't smell like dirty gym clothes. It was only after I did the deed and saw the look of disappointment in my date's face for the little effort I had made, that I established how important it had been to her. Her breaking up with me a couple of days after was a good indicator as well.

If Beauty had guarded her virtue up to this point, whatever the reason, I had to make sure her efforts were well compensated tonight. I will care for her. I will give her the moment she's been fantasizing about, and maybe even dreading. I'll be the very definition of her king tonight.

Beauty slowly continues to wander her fingers onto the lacey fabric covering her most treasured possession and carefully pulls it down her toned thighs, all the way to the floor. Once all the garments are fully removed, she stands tall and holds her stare to mine, looking for some form of approval; she needs none since she should know by now how extraordinary she is—a true masterpiece if I ever saw one.

"Come here, pet."

She takes two shaky steps my way and stops mere inches from me, uncertain about what to do next. Up to this point, she's only been able to follow my commands, and I've yet to give any more. I'm still looking at her sumptuous naked body, and a little too sidetracked to give her the next command I have in mind. I reprimand myself for that error when I see her bite her lower lip anxiously. She needs guidance tonight, and so far, her following my simple instructions has given her some small comfort, knowing I would take the lead.

"Kneel, pet. I want you to take my shoes off next."

I see relief fly off her shoulders as she falls to her knees and does the task, effortlessly removing shoes and socks alike. I can't resist and play with her hair as she does, going as far as caressing her neck and back just so I can get a small taste of her flawless skin on my fingers. Smooth as silk, and seductive as velvet.

Once she's finished, Beauty looks up from her kneeled position, expecting my next order. I almost ask her to end my misery and spring me free, so I can have the same image of her just like this, on her knees, looking up with wide, expectant eyes, and my cock cumming in her mouth.

The thought alone gets me harder than hell and I take my hands off her to cool myself down a bit. This doesn't sit too well with my pet, as I see the look of hurt reach her eyes from my sudden withdrawal. So I quickly slap my knee instead.

"Sit here, Beauty. Come and take off my shirt now," I direct.

Her joy returns tenfold, and the fire in my chest heats up just as fiercely, seeing how much she craves to touch me, too. She sits on my knee, naked as the day she was born, and my shaft hates me for its confinement since it knows damned well I've just made him the last one in line to feel her warmth. With tender hands, she unbuttons my shirt meticulously, button by button, like a surgeon would conduct a lifesaving operation. Once every single one is completely freed, she takes the shirt off my back, licking her lips, and looks into my eyes as if pleading consent to do more.

"Do you want to touch me, pet?" I smirk, enjoying her apparent approval of her findings. "You don't have to ask permission from me. I'll ask for yours always, but tonight, you can do with me what you will. You have earned that much, don't you agree?" I cock my brow.

She blinks twice and then nods before placing a tender hand on the base of my neck. Like a shadowed kiss, she trails it over my sensitive flesh, making it heat up further still with her innocent touch. I close my eyes to let her enjoy her moment, although I'm not used to just foreplay. Here in the club, I'm more used to either keeping to the background and watching others take their pleasure, or when I do partake in my own, I take it roughly and brutally. So, This type of gentle exploration between us is unsettling. It feels oddly intimate. And just like her demure kiss on the balcony, I feel the earth rattle from beneath me, and I have to grab the bedspread in a fist to keep my bearings. Her sexual naivety intrigues me, yes, but I wasn't expecting her touch to make me feel just as vulnerable.

And when I think I can't bear to feel another burning mark, she torches me further with a simple kiss to the hollow of my neck. I inwardly hear myself grunt. Another kiss, followed by yet another, and another. Down and down she goes. So torturous, I feel my spine come very close to mimicking her delightful shivers. My brave pet surprises me further when I feel a wet, warm, hot tongue lick my right pec, taking her time to nibble on my flesh there. But her wicked tongue starts drawing a fine line right down to my navel. I've reached my limit. I can't stand it anymore. I place my hands on her arms, holding her still, and throw her on to the bed a tad too forcefully, but a man can only take so much.

"That's enough, pet."

"Mmmm," she replies, her eyes half-mast, still enraptured with her midnight snack.

I'm not sure if the heart I hear beating a mile a minute is hers or mine. I stand on my feet while her luscious perusal of me continues. I take off my pants, and even though sense tells me I should leave my boxers on for a little while longer to prolong her gentle foreplay, I take them off, too. The game has changed, and I fear that for my own sanity I will have to end this sooner than I intended. Intimacy was never on the table. Only a moment. A good time for the both of us. But I gave her my word, and I will honor it—and enjoy myself while doing it, because, without question, this woman is too delicious not to.

I crawl up to her and attack her mouth. Her wide eyes, brought on by my own nudity, close immediately, and all I hear is her moan, and I fall back into our whirlwind desire.

Her damned kiss. It gets me every time. I should expect how lethal it is by now, and yet when her lips touch mine, I am blown away by it every single time. I eat up her gentle sigh, and roar as her body rubs itself against mine, fitting ever so flawlessly. Every soft curve aligning itself perfectly to my hard edges. Her core, wet and aching, pleading for me to enter her, but I'm too enthralled right now just kissing my Beauty to take this to the next step.

"Oh, God," she whispers.

"King, pet. Always say my name when I'm about to fuck you," I tell her possessively, wanting her words and thoughts only to have me in them.

"Yes, my King," she concedes eagerly.

I gain courage to break free from her lips and start my own exploration down her body with my own. Her long neck first gets my attention, so I pepper it with the same sweet kisses she bestowed on me earlier. I then take them down to her breasts and those enticing pink nipples which beg me for their playtime. I pull and bite just as I silently promised them I would, only to have my pet quiver on the bed, aching in need.

"Be still, pet," I sternly command, and slap her thigh to make her understand I mean business.

Her cheeks turn the usual rosy shade, and I see the mirror image on her thigh. Oh, what wondrous things I could do with this body if given the chance. I continue nibbling down her body, just as she did mine, and the whimpering coming from her mouth lets me know just how her torturous ways being reciprocated have a similar effect.

Good.

Once I reach her shaven mound, an unexpected resentment of Con being the first to taste her hits me. But just as the feeling surges, I quickly kick it away by having a taste of my own—fucking honey, just like he said.

"Oh, God… I mean, King! Please, no!" she screams.

"Why not, pet? Didn't you enjoy it?" I ask, lifting my head to look her in the eye, curious to learn why she's so against this.

"Yes," she replies sheepishly.

"Then why are you denying me, but most importantly yourself, the satisfaction?" I query, intrigued. She lets her head fall back onto the pillows and places both arms over her eyes since the mask she's wearing does poorly in concealing her discomfort. If the eyes were the window to a soul, then hers were floor-to-ceiling glass, letting everyone have a full view of hers.

"I'm waiting, pet." My stern tone suggests I'm growing tired of her silence, but in all honesty, I'm quite enjoying the view from down here.

"I don't want to pass out again. Last time *that* happened, I did. And if I pass out, then maybe you won't wake me a second time," she finally relents, huffing out exasperated in the end. I kiss her inner thigh to camouflage the small chuckle I let out.

My Beauty, ever the eager one.

"You won't pass out, pet. Trust me. I intend to keep you fully awake the rest of the night," I swear.

Her arms fall to the side, revealing a smile spread wide from ear to ear, and fuck me if it isn't the most glorious thing I've seen. I place my head in between her thighs just to hide my own satisfaction to her response in spending the night with me, and as I eat her out, I don't think I have ever tasted anything sweeter. I could easily make her cum just like this. Hell, I could easily make myself cum just like this, but my intention wasn't for an orgasm, but to prepare her body to take me. As she withers away, I insert two fingers in her, happy to see my pet is too eager to have them there. Once she is comfortable with the rhythm of my tongue on her clit and the thrusts of my fingers, I add another digit. Her moans start to build up their tempo, but I need her pussy just a little bit better prepared for me, so I enter her deep into her walls. No sooner do I do this, as I lavish on her clit, my pet cums like the early sun on a gorgeous summer day. Apparently, my calculations were off a smidge, since I believed she could have held on a few more minutes, but it seems my Beauty is extremely sensitive to me. She wasn't with Connor, but with my touch, my pet doesn't need much. Another feature of hers, which feeds my already hungry ego where she's concerned.

"My King, I need you. I need you so much," she pleads.

Fuck, if that isn't poetry to my ears. I crawl my way back up, placing a chaste kiss on her damp forehead when I finally reach her.

"Your body seems ready for me, my Beauty, but this will still hurt. Are you sure you want to do this?" I ask, wanting to make sure her resolution still held true.

"More than I want to breathe," she answers in one exhale.

"So dramatic, pet," I tease, not forgoing my chuckle this time. She places her hands on my face, careful of my own golden mask, and looks into my eyes intently.

"I want you so much," she says in earnest, and there is a tightness that occurs in my chest because I believe her. The honesty to her words, accompanied by an unknown sentiment behind her crystal eyes, is too damned appealing not to be consumed by it.

"You have me," I tell her. For tonight, she will have the best of me.

This will hurt her, though. I remember that much at least. So the first time will probably not be as pleasurable for her as it will be for me, but I will try my best to make it as pleasurable as possible. By the night's end, maybe by the third or fourth try, she'll be able to have an orgasm from sex alone.

"I'll go slow, Beauty. Tell me when to stop if it gets to be too much, alright?" I explain, getting only a nod and a bite of the lip as her only response. "I'll need you to be more vocal than that, pet. Use your words," I reprimand softly.

"Please… I need you now, my King," she says, and those mere chosen words end me.

I crush her with my mouth, seeking yet again my precious nirvana from her lips, and join her core with my restless cock at last. I pull away from our kiss, unable to concentrate otherwise, and enter her slowly, and even though I prepared her so thoroughly, I know I'm bigger than most, so such delicate preparations would have been needed for more days at a time before this big event.

One night of prep work to get this right is asking a lot from a man, but she did insist on a king's performance, after all. Ever so gently, I push through, slowly and carefully, always picking up on any resistance, or signs of pain she could be suffering.

"My King. Look at me," she begs, and that's when I establish my eyes have been closed this whole time, too focused on the task at hand.

I nod, wanting to appease her and give her this small solace. But in doing so, I see that foreign feeling in her eyes yet again, one I recognize as adoration, so my vulnerable state comes back like a hurricane breaking down cemented walls.

I start to turn my head, but she grabs it and kisses me, gently overpowering my will. I concede and lean into the kiss, desperate for it, and before I know it, I feel myself breaking her barrier. She lets out a small shriek of pain, but I devour it as well, as her tongue continues to dance with mine.

I kiss her violently, each of us keeping our eyes fixed on the other. Passion, lust, and that damned intimacy transpires through our stare. The very thing I never wanted to share here tonight is screaming at me to stop. Yet, willingly lacing itself around each diamond that her blue eyes are crested with.

This kiss is too damned powerful. Like a dream

you don't want to wake up from, I relish in it. I cherish it, just as much as I'm cherishing how her body is responding to me entering it and owning it as mine. With each movement I make, her hips start to meet mine slowly, and as our tempo syncs in harmony, so does her forcefulness in seeking me. When she begins to pant and sigh, and her pussy starts to clench on my cock like ivy on a vine, bright lights blind me as my own orgasm starts to come through.

"Beauty—"

"Oh, God! KING!" she yells out, cumming, and I follow right along with her. She meets my every thrust to perfection. Pure fucking paradise. I have found a fucking treasure in a place that holds little shine. My drumming heart can't seem to slow down as I take a minute to look at this incredible fortune under me. My pet is sated, her brows wet, and I'm sure the mask she's wearing is a great discomfort to her blissful state. But aside from that, the joy plastered on her face is too overwhelming to maintain my watchful eye on her. I kiss her forehead and unlatch myself from her hold to get a wet towel to clean her off. When I return to the room, my pet is sitting on the bed, hugging her knees under her chin, her joy no longer visible.

"Did I do something wrong?" she asks, her voice so low I almost don't catch it all. I place the towel by her side and gently cradle her chin in my grip. When I see unshed tears threaten to break free, a need to tear the bastard who caused her pain overpowers me, and it takes me a minute to realize I'm the villain in the room.

"You were perfect, my pet. More than I could have ever hoped for in a lover," I answer honestly, and kiss each wet cheek tasting the salt of her tears

Even though it pains me I've hurt her with my urgency to flee and give myself pause from what we shared, my cock doesn't seem to be on the same wavelength, since he *tells* me that just by the taste of her tears alone, for *him* round two can commence sooner than I anticipated.

"Now, lie back so I can clean you, pet," I coo, hoping to ease her back to her previous gratified state.

"M'kay," she replies, doing precisely as I said.

I gently pass the wet towel on her sensitive center, knowing I should probably leave the night's activities as they are, and bid farewell. Duke's warning comes to me like a slap on the back, and I know I should take caution. But I don't believe I'm dealing with a psycho or a clinger. I'm not sure what I'm dealing with, but I've always fancied myself a good judge of character. The only flaw I find this woman to have is her naiveté and innocence, something that should have never been born in After Hours. But it was this same characteristic that appealed to me and caught my eye. However, if I am to prolong this evening any further, I should know more about my pet, shouldn't I?

Once I'm done, I place the towel on the nightstand, not wanting to leave her alone again with her thoughts. I lie beside her, pulling my pet toward me, and gratefully she comes willingly. I begin to play with her hair, lulling her until I feel her relax. Her naked body, still warm and vibrant, is wreaking havoc on mine, but I need my answers first.

"How old are you?"

"Why?" she asks, lifting her head and placing her chin on my chest for balance.

"Just indulge my curiosity, pet. How old are you?" I repeat, teasing her uncovered cheek with my thumb.

"Twenty-four."

"Hmmm."

"What?" she asks, suspicious of my own reply.

"That's a long time to be holding off sex. Why the change?" I ask, wanting to know the real reason behind her membership in this elite club, but all I end up getting is a whole lot of silence.

"Now pet, no need to be shy with me. Especially after what we've just done," I coo again, reassuringly.

"Promise you won't laugh?" she says, worrying her lip.

"I'm not the laughing type, Beauty. Tell me," I

reply, although with her I have found myself chuckling more than not.

"I guess I was looking for the right guy. I didn't want to have sex for the first time just to be done with it," she answers, shrugging her shoulders. "I wanted it to be special."

"Is that why you came to After Hours, then? Had you given up hope?" I ask, puzzled.

"No. I got exactly what I wanted," she remarks, a small smile on her lips.

"I'm a stranger to you, pet. I'm sure I'm far from being the ideal you were dreaming of." I cock my brow and stare into her eyes, searching for something, anything, to understand how she could have gotten what she always pictured.

"Yet, you were exactly what I always wanted," she deadpans matter-of-factly.

"You wanted to lose your virginity to a stranger?" I ask, still confused as hell.

"No. I wanted to make it special. To share it with someone worthy of it—you."

"Me?" I ask, astounded.

"You sound surprised?" She grins.

"It takes a lot to surprise me," I answer stoically.

"Yet, you are," she replies, with her grin beaming out proudly.

I feel a smirk of a smile start to form on my lips and the promised second round knocking at the door.

"Yes, pet. Yet I am. Let's see how many more surprises you have for me tonight."

Chapter 12

EDIE

When I open my eyes, the first thing I encounter is how cold I feel, which makes sense since I'm buck ass naked in a king-sized bed with nothing to warm me. The King has left the building, y'all, and left with no forwarding address. Not what I expected, but neither was last night.

Should I be pissed he left in the middle of the night after plowing through my body three—oh, that's right, ladies and gentlemen three—freaking amazing, glorious times?

You know what? I'm not angry he's gone, and I'm sure as shit not one bit sorry for any delicious moment we spent together last night.

So he bailed. So what?

The man has an empire to run, and I'm positive that spending any of his precious time locked away in a clandestine nightclub with a woman he hardly knows isn't high on his priority list of demands for the day.

Still, it does taste bittersweet. Or maybe that's just my morning breath. I put my hand over my mouth to double check. Yep, could be me. There're no clocks in this room, but by the light just threatening to crack outside the window, I'm guessing that I'll have to haul ass to work pretty soon, and all I have here is last night's getup. Shit. It's going to take me at least half an hour to get to my apartment and ready for work.

But just like Dean, I have to kiss the night away so that I can tackle what everyday life has in store for me, which means forgetting, for the time being, After Hours, its King and his Beauty.

Beauty.

Sweet baby Jesus!

Didn't that make you all swoon like a schoolgirl?

No? Just me?

Whatever.

Bet you guys a million if you had the King himself all lovey-dovey, looking into your eyes like he did last night, making you all hot and bothered, and then nicknaming you Beauty because he thought that was the only name which did you justice, you'd be all weak in the knees, too. I'd like to see how well you guys could hold in your swoon abilities in such a scenario.

Focus, Edie!

Okay!

Out with living a fairy tale, and in with… well… life as the personal assistant to the almighty Devina Richardson—basically the only title people know me as, and not much else. Edie Vanderwalt might as well be a ghost outside Royal's walls, but at least there, she's level-headed and doesn't look like the kind of girl who almost engaged in a foursome.

Jesus, Edie! FOCUS!

After my third—okay, *sixth*—reprimand, I get dressed and out of the swanky building. I still have a hint of luck from last night, as I'm able to hail a cab right away, and within twenty-five minutes flat I'm opening my front door. I get my butt in the shower, wash my hair and clean my body thoroughly, erasing all evidence of Dean's touch. Isn't that a bitch? 'Cause I would have loved to have his scent linger on my skin just a bit longer. But no way could I have gone to work smelling like I'd gone three rounds with Mike Tyson. And believe me, Dean made sure I went through the wringer. He said he'd be cautious and take care of me, but if that was his delicate touch, then damn! I can't wait for his rough stuff.

Oh, yeah! There won't be rough stuff, because this was a one-time event!

Well, that sucks!

I was just getting used to this rolling-in-the-hay thing. I mean, who would have thought I'd be good at it? If I had a way of recording when he said I was a good lover, believe me when I tell you I would have pulled out my iPhone and pressed record on that sucker just so I could play that shit until the cows came home.

It is memorized in my brain. Burned through.

I'm sensing judgment.

Can you imagine your crush saying that to you? For perspective purposes, put it this way; imagine you just done the dirty with Henry Cavill—since he's the closest man I know who can come close to Dean Knox's likeness in flair, style, and hotness—or if he doesn't do it for you, I don't know, Channing Tatum—because c'mon, Mr. Magic Mike himself is every woman's eye candy—or whoever gets your motor running, and he looks deep into your eyes right after your very first time and says that you were perfect, that you were more than he could have ever hoped for in a lover. Let's see how fast you'd be running to your phone to play it over and over and keep it as your ringtone. It does your ego good, right?

Okay. So where was I?

Oh, yeah. Shower done, hair done, towel on. Teeth thoroughly brushed.

Now all I need is a good cup of coffee.

I walk to the kitchen and feel a hand creep on my shoulder out of nowhere.

"JESUS CHRIST!" I yell and throw my left hook behind me, but luckily, Lexi takes a dive to the left. "I told you, Lexi, one of these days you are not going to get so lucky, and I will punch you in the face. Shiners don't exactly scream out *professional journalist*, that's all I'm saying," I quip with my hands placed on top of my chest, so that sucker doesn't drop out with the fright my roommate just gave me.

"Yeah, like you could ever sucker-punch me, *chica*," she snickers as she passes by me, grabbing a water bottle from the fridge. "I'm from the Bronx," she says, swaying her hips and bumping her ass to mine, in true J-Lo fashion. I roll my eyes because I feel her sass coming in three… two… one… "And you're from Jersey. And not even the part that's scary, but the nice one, where hipsters reform, turn WASPs, and have babies." She winks. "No way could a Jersey girl ever knock me out."

"Yeah, Yeah. Whatever. Heard it all before. It's all a bunch of laughs until I have to drive you to the emergency room for a busted lip," I shrug, tucking my towel in closer.

"My little slugger is up so early this morning. What happened, E? Had some bad pizza or something?" she teases back.

"Hmm… or something," I reply, turning my back to my inquisitive friend, and instead search for a mug so I can get the brew I desperately need.

"Or did you want to surprise me and finally

accompany me on my morning run? Huh? Bet those muscles haven't seen a good workout since their PE class in high school. Might do them some good," she goads.

"I'd rather not," I reply almost in panic, thinking about how my muscles are sore enough from Dean's attentive care, so going for a run is the last thing I want Lexi to wrestle me into doing right now.

"Babe, all I'm saying is if you don't get a workout here and there, that body, once it reaches thirty, it's going to go downhill fast," Lexi explains, in full-concern mode now.

Yeah, cue in eye-roll, because c'mon, it's not like the saying 'if you don't use it, you'll lose it' is an actual scientific fact. I get Lexi wanting me to be healthy and strong since she is the energizer bunny, but I am not that girl. The only exercise I see myself doing, ever, would be a repeat performance of last night. I'm sure I burned more calories with Dean than any ten-mile run through Central Park could ever provide. It all comes down to incentive. Running at five-thirty on a cold November morning has zero incentive for me. Having Dean Knox making me work for every orgasm he so expertly provides, is definitely more appealing.

"I'm still twenty-four, Lexi. I think I got time before I have to think about going downhill."

"Well, someone should be thinking about going down, if you get my drift." She winks, and for the life of me, the first thing that pops into my head is Dean's mouth on my core, licking and teasing me until I couldn't take it anymore. My stupid cheeks must give me away because Lexi starts looking at me funny.

"What's going on here?" she asks, pointing at my face with her finger in a circular motion.

"Huh?" I murmur, turning my back to her yet again, looking anxiously for that damned cup of coffee.

"I just made a sex joke, and you got it. You never get my sex jokes."

"I get your sex jokes." I hiccup, hiding my face behind the cupboard door.

"No, no you don't. You don't get them because you've never gotten any action. What's up, Edie?" Lexi asks, now with her investigative-reporter hat on.

"Nothing's up," I mumble.

"Don't bullshit a bullshitter. Something is up."

"Nothing is up," I insist, but the woman doesn't let it go, so I say the first thing that pops into my head, "Okay, so if you must know, I've been checking Tumblr more often. You know, checking things out a bit more, like you said."

"Really?" she asks, more enthusiastic upon learning I took her advice to go online and just look at porn to get acquainted with sex—or as she likes to say, 'you need to get your freak on, E. Even if it's you and a battery-operated boyfriend.'

"Mm-hmm," I nod, taking a sip of my coffee.

"Well, good for you," she stares, giving me a slap on the rear. "Next app you got to download is Tinder, E. It will change your life. Swipe left, swipe right, free cock at every turn." She grins, eyebrow perked up.

"Jesus, Lex."

"What? Guys can say free pussy, and I can't? That's a double standard if I ever heard one. If I want some, I'll get it, and there ain't no shame in how I go about it."

"So I take it Diego is no longer in the picture?" I ask, even though the writing was on the wall pretty much from the first day she started dating the Don Juan from her gym.

"Not if he's still two-timing me with that skank Regina." She smiles bitterly.

"Oh, jeez. I'm sorry, Lexi."

"I'm not. He was a good lay, but a boring conversationalist. If I had to hear any more about CrossFit, I swear I was going to bash his head into a wall," she laughs, and I'm in awe of how she can so easily dismiss her latest fling's crash-and-burn fiasco. If that ever happened to me, I would probably be curled up in the fetal position for a solid week, eating Ben & Jerry's out of the tub. Not Lexi. She's as right as rain.

"So I take it Regina is a good thing?" I ask, wanting to make sure my friend's feelings aren't hurt by the scumbag's traitorous actions.

"Yeah, E. I'm good. I got to concentrate more on my job anyway. That Pulitzer won't be won by itself, you know?" She grins.

"Oh, shit. I got to run, Lexi."

"But it's not even six," she bellows, looking at her phone.

"I know, but I want to get an early start today," I explain, washing my mug, and letting it dry by the sink.

"Jesus, Devina is running you kind of hard, don't you think?" I shake my head, making haste to my bedroom, mumbling how I need to run, all the while thinking how wrong my friend is. Devina isn't the one I want to run me hard.

I need to get to work and do what I need to, and simultaneously come up with a reason to go back to After Hours tonight and talk to Dean. I will thank him, of course, but I refuse to keep what we had last night as a one-time thing. There needs to be more. If not for the craving of having to get my Dean fix, then at least for my own sexual awakening experience. I mean, Lexi's morning astonishment at my awareness of a dirty joke was a great example of how I'm lacking in intellect in that department. I'm still way too naïve when it comes to sex, and if it weren't for his small, simple commands last night, I would have felt inadequate right from the get-go. He made me feel safe and genuinely cared for. Not only do I want to be with him, but I also need him, too.

As I get dressed and in a cab to go to work, the pieces of the puzzle start to form the answer I need, becoming clearer and clearer. By the time I get to the office with Devina's steaming latte in one hand and mine in the other, I think I might have the solution which will get me a second chance at Dean Knox, and also at shedding the old Edie Vanderwalt's unblemished sexual reputation.

Chapter 13

DEAN

"But Mr. Knox, the designer insisted we use the black piece instead."

I roll my eyes because the photographer is wasting his time and mine with this back-and-forth discussion. I made my opinion perfectly clear on how I envisioned next month's Royal cover to look, which he completely disregarded. So, him looking at me all astonished and hurt because I've told him to do it all over again is his own damned fault, not mine.

"I don't give two fucks what the designer wants, and that goes double for anyone else who thinks they have creative control on this set today. It's still my magazine, and I'm the one to veto the cover. If you want your name to be attached to the picture, I suggest you listen to me and tell the model to change."

The asshole has the nerve to look behind me, where I know Devina and her shadow stand, quietly observing. Luckily Devina doesn't give him an inch, and he comes back to face me like the half-man he is, searching for another chance of getting his way. I'm growing tired of his diva-like antics. I don't care if he is one of the hottest, up-and-coming photographers around—if he gives me more shit, I'll not even bat an eye at calling in one of the many other well-known artists who would cut off a limb to get a chance at working with us. I have Leibovitz on speed dial precisely for these types of emergencies.

"Mr. Knox, with all due respect, this shot called for class and elegance. Don't you believe the color you've chosen contradicts that? Isn't red a bit too much? Black is a classic, after all, and the designer has sent us enough samples to choose from. You must agree, every woman has such a black dress for a reason," he continues, trying to make his point and, in turn, only making mine that more obvious.

"My point exactly. A Royal woman doesn't need to hide behind a black dress. We sell a lifestyle. In our own way, we sell a fantasy. While every woman has a little black dress in their closet, they secretly yearn for a red one. Black fades to the background, while if a woman enters a room wearing red, all eyes are on her," I counter, crossing my arms over my chest, pinning him down, frozen with my stare.

"For *my* cover, I want every woman to feel *that* special. I want them to believe that they can be brave enough to dress how they want to dress, not how society dictates. Fashion is a form of expression where anyone can voice who they are, without fear of standing out from the mold. I want every woman reading my magazine to feel bold and alive, and not dead inside because they held back on their true selves. Change the dress, or get out of my shoot. The choice is yours. Are we understood?" I deadpan, already turning my back to him, finished with his little debate on what he thinks *my* magazine should feature. If in five minutes I don't see a change in scenery, I'm making the call to both a new photographer and security to get this one out of my sight.

Of course, when I turn around, I come face to face with my partner's smirk, her own attention on her phone as she's probably sending her fiftieth email of the day. If I'm a workaholic, then Devina Richardson is obsessive-compulsive. And as I predicted, her attentive personal assistant is just as busy on her iPad behind her.

"Little rough on Pierre, don't you think, Knox?" she asks without once looking up from her phone.

"I thought I was quite civil, actually. Didn't threaten bodily harm once, nor did I insinuate I would ruin his livelihood should he not comply. I believe I heard you do both just this morning from your office," I goad.

"Hmm, only threaten? Guess it's been a slow morning," she replies, with a twinkle in her eye. "Still, Pierre does good work. It wouldn't be a bad thing to play nice with him," she adds.

"Oh, please. This from the person who is pissing off every writer we have on our roster. Pretty rich, considering you're snubbing almost every piece of content we're printing," I exclaim.

I've recently been getting all sorts of complaints

because of Devina's crusade for the perfect story. Even Sam, our editor-in-chief, is growing tired of her search for literary recognition. I, however, understand Devina completely. While I am more visual in nature and want every picture to hold power, she wants the same done regarding the words we print. Our fathers' partnership worked well and got this magazine up to a certain point. Devina and I, though, we seek greatness, and with her thirst and my hunger, we'll achieve what our fathers were too accommodated by wealth and power to even dream to aim for.

The two men ran Royal like they did every other business they had their hands on—successful enough to make their mark in the industry—and in Royal's case, media. But they played it safe enough that no heads were ever turned, or boats were ever rocked—metaphors which represent neither Devina nor me very well. We are both trailblazers in our individual way, intent on making Royal a household name. Even if assholes like Pierre will bitch and moan about their treatment to the whole world about it, at the end of the day, only Royal matters.

"I only want the best for Royal, Knox. I doubt a red dress will make much of an impact," Devina chides, lifting her head from her phone and fixing her glare on me.

"Miss Vanderwalt, tell me, do you own a black dress in your wardrobe?" I ask Devina's number two without looking away from my partner. I think I hear the demure woman curse behind Devina but then hear the faint yes I expected.

"And a red dress? Do you own one of those?" I ask, knowing full well that a woman who wears pastels to work, with little to no makeup and a grandmother's bun on the top of her head would most probably shy away from such a bold color. When I hear her say no, my winning smile is too evident for Devina not to notice.

"Of course not, because most women tend to have the famous little black dress as their go-to dress when they want to go out. It's comfortable and safe. Royal is not safe, Devina. It's our own motto. You keep with what you got going, and I'll stand behind you to make it so. I expect you do to the same for me," I remind her.

"Yeah, yeah, Knox. I hear you. Red dress it is. Very revolutionary idea. Whatever. Just don't be late for the meeting we have at three," she replies, giving one last look at the shoot before making her way back upstairs.

When I turn my back to face the shoot, I'm happy to see the model we've chosen is now delightfully wearing one of the red pieces the designer had sent us, and it will make for a spectacular cover.

"It's not only for going out," I hear behind me. I slant my head to the side to come across the pale face, almost fully covered by dark-rimmed glasses, of an annoyed young woman.

"Come again, Miss Vanderwalt?"

"You said a woman has a black dress for going out, but that's not true. A black dress is a woman's most-needed fashion accessory in her closet for numerous reasons, and implying it's only for dating purposes is just foolish on your part. Sometimes, blending in is exactly the point of the dress," she argues, fidgeting in place.

"Really? How so?" I ask, intrigued.

"Well, it can be used in all sorts of scenarios, but the one that comes to mind is more frequent than you think. Last year alone, I wore it a bunch of times. You'd be surprised how many funerals Devina has been invited to. Highly doubt any woman wants to be the center of attention in such circumstances. Don't knock the little black dress, Mr. Knox. I'd be lost without mine. It's a true life-saver," she remarks with a hint of laughter at her own joke.

"Funerals? That's your defense for the black dress?" I ask, trying to hide my own amusement.

"Well, I couldn't wear *that* red one, now could I?" she shrugs her shoulders, her head tilting at the model getting ready for round two as I ordered, before trailing behind Devina as usual.

I stand there looking at the woman in a Hillary Clinton pantsuit and catch myself chuckling at the absurdity of such an idea of Miss. Vanderwalt arriving at a funeral wearing a red Vera Wang ensemble. Very scandalous indeed. I'm instantly reminded of another woman who was able to make me so lighthearted, with so little effort.

Beauty.

Thoughts of deciding if I should return to After Hours this evening have been tormenting me all day. Maybe I've been on edge because I'm still unsure of my next move. With other members, this would have been easy. There wouldn't be such a debate in my head if it were wise for me to have another go at my new favorite pet. Even though it was a rare occurrence to have a repeat performance with any member, sometimes it happened, and there was never an actual discussion about it. The encounters happened a few more times organically until the thrill ran its course. Usually, this took me just a couple encounters more for the excitement to wear off, but something tells me that with Beauty, the shine on this new toy will take longer to dim. Worse yet, her ingenuity tells me a talk is necessary. The very thing about After Hours that appealed to me, with their no-strings policy, held no weight where Beauty was concerned.

On the other hand, I could just abstain from the club in its entirety for a while. She got what she wanted. I didn't need to rush back and see what her next move would be. Maybe she won't even go back to After Hours after last night. After all, wasn't what we did the sole reason why she went through the trouble of getting a membership in the first place? Losing her virginity. Or was last night only the beginning? She might wish to find a new partner altogether now. But just the idea of her broadening her sexual horizons tightens my chest in a vise grip, and I don't know what to make of it. I just know I don't enjoy the feeling.

No.

Even if Beauty does go back to the club, to do God-knows-what, she'll need someone to watch over her. And God help me, but a small part of me is invested in her. Maybe it's because I was her first and I feel somewhat responsible for her now. I'm not sure. Or perhaps, if I allow some truth to color my thoughts, I might admit I'm somewhat infatuated.

She first caught my attention with her bold silver dress and her innocent crystal blue eyes. Then she caught me off-guard with her kiss. But after last night, I've been consumed trying to remember the last time I fucked a woman senseless and, at the same time, feeling that we were sharing something so intimate and passionate. Not one single occurrence comes to mind. Beauty has immense power inside her, but she also holds true burning fire, which is too addictive not to want to fall into those flames.

So, I guess, no matter what argument I make, my decision has already been made. Tonight I'll be in attendance yet again at the club to see if my Beauty makes an appearance, and if so, what her disposition is. But most importantly, I'll be on the lookout for her next move.

The King

Be careful what you wish for.

I've heard that saying a million times over the years, but as I've hardly wished for anything in my life, I never paid it much heed. I've always been a man who thought that wishes were for people who believed in fate and destiny—ideologies which, for me, made no sense whatsoever. A man makes his own fate with work and effort. Wishes are for fools. Yet for the past hour, I've been twiddling my thumbs wishing a certain blonde would walk through those doors, and praying to an unknown deity that she doesn't, all in the same breath.

When my wish is granted, and not my prayer heard, I'm not sure if I'm elated or fearful, because the woman in red entering this club is the very definition of fierce and vibrant, the very same one I described earlier in the day for Royal's cover. Even the mask she's previously worn is forgotten, and in its place, red and black crystal beads cover the upper half of her face—almost translucent, save for its color. Yesterday, Beauty came to me dressed like a sacrificial lamb; today, she's a vixen temptress. And as I foretold this afternoon, this dress, or the woman wearing it, has gained the attention of every man in here. My instinct tells me to stand and go to her before some other asshole does, but my ego and pride prevent me from taking a step. When her head tilts my way, and our eyes meet, the damned woman robs me of all thought, and with one shy smile thrown my way, my chest tightens all over again.

However, my brief euphoria quickly plummets to the ground when Beauty makes her way to the bar instead of parting the crowd, like the Red Sea, to meet me at my regular spot. Not used to the bitter taste of disappointment, I lean back in my seat and watch as she goes over to greet Poppy, who is all too happy with her friend's arrival. After ten minutes of watching Poppy go on and on about one thing or another, I've had my fill of being just a spectator of their chit-chat, and get my ass out of the seat toward where I've been dying to go since the minute my pet walked in.

"Good evening, ladies," I say once I am close enough to touch my pet. Her dress is really stunning. It is almost identical to one of the other dresses we were unable to use for the afternoon shoot. The first three dresses were hits, so we still had a couple to spare, but I was curious as to how this backless silk one would have turned out.

Now I know.

Perfection.

"It was," Poppy replies sweetly, not hiding her *affection* for me. "You lost, King? Did your throne get lonely from way up there without your two lackeys to keep you company?" she adds with a sarcastic grin.

Tonight, Poppy looks like she stepped out of an anime cartoon. She fits the Asian schoolgirl look to a T. Only while my Beauty chose red and black beads as her camouflage for this evening, Poppy decided to divide her whole face equally with a similar accessory. One side decorated in black pebbles, and the other with white crystals. Give the petite woman a sword, and she would look deadly. A quality I'm sure her suitor quite appreciates.

I ignore Poppy's greeting, and instead place my hand on Beauty's back, making sure she feels my full palm caressing her naked skin evenly. Immediately, I'm rewarded with the view of how her body responds to my touch—from the goosebumps on her arms to the rosy cheeks on her face. I try to ignore how her reaction ignites my own tempestuous thoughts.

"A word, Beauty?" I lean in to whisper. My pet looks deep into my eyes, licking her lower lip and giving me her answering nod. It takes me a second to register she's conceded to my request since I'm still spellbound by her wicked tongue and the tricks I desperately want to reenact with it. I start to usher her away, but the ever-insistent Poppy holds my pet's elbow in place.

"Lady, you sure about this? You know you don't have to go anywhere with this guy. Remember, we make the rules here," Poppy states, giving me the old stink-eye. I almost want to growl at her petulance.

"It's okay, Poppy. I want to go. The King and I have things to discuss. I'll talk to you tomorrow. Promise," Beauty replies, giving a soft squeeze to her friend's hand in comfort. However, I'm the one who is comforted by the knowledge my pet already intends to have some sort of discussion with me, preventing her from going back to Poppy this evening.

"Okay, Lady. Just be careful. You know where to find me," Poppy adds as if I'm some sort of boogie man aiming to steal Beauty's virtue. Well, maybe I am. Perhaps I am some sort of villain and Poppy is just being a good friend to my pet. Yet, my resentment toward any vile nonsense she can fill my pet's head with, regarding me, is strong. So of course, I can't leave without adding my own two cents.

"Oh, Poppy, since you care for *my* pet's welfare so much, at least get her name right. It's not Lady. It's Beauty." I smirk. She, of course, flips me off with both hands and goes off to look for Panther, most likely. I turn to look at my pet, feeling a bit lighter now that I've put Poppy in her place, but Beauty doesn't seem like she wants to budge.

"Was that really necessary?" she asks, looking at me disapprovingly.

"Probably not. But does everything that feels good need to come out of necessity?" I question with my own brow up high, making my point.

"Maybe not," she answers, with a faint smile reaching her lips and those damned diamonds shining brightly in her blue eyes.

"You came back," I state, taking all of her in. Every piece of memory from last night comes back to me, and I wonder if she's recollecting the same images right now. How can a simple one-night stand, which occurred just the previous night, feel as if it happened a lifetime ago? It's been mere hours that I haven't been in her presence, this mysterious creature, yet it feels like an eternity.

You're so fucking losing it, Knox!

"Did you think I wouldn't?"

"After last night, I honestly thought you'd achieved what you wanted from your visit to this club," I answer honestly.

"I see." She looks to the ground, and I fucking hate it. Every time she shies away from me, a true revolt is born within me. She can hide from whoever she wants, but not from me. This new innate possessiveness is alarming. Therefore, I reel it in as much as I can, but still, I find myself gripping her chin gently, so I'm no longer deprived of her. Even if she is concealed in her mask, I will not have any other barriers between us.

"Seems I was wrong, though," I add, my thumb softly caressing her uncloaked chin.

"You were," she replies more confidently.

"And why is that, my pet? Why have you returned?" I ask curiously. I'm thankful she has, but wary of the reason. A small part of me wants her answer to be me, while the other part, the logical one, is looking sideways in confusion at why I would want that answer in the first place.

"I've realized that although I am no longer *untouched*," she starts off, using air quotes for the word while looking side to side to see if anyone is hearing our conversation. I almost want to interrupt her right here and remind her that we are in a sex club, after all; I'm positive if she took the time to listen to half of the conversations people were having around her, she would hear far worse. But her use of bunny ears is just too cute while looking like the most sophisticated, elegant woman I have ever seen, so I just keep my mouth shut and let her continue. "If the circumstance ever presented itself again, I think I would feel just as naïve as before," she mumbles in the end.

"Experience comes with practice." I try to soothe her insecurity.

"Perhaps that's why I'm here, then. To practice and learn," she retorts more sternly, her back straight as if she is ready for battle.

I, in turn, feel as if I just lost a fucking war. So this is why she's here. She wants to learn. To fucking practice. She sure is in the right place for it, then. Why do I feel like I want to hit something and throw up at the same time just at the mere idea of it?

"I see. The members here will be very pleased to learn how you are greedy to broaden your horizons," I reply, a bit more coldly than I intended. I aimed for aloof, yet my tone sounds as bitter as I feel at the idea of Beauty getting her sexual education here, of all places. I remove my hand from her back immediately, no longer feeling as if it's allowed to be there if she's willing to let so many others enjoy her softness the minute I walk away.

"I'm not interested in any member this club has to offer, but one only, my King." Her tone is as clear as day, making her intent unquestionable. Yet, I see a small trace of hurt behind her crystal eyes. No doubt brought on by my harsh reaction to her initial statement. This one, however, has me doing a one-eighty.

"Are you propositioning me for the role of a tutor, pet?" I try to conceal how this plan of hers delights me a great deal better than the one I had conjured up in my mind.

Oh yes, I like this idea a lot better.

"Is that so absurd? You seem to know exactly which buttons to push already. All I'm asking is for you to teach me what they are," she answers plainly as if conducting a business arrangement. She can try to simplify it if she must. I'll do the same since it will give me what I want in the end. Some extra rounds with my pet until this infatuation takes its course.

"How long would this tutelage be?" I ask, wondering what her timeframe looks like.

"Until the end of the month," she answers, biting her lower lip. I'll have to curb that instinct of hers or start biting it for her. Until the end of the month, huh? That's just two weeks. Fifteen days. Yeah, something tells me even if I had my pet roped to my bed for those fifteen days, my infatuation wouldn't be gone by then. I'll need at least another month. Maybe two. Have I ever been interested in a woman that long? Hmm. None come to mind, but I'm sure I must have. I think. At least a full week. Of that I'm positive. Anyway, the issue at hand is that two weeks is not an option. However, I won't argue now. I'll just have to come up with an excuse to extend our education a little longer when the time comes.

"I could always ask your friends if they'd be interested in the job if you're too busy for it," she adds with a hint of cockiness, which she doesn't naturally possess, undoubtedly taking my silence as resistance to her proposition.

I raise my brow and cross my arms over my chest, showing how her little remark backfired, making her fidget in place. Her unsettlement of wanting this to happen so badly is heartwarming. Defeated, she slumps her shoulders, looking worse for the wear.

"I'll give you until tomorrow to think about it," she says, holding on to hope.

"No," I deadpan.

"No?" she squeaks.

"No." I shake my head.

"Oh," she whispers, crushed.

"Have you ever seen a show here, pet?" I ask her, placing my hand back in its rightful place—the small of her back—and gently urge her to walk toward the exit of the nightclub.

"Huh? What?" she asks, gawking at me as if I'm speaking a foreign language.

"A show, Beauty. Every night, there is a show in the theater room. Would you like to escort me this evening?" I ask, even though I'm already ushering her into the elevator and placing my card on the panel for the desired floor.

"Hmm, okay," she answers, confused.

Once the elevator starts going down, I move over to my vixen in red. How can a woman look so tempting and yet so innocent at the same time? I place one hand on her waist and the other on her chin to lift her face up to meet mine. Once our eyes are firmly fixed on each other, away from loud music and prying eyes and ears, I feel better. The next words to leave my mouth will also have a more intimate resonance, which would not be as effective upstairs.

"I don't need a day to give you my answer, pet. If you need schooling, you'll get it from the King himself and no one else. While you're with me, you'll only *be* with me. Is this understood, Beauty?"

Her face brightens up with a nod, followed by one

stray tear. As it falls down the beads and hits her bare cheek, I catch it with my tongue, to which I hear a small sigh leave her lips in contentment. My cock twitches in delight, being pressed so close to her warmth and feeling her arms naturally wrap themselves over my shoulders as if they've done it a million times before.

Too soon do the elevator doors open, stopping us from the reunion we so yearn for, but I promised my pet a show, and thirty minutes later, we are in our own little private booth, watching tonight's performance of one of the country's finest burlesque dancers.

"She's extraordinary," my Beauty exclaims, looking at the stage, thrilled with the performance taking place.

"That she is," I reply, never wavering my sight from the woman at my side. "Are you enjoying the show, pet?" I ask, even though her genuine rapture is too palpable to be ignored.

"Yes. Very much," she answers, her rosy cheeks revealing her red beads.

"Good. I'm glad."

"Aren't you?" she questions, turning her back to the stage to look at me head-on.

"I was actually thinking about your tutorage," I tell her.

As if I could think of anything else. The dancer on stage could be doing God-knows-what, naked as the day she was born, and my eyes and thoughts would still only be on one person alone—my new protégé.

"Oh," she whispers, rubbing her lower lip raw. Images of body parts that I want to have the same treatment immediately come to mind. Her curious brows are up questioningly. Ever my inquisitive pet.

"Yes?" I tease.

"What part?" she hushes, leaning toward me, even though we are the only ones in this booth.

"I was thinking about feeding your curiosity, for one," I answer truthfully.

"My curiosity?" she mimics.

"Are you going to repeat everything I say, pet?" I jest.

"No." She pouts erotically. I don't think this was her intention, but seeing her full, pouty lips like they are now, just begs me to give them some attention. My cock, which has been hard as steel since she pressed up against me in the elevator, also seems to agree it's time to feel those gorgeous red painted lips mark him, too.

"Yes, your curiosity. For one, I saw how curious you were last night when Duke so ungracefully came on your hands. What did you want to do, pet? Tell me honestly," I order.

"I wanted to see how it tasted." She blushes.

"I thought as much."

I knew it the moment it happened when the thought crossed her mind, but something came over me then, so I stopped her before letting her get that far. I couldn't explain it at the time, I just knew I didn't want her first taste to be my best friend. Ironic, since I was the one who set last night's events in motion. When the possibility of Beauty's first time of tasting a man struck my mind, a streak of selfishness rose within me, and I knew I wanted to be her first in this way, too.

"Are you still interested, pet?" I ask with a calm tone, contradicting my restless thoughts. She gives me a quick nod, never removing her eyes from mine. I'll have to remind her to keep this trait, as I know I'll enjoy it even more with her lips around me.

"On your knees, then," I command, not moving an inch from my seat.

"Wh-wh-what?" she stammers, looking from side to side, to the other booths around us, as well as the crowd seated below, appraising the exceptional performance I'm sure the dancer is exhibiting with all the *oohs* and *aahs* coming every so often.

"You heard me. On your knees," I repeat, using

the same tone one of my college professors excelled at when he had an unruly student in attendance.

"But… but… but people will see. Anyone looking at us will see what we're doing," she explains, justifying her resistance.

"And your point is? They'll see a king being pleasured by his beauty. Nothing more, my pet. No one knows you here. Remember that," I explain, trying to remind her where we are.

This is not a show at the local theater. We are still very much in After Hours terrain. Hence its appeal. Anonymity above everything else. Freedom to be you above everything else. No judgment. No persecution. Nobody's fucking business but our own.

"Do you trust me?" I ask, sensing maybe I'm going about this the wrong way. Beauty is different, after all. She's not like the other women the club is known for. Maybe I'm asking too much, too soon.

"I wouldn't have slept with you if I didn't," she answers in earnest. She doesn't even know my real name, and yet I believe her. Maybe I'm as foolish as she is naïve.

Oh, what a pair we make, pet.

"Then what is it, pet?" I query, bringing her chair closer to me, reducing the gap between us. She's nervous. It radiates around her in volumes. I put both hands on her face since it seemed to comfort her the last time I did this. I feel her relax and gain the courage to confess her worries to me at last.

"What if I'm not any good at it? I've never done anything like it before. What if I suck?" I watch her squint her eyes at the choice of her last word, and I almost chuckle, since it's exactly what I'm proposing her to do now.

"Last night you had no clue what to do, either, and yet it was one of my most memorable experiences to date," I tell her, my words aimed to soothe, yet I'm overwhelmed by how honest my remark truly is. She opens her big blue eyes at me, and even though her face is only half covered with the intriguing beads, it's the first time in this club that I've wished I could see someone's face to its full extent.

"Really?"

"I'll cherish it, as I'll cherish the opportunity you're giving me now to teach you." I place a chaste kiss on her forehead, ending any other words I may be inclined to say this night.

She's bewitched me somehow, so I must hold my tongue before it leads me to those messy strings I tend to avoid, like the plague. A tender smile reaches her lips, which only provokes a grip to tighten in my chest. A heart I forgot I held beats profusely, watching my pet kneel before me bravely, never once straying away from my fixed stare. I do her the courteous thing of freeing myself from my constraints, not wanting her to feel even more intimidated by undressing me. I'm fully erect just with the image of her small, warm mouth inches away from me.

"What do I do now?" she whispers.

"Touch me first, pet." I hear myself beg.

To her, it was probably just another order, but to me, I hear the desperate plea in my words. Thankfully, she has mercy on me and does as asked, ever so teasingly. Soft at first, lovingly taking her time with each long stroke. Getting acquainted with my skin in her grip, the smooth head on her fingertips, the aroma of sex and arousal she invokes. As she becomes more confident, so do her smooth rubs get bolder, more aggressive, and stronger. Her breath quickens with my own, exhilarated with how my body is responding to her. If she keeps this up, I might cum sooner than intended, blowjob be damned. But that's not what I promised my pet.

"Pet, I need you to look at me," I order.

My good girl does as ordered, and on hands and knees she looks up at me, her face inches away from my crotch, and I know it won't take long for me to cum in her mouth. Something tells me I'm going to break rule number one of After Hours tonight. Shit! That can't happen.

Focus, Knox!

Fuck!

"Lick the seam first, pet. When you get comfortable with the taste of me, take me in and treat me the same way you would like me to devour you," I explain, playing with the strands of her golden locks through my fingers.

Again, ever the clever pupil, she begins carefully. Her pink tongue caresses my tip, and my eyes almost roll to the back of my head with how delicious the sensation feels, fucking paradise and hell all rolled up into one languished stroke of the tongue. She continues her soft, explorative ministrations, licking and teasing my tip, then my length. Before I know it, her warm mouth envelops me fully as she takes all of me in, which is incredible since I know I'm not a small man, and I'm incredibly turned on by discovering my pet does not have a gag reflex. She pumps me to her, using her mouth and her hand alike, and as she hums her satisfaction, I start to lose it.

"That's good my, pet. You can let go now."

"Huh? Let go?" she wines as if she misheard. I see her lust-filled eyes suggesting that my wish is an unacceptable one. Especially since she's right back at licking my cock from balls to tip. So fucking good. The woman was made for this.

"Yes, pet, you've tasted me well enough for your first time, don't you think?" I try to reason with her, even though my cock is loving how her mouth is worshiping him.

"Just a little more, my King," she moans, taking me deep into her throat, making me powerless with her merciless kiss.

Fuck, but this was not what I intended. I don't exactly relish the idea of blowing my load in her mouth the first time around, with all these spectators. Our little show has caught the attention of a few wandering eyes from neighboring booths, and as much as I told her that no one gives a fuck, I give a fuck as to what they think they can do with her after we part ways. The thought of another asshole thinking he could open her mouth this way, pump her the way I am, cum in her mouth, and make me watch, is too painful for words.

"Pet, stop. Enough!" I whisper-yell, too upset to where my own thoughts are leading me.

She freezes in place, uncertainty plastered on her sweet face, imagining the worst; concluding my switch in mood could only be brought on by her inadequacy. I feel ashamed at how I could ever make her feel this way. It isn't her fault. If she were any other woman, I would have enjoyed watching such a scenario and even giving such a show. I wouldn't even care if any member in this club fucked her right in front of me afterward. But right now, just the idea of another man's hand on *my* Beauty is driving me to the brink. I'm feeling a bit too possessive of her, and perhaps that's my problem. Maybe I shouldn't be feeling this way at all. I've known this woman for only a New York minute, and I'm already acting insane.

So I do the total opposite of what every fiber of my being is telling me to do. I grab her hair in a fist and place her perfect mouth back on my cock, and like the good girl she is, she starts to mouth-fuck me like it's her mission. Only this time, I don't think about the consequences. I don't think about what will come after me. I don't think about anything at all. All I think about is this moment. The moment of ecstasy she's giving me right now. Of her abandonment to this exquisite thrill and mine. Of how good it feels to have her lips wrapped tightly around me, and how this is the best fucking blowjob I've ever had, and it's her fucking first. I can only imagine what she can do with a bit of practice. She will bring men to their knees. They'll beg, bribe, and promise her the world for a chance to have the view I have now. But fuck them! This is my turn! My shot with her, and by God, I will be the first one who will cum in her pretty mouth. I will be the first one she will ever taste. Like her sweet cherry, she will remember me for eternity since I will be her first in this as well. Her sultry moans and lust-filled glare let me know how much this is turning her on, maybe just as much as the irrational greed I have to own all her firsts, branding her in any way I can. I pull her hair tighter, this time giving her a bit of pain to mix with her pleasure and bring her down further and further onto me. Her humming increases and I'm so close that I start to go blind.

"Fuck!" I groan, unable to contain it any longer.

My Beauty's pussy is too far from me, but by the

way she's rocking, I feel her ache as much as I feel my own need to combust. We're both close to the finish line, and one more stroke or bold move will get us there. My grip still firmly wrapped around her hair, tilts her head just enough for me to have a perfect view of her supple exposed breasts. With my other hand, I lower it to caress her left bosom, while savagely thrusting my cock into her mouth, and then surprise her peaked nipple with a painful tweak. I don't need to be inside her to know how this simple act is enough to have her wet pussy clench and explode to new horizons.

"Oh, God! Yes, my King," I hear her slur between spit and cock and I'm gone, gone, gone, as I cum in between two luscious red lips. My studious pupil surprises me further by swallowing every last drop.

Fucking perfect, this woman.

Where have you been all my life?

And where will you go when you get tired of me?

These are the thoughts that pass through my head the moment she looks up at me, carrying stars in her eyes along with the diamonds I can't get enough of. Now I will have to add yet another item on my list of things I yearn to repeat with her. Her looking at me as if I hung the very moon in the sky just for her, is too addictive not to actually want to do it for real, no matter how inconceivable and unrealistic the scenario.

"Was that good, my King?" she asks, breathlessly.

I lean down and kiss her deeply, loving how she falls into me with ease and eagerness to respond to my affection. I end the kiss with another chaste one to the tip of her nose and sit her back on her seat.

"It was perfect, my pet. Perfect enough for your own reward," I explain to her, raising the little devil's dress up her thigh, while I kneel before her.

"Remember tonight, my pet. You had a King on his knees for you. You deserve nothing if not the best. Never settle for less, my Beauty. Are we agreed?" I try to order her stoically, but to my ears, my own possessive and selfish thoughts cloud my heartfelt command.

There is a deafening silence between us, as I watch her replay my statement word for word. The crease in her forehead tells me she heard me, but the way she refuses to meet my eyes tell me I've touched something sensitive inside her.

"All that matters is I have my King now," she replies in a soft whisper instead of conceding, and the same look she had last night in bed returns with its full force.

Yesterday I thought it was adoration, yet tonight it looks like more. I wish I knew this woman better, in order to decipher her mysteries. But as luck would have it, I have at least until the end of the month to learn some of her tricks, while I teach her some of mine. Two weeks, maybe more. But if this is my intention, I can't get as sidetracked as I've been all night. I part her legs, which gets me a gasp from her. I almost laugh since not five minutes ago, I was balls-deep in her mouth, but me opening her up so I can get a nice view of her wet pink pussy is what shocks her.

"Now, pet, don't be shy," I tease.

"Mmm," she mumbles, looking from side to side. The show is going on strong, and the music is too loud for anyone to hear her moans. The previous spectators we had are having their own sexual interval, so her delight will have but one witness.

Me.

"Beauty, let me show you how perfect you are," I say lovingly, and this is the only persuasion she needs to offer herself to me. Honesty is always the best route, in my opinion, and here is the evidence glistening at me. I lick my lips in hunger at the sweetest dessert staring me in the face. Two weeks will not be enough to fill my craving. My cock is fully awake again, just with what my eyes promise to be in store for him.

I doubt even a month is enough.

"Hold on tight, pet. This may take a while."

And I'm not sure if I'm warning her about how long I'm going to be in between her legs, or how long I intend to be in her life.

Definitely more than we both could ever imagine.

Chapter 14

"Oh good! You're here," Devina says as I walk into her office. She's wearing a full grin on her face, looking ever so graceful in a white Dolce & Gabbana number, which looks tailor-made to accentuate her tall, shapely figure.

Me, however, I look bland as usual, in desperate need of a few more hours of sleep, thanks to a certain Royal figure who kept me up most of the night—not like I'm complaining—but now my face is also sporting a puzzled expression, too, since I wasn't expecting to find my best friend so cheerful this morning. Usually, Devina rivals Miranda Priestly herself from *The Devil Wears Prada* before she's had her coffee fix, and since I'm the one carrying her precious caffeine in my hands, her unexpected giddiness means something stinks in Denmark, people.

When I turn to close the door behind me and catch a glimpse of a young woman sitting across from Devina's desk, wearing a similar glowing smile, my suspicions increase tenfold. I know for a fact Dev didn't have any meeting booked this early in the day, or any day for that matter, unless it was to fire someone's ass so they could feel her full wrath.

Yep, she's cooking something all right.

"Sorry, I didn't mean to interrupt," I tell her, placing her macchiato on the desk and doing a piss-poor job at concealing my own in my other hand.

I have no clue who this young woman is, so I don't want to come off looking unprofessional, especially since she's looking far too sophisticatedly put together and I already look like a hot mess, so slurping my cup of joe in my boss' office is a big no-no.

She also doesn't need to see the disappointment in my face or my lack of enthusiasm at her being here, as I was looking forward to my time with Devina this morning. Dev and I usually take our morning coffee together and just talk smack for twenty minutes until she's human again. I'm doing a public service by calming the dragon. If I let Devina on the loose without our little morning pow-wows, I fear for mankind.

LOL!

Nah!

Devina is a pussycat.

It's just the people who piss her off who need to worry about her claws. But most of all, it's our little sacred time we make for one another, and even though I haven't been exactly honest with her on what's going on in my life, I miss my friend. I need Dev in my corner more than ever. There are so many emotions and experiences that I've been going through lately which have turned my whole world a bit off-kilter. I'm genuinely trying to gain enough courage to come clean with Dev and just tell her what's happening. But since I'm a big wuss, all I've accomplished in doing is talking in metaphors. I might have even suggested that Lexi is fooling around with her boss, or even hinted she was falling hard for him, so getting advice from Dev to counsel my roommate was crucial since she knew I had no experience in this area.

Yep! I know! I know!

I'm a fucking terrible friend!

Bad Edie!

But guys…. c'mon!

You know I can't tell Devina outright without at least preparing her for it.

She'll kill Dean if she thinks he'll hurt me somehow. And I can't allow my best friend to go to jail for murder, nor can I allow her to kill the man who makes my heart melt into warm goo every time he smiles at me.

Oh, you think I'm exaggerating, do you?

Cough. Cough.

Pushing glasses back to the temple for dramatic effect

Let us go back to my thirteenth birthday party, shall we?

It was an enchanted day, where I innocently let Christopher Jacobs kiss me behind the Richardson's pool house. It was just a ten-second peck on the lips, but to me, it was magical and a defining moment in my young pubescent life. I thought this meant Chris, who was the captain of Ridgefield Junior High soccer team and resembled a young version of Justin Bieber at the time—HEY! What did I say about no judgment? He was dreamy, okay? Jeez—meant that he liked me.

That night, Devina heard me gush and swoon all about Chris, with his wavy hair and killer smile, and laughed as I dreamed up of our future babies' names and joint wedding invitations. Yep, I was that far gone with the Biebs lookalike, but Devina was right there with me, plotting away every little detailed of my fairytale wedding. Collages and all.

Yep. I was a nutter even then. But Devina never made me feel any less for my wacky behavior. On the contrary. She fed my brand of crazy at every turn.

The following week at school, Chris was still very polite to me, but he never initiated or even tried to talk to me, which confused me a bit. I was, however, getting other boys' attention, which just added to my puzzled state. Popular boys that didn't even know I existed before were trying to carry my books, opening doors for me, and trying damned hard to get my phone number. It was all a little intimidating, to say the least, and most of them were so not my style. The only popular boy I was into was Chris, but after our kiss, it seemed he lost interest, and I couldn't fathom the reason.

When Devina got three days suspension from school for breaking Chris' nose with her History book, I found out why fast. Apparently, dear old Chris had been going around telling every guy at school he had gone to third base with me at my party. To my naïve thirteen-year-old mind, I had no idea what that consisted of, but I knew it wasn't good when he got Devina to go all Hulk on his ass. I was heartbroken, but having Chris walk around with two shiners and a busted-up nose did lessen the blow.

Devina did that for me. Like the big sister she is, she will always look out for me. So you see my dilemma, guys? Dean is too pretty for Devina to bust up. And she would have no qualms about going into his office the minute I told her I joined a sex club just so he could take my V card. Oh, and by the way, me telling her I had to go through his two best friends beforehand, won't get him any brownie points either. Yeah, I can see that conversation going down brilliantly.

No thanks!

Devina would kick his ass!

And Dean is a big guy, but hell hath no fury like a pissed off Devina! You can count on it.

"E? E? You spaced out there a bit, babe," Dev remarks, and I realize I'm still planted in front of her guest, looking blankly frozen at her uncomfortable state.

Shit!

"Sorry. I guess I did. I didn't realize you had company this morning. You want me to come back once you're finished?" I ask, looking at the bright-eyed and bushy-tailed young woman sitting across from my best friend, trying hard to offer a smile at the wacky woman who just went to la-la land on her watch. I give her one of my own grins, hoping it looks somewhat normal, but at this point, I'm not sure if I'm fooling anyone anymore regarding my sanity.

"Don't be silly, E. In fact, we were just waiting for you. Edie, this is Tatiana. I just hired her to be your assistant. Isn't it marvelous?" Devina shrieks with joy, while I'm too speechless to say anything, and I almost suffer whiplash from turning to stare at her instead. Guess I'm not the only one who has a few loose marbles in this room after all.

WTF?

"Well, say something?! I thought you'd be hugging me right about now, not glaring at me like I just ran over your puppy," Devina jokes, but I hear the trace of hurt in her voice that I'm not more thrilled with her kind gesture than she hoped. I take a deep breath because we're in mixed company and this poor girl has seen enough crazy as it is. She shouldn't have to witness my next meltdown.

"Tatiana, is it? I'm sorry we've gotten off on the wrong foot. It's lovely to meet you. Welcome to the team, and to Royal. Do you mind if I could just have a quick word with Ms. Richardson?" I ask, this time wearing my professional game face, sticking my hand out, offering a welcoming handshake to who will now be, for all intents and purposes, my new personal assistant.

"Of course. I'll just wait outside," Tatiana replies, a bit too eagerly, giving a side-glance to Devina and then lowering her head toward me. So, although Devina is technically her boss, I just became the bad guy and the woman to fear in her mind. Great!

Both of us watch Tatiana make haste out the office door in record time. I look over at Dev, who is now sitting crossed-legged on her white couch, mocha in hand, and a firm scowl in place. I wish I could take the last ten minutes back to redo this whole scenario again and do it right.

"What gives, E?" she starts off, never one to vacillate.

I walk behind her desk and sit down in her chair, twirling it around and around and around, looking at the ceiling, thinking what answer could I possibly give my best friend that would satisfy her enough not to dig for the real reason of *what gives*.

Denial is always the route most traveled. So are misdirection and blatant omission of truths. Best not uttered to prevent jail time and certain death.

"What do you mean?" I ask, my eyes still fixed on the tall ceiling, trying desperately not to make eye contact.

What can I say? Lying is easier when you don't have to face the person you're doing it to. Especially if you love them with your whole heart like I do Dev.

"I mean, these past few weeks you've been exhausted. I hardly see you anymore outside of these walls, and when I do see you, you look like you're about to keel over at any minute."

"You're exaggerating." I laugh off her concern.

"Am I?! Yesterday I caught you napping at your desk. Napping, Edie! You're tired, just admit it. And I got it, okay? I've put too much on your plate, and it's caught up with you. It was bound to happen, and it's my fault I let it get so out of hand. I take full responsibility for it, E. So here I am making things right," she explains with such affection, my guilt is actually choking my windpipes, preventing me from getting a word out to stop her rant.

"Tatiana will ease your load, babe. She's not here

to take your job in any way if that's what got you so riled up. There is only one E, and you know, for me there will only ever be one E. But you're not Wonder Woman, and I shouldn't expect you to act like one. So, just take Tatiana. Let her do the grunt stuff you hate, and those minuscule tasks that end up eating up your day. Let her deal with them. Focus on the big things here while she deals with the pesky little ones. I mean, take this for example—" she says, pointing at her precious mocha goodness. "You don't have to get my coffee, for crying out loud, E. This takes thirty minutes of your life every morning, during which you could be doing other things, like sleeping, since you look like you still need it," she jokes, pointing at my drowsy state to make her point.

It would have been incredible to have an extra half hour in bed, but I'm not thinking about the one I have back in Queens. I'm thinking about the one that Dean has back at his private suite and what he could do to me with an extra thirty minutes in his bed. It's official. I've turned into a sex fiend.

I shake those thoughts out of my head as quickly as they came, just in case Dev has some super-duper X-Ray vision sensor that can pick up on R-rated images dwelling in my mind. Hell! I don't know! It could be possible. She has so many new gadgets sent to her office every day, who knows what each one is for.

"Tatiana can bring us both our morning coffee. Take advantage of her and start working from nine to five like everybody else," she ends proudly as if she's just cured the world's largest epidemic.

God, I love her. But the thing with Dev is, she'll always put my happiness first and never once think of her own. That's why she needs me, too. As much as she looks out for me, someone needs to look out for her, and that's where I come in. In other words, if she ever called me up one night saying she went all Mad Max on someone's ass—my bet would be Connor Walsh, but hey, it could be anyone who crossed Dev the wrong way, really—and she needed to hide a body in the middle of the night, I'd be at her place with a duffle bag, large enough to dump a stiff, and two shovels in the trunk of my car. I even know a spot in Long Island where no one would even think of looking.

What???

That's what best buds do for each other.

"Oh yeah? Like everybody else, huh? Does that mean you're going to start working from nine to five, too?" I goad, knowing perfectly well the answer to that question, even though she suddenly expects it from me.

"Don't be absurd. This place would fall apart without me," she retorts as if the mere idea is preposterous.

"So your whole speech about Wonder Woman was only for me. But what about you, D? You thinking about wearing a cape around New York City anytime soon? Think that number would look good on you?" I tease.

"She didn't wear a cape, dufus. Did you even see the movie?" She rolls her eyes, trying hard to hide her smirk.

"No, I didn't have time. I work for you, remember? The real superhero, who spends every waking hour at Royal headquarters to ensure world domination," I joke.

"Hence the assistant. This way you'll have more time to do normal stuff like watch a damned movie. Even I watched it while plotting and raising my empire," she kids back with a cheeky wink.

"Fine, D. You win. I'll give Tatiana a try. But does this mean I get an office, too?" I ask with a naughty grin.

"The moment one opens up, it's all yours. As long as it's not too far from me and not too close to Walsh's. No way am I going to have to pass through him to get to you."

"Save it, Dev. For me, you go against anyone," I reply, giving her a wink of my own while standing up from her desk chair. I grab my coffee and make my way to the front door, so I can get to my new protégé and get her acquainted with our own little kingdom here at Royal.

"Love ya, E," she sing-songs.

"Love you, Dev," I tell her honestly, and pray that she'll forgive me for lying to her as I have been.

True to form, my new assistant stands patiently waiting outside Devina's office. The brown-eyed young woman, who by my guess must be fresh out of college, looks as green in the face as I did on my first day of work here. It probably didn't help matters that I literally froze in place staring at her in Dev's office, or my displeased attitude in the announcement of her hiring. Two things I need to rectify if I'm to make her feel welcomed. If she is going to do shitty jobs on my behalf, she isn't going to like me much anyway, so no need to start off on the wrong foot. Dev said she should bring us our morning coffee, but something tells me I'd better get my own. Once she gets a feel for what she has to deal with here, I'm sure she'll be far too tempted to spit in my Starbuck's cup, and I prefer mine spit-free, thank you very much.

I show her to my cubicle and make a note to send an email to IT and Facilities to add a new compartment at my side so she can have some privacy of her own. I look at my phone and see that it's just shy of eight o'clock. HR should be fully staffed by now. Might as well send the poor girl there and get her affairs in order first.

"Tatiana, I want to apologize if I came off as aloof in any way earlier. Ms. Richardson surprised me, that's all. I wasn't expecting you, but this doesn't mean I'm not grateful, and I'm looking forward to you helping me with the current workload I have. Ms. Richardson runs an onerous schedule and is very demanding in her endeavors. Therefore, we must always strive to make sure she gets what she needs at all times," I explain politely.

"I understand, Miss Vanderwalt. I will not let you down," she replies shakily, turning all shades a crayon box can contain.

Oh boy. I must really have scared the poor girl in there if she's looking at me like I'm Medusa reincarnate.

"I'm sure you won't. Now, first things first. It's best to go down to HR. It's on the third floor. Ask for Mrs. Carol Smith. By the time you get there, I'm sure Ms. Richardson will have already sent an email detailing your employment. After you've read your contract and signed everything, you can come up, and I'll show you around. Unless, of course, you'd like to start fresh on Monday." I sweetly offer a way out to the jittery girl in front of me. Giving a few extra days so she can get her wits about her, must get me a little bit on her good graces, and appear to be a less threatening superior. Right?

"Oh no! No, Miss Vanderwalt. I'd like to start today, please," she pleads, concern marring her features that I even suggested such a scenario.

"Very well. I'll see you back here in an hour or so." I shrug.

Hell, I tried.

"Thank you, Miss Vanderwalt," she answers with the same bright smile I saw her wearing when I barged into Dev's office thirty minutes ago.

"No worries, Tatiana. Go on, then. I'll be here when you get back." I give her a small grin, and I see a bit of the paleness in her face disappear as she moves through the open office area and makes her way to the elevator as instructed.

I sit at my desk, coffee in hand, taking the first sip of the cold brew. I'll have to pop downstairs and get a new batch if I want to make it today. Apparently, I can't take a nap like I did yesterday without running the risk of getting caught again. And since Tatiana is going to be my new shadow for the foreseeable future, it would set a bad example to see her new boss drooling over her keyboard taking a power nap.

Desktop on, I start rummaging through my emails to see what's on today's order of business. Everything looks up to standard until I get a ping on my phone— a new email which isn't showing up on my desk screen.

Odd.

When I pick up my phone, the reason is made all too clear, and my heart starts to make erratic palpitations, which I'm sure the whole floor can hear.

It's an email from Slevin.

And not just any email.

It's an End of Trial email.

Shit!

Shit!

Shit!

The email consists of congratulating me on an excellent attendance and the hopes I've been able to offer a satisfying report to Ms. Richardson so she can become a member this month. I look at the calendar, and lo and behold, it's fucking December first.

How the hell did I miss that?

My mind is a blank, but all I'm thinking about is how I made plans with Dean to go to dinner tonight.

Yes, you heard me. Dinner!

Because apparently, After Hours is Willy Wonka's pleasure factory for grown-ups. Each floor is designed to have its own purpose and use and to bring what members relish most. Dining out and eating aphrodisiac foods is right up there with going skinny dipping in a heated pool or soaking up in a bubbly, steamy jacuzzi on a snowy winter night. Which this girl has done, by the way, and highly recommends.

Ah! Fuck my life!

Okay, Edie! Think girl! Think!

Okay, this is a no-brainer. Slevin is a businessman after all. I'll just appeal to his entrepreneurship savvy.

My fingers tremble as I start to punch each key, but my will is too strong to back out now.

Dear Slevin,

First of all, I'd like to thank you for your kind words and the hospitality After Hours has bestowed upon me this trial month. Its services have surprised and delighted me in many aspects and I'm thrilled to inform Ms. Richardson is also quite taken with the information I have provided.

However, I'm saddened to inform you, she still feels my research is inconclusive to make an informed decision as to whether she should, in fact, become a full-fledged member of your prestigious club.

I have, however, come to a solution that might satisfy both parties.

You offered a trial period of thirty days, but as you can see, for Ms. Richardson, this was insufficient, even though I have tried my best to attend every evening as per the professional etiquette expected of me.

What if this trial period was to be extended, as a one-off, for sixty days?

Let's say ninety at the most, should these extra thirty days not suffice (it is the holiday period, and as much as I would love to perform all my professional duties, there are some family obligations this time of year that cannot be rescheduled).

Could this be something that After Hours would be willing to accommodate for Ms. Richardson?

I look forward to your reply and will do my best to ensure your success from my end.

Sincerely,

Edie Vanderwalt

Aka Beauty

And... Send.

My whole body shakes at the pack of bull I've just sent.

What type of person am I becoming?

I'm lying to the whole world, and the worst part, I'm getting too damn good at it.

Guilt.

That is the only little thing that tells me I haven't lost my soul yet. If I didn't think my ass would burn the minute I stepped foot in a church, I'd be there twenty-four-seven, begging for forgiveness for the web of lies I've been spewing off lately. The constant sense of guilt I carry on my shoulders, like dead weight, is the very knowledge I cling to, which reminds me that I'm still not entirely gone to the dark side yet, like Darth Vader or Kylo Ren. See? I do go to the movies! Dev doesn't know what she's talking about. Okay, maybe it was a midnight show, and yes, maybe I thought I was going to see Adam Driver shirtless, but still, I saw it, didn't I? But I digress.

Slevin's reply is instant, but my reaction on opening his email isn't. This little electronic piece of correspondence contains the answer to whether I will be in Dean's arms ever again or not. So excuse me if I'm not rushing to read it, you guys.

I need a minute, okay?

A quick intake of breath, a mumbled Hail Mary, and I finally click on the sucker that will determine my destiny.

Dear Ms. Vanderwalt,

Thank you kindly for your gentle support of our enterprise with your employer. It grieves me Ms. Richardson is still on the fence, even after what I'm sure was a stellar report made by such a professional woman, as you appear to be.

The suggestion you have made does seem the most appeasing one, which I'm confident I can arrange with my own superiors to allow an extension to the trial period as a one-off event.

However, they will want each extra month to be paid in full as a regular member, just to avoid any precedents. If word got out there was any leniency given in this regard, well then, existing members may take offense. We treasure our loyal members and ensure their satisfaction is always maintained in accordance with our services in all accounts, as Ms. Richardson will soon attest by this show of faith we are providing now. You understand, my dear.

Please advise us if Ms. Richardson agrees with this proposal. If so, we expect you this very evening as per usual to continue your research.

If not, it was a real pleasure meeting you, Miss Vanderwalt. If this arrangement does not go forth, at least I've had the great pleasure of meeting such a charming and intelligent woman.

Sincerely,

Slevin

P.S. I never did tell you, but I do believe you chose your pseudonym to perfection. The name suits you marvelously.

Take care, my dear.

Fuck.

Fuck.

Double Fuck.

I'm hyperventilating now!

How the fuck am I going to get twenty-five thousand dollars by tonight?

There is just no way. This is it. The final no. The dreaded no I didn't want to read.

Dean and I are through.

Actually, The King and Beauty are through.

I mean, well… you get what I mean.

I want to slip under my desk and cry, but it's almost nine o'clock, which means everyone is busy running all over the place, talking loudly on phones, typing furiously on keyboards, but still not hectic enough for a crying Edie to go unnoticed. You think I'm blowing things out of proportion, right? I mean, it's just sex, huh?

But it's not.

Well, at least, not for me.

Let's have a heart to heart here.

When I'm with Dean—or the King—I'm the most alive I've ever felt. He makes me feel special. Like he sees me. The real me. Ironic, since he only sees Beauty and the mask I wear every night. But it's true. I don't have to hold back when I'm with him. I can show him my shy side and my crazy one. Not like here at Royal, where I have to act like I'm a silent fly on the wall. Or, in most cases, a total bitch just to make sure the job is done up to Devina's standards. I don't know where I wear the true mask anymore—here at Royal, or at After Hours.

But with Dean, I don't feel like that. Just like I am with Dev, with him, I can say what I want. Ask what I want. Do what I want. Without fear of judgment, or ridicule, or even malice. And when we make love or have sex, whatever you prefer to call it, I feel whole. As if this is the person I was supposed to wait for, all along. The one guy who gets all my quirks without me having to explain them to him.

After we're done, and completely sated, he holds me as if I'm precious to him. Those are the moments I live for. We talk about everything. Big things like global warming and state affairs, to little things like where to find the best slice of pizza in New York City. I swear, when he said Joe's, I almost proposed right then and there. These past two weeks have been my wildest fantasy turned reality. How can I give it up? We were just starting to get to know each other.

I know what you're thinking. This is going to blow up in my face. Sooner or later I'll have to either tell him who I am or walk away before he realizes he's been screwing his partner's assistant. Fraternizing with the staff is frowned upon at Royal, and if word got out the boss was jutting his pen in company ink, it would be quite the scandal. But it's not time yet. For crying out loud, we just started enjoying ourselves, we can't put an end date on fucking happiness yet, people!

Okay. No biggie.

Twenty-five grand. All I have to do is come up with twenty-five grand.

Prostitution comes to mind, but since I only want to sleep with one guy, that's out of the question. Stripping won't get me twenty-five Gs by nightfall either, and I highly doubt anyone would pay that kind of dough to see me fall on my ass anyway. Trust me, after watching some burlesque shows at After Hours, I've seen those girls work a pole. That shit is hard work, and I bow down to their amazing talent in making that shit look easy.

Shit.

Focus, Edie!

With those two options out of the way, and having zilch in my savings account thanks to the added expenses of new finery masks, and makeup to use in my new nighttime adventures, my options are looking pretty bleak. No bank will loan me that amount in such a short time frame, either.

But my company's black Amex will.

The one Devina gave me for 'emergencies.'

Yeah, I think she meant for me to use it to fly

across the world to meet her, in case a real emergency was needed, at a conference or a shoot. Or that alibi scenario I told you about earlier of getting rid of a dead body. I highly doubt she meant it for me to pay for a month's use of a swanky sex club so I could continue my affair with her business partner.

But it is the solution I have for today. It buys me enough time to get twenty-five grand later on. I mean, it is almost Christmas, so I'll get my bonus in a few weeks. Devina is usually very generous with it, and no doubt I can count on at least ten grand there. If I max out all my other credit cards, I might get another thirteen, give or take. The rest I can account for with my wages. Might have to ask Mom for a few bucks to tide me over if not for extra necessities—like food and my half of the rent and bills—but at least I'll be able to pay the full amount before anyone is the wiser for it. No harm, no foul. And I got my thirty days, which means my happiness really does have a timeline, as it ends on fucking New Year's Day. I thump my head over and over on my desk—physical pain is preferable to the one growing inside my lungs.

A looming figure clears her throat, stopping my repetitive self-abuse.

"Hgh, hgh. Miss. Vanderwalt, are you okay?" Tatiana asks, looking at me like I've completely lost it.

And I have. Or am about to, anyway. In thirty days, I'm about to lose everything. My mind. My heart. Everything. But right now, I have to put on my day mask and show this girl I'm not as insane as she believes me to be. On the inside though, I'm dying.

"Just need some coffee. Let me show you around, and we'll get us both some much-needed caffeine." I replay stoically.

"Oh, okay," she mumbles, not entirely sure I'm fit to stand, let alone show her around, but I feign ignorance to her burdened appraisal of me and gather my things.

"Just let me send this email really quickly, and we'll be good to go," I explain, already standing from my seat, phone in hand, clicking on reply to the email which shattered my hopes.

Dear Slevin,

Your terms are more than acceptable.

I'll see you tonight to start off my extra thirty-day trial.

Sincerely and affectionately,

Beauty

My reply is short, sweet, and to the point. Just as the remaining time I have with the only man I have ever felt a true connection with. I'll just have to make each night count.

For the next thirty days, my King awaits me. I just have to make enough memories to last me a lifetime, because I don't doubt that after a month of loving a

The King

King, I could never be content with anything less.

I guess he did try to warn me.

Chapter 15

DEAN

Bash is about to run through some numbers on expenses that he thinks Royal can cut down on, such as the Web Design Department, when a red-faced Connor barges into my office looking like he's about to murder someone. When his eyes land on the Ice Queen herself, you don't have to be an Einstein to figure out who his murdering instinct has been inspired by.

"You fired Lloyd?!" he roars, gaining an audience from outside the room. Sebastian must read my mind, as he places his tablet on the coffee table and calmly walks behind our enraged friend to close the view for the small gawking crowd pretending to work, but in reality, hanging on every syllable Con will spout out next.

"I did," Devina answers coolly, observing her manicured nails as if Con's reaction is of no importance.

"Why the hell did you do that? What did the poor schmuck ever do to you?" he spits out, his fists gripped at his side, and his chest rising and falling with every erratic intake of breath.

Devina rolls her eyes and turns her chair to face the beast before her. Any other woman would be intimidated by the sight of such an aggressive, unhinged man, foaming at the mouth, with thoughts of wringing her little neck as the only thing that would satisfy his rage. Devina, though, just looks plainly bored. I force myself to clear my throat, instead of the chuckle that threatens to come out. Unfortunately, I'm not fast enough, since Bash catches me red-handed and gives me a suspicious squint of the eye. I straighten my back and control my features, letting these two fools get their foreplay on and over with.

"It's not what he did to me, Connor, it's what he did to others in a lower position than him on a daily basis. I always found his performance less than stellar, but you always seemed to think otherwise, so I overlooked it, letting you take the lead. But some things cannot be overlooked. I fired said schmuck, as you called him, as I wasn't pleased with his sexist tone and repulsive behavior. Edie's new assistant, Tatiana, was disgusted with the things he said to her when she went to your department to hand over some files yesterday. The fool was under the illusion she was a temp and thought his actions wouldn't get back to his superiors. He was wrong. After careful due diligence, I found out his remarks and grabby hands were well known in the office, and I will not condone that type of behavior. Nor should you have, for that matter." Devina states coldly, daggers in her eyes as if Connor was the culprit for Lloyd being a douchebag.

If I'd known I had such a man employed at Royal,

I'd have fired him myself and would have had security roughen him up a bit when showing him the door. Con should be relieved, in my view. Devina did him a solid.

"First of all, Devina, I was well aware of his antics and had already talked to him about it," Con replies, his face passive. *Goddammit, Con! Not everyone deserves a second shot,* I want to scream at him, but doing so would only anger the beast further. Best to give him a piece of my mind when he can hear reason. Right now, the only thing he's focused on is her. Nothing new there.

"Apparently, not severely enough. And as we both know, talk is cheap," Devina quips.

"I was giving him time to redeem himself. That's why I gave him the L'Oreal project. He might have been an asshole, but he was a talented one."

"Well, that's exactly where you went wrong. Some people are irredeemable. And you should never reward bad behavior. It sets a bad precedent." Devina counters, still impassive from her seat.

The woman is looking up at my blond friend—who in body would give Tom Brady a run for his money—and yet, it's as if they are both on an even keel. This is one of the many reasons Devina makes an excellent partner. Even sitting down, she can make any man in a room feel ten inches small. I would much rather have Devina on my side than as an opponent. Right now, I'm betting Con can attest to that, too.

"Oh! So now you want to do *my* job?" He smirks unapologetically.

"No, I want *you* to do your job *efficiently*. He was a bad apple, so he had to go," she announces matter-of-factly.

"You should know since you're the expert on letting go of things once they go bad. But you can't fire everyone you don't like, Dee," Con roars, running his fingers through his hair, exasperated.

"Oh, I know that, Connor! If I could, you wouldn't be standing here in front of me! And don't call me that! Ever!" Devina wails on her feet, showing her stormy spirit, which had been inert and calm throughout this whole conversation. I guess Con using a previous pet name summoned old demons best laid dormant.

"Fine! Just stay out of my department! Deal with your shit and stay out of my way!" he growls ten inches from her face.

"Your department belongs to me! You seem to forget that, Walsh." Her smile looks perversely wicked. I look over at Sebastian, and he's just as enthralled by their melodrama. Feels like we're all back at school, assisting one of their meltdowns in the middle of the quad. Old habits die hard, I guess.

"So *your* shit is *my* shit! If you drop the ball, I'll

have to pick it up," she adds, bitterly pointing her index finger repeatedly to the center of his chest. I swear, I see him puff out more to make himself look even bigger.

"Babe, not in this lifetime or the next will I let you anywhere near my balls. Stay away from my department and me. If I need help with anything, I have Dean. I don't need you, Richardson. I never did," Con replies, giving her a departing kiss to the cheek, which she immediately scrubs off, as if his saliva alone contained every STD known to mankind. Of course, the asshole has to leave my office the same way he came in—like a fucking typhoon, almost slamming the door off its hinges.

"I fucking swear, if either of you two breaks my fucking door, you are paying for a new one—made of steel or something to withstand your abuse," I huff out, pinching the temple of my nose, feigning annoyance.

A month ago, this little display of theirs would have given me a migraine that could only disappear with a handful of Advil and a bottle of scotch. Lately, however, it will take much more than their childish antics to sour my cheerful mood. Whatever shitshow I have to endure and fix at Royal during the day is all worth it, because the sooner I'm done here, the sooner I get to play with my favorite pet.

Bash walks over to the corner bar I have set up in the office and fills up two glasses of whiskey, no doubt thinking I'd need one after this little fiasco, even though hard liquor before noon isn't my thing. But like I said, Devina and Con's interactions have a way of making me seek out a glass or two.

Surprisingly he doesn't offer me one, but hands it to Devina instead, and sits back on the couch to enjoy his own. Devina is back to her calm and collected form. Anyone looking inside my office through the floor-to-ceiling windows wouldn't even suspect Con had rattled her in any way. The only telltale sign is witnessed by Bash and me alone. After downing her whiskey as if it's water, her shaky hands tremble, placing the glass on the table. Cursing under her breath for showing the one moment of weakness, she pins both hands between her crossed legs, hiding any evidence that Connor Walsh got to her.

"You shouldn't antagonize him so," I advise her for the umpteenth time.

"I'm not antagonizing anyone, Dean. He's a big boy. He can take some constructive criticism," she answers bitterly.

"Not by you, *Dee*," Bash adds stoically.

Devina's back stiffens in her seat, her eyes growing colder with every passing minute. The transformation is uncanny. The Ice Queen is back in full force, and it took little but a few minutes for her to regain all her composure. A true sign of a warrior ready for battle, no matter the wound previously inflicted.

"Gentlemen, I believe we've wasted enough time

as it is. *Mr. Kelley*, you were about to show us some data, as I recall. Please proceed," she orders, taking her tablet back onto her lap to follow Bash's data analysis.

Bash throws me a knowing smirk and starts from where he left off before Con interrupted us. Any other person might have asked to postpone this meeting. However, Devina is all business in no time as if no row had taken place at all just five minutes ago in this very room.

The woman has bigger balls than most men I know. You have to admire that type of gumption and professionalism.

An hour later, our meeting comes to a successful close, with a few new added ideas by Devina herself, by which I believe not only can we decrease expenses, but increase revenue by ten percent. All in all, not a bad way to break before lunch.

Bash and I head out to Luigi's, an Italian deli around the corner from Royal, which makes the best meatball subs. Sure, it's usually packed, but the owner, Luigi himself, usually reserves us a booth around this time, just in case we show up. His loyalty is always rewarded with our asses sitting here at least twice a week. If we're too busy to show up, then he delivers happily, knowing the tip will be a cool Benjamin every time.

"Those two should just fuck and get it over with. Their constant back and forth is getting worse as the years pass. Both too stubborn to their core, and neither willing to submit to the other," Bash groans, taking a huge bite into the tomato, basil, and oregano seasoned sub.

"I'd say give them time, but I'm not sure anymore. However, I'd rather not spoil my appetite in overthinking how Con and Devina might go nuclear one day and fuck up Royal. I'm in too good a mood," I add my own two cents.

"So I've noticed," Bash replies, with a concerned look in his eyes.

"What the fuck is that supposed to mean?" I ask, feeling defensive all of a sudden. I know Bash. He's not one to mince words or insinuate to stir shit up. He's got something on his mind, and apparently has decided now is the time to speak about it.

"Just saying, I've noticed a few changes in you these past few weeks. I'm not knocking them. For the most part, I'm happy to see you're no longer thinking of work twenty-four-seven. I also like seeing that thing you do with your lips now. It's been a long time since you've done one of those. Thought your muscles forgot what a smile was, but guess it's like riding a bike, huh?" he teases.

"Fuck you." I flip him off and take a pull of my beer.

"No, I believe it's the pretty little sleeping Beauty who has been able to perform such a miracle," he retorts, and I take another sip of my drink, so I don't have to answer him. It's not like it's a secret I've been seeing Beauty. I know both he and Con have seen us at the club together. But it's not as if I've had a conversation with them about it, either. I'm not sure how I would act if they approached her. I'm all fucked up in so many ways it's not even funny anymore.

"You're conflicted," Bash says as if reading my mind.

He's always been able to do that mind-reading thing. Case in point, back in the office, he knew I was okay with what went down between Devina and Connor, forgoing my usual drink to forget their nonsense. Devina, though, needed something to take the edge off, stat. He read us to perfection then, just as he's reading me now. I've learned a few tricks from him, but he's always been better at it.

"You've also been absent recently," he continues.

"Aw, Bash, you feeling neglected?" I goad, playing off his previous spot-on observation.

"Fuck off. I'm not Connor. I don't have abandonment issues. I'm all good going solo," he replies with a wolfish grin and a glint in his feline silver eyes.

"So I've heard. Con doesn't seem to be minding it, either."

"No. He lifted his ban on blondes in a big way after he tasted your Beauty. Can't seem to get enough of them lately," he mocks.

I shift in my seat, not comfortable with the intimate way my two best friends have such carnal knowledge of my pet, especially Con. Bash, the perceptive bastard, picks up on my discomfort immediately.

"You know, it was always *you* who set that game in play. You could have always stopped or changed the rules whenever you wanted to," he asserts, adding salt to an open wound I've been trying to ignore.

"I'm aware," I reply, as if unaffected.

"But you didn't. So don't be hating on a brother for something *you* let happen and instigated yourself." His brows lift up high, jaw tense, awaiting my response.

"I'm not," I answer, hoping I'm not lying to my best friend.

"Good." He nods solemnly.

There is an uncomfortable silent pause between us, one I wish would disappear and bring back the old friendly banter of two brothers who held no secrets from one another. Yet, I fear I'm the culprit for creating such a silent barrier.

"But that's not what I wanted to talk to you

about," Bash gives in, running his fingers through his dark ebony hair.

"Oh?"

"Like I said, I've been seeing a lot more changes in you of late."

"Yes, the smiling and shit. I get it, asshole. What else?" I say, trying to lighten the mood.

"Well, what happened in your office just now, for one. Con and Devina going at it and you not giving a *Royal* fuck. A month ago, you would not have been as calm," he explains.

"I guess I just got accustomed to their brand of bullshit. Bound to happen." I shrug, taking a bite of my neglected lunch.

"Or you're happy," Bash says out of the blue, and I almost choke on my meatball.

The fuck!

Where did that come from?

"Come again?" I say, once I've established a Heimlich is not needed, and down my mouthful of the sub with the rest of my beer for good measure.

"You heard me, Dean. I think for the first time in your life, you might be happy," he declares as if he's forecasting tomorrow's weather—a matter-of-fact expression on his face—with an exaggerated tone.

I feel a tug of a smile coming on, but don't want to show it just yet, since I'm not entirely sure if Sebastian pointing out such a fact is a good thing or a bad one.

"From what I've seen, you've wined and dined her there most nights. I've seen you on the common floors, not much else," he affirms.

"What are you insinuating?" I straighten my back to face him head-on since I'm not thrilled where this conversation is suddenly leading.

"Are you worried she might run off if you show her who you are? Scare her away? Are you wearing another mask behind the one you use every night around her?"

"Your point?" I quip sternly.

"My point is but one, *my King*. Is this new-found happiness based on something long lasting, or a fleeting illusion of your making?" He glares at me intently, making it known he's not going to pussyfoot about the issue any longer.

"Does it matter?" I ask since I'm unsure of the answer myself.

"It does, Dean. One will build you up further, while the other will only break you apart. I'd rather prevent that if you don't mind. It's kind of written in my job description." He slumps back in his seat, done with the brotherly advice, for today at least. God only knows how long it had been lodged in his throat, ready to burst in my face anyway.

"Oh yeah? It's in your job description as my finance director?" I quip back.

"No, fucker. As your best friend."

Chapter 16

EDIE

"Where are we going?" I ask as Dean pushes the button to the eleventh floor, one that we've never been to before. He was disturbingly quiet through dinner, and my intuition is yelling to be cautious approaching my King this evening.

"I haven't been much of a tutor to you, pet. This club has many activities which can immensely benefit your education, and I've been foolish to neglect them as long as I have," he states harshly.

I don't know why his tone hurts my heart, but it does. And in more ways than one, I'm thankful to hide behind the black lace mask I'm wearing tonight. If any tear should fall, the fabric will surely soak it up before he has time to witness how his callous tone affects me. His back is to me, standing still, facing the elevator door, almost as if he doesn't even want to look at me.

"Did I do something wrong? Offend you in any way?" I hear myself ask, and hate how vulnerable this man makes me feel. Never before was there a person, alive or dead, who could break me with just a word. Yet, one cold sentence from Dean thrown my way, and I want to crawl into the fetal position in the corner of this elevator and lick my wounds.

I see him fidget in place, and his hands pull into hard fists.

"No, pet. I'm the one who's been wronging you. Tonight it ends," he whispers softly, and I get an eerie premonition that whatever he's about to show me on the eleventh floor will make me want to run away instead of huddle down on the ground in misery.

The ding sound of the elevator comes too soon, and my frozen state comes to an end, beckoned by his strong hand on the small of my back. The lighting is odd here—dark, but golden at the same time. It's as if all the lights were turned off, and only glimmers of a faraway lamp is giving off a faint light. There are no chairs or sofas, or any furniture I can see in this place. But Dean seems to know his way perfectly down the long path. And that's when I see it's a long, wide corridor, and not an empty room as I presumed, but I don't see any doors to speak of.

"King?"

But he doesn't answer me, and instead, he just continues to push me along, guiding me to the unknown destination.

Something tells me I shouldn't have eaten the oysters, people. I wanted to be sexy and provocative, but Dean is freaking me out right now with his secrecy. Thoughts of big-bellied bald men, with ball gags, being whipped into submission by their dominatrices in leather unitards, might make each and every oyster reappearing on this lovely imported carpet. I shit you not! Poppy said there are all sorts of nasty floors, doing crazy kinky stuff, and as much as I would do anything for Dean—and let's face it, I think I've done quite a bit—there are some lines I will not cross.

When a door finally appears on the right side of the wall, Dean presses a few buttons, then runs his card through the panel, releasing an unlocking sound. He pulls the door open, letting himself step in first. I take a few breaths, gaining courage for whatever I'm about to face on the other side.

"Pet?" he summons, reaching out for my hand.

Now he calls me. Yeah, well, just hang in there, will ya, King? Not really excited for this next part.

Another quick intake of breath, pulling up my imaginary big girl panties—or in my case Victoria's Secret thong, but whatever—and I clasp my hand in his.

Of course, once again, my imagination doesn't compete with the real thing. The first time I let my imagination run wild concerning After Hours' affairs, I was pleasantly surprised. This time? Let's just say this time I'm more confused.

I'm in a spacious theater room, but the stage is smaller than the one used for shows upstairs, and it doesn't have two floors or private booths. Instead, it has one small stage, where the audience is separated by a thin glass of sorts. By the look of it, it almost gives the impression it's a two-way mirror, like the ones used in interrogation rooms seen in detective TV shows that Lexi devours and binge-watches. Inside the stage area would be where the cop would take the perp for questioning—or beat the confession out of him, as Lexi liked best—while on the other side, cops would observe the perp having no clue to who was watching him at his weakest.

Dean moves closer to the stage and finds us two empty chairs. I look around and see at least thirty couples. It's a quaint audience, compared to the high volume of members this place has. Yet, something tells me it's not because of the lack of popularity since I don't see any other seats available.

"This isn't a free-for-all show, is it?" I hush under my breath, my eyes still looking around the room.

"No."

"Yeah, I didn't think so."

My suspicions were right; you must have clearance to see this show, and you need to pay extra to come, which means Dean must have paid a pretty penny for my so-called tutelage. With all my appraisal of the audience, I forget to focus on the center stage, but when everyone stands and claps, I mimic their actions, even though I have no clue why they seem so happy all of a sudden.

My eyes trail to the stage, and there, right at the center, stands a woman in a white silk robe decorated in delicate cherry blossoms. She turns around, letting the robe fall down her slender shoulders, revealing milky white skin and a snowy figure from neck to ankle. Her red hair looks like flames falling down to her petite waist, and it takes me a minute to notice she has just disrobed and gotten completely nude, with the full knowledge there were about sixty people watching her do it. She walks over to the middle of the room, and this is when I register how bare it is, save for a pole standing intimidatingly strong from floor to ceiling, and a chair beside the door she must have used to make her grand entrance. When she gets close enough to the pole, she turns to her spectators, who praise and applaud yet again her bravery, and I'm sure her physique. The woman is in fact quite extraordinary. I work with models all the time, so I'm not a prude, or shy when it comes to the female form. I can appreciate beauty when I see it, and this red-haired exhibitionist knows God was generous with her in bestowing all her assets.

She's holding something in her hand, a type of cloth, but it's too far to see what it could be. My question is answered when she unravels the long black material, placing it over her eyes and tying it behind her head. She makes sure her mask and blindfold are in place before locking her wrists in front of her. I see her say something, but the glass is soundproof. We can see what she wants us to see, but we won't be able to hear a thing.

A man in a dark blue suede suit enters, looking

more like one of the New York Giants defense player than anything else. He also asks her something from the door, to which she replies and nods. He comes to her side, gently leading her closer to the pole, and stretches her arms up high, binding both wrists with a similar black cloth. He gives it a pull, making sure it's tight but also comfortable to the bound woman. I see his lips moving, his features look concerned for the woman's well-being. I see her nod again and saying something in return that lightens the spirits of the heavy-framed bouncer. He then goes back to the door and takes a seat at the one single chair.

I don't know what's coming, but I think I've seen enough for tonight.

"What is this?" I ask under my breath, not wanting the other spectators to be disturbed by the argument I'm sure will unfold in the next two seconds.

"What does it look like?" Dean answers, his eyes on me.

Were his eyes always on me as I was taking all of this in?

"It looks like a naked woman bound up to a post in the middle of the room, while her boyfriend, or whatever that guy is, is just going to sit there and watch. Is that who we're all waiting for now? Her lover to arrive?"

"That's not her boyfriend. And yes, she is waiting. She just doesn't know who she's waiting for," he explains, still looking intently at my reaction.

"I'm sorry, what?" I whisper-yell, gaining the attention of the couple next to us. I squirm in my seat, giving them a view of my full back, but really what I'm giving them is my big Jersey kiss-my-ass move. Yeah, go ahead and kiss it, Mr. and Mrs. Kinky Weirdo. I'm trying to talk to my... whatever Dean is to me in this crazy-fucked up scenario right now.

"It's her fantasy. She willingly came into this room and blindfolded herself. It's all part of the game, you see?"

"So, you mean to tell me some stranger will come into the room in about a minute or so, and have his or her way with that woman, and she is a hundred percent fine with it?" I gawk.

"Not only is she fine, but she's the one who auctioned herself off," he states, pretending to clean some imaginary lint off his cuff.

"Auctioned?"

Did he just say auctioned? Are we fucking cattle now? This is so wrong.

"Hmm. Usually, the money from the auction goes to some institution she's passionate about. Domestic abuse or rape victims support units are the most popular," he adds, still unable to look me in the eye. How quickly he did a one-eighty there. First, he was gauging all my reactions, but sensing my displeasure, he's no longer interested in keeping such close vigil.

"Really? Even though she's put herself in a similar environment?" I scoff.

"A fantasy is a fantasy, pet. The real thing is much different. She knows it. She knows she's protected. There are eyes on her at all times. Some prefer this type of scenario to be more discreet than this, but apparently, she wanted an audience, and the house always provides. And let's not forget the fact that she's there willingly."

"So who's the goon then? You said he wasn't her boyfriend, so who is he and why is he in there with her?"

"He's her protection. He will stay in the corner of the room at all times and listen in. Should the woman even hint at using the safe word she provided him, whoever won tonight's auction is off her in record time, one way or another."

I've heard enough. I stand from my seat, not waiting for this so-called show to begin. I get that this club is in the sex business, and I get that this woman is just getting her kicks, just as the people who are sitting here in anticipation for her guest to arrive are getting theirs. But some things are beyond my comprehension.

I know I'm not as experienced. And compared to Dean and his vast knowledge in this field, I'll never catch up. And right now, I don't think I really want to. I don't want to make love in front of spectators. I don't want to share something so intimate without looking my lover in the eye, as that woman is about to do. And I sure as hell don't ever want to be in a situation where I need someone to be standing close by for protection, in case things go sour. The man I'm making love with should be making me feel cherished and protected enough.

So call me foolish. Call me naïve. Call me a prude if you must. But for me, some things should remain sacred and not a show for outside viewers enjoyment.

I make my way to the back of the room, ignoring the ugly glares I'm getting for interrupting tonight's show. I don't look back once, too afraid Dean is still at his seat, patiently waiting, like the rest of the crowd, to see who will come onstage. But when I feel a warm hand settle yet again on the same spot it seems to always find on the small of my back, my anger simmers to a low boil. Dean opens the door, offering me my blessed escape from this God-awful room, and a new round of applause ensues. My curiosity gets the best of me, and I give a backward glance to see if the redhead got a girl or a boy at least.

Ohhh boy. Definitely male, alright.

It's a good thing you ain't watching, Red. 'Cause the Russian coming at you is going to eat you alive, I think to myself.

I've been lucky enough to stay clear of Panther's Russian friend. One look at that man and I knew all I needed to know—he was trouble, in and out of After Hours. Just another reason to put some added distance between me and this stupid room.

What was my King thinking about bringing me here in the first place?

Instead of going to Dean's suite, I ask him to escort me to my own room. I haven't seen the need to be in here that much. Dean's room is easily three times the size of mine, and his bed is definitely more appealing, so of course, why would we ever choose my temp room for our rendezvous, when his offered so much more luscious comfort? But tonight I'm not feeling it. Actually, if I had any sense, I would have left his ass behind and just caught a cab back home, rendering this as a lost night.

But you guys know me by now, right?

I wouldn't have slept a wink, replaying every minute of what happened upstairs the whole night through. I would have gone to work the following day and do it all over again, just to find myself right here in this exact spot, demanding answers to what the fuck he was thinking in the first place.

So yeah, I'd rather spare the predictable twenty-four hours of miserable torture and get this over and done with.

"I think you wanted to shock me tonight. Why?" I ask, holding the gun point-blank to his chest. And when I say gun, I mean the venom in my tone and stare.

"I didn't want to shock you. I wanted to teach you," he answers, taking his coat off, and proceeding to turn his back away from me. I have to bite my inner cheek to keep my cool. He's trying to gain some distance, but hell if I'm going to give it to him.

"Teach me what? That there are people who get their kicks at being tied up? Yeah, I saw the movie and read the books; I don't need an actual live visual," I snap.

"You're upset," he states, still with his back turned, but I can see him filling two chalices of expensive scotch from the room's mini bar.

"I wonder what gave it away?!" I bark back. Oh, buddy! You think a sober, pissed-off Edie is something unpleasant to deal with, you do not want to see the drunk version!

"But you shouldn't be. Wasn't this the whole point to your tutelage in the first place? To learn what your limits are? What drives you? What turns you on?" he replies dispassionately and offers me his prepared drink. I slap it out of his hand, and it crashes to the floor in shattered pieces.

Fuck!

I'm losing it.

This is it. The point of no return. The exact

moment when level-headed Edie Vanderwalt loses her shit because the man she's hung up on lives in a whole other world different to hers. Who was I kidding? Here I am dressed in couture from head to toe, but it's a sham.

I am a sham.

"You turn me on. I don't need to learn anything else," I whisper, defeated, walking over to my twin bed, and sitting down as solemnly as I feel.

"That's very flattering, pet. Still not the point of the lesson today," he replies, eyeing me up and down.

"I lied," I tell him.

Oh, how I've lied.

"Lied? About what?" he asks, taking a few steps closer to me.

"I made up the whole tutelage idea just so you would spend more time with me," I explain truthfully. One less lie to worry about. But a hundred more where that one came from yet to tell.

"Did you, now?" I feel him sitting by my side, and I don't need to raise my head to see he must be wearing his panty-melting smirk I adore so much.

"Yes. I mean, after you insisted on your so-called 'court' to take place, I was left with the impression it was just a one-off type of thing for you. I guess I got a little creative for a repeat." I shrug in my defense.

"I guess you did." He's definitely smirking, alright.

"Are you mad?"

"I should be, shouldn't I?" he replies, but I don't hear any malice in his voice.

"Tonight didn't go as I thought it would. Maybe it's best I went home," I relent, raising off the bed, but Dean catches my wrist and brings me back down to sit by his side.

"No, pet. I prefer you'd stay. I'd prefer you stay here with me." He wraps a strand of my hair around his fingers and becomes mesmerized by it for some reason.

"Are you sure?" I question since, for all intents and purposes, I think we just had our first fight.

Sure, I still haven't told him the real reason why the scene upstairs upset me so, and I know his explanation has more holes than a fishing net, but I'm pretty sure we skipped the yelling stage and are jumping straight to the making-up portion.

"I guess you're not the only one who used the tutelage angle as an excuse. I've grown fond of our encounters, too." He smiles.

He fucking smiles! I have told you how the smiles from Dean Knox are like meteor showers, right? Rare like motherfuckers, pardon my French, but the most majestic sight you will ever witness.

"So does this mean you're keeping me?" I let out without thinking, but the smile knocked the wind out of me to have time to put in place my think-before-you-speak skill set. His face looks almost pained, and I realize just what a stupid question it was.

"I mean for tonight, at least," I rephrase, hoping it's enough to do damage control.

"Yes, Beauty. I am."

I'm woken up with feathered kisses along my jaw and neck, and I stretch like the kitten my King takes me for.

"Tell me something real, pet," he whispers in the dead of night.

"You know the rules. No information about our real lives, remember?"

I bite my inner cheek when I see hurt reach his green eyes, of how the barrier is still there between us, and my insistence of maintaining it skyscraper high and out of reach for him.

"What do you want to know, my King?" I concede.

"I can ask anything?"

"Within reason," I affirm.

"Define within reason," he taunts.

"I might plead the fifth if the answer embarrasses me in any way," I answer honestly, and his eyes start to sparkle like the jewels they are.

"Hmm. My shy pet returneth. I do like seeing her from time to time," he mocks.

"Ask your question before I change my mind. But you'll have to tell me something about you, too."

"Can I plead the fifth also?" he goads.

"Sure." I shrug. "But then I'd have to ask my question first."

"Hey, now. I started this game, I think I should go first." He pinches my sides, releasing a mouse-like squeak from me.

"Well, you took too long," I assert, slapping his ticklish paws away from my naked and sensitive flesh. He bites my shoulder, hard enough to leave his mark, but then eases the pain with tender kisses and a flirtatious tongue.

"Fine, you cheat. What's your question again?" I consent.

"I want you to tell me something real about yourself. Something you've never admitted to anyone."

"Anyone?"

"Anyone."

"I'm a coward." The honest admission is out of my lips before I have time to think of an acceptable alternative.

"What?"

"I am. I'm a coward. I'm genetically defected. I have deep-seated trust issues, yet at the first show of hardship, I'm the first to bolt. So I just don't try. On anything. I build walls of invisibility, so people don't see me, and the ones who do and come into contact with me either think I'm a heartless bitch or sweet like apple pie. I think somewhere in my job description there is a line which says just that. Be callous to some, and graciously pleasant to others. I actually get paid to either be invisible, a ball-breaker, or to make everybody happy. And the funny thing is I'm good at all of it."

He places his chin on my chest, his green emerald eyes fixed on mine, and delivers a grin I haven't seen yet on his glorious face. Demure, and almost shy-like, but still as earth-shattering as its brethren.

"You sure make me happy."

"I do?" I stutter, feeling my heart want to leap from my chest.

"Yes. Very." His tone is just as soft as the look in his eyes and smile on his lips.

Oh dear lord, I'm in so much trouble.

"Good." I have the sense to reply, even though my mouth is dry and my ears are ringing, and all my organs have literally stopped working, save for the one beating a mile a minute.

"But you're not a coward," he continues on.

"I'm not?"

"No. It took guts for you to come into this club. It took guts for you to ask to hold court with my friends and me that first night, and it took guts to ask me to tutor you. You are anything but a coward. In regards to you being invisible, the first night you came into this place, I couldn't take my eyes off of you, which tells me that when you want to be seen, you command it to be so. And I'm glad to say my balls have never been busted in your care. Quite the contrary. Therefore, whoever saw that side of you must have warranted it in some way."

"Huh? I never thought about it that way."

He snickers softly and I'm a gooey, hot mess.

"Okay, now your turn," I say, trying to regain

some decorum.

"Mmmm." He murmurs, kissing the tops of my breasts.

"No, no! None of that! I answered your question, now you have to answer mine." I grab his chin, stopping him in his tracks.

"Very well, then. Go on," he replies, amused by my sudden assertiveness.

"Why come here?"

He looks at me, confused, then starts looking around the room and our naked states, thinking that the answer to my question is rather obvious.

"No! I mean why come to After Hours? You're attractive, intelligent, and just by your poise alone, I'd know you're a successful man, too, if not your arrogance in some cases being a dead giveaway," I chide. "You can have any woman you want. Date whoever you choose. Why come here?"

He closes his eyes in contemplation, and I wonder how much time he really needs to remember what brought him here in the first place.

"I think for a time I thought I was empty."

"What?" I stutter again, trying to grasp what he can mean by such a depressing statement.

"Empty, pet. Shallow. I thought there was no real depth in me, beside the deep pockets I had."

"That's not true," I try to argue, but he places his finger on my lips to silence me.

"It is, pet. Or at least I believed I was. If you knew me, the real me, you would have seen it, too."

"I don't believe that." I shake my head, tears threatening to make an appearance in our whispered confession.

"Believe what you will, but for a time I knew what I was, wholeheartedly. A man with no actual worth. Dating meant commitment. Meant promises I could never give. A woman's time is precious, pet. It shouldn't be spent on a man who knows his mind and will never give her the life she dreamed for herself. I couldn't have it on my conscious to have someone feel worthless because of my own barren state. It wouldn't be fair. And I pride myself on being honest in all aspects of my life. When After Hours presented itself to me, I saw it as a diversion. Nothing else. A game where no one got hurt since all the players were just as devoid of worth, emotion, and as desolate as I found myself to be."

"Hmmm. Can I ask you something?" I ask after a pregnant pause and making sure that my voice is strong enough to speak.

"Yes."

"If anyone asked your closest friends, the Prince or the Duke for instance, if push came to shove, would they take a bullet for you?"

He lets out another low laugh and kisses my chin after he's composed himself.

"That's a stretch, pet."

"Humor me," I insist.

"I guess."

"Well, then I guess you have worth to someone, don't you?" I state proudly, believing I've made my case.

"It's not the same. But yes, I see your point," he says, rewarding me with another kiss.

"Hmm. But you said you don't think you're empty anymore."

"No, I don't think I am."

"What changed?" I ask, curious, wondering what could have woken him to the truth.

"This place, for one. It showed me what true emptiness is. What people do when they have lost hope or have become too jaded. They don't even care to learn the name of the lover they're with."

"Oh."

"And innocence reminded me I was once just as naive. Just as hopeful and curious. If the aloofness of these walls showed me I'm different from the people it surrounds, then it was innocence that popped the roof off the whole goddamned building for me and showed I, too, am not lost yet."

"Oh."

"Yes, pet. *Oh*."

After another embarrassingly long pause, partially due to being brain dead from his last remark, an idea pops into my head. One that might just help him, if he ever starts to feel this type of empty feeling again. Lord knows it's been my saving grace more times than I care to admit.

"I think you shouldn't be concerned about your own worth, but how you might be worthy to others instead," I state sharply.

"I don't follow." He squints his eyes, almost cruelly, as if I've hit a scab best left untouched. But I've started my reasoning, and he would be disappointed in me if I cowered away now.

"Well, my King," I take a quick breath, "have you ever thought about how to better this great city of ours?"

"You're talking about philanthropy? I do that already, pet. I donate thousands each month to various charities."

"Oh, my King, but that's only money. Kindness and love last much longer than any dollar bill will."

"Hmm."

"And if I'm any indication, just being with you makes my day better. It would be awfully selfish of me to keep you all to myself," I try to play off.

"A selfish pet, now? Doubtful."

"Just think about it. You'd be surprised how sometimes, just giving a piece of yourself to someone who needs it, be it a hug, a smile, or a kind word, gives you so much more in return. I doubt you'd see an empty day in sight, my King."

"Ah, my pet. Of that, I don't doubt. I bet the world through your eyes is rainbow-colored and cotton-candy flavored with potential."

"Are you mocking me?" I ask, injured.

"No, Beauty. I envy you. Envy not knowing true hollowness, ugliness, and loneliness."

"You are mocking me. I've felt all those things," I tell him truthfully.

"Yet you've never given them any weight. Or maybe you did, didn't you, pet? Otherwise, why would you have kept yourself hidden away, untouched for so long?"

"Because I'm a coward like I told you."

"Then fate is kind after all. It gave you the courage to break your chains to seek me out when I needed something to release me from the prison of my making. What a pair we make," he states, going back to kissing my neck, his hands already seeking the warmth of my body, freeing himself further from his burdens, yet binding me deeper to him with every touch.

"Yes, my King. What a pair we make."

Chapter 17

DEAN

The dress she's got on tonight accentuates the golden goddess that she is, and the glitter painted on her face only heightens the pure blue of her eyes. I love it when she forgoes the mask and goes with her paints instead. It's as if I'm almost seeing her true self. Well, as close to it as I can get—for now, at least.

"What is this place?" she asks as she continues to walk into the secluded room where only the sound of her stilettos on the varnished floors echoes. The room is exactly the same as I remember it. And I certainly should, since I've spent countless hours here. It's smaller than most of the playing areas After Hours provides, and there is good cause for it, too. It's supposed to have this more intimate feel to it. With only a red velvet couch in the middle of the room and four lounge chairs surrounding it, there really is little else to focus on, save for the monstrosity of a chandelier hanging from the ceiling, giving the room enough mood light for each spectator not to miss a single moment. Much more intimate than the auction room of last week. Bringing her there was a mistake I won't repeat again. But bringing her here, to a place I once spent hours in, needs to be discussed. She might not like it, but I don't want to keep any secrets from her, either.

"You asked me once what brought me to After Hours in the first place, remember?" I start walking her over, my hand remaining on the small hollow of her back.

"Yes," she answers, looking up at me with trusting eyes. A man can get lost in them for days on end and still not want to find his way back to the real world.

"I told you it was because I was empty. But in a way, I guess I was still searching. Searching for something. And for a long time, I thought I had found it in these four walls," I explain. How foolish of me to ever think that I would ever find it here, when only now I'm getting a taste of what I truly want.

"But it is empty. What is this place, King?" Her brows furrow, genuinely perplexed, and I feel a small tug of my lip lift in amusement at her frustration for not being able to put the pieces of the puzzle together quickly enough without me having to explain it to her.

"Sit down, pet," I tell her and give her a little nudge. She plants her luscious-looking ass on the couch as ordered, while I walk to my preferred spot and sit in my usual lounge chair. As soon as I relax into my seat, she tenses in hers. Her frustration for not understanding this room has increased now with the distance I've just created between us. My pet hates not being in close proximity to me. But I want to just stay here a bit and take all of her flawless beauty in.

Such innocence. Such eagerness to touch me and know my every secret. As her scowl deepens, so does her ache. It's as if being away from me hurts her. And in the ten steps that separate us, I realize just how much it pains me, too. I honestly have become addicted, and it's incredible that it's taken me this long to acknowledge the truth of how much this woman has crawled her way under my skin.

"Lean back for me, pet." And as a truly obedient, loyal subject, she abides my every command.

"This place used to be my sanctuary. It had everything I thought I craved. You see, these four walls used to host a certain type of spectacle. A place where a woman would come, either alone or with a partner, be it male or female, and she would have an audience waiting for her. At her demand, she would allow said audience to watch her while she made herself cum over and over in front of us. Or if she were truly daring, she would allow that audience to assist her and participate in giving her the desired orgasm she was entitled to for the great performance given to us. Mind you, this was a very intimate affair, and a very small audience was ever in attendance. But still, this room was what I enjoyed best. And although I liked to play, I always liked it more when the hostess denied me my time and made me only watch her."

"You mean you preferred to only watch her play with herself or have sex with someone else?" she asks, genuinely intrigued.

"Yes," I answer, placing my elbows on my knees,

and my clasped hands under my chin, just watching her curiosity blossom.

"Why?"

"Because it allowed me to see everything. Especially if she brought a partner with her. It allowed me to see how they clicked together perfectly. It was the bond they shared that intrigued me most. How their attraction for each other was so palpable sometimes, that you could almost feel the electricity in the air flicker—especially if they were in love. Those were the shows I enjoyed best. The union was more than physical, and everyone in the room could taste it. How they would keep eye contact with each other at all costs, not wanting to lose the invisible bond that held them together. I witnessed how the woman's breath would become shallower as she was getting closer to her peak. I was able to get a better view of her hardened nipples, and tightening her thighs around her lover, binding him to her in every way she could. All of it. There is so much we miss out on when you're actually having sex, that you forget how erotic it is from the outside. Every little aspect of it should be appreciated. And I've always been a man who likes to know what makes a person tick." I wink.

"Oh," she whispers.

"Does that shock you? Or does it repulse you in any way?" I ask, after a few minutes of silence, wondering if it was too soon to share this with my innocent pet.

"Should it?"

"I brought you here because I want you to see what turns me on—for you to understand that if you want to acknowledge what turns *you* on, you have to be honest with your feelings and your desires. I'm being honest about mine with you now. This is me," I answer softly, not wanting to scare her away.

Another pregnant pause transpires, and my skin starts to prickle in warning, telling me that this might have been too much too fast for such an angelical creature. She's still learning her way, and although she's getting more confident and brazen, there are just some things she will need time to get used to, my particular tastes being one of them.

"Do you think that's why you used to hold 'court'? Because in some way you might not have a bond with the woman in question, but rather with the two men at your side?" she asks, worrying her lower lip.

"Such a perceptive, clever pet," I beam proudly, letting out the breath I had been holding since the last time she uttered a word.

"So, do you always prefer to watch?" she queries.

"I have my exceptions," I smirk.

"Do you, now?" she replies, coming closer to the edge of the couch and opening her legs up wide, showcasing those toned, long legs of hers. "So when these women came in here, did they just start the show without even talking?" she asks, but it takes me a minute to register since I'm fixed on the way her hands are slowly moving up and down her calves, right to her outer thighs.

"Yes. Mostly," I finally hear myself answer, my voice now nothing but a husky moan.

"Hmmm. Yeah, I'm not going to do that," she says, this time running a hand over the top of her full breasts.

Sweet Jesus.

"No?" I ask, feeling my throat close up all of a sudden.

"No, my King. I like to talk. And I like your eyes on me, too. I always like your eyes on me," she continues, licking her lips, her lids half-mast.

I've seen that look before. It's the look she has on half of the time we're together. The one that tells me she's game for whatever I have in mind for her. She raises her dress a little further up with one hand as the other continues to caress her breast over the flimsy material of her dress, making her nipples hard points directed at me. My cock never goes down with this woman around me, but now it's too hard to keep it confined. I pull my zipper down and let it out from its prison cell. The moment it hits air, my Beauty hisses in delight, and my cock tears in satisfaction at her sighs.

Unhurriedly, she slides one of her gown's straps down her shoulder, giving me a peek at her bare breast and its pink nipple, which is already taunting me to give it a good, ruthless bite. My temptress continues torturing me by doing the same to her other strap, leaving her full breasts now on display for my eyes alone. Her breath quickens its pace when my hand comes in contact with the one thing she wants desperately from me, and each time I slide it up and down, she can't help but follow each leisured stroke.

"Like what you see, pet?" I smirk, jerking my shaft just slow enough to drive both her and me wild.

"Yes," she huskily replies.

"But I'm not the one supposed to be giving a show, now am I?" I wink at her again, in jest, and the soft crimson hue that follows, almost makes me want to get off this chair and run to her, impale her right now, and fuck her until she sees God himself.

But it only takes mere seconds for her to recover, and my little vixen is back in the game. She places both of her feet on the couch, keeping her legs spread wide and letting me see that my girl not only forwent her mask tonight but her lingerie as well. Her sweet pussy is already dripping with need, and she parts her lips with her fingers, letting me see all of her. I can't recall when I wanted to end one of my games so quickly before, just to get a taste. She starts to tease her little bud with one hand, while the other continues to pinch her nipples to the point of pain, but her eyes never leave me.

"My King," she whispers repeatedly.

"Yes, pet?" I answer, more in control of my tone, at least.

"I need you."

"Why, pet? When you look so good just like this." And she does. She looks heavenly beautiful—rosy cheeks, glazy eyes, filled with lust and want, sweat falling down her neck, while her breasts get fuller and perkier with each second of her getting closer to cumming. She is the most beautiful thing I have ever set eyes on, and I will treasure this moment forever. This and every other one she has given me.

My star pupil.

My pet.

My Queen.

"Please, my King," she begs, so close to seeing fireworks, but frustrated that her own hands can't get her there fast enough.

"You need me?"

"Yes!" she howls.

"Then cum for me," I order.

"What?" she asks, puzzled and disheartened all in

the same breath.

"If you need me, you will obey me. Cum for me and you can have me," I deadpan firmly.

"Oh, God," she sighs, pushing herself further.

"What do you want, my pet?" I aid her, knowing my voice has the magical effect to get her to her destination.

"You. I've always wanted you," she says, so matter-of-factly that it soothes my icy interior. I don't even know her name, yet she holds the same effect on me as I apparently have on her. She is not shy in telling me who she wants. She's been telling me so since day one. Only now, I want her just as much. I need her just as much.

"I want you, my King," she repeats again in a jagged breath.

"You have me, my Queen," I answer honestly.

You'll always have me.

And just like that, her yell of ecstasy reaches every corner of this room, bringing light to every dark element in here and bringing me almost to my own brink of madness. I stop my own ministrations, too enthralled with her orgasm to focus on anything else but her—this perfect creature in front of me; this miracle. It takes her forever to come back to earth from such an earth-shattering explosion, but when she does, her smile is just as bright as the beam she created.

I stand from my seat and take those ten steps, which should have never been between us in the first place, and grab her waist to lock her legs around me. She wraps her arms around my neck and looks intently into my eyes.

"So, is that what you're used to watching? Did I pass your test, teach?" she teases, her brow still damp from her little performance.

"I can honestly say I've never watched anything like that before," I tell her, and I feel her slump in my embrace.

"Oh?" she questions, unsure of herself, with a little frown on her lips too cute not to kiss away.

"That was the best performance this room has ever seen, pet. And I'm the lucky bastard that was privileged enough to be in the audience."

"Hmm, maybe I should do a repeat, then? You know, to get an outside opinion. Just in case you're biased and all," she taunts, biting her lower lip provocatively.

I slap her ass and sit down on the couch in one quick move, aligning her bare pussy with my aching cock, which has been deprived of her long enough. Before she has time to utter another smart remark, I thrust into her, hard and without mercy.

"Enough talk about any other men, pet. The only one you'll be fucking is me."

Thrust.

"The only one who will know how good this pussy feels is me."

Thrust.

"How it tastes."

Thrust.

"How it feels wrapped tightly around my cock."

Thrust.

"And how it cums when I pump it hard like I am now. Only me, pet. Are we understood?"

"Oh, God," she moans, her head hanging back already too lost to the world, but I need to nip this shit in the bud now. I grab her chin while keeping up with our brutal tempo.

"Are we understood, pet? I am your King! I rule this pussy, and no one else will touch what's mine! Do you understand?" I growl this time, feeling desperate for her to acknowledge me in this way.

But while I feel manic and going crazy with rage, my temptress only smiles and looks at me with stars in her eyes.

"That's because I'm your Queen," she says breathlessly.

"Yes, pet. You are. And I'm your King," I reply, just as crazed as before, still thrusting hard into her, marking her in every way until her body remembers that it belongs to me. I see her eyes soften, and she unwraps her arms from my shoulders and places her hands on my face, looking intently into my eyes.

"Yes, you are. You've always been my King. My one," she whispers, and I stop my ravishing as she pushes me back into the couch. Without skipping a beat, she takes over, slowly, moving up and down my shaft, lovingly, while never breaking eye contact. Her hands continue to stroke my face as her eyes seem to pierce my very soul.

"You are my King," she breathes out in a whisper, mesmerizing me.

Up and down she goes, and my hands find her waist to guide her tormenting rhythm.

"And I am yours," she moans, and I mimic her song here, too.

Up and down.

"Always yours."

Up and down.

"My King," she vows, never once tearing her gaze from me, but the emotions bubbling in my chest are just too intense, and my lids close for a few seconds just so I can take this all in—take this act of divine surrender and keep it safe and locked away, so I can visit it again on those lonely nights where I don't have her lying beside me. Just the idea alone, of an empty bed without her body next to mine, crushes my lungs into shards of glass, too prickly to breathe in right. I quickly open my eyes, not wanting to be anywhere she isn't, and I am met with crystal blue eyes, looking down on me with nothing but desire and—if I let myself believe it—even love.

"Tell me again, pet. Who am I to you?" I grunt, this time quickening her slow pace, but just by a smidge, since the masochist in me is loving this too much.

"My King," she sighs again.

"Is that all, pet?"

"My tutor."

"And," I provoke. I want it all from her lips. "Repeat it all, my Queen," I order, giving her what her own heart desires to hear me reveal to her again.

"Oh, God!" she moans, removing her hands from my face, grabbing my shoulders for dear life, trying to keep her balance. Her newfound title seems to bring her too close to the edge, but I still need to hear those words.

"No. Not God, but I'm flattered, pet. What else am I to you?" I groan, feeling her pussy clench on my cock in such a sweet way that I know I won't last too long, either, with or without her words of endearment.

"My one. My only! Oh, God!" she cries, as I pound into her now, loving those words flying from her lips. I bite her breast, getting another moan out of her, and her sweet taste in my mouth and her voice still in my ears, while all of her is wrapped around me like a vine, is pure nirvana.

"Cum for me, my Queen. Cum on your King's cock as you've always been meant to," I command, and like clockwork, my gorgeous Beauty yells from the top of her lungs the most glorious melody a man can hear, and reaches the sky, picking apart each star, since they can never compare with how extraordinary she looks right now.

Her *one*.

Her *only*.

Her words on repeat in my ears and her orgasm milking me for all it's worth, take me over the edge and into unchartered waters as I release my own explosion. Yes, I was the one who took her sweet cherry for the first time, and for the time being, I am her only. Her only King and lover. And by God, I will do everything in my power to keep it that way.

As I calm down my beating heart, I hold her to me, loving how our wild organs beat erratically to a similar pulse, as if they, too, recognize each other. Her whole body is too blissfully limp for any further movement, so I carefully lay her down in front of me and grab her tightly. It's only now that I see that I'm still fully dressed, while my goddess has her little golden number bunched up in the middle of her belly. I relieve her of her dress in mere seconds, getting her nice and comfortable. Of course, the moment her back meets my belt and my pants, I hear her little frustrated growl, so I take care to please my little pet by getting undressed, too. When she's perfectly situated in her spooning position, I swear I hear her purr.

What am I going to do with this woman?

"Pet?" I whisper in her ear after a few minutes. The bright smile on her lips is the only giveaway she's still awake.

"Yes?" she asks, no longer hiding the purr of contentment behind her reply.

"What's your name?" I ask, cautiously hoping she's too out of it to overthink my question.

"I thought we weren't supposed to tell each other our real names here?" she replies, more awake now, my question making her body tense immediately.

"I won't tell if you don't." I try to joke, not liking

her sudden alertness one bit. This was not the reaction I was hoping for.

Even though I'm behind her, I can still see fully well how she rubs her lower lip raw.

"Come on. Humor me," I continue, but this time I remove my hand from her stomach and start to stroke her outer thigh, using small, hypnotizing circles, hoping to get her back to her relaxed state, even though mine is no longer in sight.

After a pregnant pause, I hear a small sigh leave her lips in defeat.

"It's Edwina," she hushes.

"Edwina, huh? Very grown-up name. You don't hear that name very often," I state, not acting at all surprised at how unprepared I was to hear such a unique name, although I really shouldn't be. The woman in my arms would never bear just any name; it had to be special. Just like her owner.

"I used to hate it as a kid. I got teased a lot growing up," she confesses, looking down to the floor, away from me.

"Well, I love it," I remark honestly, pulling her face to me and kissing the top of her nose.

"Thank you," she says, with a tug of a smile threatening to reach her lips.

"Should I be offended you didn't ask mine? You're usually such a curious pet." I state, still holding onto her chin.

"Hmm, sorry. So what's yours?" she asks, blinking quickly and reddening further still.

"It's Dean." I chuckle.

"It suits you." She grins.

"Thank you, Edwina."

She scowls and scrunches into my chest.

"Wow, you really don't like your name, do you?"

"No, not so much. You mind if we don't use our real names? I want to keep things as they are. Is that okay?" she pleads, looking up at me with true urgency in her eyes.

"Sure, my pet," I reply with a grin, even though a small part of me deflates with her answer of keeping our current circumstances the same. She nudges back into her favorite position, and I pull her to me, offering her the beloved cuddling moment she's so fond of after two mind-blowing orgasms.

"My King?" she asks, breaking the new silence around us.

"Yes, pet?" I answer, returning to stroking her thigh in tender loving strokes, seeing how her skin pinks and heats up as I do, promising a second round in no time.

"Why did you want to know my name?"

I continue to let my fingertips feel the softness of her skin, while my lips open and give her the only lie I've ever given to her to this day.

"No reason, pet. Merely curious," I pronounce, never skipping a beat with each brush of a finger.

"Oh," she says, and I hear the small disappointment in her tone, too.

But if my pet wants to keep things as they are, she wouldn't want to learn the real reason behind why I wanted to learn what her name was in the first place. If I uttered those words, she might want to end this arrangement we have going altogether, and that was a risk I was unwilling to take. Especially considering the real reason her name had become so important to me. If she hadn't stated how reluctant she was at changing our dynamics, then maybe I would have said something much, much different.

In my mind, when she asked why I wanted to know her name, my answer would have been instant and one-hundred-percent heartfelt.

"Because I want to know the name of the woman I'm falling in love with."

I have a name for my love now.

However, I also have an answer to a question I wasn't expecting to get so soon.

My Queen only wants her King.

Edwina doesn't want Dean in any way.

Chapter 18

EDIE

What was I thinking?

What in God's name was I thinking of giving Dean my real name?

It was a moment of weakness. A lapse in judgment provoked by a muddled brain still clinging to the aftershock of the most incredible orgasm I'd ever experienced in my life. He was looking into my eyes, ever so earnest, searing into my very soul with his tender gaze, and I lost all sanity. I just gave in to his will, and before I knew it, the six-letter word, which might condemn my happiness, sprang from my lips.

I gave him my name.

My real fucking name.

I've lost my mind.

These troubled thoughts are pounding away in my head, as I fumble with my keys to get the apartment door open. In retrospect, if I wasn't in such shock, I might have caught on faster to the surprise awaiting me inside. I should have been paying attention. I should have expected Lexi to be up at this time of hour.

If I had at least looked at my phone to check the time, I would have seen that I was beyond late getting in without risking getting caught. It was six am, and my roommate was either on her morning run or already getting ready for work. But since the apartment was dead quiet and my mind was loud enough with the repetition of telling Dean my real name, what happened next took me completely off-guard.

"What the hell?" I yelp at the sight before me as I slam my bedroom door open. Lexi, still donning her Alice-in-Wonderland pajamas, candy-pink hair all over her face, continues on her mad rush, rummaging through every drawer in my dresser, as if she'll find hidden treasure amongst my lingerie. Even with my sudden appearance during her snooping of my room, doesn't make her stop. She just looks up, gives me a snarl, and carries on as if I'm not even there.

"Hello???? Lexi? Are you for real? Or are you seriously going through my stuff?" I ask a bit pissed off that she doesn't even have the decency to look contrite at getting caught red-handed while turning my room into a battle zone. "Helllloooo??? Lexi!"

"The answer to your question is yes! Yes, I am ransacking your room. Because I don't trust that you are actually going to tell me what the fuck is going on!" she shouts back at me, putting her hands on each hip, finally stopping long enough to face me head-on.

Yeah, maybe I liked it better when she was pretending I wasn't in the room. Her livid scowl is a living, breathing monster, and I know if I say the wrong word right now, it will eat me alive, you guys. If I don't make it out of this alive, delete my internet browser history and trash *Mr. Knoxy*—aka my previous nighttime battery-operated lover before the real one came into my life and made his use redundant. I'd hate for my mom to find my treasured toy amongst my things as she prepares my funeral since Lexi looks like she's about to murder me in three… two… one.

"You've been acting shady for weeks! Been coming home at odd hours, doing Lord knows what! Wearing stuff I know you can't afford, gunk on your face which makes you completely unrecognizable. It baffles the shit out of me since you're the type of girl who only carries cherry lip balm in her purse and considers it makeup. I want to know why the fuck you leave the apartment dressed up like you're going to a high-class masquerade ball every night," Lexi huffs out in one dragon-like breath, and inside I'm slapping myself at being so stupid for thinking she was totally oblivious to my comings and goings.

Stupid, stupid Edie.

"Now, if it were *me* doing this shit, I would understand. I was probably going undercover for some job or whatever. On the other hand, I highly doubt Devina has suddenly added such a task to your already busy schedule. So, since you haven't told me what's going on out of your own volition—which I have patiently waited on for WEEKS, I might add—I've given up waiting, so this is me getting answers," she explains, her scowl growing deeper, making each crease on her lovely forehead hurt my insides even more.

Shit!

This can't be happening.

Think, Edie.

"Lexi, you're being ridiculous," I hesitate, unprepared to think of anything to say to her which could justify her sudden suspicions.

Shit!

I could just tell her the truth, couldn't I?

No, Edie.

Best to keep things on the down-low as they are for now. My loose lips have already gotten me in trouble today with Dean as it is. I can't risk exposure again by telling Lexi and giving her information that might get me in hot water later. Right now, she has nothing but a few expensive dresses, fancy lingerie, makeup, and masks that don't make any sense to her.

Yes, she's a good detective.

Yes, she's a great journalist.

And yes, she's an even better friend.

Especially when she's worried about me, which I know she is since she went all nuclear on my room to find clues to what I've been up to. But regardless of all this, there is no way in God's green earth she is going to add all those clues up and come to the realization of what I'm currently involved in—me spending my nights in a place such as the After Hours club. No way is she ever going to suspect that I, Edie Vanderwalt, would ever be a member of such an establishment. It would be so inconceivable, too far-fetched an idea for her to even imagine as a possibility, even if she has heard a rumor of the existence of such a place.

So all I have to do is play it cool.

Loose lips sink ships, after all.

Everything is totally fucked, but it can get ten times worse if I don't do damage control, and stat. I can deal with a pissed-off Lexi, I just can't deal with a disappointed one.

I take off my heels and walk to the corner of the room, trying to find some free space where I can place them. I then walk back to my door and grab my bathrobe, happy to see it survived the battle which occurred this morning, conducted by my over-imaginative BFF.

"Lexi, nothing is going on. I've just been going out

with some new model friends whom I met on a few photo shoots that we've been doing for Royal. I've been showing them around the city, since they don't know anybody else, and going to a new themed costume club in the meat district that they are fond of. They'll be back home after New Year's. I'm just babysitting them, Lexi. If you were worried all this time, all you had to do was ask," I explain, sounding exhausted.

My debilitation isn't an act. It's one-hundred-percent real since this lying crap is all slowly taking away all my vitality. The way I've been lying to Devina twenty-four-seven, and now to Lexi, is eating away my soul, taking large chunks out day after day, leaving me feeble-hearted.

"But since you're usually working so late, I didn't think you would notice. The dresses belong to Royal, of course. They're loans because, technically, it's still work. Are you satisfied now? Because I'm dead on my feet. I've got to take a shower, grab some breakfast, drink a gallon of coffee, and do it all over again. Hopefully, I'll be able to take a nap this afternoon. Like I've been doing every afternoon this month, which you would've known if were here, but you're just as much a workaholic as I am. So please, stop messing with my stuff, 'cause all you're doing is giving me more work to do. Or are you going to clean this up?" I try to joke, but it comes out flat. I can't even fake humor when I know I'm feeding such bull to a beloved friend.

"Babysitting? You're telling me for the past few

weeks you've been going out dressed to the nines, coming home at ungodly hours because you're babysitting a bunch of models? And going dancing at some swanky costume party nightclub?" Lexi interrogates, full brow raised in the air.

"*Very* important models. Kendall-Jenner-important," I answered sternly, wiggling my eyebrows.

Lexi appraises me silently, and even though I'm fibbing with the best of them, somehow the deep root of suspicion in her eyes just won't go away. A small voice inside her must be warning her to my deception, but my shoulders go limp and relax as I watch, before my very eyes, her making the decision to allow me to continue on this charade. She's going to pretend that she believes me when I say everything is fine. I don't doubt she's probably doing it just to allow the noose to tighten further around my neck— with the amount of lies I'm spinning—until I have no choice but to seek her out. In the meantime, she's going to continue to skim and snoop around until she gets the real answer. Either I tell her of my own accord, or she'll find out one way or the other.

Lexi has just found a story that is better and more important than anything her boss could ever throw at her back at the newspaper. I'm officially screwed in more ways than one.

Shit!

"Fine, *chica*. Go and take your shower. I'll have

your breakfast and coffee done for when you get out," she replies. "And don't worry about the mess. I'll deal with that, too." She shrugs, trying to look apologetic, but I know her all too well—her cleaning is just another way of seeing if she missed something in her haste.

"Now, there is the roomie I love," I quip, going to her and giving her a quick hug, but before I have time to let go, she holds me in place.

"Edie, you are one of my closest friends. I love you like my sisters. Actually, I'm pretty sure I love you more than Carla." We both laugh at that because it's probably true.

"You'd tell me if there was something serious going on with you? If you were getting involved with people who might do you more harm than good, right?" she whispers, holding me protectively.

Lexi is approximately five-foot-five to my five-foot-eight, so she just about reaches my nose. Then why do I feel like she's the momma bear in this equation, towering over me, trying to protect her cub, while I am grasping at her fur, warm in its security, yet still unable to give in, like an unruly child? Tears prickle behind my eyelids since I want to spill every last word here and now. But I know I can't.

If I tell you, Lex, you'll make me give him up.

She'll'll try and shine a light on truths and reality versus my beautiful fantasy.

And I want to live in denial just a little longer.

Let me live this dream just a few more weeks.

Please.

My body must give her the answer that my lips refuse to say, and she backs away sheepishly.

"I'm here for you, Edie. Always," she states and leaves me to deal with the mess of my own creation.

My life consists of wearing masks.

I feel like I'm living in Cinderella's shadow, good and bad parts alike. I wear a mask when I'm face-to-face with my King—behind its protection, I am freer than I have ever been, living my fantasies and wildest dreams to their fullest extent, and yet never letting go of the shelter it brings.

I continue with the charade in the daylight, too. Looking behind curtains and shadows. Even when I'm in the same room as the man who makes me thrash in ecstasy every night, he doesn't see me. Doesn't know how close I am. I control the urges I have to walk into his office and offer myself up as his midday snack, knowing full well that he would fire my ass for such an action.

He only sees what I let him see and what everyone

else sees—a woman who tends to everyone's needs but her own. Yet at night, he's the one on hands and knees catering to me. Last night he asked my name, and the shock has worn off regarding some of the foolishness of actually giving it to him. The feeling now living in my heart is elation. I was so focused on my little mishap I forgot to pay attention to the biggest detail of all—Dean gave me *his* name. He wanted me to know who he was. That has to mean something, doesn't it? Oh Lord, please let it mean something, because if I ever doubted I loved him before, well I sure as hell know now. This is no longer a crush. I'm not even sure if it ever was, to begin with.

Dean.

He told me his name.

And asked for mine, going against all the rules.

He played it off as mere curiosity, but the words falling from his lips felt false. There was electricity in the air as he waited to hear me say my name as if his heart had stopped beating and could only be revived with one word.

Am I reading him wrong? Am I infatuated to the point my senses are betraying my very intuition and perception of reality?

I wear a mask every night, as does my King, yet when we join together as one, it feels like we see each other for who we truly are. No pretenses. No camouflage. No smoke and mirrors to distract us. We are true to ourselves as much as we are true to each other. Last night, him taking me to that room was a vote of trust in that regard. He trusted me well enough to know I wouldn't judge him, as he has never judged me. He gave me his truth and yearns for all of mine.

So he started with a name.

And I wanted so badly to give him all he's ever wanted that I gave him even that.

Such a dangerous game we are playing.

'Oh, what a pair we make,' he said. I fear he called it.

I feel a shadow lean over me, and someone clears their throat, trying hard to grab my attention from my obvious daydream state. I must have been staring at the same document on my computer for the past twenty minutes.

Employee of the month right here, people!

Shit.

I look up, and thankfully it's only Tatiana. I actually owe Dev a thank you for getting me an assistant of my own. Tatiana has been a blessing. She's sharp, motivated, and a quick study. I've actually been able to do eight-hour shifts instead of my usual twelve, thanks to this girl. Of course, once I no longer have a social life, I probably will be back to punching in my previous hours, but it's good to know that, when push comes to shove, I got back up.

"Yes, Tatiana? Do you need something from me?" I lean back in my chair, trying to look like I've been busy at work and not trying to sort out my messed-up life's conundrums.

"Umm, sorry to interrupt you, Miss Vanderwalt. It's just that it's twenty past ten already, and I know how you like to be on time for your meetings," she mumbles, looking down at her feet.

She still has a hard time looking me straight in the eye. With Devina she has no issue, which astounds me since most people run the other way when she so much as passes by. But somehow, my first impression with this girl was such a clusterfuck, she still thinks I might hit her upside the head or something.

"I don't have any meetings today," I state, confused as to what she's on about.

Devina only had one meeting this morning, and that was with Dean himself. And usually, those one-to-one's are closed off, even to me. Thankfully so, since today I would be all loopy and could not handle being in a closed room with that man without giving myself away.

"You do, Miss Vanderwalt. Mr. Kelley himself called early this morning and scheduled it in for ten-thirty." She looks at her wristwatch and then gloomily back at me, "It's in five minutes, in his office."

"What?!" I ask, already picking up my things from my desk.

What would the finance director of Royal magazine want to talk to me about? Damn it all to hell! His office is only four floors down, but I have a better chance of taking the stairs than waiting for the elevator. I'm already flying down the aisle of desks and cubicles, but I can still hear Tatiana howling her apologies behind me.

By the time I get to Sebastian Kelley's office, I'm sweaty, pissed off I didn't check my office calendar like I always do, unfocused, and looking worse for the wear. A hot mess if I ever saw one. I'm late as it is, so instead of making my presence known, I go across the hall and pop into the ladies' restroom to make myself somewhat presentable. Two minutes later, I'm knocking on the dreaded man's door.

"Come in," his deep calm voice should tranquilize me, but instead all it does is send trepidation and cold sweats down my spine.

"Ah, Miss Vanderwalt, thank you for coming. I thought perhaps your secretary failed to mention the urgency of this meeting," he remarks, gesturing me to take a seat.

"Tatiana isn't my secretary, Mr. Kelley. She's assisting me with keeping up Ms. Richardson's demanding workload," I state defensively.

I'm not sure why I'm uncomfortable with the idea of people thinking Tatiana is stationed at a lower rank than mine. From my perspective, the only thing which separates us in this business is time and know-how. Give her a year or two, and professionally, she'll be exactly where I am today. Not sure if it's what she wants, but she's working hard to achieve it.

"Very well. However, I'm less concerned with Ms. Richardson's workload, and more with her unusual expenses recently," he starts off, and his cool tone takes an even graver effect.

He takes a long pause, and for the first time, I'm reminded that the prim and proper man sitting at his mahogany desk is just like me—Sebastian Kelley is a man who wears a mask every day, too.

During the day, he hides his dark side beneath his conservative suits and stoic demeanor. His dark ebony hair is silky-sleek and just long enough to hit his left brow, perfectly hiding his long scar, which begins at his scalp and ends just above the same brow. His blue shirt, with its long sleeves, conceal what I know are detailed tattoos, evidence of a misspent youth. And how will I ever forget his silver eyes turning to deep black pools behind his evening mask when I was on my knees beside him? His smug smile, and his pure enjoyment at seeing me beneath him? Even a mask could not disguise how much he enjoyed the mere act of seeing someone so vulnerable and at his mercy.

It had been an offering the man I love gave to his

best friends since it was the only way he knew to get close enough to touch the real thing—love.

But he doesn't want to share me anymore, now does he?

That has to mean something, right?

"Miss Vanderwalt," Duke—I mean Bash—says, knocking me out of my haze.

"I'm sorry, Mr. Kelley. You were saying?" I reply, straightening my black skirt, as well as the chaotic noise in my brain.

Shhh!

Keep quiet!

I need to act normal, for crying out loud!

Not you guys. You are all cool. I'm barking at the voices in my head. They're the real troublemakers right now, and by the way Bash is looking at me, like I've lost a screw or two, I think I'm not fooling anyone.

"Please, go on, Mr. Kelley. I'm all ears." I smile sweetly.

"As I was saying, Miss Vanderwalt, our department is very thorough with all expenses, including that of each CEO. It really doesn't matter to us which title a person holds here at Royal, we need to account and explain each expense come tax month. The IRS is impartial that way."

"Oh, of course," I add, my stomach cramping at the sudden theory as to why I was called here.

"I'm aware you have access to all Ms. Richardson's business cards, both credit and checking accounts, is that right?" he queries, although the question is asked out of courtesy since I'm positive he already knows the answer to it.

"I do." My reply is short and precise. Isn't that what Lexi always tells me when she's getting info from her informants? The rotten ones are those who only give her yes or no answers, which for her is the same as giving her a paper bag filled with a warm pile of dog poo.

Hey—her words, not mine. Well, someone pass me a paper bag, then, 'cause I'm going to start filling it up for Mr. Kelley here.

"The transactions in all of Ms. Richardson's credit cards and accounts have all been quite standard Miss Vanderwalt, save for one, and I was hoping you could shed some light on the matter," he explains, his features always expressionless, never hinting what is going through his mind.

But the one thing Bash probably didn't account for is that I'm more like his best friend than he realizes. I take into account what I've seen and heard when I've been in the presence of a person, and years of being a fly on the wall for Devina has taught me enough to pay close attention to detail.

When I see his light gray eyes tinge to a darker, thunderous shade, I know Bash is holding all the cards, and he's got me at his feet. To anyone looking in through the windows, I might be sitting on this leather office chair, looking respectable and attentive to his every word, but in reality, I'm in chains, gagged and bound, dreadfully awaiting a sentence to be carried out from the executioner before me.

I've been caught. All there is left to learn is what mask has Bash uncovered. The one who used Royal's funds without permission—or if I'm being real, committed the crime of embezzlement? Or the one who used said funds to gain access to an underground club to seduce his best friend?

Which mask did you uncover, Duke?

Which one?

"Which one?" I ask plainly, with all the courage I have left. My back is as stiff as a board. I know he thinks he has me pinned to the wall, yet I will not give him the satisfaction to see me break. He doesn't know why I did what I did. Has no clue to my motivations.

The thing is... even though I might end up in jail, break my mother's heart, and lose Dev's and Lexi's trust, when it comes right down to it, I'd do it all over again.

These weeks spent with Dean have been the best of my life. I have never lived until now. I have never loved and felt truly cherished the way I feel in his arms. Call me a romantic, call me foolish and naïve, call me a damn idiot. I don't care. I still would. I'd do it all over in a heartbeat. And it won't be Bash or anyone else who will make me feel any less for finally being brave enough for going after what I wanted all along.

I wanted Dean Knox, and for a brief time, I can say I had him. It was all worth it.

And anyway, orange is supposed to be the new black, right? I think I can pull off an orange jumpsuit. Don't know if I can beat up the scariest bitch on the cell block, but I'm pretty handy with my fists. I think I can do a shiv with a toothbrush. Better practice at home, just in case.

"Edie? Edie?"

Shit.

I spaced out again. Well, so much for acting all chilled and steadfast. Bash stands from his seat and goes over to his door, then pushes a button which immediately closes the blinds of his floor-to-ceiling windows. No one from outside the ample, open office space has further view of what will transpire between us, and my nerves skyrocket to the roof.

"Mr. Kelley…" I stammer.

"Edie, call me Bash. I think we've surpassed such formal greetings, don't you?" His smile is genuine as he takes the seat next to me.

The fox-like eyes are back to their light-gray shine, and although my breathing is altered, it slowly begins to steady. At least now I know which truth he's unraveled.

The Duke has unmasked the King's Beauty before he did.

"We've got ourselves quite a situation here, Edie. I have proof you used Devina's account and transferred twenty-five thousand dollars to your own personal checking account," he informs me, concern marring each pronounced word, and continues, "I also have proof that yesterday, ten days after the withdrawal, the same amount was deposited back to her account from yours. Care to elaborate what made you do such a careless thing? One that will not only harm the respectable reputation you've worked so hard to achieve but also damage your relationship with Devina herself, a trusted dear friend, from what I've been able to observe. What could have ever been running through your mind at the time you decided to commit such a felony?"

"That I couldn't use the emergency credit card after all, since I had no way of putting the money back without getting caught?" I laugh out sarcastically, slumping down further still in my seat, cradling my face in my hands.

"Yes, the credit card would have been a worst-case scenario," Bash retorts, and I hear him shifting in his seat. "Devina's disappointment is not my only concern," he adds, and my tears can no longer be kept at bay, fogging up my glasses, just with the mere idea of who he's referring to.

"I'm not sure what he'll think of this, Edie. I'm going to be honest with you, I'm still unsure of how I feel about this myself," he adds with a gruff.

Oh, God!

No!

Please.

In a panic, I let go of my head and grab onto his sleeve instead.

"Please, Bash, you can't tell him. Please," I croak, desperate for him to hear my plea and do this one solid for me.

"Fire me! Send me to jail! Do what you must, but please don't tell him. He'll never understand," I cry, tears falling unashamedly down my pain-stricken face.

I'm genuinely in love with Dean, and he can never know who I am. He would think that every moment we spent was a lie. Something rehearsed or fabricated by an employee with a sick obsession with her boss. Maybe even think I played him to rise up the corporate ladder. If Bash shows him his findings, he'll never believe my feelings for him were real and not some calculated ploy.

Oh, God, I'm going to be sick.

What have I gotten myself into?

If he learns I've stolen from Devina to get myself into After Hours, he'll think I pinpointed him all along. I just know it. And let's face it, it's not a lie. I did do all those things. But my reasons came from an unknown force within myself. I can name it now. Before, I might have called it an infatuation, but now I know the specific name of the culprit that made me commit all this madness in the first place.

It was love.

Crazy, stupid, maddening love.

I love Dean Knox.

And even though my reasons came from a pure place, it has been tainted with all the lies, theft, and games I've played, turning it into the ugly thing Bash must see plastered on my face now.

Oh, dear Lord.

Please strike me dead now, because I am the world's biggest fuck-up.

I did this to get closer to Dean, but what I've done

in reality is lose any chance of ever being with him. Even if he could care for me in any way, it is his Beauty he cherishes. The minute he learns who I really am, all the sparkle on his treasured jewel will dull and taste like ash on his once loving lips.

"Breathe, Edie. Breathe," Bash insists, patting my back in smooth strokes, trying to get the professional woman who walked into his office ten minutes ago, instead of the neurotic, weeping mess he has to deal with now.

"You don't understand..." I begin, taking my glasses off and wiping the teary glass on my skirt.

"I think I'm beginning to, Edie. Sit tight," he coos, raising himself from his seat and walking somewhere behind me. When he returns, he hands me a bottle of water, and I accept gratefully with shaky hands.

"Only I and another employee of mine know of this small irregularity, Edie. I don't want you to have a second thought about it. I'll make it go away. For a criminal, you are an extremely honest one. I wouldn't have given it a second thought myself if you hadn't deposited the money back so quickly. I had assumed it was a perk Devina had given you for the Christmas holidays. See? Sometimes honesty is what gets you caught, *Beauty*," he teases, petting my nose teasingly.

Even through bloodshot eyes and blurry vision, I can see the predatory Duke is not in this office with me; Bash—Dean's right-hand man—is. He's trying to protect me, even if this means covering up for my own foolish mistakes.

"I don't know what to say…" I hiccup, still a bit incoherent.

"No need to say anything at all. Drink your water, Edie. I can't have you leaving my office like I've just told you I ran over your dog or something?"

"You and Dev have very similar senses of humor," I tell him, finally feeling something different from desperation.

"I remember, but I think she was sassier in college, though. I think I'm wittier by far now than she could ever be," he quips, with a crooked, wolfish smile.

"Oh, that's right, you went to Harvard, too." I sniffle, trying to recollect any tidbit Dev could have told me about Bash and their time together back then, but I'm drawing a complete blank. The only one I knew she had grown close to had been Dean right from her freshman year, and closer still during his senior year, when she was a sophomore since he would be starting to prepare ground at Royal for the both of them.

"Did Dean introduce you?" I ask, his name feeling right on my lips, even if it's the first time I've ever been so informal in Bash's presence. My blush must give me away because Bash's tender appraisal of me softens further. Hard to believe those same feline eyes can hold such crude dominance in them. He lets out a smug laugh, covering it with his fist, trying to maintain his cool exterior once more.

"No, not Dean. Her ex-boyfriend used to be my roommate. There were plenty of nights I came home, greeted with a sock on his bedroom door, and none of us got much sleep, thanks to your friend," he chuckles. My eyes go wide, not because of Bash insinuating Devina is a hellcat in the sack, but the fact she had a boyfriend back in college.

My Devina has never had a boyfriend in her life, much less in college. Bash must be mistaken. Whoever Dev was involved with at the time must have been blowing smoke up his ass, because there is no way Devina Richardson was in a committed relationship with a boy back in college without me knowing about it.

You mean, like the way she doesn't know about you and Dean?

"Edie, am I to assume a similar bill might show up on Devina's account next month?" Bash watches me intently.

"I think it's best this be my last criminal act since I'm so bad at it." I offer a weak smile in return.

"I see. Maybe it is for the best. It would be a shame for anyone else to find out about this. They might come to different conclusions."

Bash was able to list the cons and pros of my dilemma in less than thirty minutes and come to the same bottom line. This will end badly one way or the other. Best to cut my losses now, lick my wounds, and carry on as if nothing happened. If I continue with this farce, all I'll end up doing is hurting myself further, hurt the people I love most, and worst of all, hurt the man I hold dear to my heart. I couldn't live with myself if that happened.

Feeling in better control of my emotions, and hoping I look presentable enough, I rise from my seat, put on my black-rimmed frames, ready to put this painful meeting behind me. But I can't leave yet. Not until I thank the man who's brought me my moment of clarity. Lexi had tried to shock it out of me this morning, but I held onto my denial with bared teeth and a lioness' grip. But against facts, my resolve shattered like confetti. I have been lying to everyone, I know, including myself.

Dreams are to be dreamt asleep, not lived awake.

I was a fool to believe to the contrary.

"Thank you, Sebastian. For your help and your discretion." I tell him in earnest, hoping that even though he knows I'm a liar, he hears the truth in my words. "I'm forever in your debt, kind Duke," I jest weakly, offering a tiny curtsy, for which he rewards me with a hint of a smile.

"I'm sorry to see it end this way, Edie. But you still have a few weeks left with him. Make them count, *pet.*"

My chest hurts just at the reminder of my King's endearment, threatening a new batch of waterworks to flood my eyes anew, but I shake it off as best as I can. Edie Vanderwalt does not cry on the job. She kicks major butt. Can't go setting a precedent, no matter how hollow I'm feeling. I place my hand on the doorknob, but just like lightning, a bolt of energy raises my curiosity and dims my sorrow for a fraction of a minute.

"How did you know?"

Bash was already heading to his seat, and my sudden query stops him in his tracks.

"How did you know it was me, Bash? That I was Beauty all along?"

He sits in his majestic chair, giving me a once-over, and his wicked smile is once again fixed firmly on his face.

"Ah, Edie, the answer to that question is simple. Dean's emotions are blinding him to truths he's unwilling, or not yet ready, to see. Dean is wearing blinders right now, too focused on his Beauty to even consider looking at any other woman. Where he is blind, I am not. I see perfectly; twenty-twenty vision. I see you just fine, Edie Vanderwalt. Enough to know the lovesick look you have been giving Dean for the past two years to be the same one of the woman he can't go without for one single night."

"Oh." I swallow dryly. I nod and start my retreat

yet again, only this time, it's Bash who stops me from taking another step.

"And Edie, just so you know, that lovesick puppy-dog look, it's only gotten worse. For both of you, it seems." Bash cocks his brow, making it clear how my entangled lies have created such a dangerous web, that getting out of its sticky confinement will not be without peril and injury. One, if not both of us, will end up screwed up by this mess I created. And it's not the kind of fucked-up I've been accustomed to lately.

I leave Bash's office, closing the door behind me in haste. I run to the ladies' restroom, yet again, and lock myself in, dropping to the floor, hugging my knees under my chin. I know staring at a toilet bowl isn't the best catalyst for prayer, but still, it's what I find myself doing. Praying to the big guy upstairs to get me out of this mess without hurting my friends, and most importantly, without hurting Dean in any way.

Bash was right, I do have a few more weeks with him. Two, to be exact. I'll just have to come up with a story as to why I have to disappear on him. Another lie. And praying to God, asking him to help me come up with a lie good enough to spare someone's feelings, feels awfully wrong.

But I'm desperate here, you guys!

After New Year's, this will all be done and over with.

I won't have to lie anymore.

Dean will forget all about his Beauty and move on.

And I'll probably die of a broken heart.

But at least everyone will be happy.

And all will be right with the world.

Awesome.

Chapter 19

DEAN

"So tell me, what are your plans for this week?"

"This week?" she asks, her brow suspiciously rising to her forehead.

"Yes, silly. Christmas? It is just a few days away, isn't it?" I tease, lightly touching my forehead to hers.

Her eyes flutter closed, breathing me in, and I take advantage and do the same by running my nose up and down the small space behind her ear. Her jasmine scent is so much more intoxicating in this one spot. I picture her standing in front of a mirror at night and dabbing just a little of the alluring perfume on her wrists, and then gently rubbing them behind her ears, calculating I'd go mad every time I found the culprit spot which teases me with her signature essence.

"You really want to know what I'm going to do for Christmas?"

She leans into the feathered kisses I'm taunting her with, shivering when I get down to the hollow point of her neck. I stop my little torture since it will only get us both excited and ready to start round seven, rather than prolong our down time.

Or is it eight?

I lost track. I always lose track with this woman. I can have her in every way, fuck her good and proper six ways from Sunday, and still not have had my fill. But I've grown fond of these small intervals, too. Where she is mush, sated, and has those diamond-shaped crystals shining brightly in my direction. Whispering secrets her lips haven't spewed, giving me hope behind her worshiping and adoring gaze, hinting on a feeling we both yearn to touch.

"Yes, pet. I do," I tell her, placing my chin on her chest, my eyes focused entirely on the parts of her face that hold no camouflage or makeup.

If you passed me on the street, would you know who I am, my Queen?

Would I?

My heart would know you, wouldn't it?

How could it not when you've done the unimaginable?

Carved your name with a scalpel and made it bleed out just for you until there was no room for anything else but your love to replenish it.

Do you love me, my Queen?

Could you ever love me away from this place?

My chest aches at my wandering, cruel thoughts, antagonizing me away from the pure moment I'm sharing with my Beauty. I scare them away as I would an incompetent and petulant employee, and dare them to return, staking claim on tonight's perfection to stay as it is.

Just perfect.

Her lip lifts ever so slightly, running her fingers through my hair, ruffling it as if I'm *her* favorite pet.

"Okay. But fair warning, it's not that interesting of a topic. Mom comes over and spends Christmas Eve with my best friend in the city and me, and on Christmas Day, we go to a soup kitchen and volunteer. It's a tradition we've had since I was little, and I guess it stuck. Then I go back home with her and just chill for a few days. Recharge my batteries to start the New Year fresh in a way. See? Nothing glamorous or stupendously outrageous, if that was what you were expecting."

She worries her lower lip, scrutinizing my stare to see what my opinion of her holiday plan might be. I give her nothing, like I usually do, since showing her how the so-called simple plans feel a world so far away from mine and threaten to bring those depressing thoughts back into my head.

"So, I gather your mom isn't from the city, then, and if you go back home for the holidays, this must mean my Beauty isn't, either. I could have sworn the contrary," I say instead, lowering my head and kissing the top of her full breasts to ease her tense state.

My lips on her skin and my fingers gently caressing her throat bring her back to the lulled and relaxed spirit I wish to keep her in.

"Nope. Born and bred from the other side of the toll bridge," she laughs. "You, my dear King of Manhattan, have been doing very unsavory things to a Jersey girl, of all people." She continues to giggle, and the sweet sound warms my fucking glacier blood, making it run rampant through me, and giving each organ brand new life.

"A Jersey girl, huh? Well then, Jersey Girl, I'm going to surprise you, too. I'm not from Manhattan, either." I smirk.

"No? I thought you grew up here?" She scrunches her brows.

"As honest an assumption as my own of you, I wager, pet. But the King on top of you was actually born in Connecticut, of all places."

"Is that so? Huh. Is that where you'll be spending Christmas, then? In Connecticut?"

"Dear God, no. I'd be bored out of my mind there." I chuckle, and she accompanies it with her own soft laugh.

"Okay, Mr. Too-Cool-for-the-Suburbs. So does that mean your parents live in the city now? Will you be spending Christmas with them?" she asks, genuinely interested.

"Oh, they have a place there and a penthouse overlooking the park here, but I highly doubt they've set foot in either in months. No, my parents aren't much of the Christmas bunch. They're more of the holiday types. They'll probably be skiing in Aspen or sunbathing in Rio. I'm sure I'll get an Instagram picture sent my way on the day, to tell me which," I explain, trying hard to leave the resentment out of my remark.

"So will you be spending Christmas alone?" Her eyes soften, concern and that tinge of unnamed emotion marring her features.

"No. I'll probably bum over at Prince's family's place," I play off in a forced chuckle. The Walsh clan, of course, do expect me to be there every year as per custom. However this year, I'd rather go to Jersey than the Martha's Vineyard, if an invite could just be uttered from her lips.

"Oh…" she hushes.

"So is it just your mom coming? No other family?" I venture, trying to get any other tidbits I can regarding the mystery of the beauty beneath me.

"Yeah. My best friend and my roommate will also join us on Christmas Eve, to help set up our tree and watch 'A Christmas Carol' on DVD, while eating enough candy canes to make us all sick for the whole year. No other family worth mentioning, really," she whispers, twirling a lock of my hair in the same way I like to play with hers.

"Your dad pass away, pet?" I ask softly, not wanting to open any hidden cuts my girl may have concealed along with the top half of her face.

"No, he's alive and well. Last I heard, he was living in Florida with his wife and two teenaged daughters," she replies absentmindedly.

"You don't keep in touch? Are you two not close?"

"At first, maybe. I remember he tried, or at least I made myself believe it, anyway. When I was five, he just walked out the front door and didn't come back. I couldn't understand why he didn't tuck me in at night anymore and begged my mother to take me to him so I could ask him. Mom begrudgingly took me to see him at his accounting firm's office once my tantrums became too intense, but he always seemed like he preferred we weren't there." She sighs as if recalling those gray days clearly through the eyes of a naïve and confused innocent child.

"Until one day, Mom packed all our things and told me we were moving to Long Island because she got a job there. I was too young to understand what was happening, but every time I brought it up with Mom, trying to wrap my head around this new life without my father, she would cry. So I stopped asking." She shrugs, looking down at me with a faint fake smile plastered on her face, the tears of a fatherless child brimming just beneath the surface of her blue sky.

"It was only later on, when I was ten, that my best friend and I found some old letters in my mom's room. There I found out my father had cheated on my mother with his secretary, as cliché as it sounds. In one of my father's 'Dear Jane' letters, he told my mother how his mistress was pregnant with his kid, and he wanted to be married to her instead. He said he was in love with her and wanted a new start at the family he had envisioned for himself all his life. Said the second time around he was going to do it right, since getting Mom pregnant in their senior year of college was the worst mistake of his life. Marrying her out of obligation and not love was his second.

"In the letters that followed, he begged my mom to sign the divorce papers, telling her he had an offer for his firm and the house we were living in. Whether she liked it or not, both were in his name only, and since he made sure Mom signed a prenup before they got married, he was going through with the sale either way. I found dozens of letters, threatening and bullying my mother into doing his will while showing how excited he was in starting his new life. In not one of them did he ask about me. So to answer your question, no. We're not close."

I move up enough to place one tender kiss between her pillowed lips, eating up her small, agonized weep brought on by a memory she didn't think she was going to relive or share looking deep into my eyes. But she did, cracking my heart in the process in recognition of how similar our broken pieces fit with one another.

"I've never met a Jersey girl from Long Island before," I tease, kissing the tip of her nose for good measure.

"You have now," she counters back, the heavy bricks of animosity and bitterness falling off her shoulders, with one loving touch, caress, and kiss at a time.

"So, when did you come to New York?" I ask, trying to move us to a safer topic, but see hesitation shadow her expression instead. Maybe my Beauty has reached her quota of strolling through memory lane tonight. A pinch of disappointment hits my square jaw at full force, yet I maintain stoic, frozen still, patiently waiting to see if she'll indulge me in one more answer to her life. A life lived away from me. When I see her roll her eyes and lean in to kiss me on the chin, as if knowing I had just been punched there, my mood lightens.

"And you say I'm the curious one?" She lets out a low-pitched laugh. It's not the one where you feel it in the gut, but I'll take it. "We stayed in Long Island until I went to college. Mom came back to Jersey, and I came here to NYU."

"NYU? Fancy," I say, impressed at her grit, and her mom's, too, if I'm honest.

"Not as fancy as some, Mr. Summa-Cum-Laude Harvard man," she mocks.

"Well that's oddly accurate, pet," I state, surprised by her guess at my University and graduation status. Her crimson blush blooms throughout her whole body, not limiting the soft hue to her cheeks.

"No… Not… o-o-odd at all," she stutters and then shakes her head as if clearing her thoughts.

"What I meant to say was, a king like yourself wouldn't bother with any other school than the best one in the country, and wouldn't rest until he graduated as the best in his class," she deadpans, making it clear how her guess was the only plausible one.

"Clever pet." I beam proudly, kissing her throat again, making my way down to her nipple, taking a quick bite at my coming dessert. My cock has been up and ready since I started our convo, and he's getting restless with me. I guess I have ignored him for a while now.

"Hmm. Hmm. What about you? It doesn't sound as if you are close to your parents, either?" She gasps as I bite her other breast.

"The answer to that question is simple, my pet. I only keep people of value in my closed circle. My parents have none for me," I state plainly, running my teeth, lips, and tongue on her pink areola. I feel a pinch in my hair, pushing my face away from my favorite candy, only to come face to face with a disturbed, outraged look on my Queen.

"Explain. You can't say something like that and start fondling me. Explain first. Playtime second," she orders, which is not only a first for my usually very submissive pet in the bedroom, but I do believe my cock could cut steel with how hard she just made me.

Fuck I love you.

"What do you mean people of worth? Like how much money they have in the bank? Or what they can do for your social standing? What?! Explain," she growls, showing teeth and claws.

Scratch that.

I'm beyond hard.

I'm a goddamn weapon of mass destruction who could cut down empires just so I could get inside my girl this very minute. My hand trails down her mound, finding it dripping in need for me.

"You're mad, but your pussy is greedier and mightier than your anger, my Queen."

Her eyes go wide and soft all in one go at the unexpected return use of her God-given title, and I use her confusion to my advantage and sink myself in her.

Heaven.

Fucking heaven, each and every time I'm inside her. Her eyes roll to the back of her head, and I'm the one biting my lower lip hard enough to draw blood, as I start slowly pushing our tempo to higher horizons.

"Not fair. Not fair," she sighs angrily, throwing her head back and meeting my hips at every turn.

So fucking good.

Will it ever stop being this fucking good?

Yeah, I don't think so either.

My Queen was made for me and only me.

"Your anger is misplaced and unwarranted, my Queen. My parents treasure things, not people. Therefore, to me they have as little value as the possessions they treasure," I explain, trying to separate in my heart and mind the two very opposed feelings I'm sharing with her.

"Family is more than blood. Blood can bring you into the world, but it doesn't mean it has an obligation to love you. My parents are exemplary in this regard. They had me just to add to their collection of prized goods, and quickly moved on when I lost my shine. Boarding schools, nannies, and their backs were how they showed me my worth to them. And when I was old enough to put away childish things, such as a father's approving counsel or a mother's bedtime story and decided to become The King I am today, they were the first on my list to be cast away," I groan, half in pain to have to go through this shit of retelling such an ugly part of my past to the woman I love, while the other half of me is in utter delight with each sinking inch I carve inside her just for me.

"I have *my* family. I have my brothers. I have the Prince and the Duke. They are all the family I need. And right now, I have my Queen. *My* Queen! Thrashing below me in the ecstasy I provide. At my mercy, complying to my every whim and desire." I lean down and catch her lips in a brutal kiss, repeating every word with my warring tongue, dominating her mouth and claiming it as mine. I break free to gain equilibrium, already drunk off this kiss alone. But she needs to hear me. Hear enough of my truth, even if only broken bits of it. Let her hear my secret hopes and the hidden meaning underlying each pronounced word.

"These are the only people whose value I treasure, pet. So enough with your questions of worth and let me show just how much yours is to me! Let me treasure you, my Queen," I growl, biting her shoulder as I thrust into her roughly and as merciless as I vowed.

Her whimpers are like an angels' song in my ear. Her nails biting down on my back are battle wounds reaped in victory. Her sighs and tears are my vows of undying affection. I pound and thrust repeatedly, bend her to my fucking will until her breathing quakes, legs tremble, warning me her crown will be replaced with a halo in just a few seconds, as she rises to meet the glowing light which threatens to blind us.

"Do you feel treasured, my Queen?" I growl.

"Yes!"

"Do you feel valued, my Queen?" I groan madly.

"Oh, God! Yes!"

"Good! Because you are!" I let out another roar, thundering down everything I have into her. It's as if I'm running a few steps behind her, praying she'll look back and reach out her hand to take me with her when she meets those heavenly gates.

"King!" she cries, grabbing onto both my hands to ground her body while our souls take flight, answering my silent plea.

"You're fucking mine, *my Queen*!" I yell, lost in her.

Completely and utterly lost in her.

My Beauty lets out another cry, loud as a rising sun at dawn, demanding the world to awake with her kiss, and yet as melodic as a closed lid whispered wish, the very one we make in secret to a full moon on a clear night sky. Our breathing and drumming hearts take forever to simmer, but the grins spread wide on both our faces will take a lifetime to erase.

"I should get you pissed more often, pet," I tease, still inside her, unwilling to leave my home just yet.

"I'd rather you didn't, my King. I don't like being angry at you," she states plainly, but still holding those stars in her eyes and my hands to her heart.

"I agree. Being angry with me wasn't fun at all. Fucking away your anger, and you bossing me about, that I could do with from time to time," I joke, not really hiding how this will definitely happen again. I'd like to play with my pissed-off pet a bit more, alright. Just get her worked up enough so she can leave her teeth marks on me.

"Whatever my King wants," she teases back.

I want you, Edwina, I almost say, but clear my throat instead.

I'd like to see her claws come out from time to time. Calling her by her name and telling her how truly I feel, might have her using said claws to hatch an escape route out of this room instead. Too many revelations have already surfaced this night.

My Queen is ready to be loved.

Edwina, though? I'm not too sure.

"Your King wants to know when you'll be back from Jersey, my Queen," I say instead, grinding my teeth to prevent any foolish words from leaving my lips. Words that can alter my current blissful reality to one which nightmares are made of.

"Will you be back for New Year's Eve?"

She's silent for less than a minute, her eyes still watery from our earth-shattering love making, lips still raised in a smile, even if suddenly faint, and gives me a small answering nod.

"It's a date," I grin, relieved she's consented, but saddened about the daunting week ahead without her.

Chapter 20

EDIE

"I swear, I can't get over how much you're glowing tonight," my mom gushes as she adds the few last ornaments to the tree. I offer her another shy smile, unable to give her any actual justification to my beaming state.

"Maybe it's a new diet, Nancy. Maybe something that one of her new model friends that she's been hanging out with turned her on to," Lexi instigates, standing beside my mom, her brow raised high, offering a hidden double meaning.

"Ohhhh, you made new friends, Edwina? You didn't tell me that?" My mom looks at me with question marks in her eyes, while I look at Lexi with daggers in mine.

"Thanks," I mouth to her. Mom is always on my case about how I never socialize enough, and here is Lexi, giving her the type of gossip Mom lives for. Lexi just shrugs and keeps looking at our tree, pretending to give a crap about whether it needs more tinsel or not, but I see the thrilled, smug grin she's trying to hide.

"Not exactly friends, Mom, more like work

colleagues, but they're going home after New Year's, so I doubt I'll see them again," I reply solemnly.

The idea that after New Year's Eve my nights will no longer be filled with my 'new friend' is too much of a horror to even focus on right now, so I push it down deep, vowing to not even visit such a troubling thought while in the presence of my mother. Especially while I have Lexi scrutinizing every word I say, and sending me jab after jab that Mom might be clueless to, but Devina, not so much. My best friend might pick up on Lexi's innuendos and see them for what they are and put two and two together.

"Well, ladies, this was fun, but I have an *abuela* who is waiting for me back in the Bronx to take her to midnight mass. Since my two sisters now have the perfect excuse of having newborns this year, they can't take her, so the task falls down on yours truly. I will have to suffer father McDowell's one-hour yawn fest and pretend to love it. Otherwise, my grandmother will kick my hide all the way back home. I swear, my sisters conspired to get knocked up at the same time just to torture me."

Mom bursts out in a fit of giggles to Lexi's whining remark.

"Oh, Lexi, I've met your grandmother. She's lovely. I very much doubt she is capable of any type of violence. Furthermore, she adores you as much as you dote on her," my mother says, clearing the cheerful tears from her eyes.

"Ah, she's a clever old woman, see? That's what she wants you to believe. That she's sweet and docile, but in reality, she won't hesitate to rip you a new one and curse you out like you wouldn't believe. When that woman wakes up in the morning, it is the devil that runs and hides, trust me." Lexi replies, already getting her purple winter coat off the rack.

"So what you're saying is that the apple doesn't fall far from the tree?" I state, wiggling my brows, making my mom snicker again.

"Funny. Very funny, Edie. Your model friends teach you jokes, too?" Lexi deadpans at our front door.

"What friends?" Devina asks, coming from the kitchen with a tray of eggnog.

"Nothing, D. Lexi was just leaving to take her grandmother to church. Ain't that right, Lex?" I counter, my eyes wide and threatening her not to say another peep.

"Yeah, right. See ya, Dev. See you tomorrow, Nancy," she sing-songs, slamming the door behind her.

"Oh, that Alexandra! So feisty for an itty-bitty thing. The girl has fire in her," my mom says, sitting back on the couch and taking Devina's offered eggnog.

"You say that about everyone, Nan." Devina

smiles adoringly at my mom as she passes me my own alcohol-laced goodie.

I love it when she calls my mom that. Mom's name is Nancy, but that is not why Dev affectionately called my mom Nan since she was seven years old. Everyone in the Richardson household was always so formal when we moved in. Dev's parents, as well as any employee who tended to the mansion, always referred to Mom as Nanny Vanderwalt. Of course, Devina thought it was a mouthful and called her Nan instead, not realizing how close to Mom's real name it was. Mom's been her Nan ever since.

"Not true. I never said that about you," Mom points out matter-of-factly.

"Oh, I believe you said something along those lines." Dev rolls her eyes like a petulant child with a teasing grin.

"No. You, my dear girl, are an element far more powerful than fire. Fire can be controlled with a cooling hand. You, my tempestuous child, are a storm. And only God himself can hold you at bay," Mom asserts, tilting her head to the heavens for a dramatic effect.

"May God have mercy on our souls, because I don't think even he can stop her," I mumble, taking a sip.

Devina leans her head back on the couch's headrest and laughs, and soon we're all giggling like schoolgirls at a sleepover.

"Okay, Mom, so what about me, then?" I ask, patting my mom's knee, genuinely interested in knowing what my mom's take is on her one and only child. "If Lexi is fire, and Dev's a storm, what am I?"

"Oh, honey, don't you know?" She looks at me incredulously, to which I reply by shaking my head in utter cluelessness. "You're water, of course." She beams.

"Water?" I ask.

Well, that was anticlimactic.

"Without a doubt. When you look at it at first glance, it seems so simple, still, seemingly unaffected, and silently at peace around us. But if you take a closer look, and truly think of all its manageable forms, it astounds you with its true potential. It can grow so cold, freezing anything in its path, or boil so hot, the steam alone is deadly. You can hold it in the palm of your hands, but you can never force it to bind to you, or it will slip through your fingers and disappear as if it never existed. It's graceful in its beauty, that way. Precious," she sighs and grabs my hand on her lap.

"But most importantly, it nourishes you. Without it, there is simply no life—a definite death sentence. And for me, a life without my sweet, darling daughter would have no meaning. So you, Edwina, are water. My life's nourishment," she ends, and my own watery eyes attack me, unshed tears hidden behind my black-rimmed frames.

"I love you, Mom," I tell her, pulling her into a hug.

"I love you too, baby. It'll be good to have you home with me this week. Maybe you'll even tell me the real reason behind the twinkle in your eye," she hushes low enough in my ear for Devina not to hear. Seems Mom picked up more than I thought.

"Yeah. Maybe."

I nod reassuringly once we separate from our embrace. But in reality, I don't know if I'll have the guts to tell the whole truth of what's happening with me while I'm back home in Jersey.

Hey, don't look at me like that!

I'd like to see if the shoe was on the other foot if you would rush to tell your mom you joined a sex club.

Yeah, didn't think so.

"Hey, you two? Is the mommy-and-daughter moment done? 'Cause the movie's about to start," Dev announces.

"What is with you and this movie anyway?" Now it's my turn to roll my eyes. "I mean, at least let's watch an updated version of the movie? This one is almost eighty years old. You know how many remakes they've done since?"

"Yes smartass, I do! But this one is the only one which is closest to the Dickens' version. And like I always say, copies never beat the originals." She slumps back into her seat, holding her knees under her chin.

This laid-back version of Devina in sweatpants and a New York Yankees hoodie is a rare sight. One that not many are privileged to witness, yet to me it's her best self—relaxed and free of all her *royal* duties, just to enjoy the night and be Dev.

"Will you, at least, tell me why you love this golden oldie, then?" I query, passing Mom a candy cane from our little basket of Christmas treats.

"I like the idea of a do-over. I wonder if a person who saw their past, present, and future, given a chance, would they do it differently the second time around? That's all. Just drop it and watch the damned movie, okay?" she says, throwing her candy cane at my face.

"Hey, that could have poked my eye out, you dork!" I warn.

"Not likely when you insist on wearing those dreadful things all the time. I know you got lenses, so I don't get why you keep hiding behind those things anyway." She smirks.

"Maybe they make me look smart," I counter, pushing my glasses further up the bridge of my nose.

"Or maybe you want one of those cool, geeky IT guys we have back at the office—who might have a naughty librarian fetish—to pin you to your desk," she taunts, humping the air.

"Dude, my mom is right here!" I yelp, my eyes growing wide.

"Sorry, Nan." Dev shrugs, not very apologetically.

"Ah, feels just like old times," my mom gushes between us, wrapping her arms over both our shoulders.

"It sure does," I smile toward Dev, to be rewarded with her mischievous wink.

Spending so much time with Dean and trying to keep up with all my lies, aside from work, I haven't had much quality time with Devina.

I miss my best friend.

So the least I can do is shut my trap and let her enjoy her boring old movie.

An hour and thirty minutes later, the movie is finished, and Mom is sound asleep. Devina was captivated the moment the title came on the screen.

Me?

Not so much.

I didn't visit my impending last day with Dean, so don't worry. That pile of pain is nicely locked in its safe like I told you. But to stay clear of the topic of King, I've been rummaging through something a Duke once told me. Something that I played off as nonsense at the time, but with my current state of affairs, I'm not sure any matters of the heart should be spoken of so lightly.

Especially if it concerns my best friend.

"Dev?"

"Hmm," she replies, stretching her arms, seeming satisfied with having watched her favorite movie.

"You'd tell me if you ever had a boyfriend, right?" I ask softly, not wanting to wake up Mom.

This type of question would be right up her alley. My mom lives and breathes for the day Dev, and I finally settle down with a nice guy, like she puts it. So any mention of the words 'date' or 'boyfriend' immediately sends her into a bridal magazine buying frenzy—both of us avoid the words like the plague around her if we can.

"Where the hell did that question come from? Did I add too much bourbon to the eggnog?" She cocks her brow.

"No. I'm serious. You'd tell me, right?" I ask, feeling somewhat hypocritical but still needing the validation that Dev isn't keeping secrets of her own. "Like… Oh, I don't know… back in college perhaps?" I bite my lower lip, trying to act inconspicuous.

"Oh, E. College and everything before and after it, for me has always been and will always be about one thing—hookups. They may be a couple of months long, depending if the guy is hot enough or if I'm lazy enough not to bother looking elsewhere, but in the end, still hook ups. No one has ever reached the boyfriend line. And besides, you know I don't have time for sappy romance. I'm all about world domination, not hearts and flowers. You know me better than that." She laughs it off, smiling, but for the first time, I see how it never really reaches her eyes.

"Yeah. You're right," I mumble, still teething my lip.

"Just like I know you," she answers smugly, grabbing my attention further. "Something has been off with you lately. And even though I don't know what it is yet, I think I know how to fix it."

"What?" I query, puzzled.

"Shh! You'll wake up Nan. Just follow me," she says as she slips off the couch, heading to our tiny kitchen. Confused, I rise from the couch, putting a blanket over my mom, and meet an anxiously awaiting Devina in the kitchen.

"This is for you. Merry Christmas, E," she says, glowing, passing me a small white envelope. Still unsure of what she's on about, and tired of her shaking the thing in my hand, I grab and open it. Inside is the answer to a question I was refusing to acknowledge all night.

Dean.

"Dev, this is a check for twenty-five thousand dollars! What the hell?!" I cry and laugh all at the same time, not knowing which emotion to grab onto first.

"Well, it's your real Christmas bonus, silly! Royal caps on what we are allowed to give as bonuses to our own staff, is a bunch of bull. But Bash runs his department with an iron fist, so all of us have to comply," she complains.

"The more reason why you didn't have to do this," I tell her while holding the dear piece of paper to my heart.

"But I wanted to, E. I know all about how that movie studio keeps calling you up, offering bucket loads of cash, cars, houses by the beach, and yet, you still tell them no. You can become something huge in Hollywood, I know you can. Still, you stay here, working for me out of loyalty. There's no price for that," she adds, her face turning serious.

Damn Lexi and her big mouth. I didn't tell Dev about the movie studio. Not because I was hiding it from her, but because I didn't even think twice about them. I mean, with everything going on, their nagging and insistence felt more like a desperate ex who I just clicked ignore on every time I saw the number on my caller ID. I honestly didn't even register it anymore.

"Dev, I don't want you to feel threatened in any way by them. The idea has never even crossed my mind, so if this generous gift is because you feel intimidated by some hotshot movie studio who could never make me leave my best friend, then take it. I don't want it," I tell her.

As much as this money would give me my heart's wish of keeping my love for one more month, it shouldn't come at the cost of my friend's peace of mind. I've done too much shady shit as it is. I couldn't take advantage of Devina's insecurities this way. Never. I love her too much.

"No. You more than deserve this and much more. You'd be pulling more than that a month anyway if you were in LA. I know it and so do you. You're staying because you're loyal and I love you for it. But if you feel that being at Royal is something you no longer want to do, I want you to know I'll understand," she adds.

"Will you stop already? I told you the thought never even crossed my mind! I'm happy right where I'm at, so just quit your martyr routine, Dev. It doesn't suit you." I wiggle my brows.

"It doesn't, does it? Yeah, fuck those LA assholes! Trying to steal my BFF from under my nose? Next time one of their execs comes into Royal, I'll have a nice, long talk with them," she snarls, menacing, but the twinkle has finally returned to her big, bright blue eyes.

"I don't doubt it." I laugh. "Still, this is way too generous, Dev."

"Oh, I'd say it's about the right amount. At least, it's the same amount you took from my account earlier this month," she deadpans, and my whole world tilts on its axis.

WTF?

"Huh?" I mumble, my words failing me.

"Oh, please, E. You think I don't know about everything that's happening in my company? Especially when it has to do with *my* money?" She laughs right as rain, grabbing a gingerbread man from the cookie plate. "One of my minions thought he would score brownie points if he snitched that my personal assistant transferred company funds to her account and then ten days later transferred it back. I, of course, cursed the fucker out and told him that anything my personal assistant did was with my knowledge and my approval, and if he came to me again with such insinuations, I would fire his ass on the spot for defamation."

"Holy shit," I stutter.

"Don't worry. I don't think Sebastian knows or anything. And even if he does, he has to come to me, and I'll tell him the same thing I told his lackey." Devina bites off the head of the gingerbread man for added effect. I'm getting a pretty good visual of how she tore her mole's ass a new one when in fact he was doing her a solid.

Shit!

"Since you didn't come to me and ask for the money yourself, I won't ask why you needed it. But I do hope you'll tell me when you're ready to talk. Don't think just because I've been busy and things have been hectic, I don't see how you've been acting differently. You've been distant recently, and I bet it has a lot to do with the reason you needed twenty-five Gs in the first place. Still, I know you too well to push you. Just come to me whenever, okay, E?" she says with a tender smile on her face.

I don't deserve her. My sister-in-arms. My best friend in the whole world knows I've been hiding a secret from her all this time, and she's willing to sit by until I get my shit together.

"Promise, Dev," I tell her truthfully, and right at this moment, I know I will, in fact, tell her about Dean and me. Not tonight, of course. I'm not mad. But soon, when the dust settles.

"Good," she continues to grin, offering me my

own ginger treat.

I take it from her hands, safeguarding the piece of paper which will give me another month with Dean. Whether I use it for that or not is still up for debate. I'll have to think long and hard over the holidays about whether it's not better to just sever the cord now, rather than prolong the inevitable. But right now, I'm just too joyful to have the option in the first place to even consider making a decision just yet, so I place the check inside my bra, right next to my heart where it belongs.

"So you've got a mole in the finance department, huh?" I ask Devina, with a sly smile of my own.

"You know me. I've got to have eyes and ears everywhere. I hate being blindsided."

The next morning, when Mom and I enter St. Mary's soup kitchen, Sister Margaret greets us with nothing but the widest of smiles. She's usually chipper on the holidays, but I've never seen her this excited. I fear her smile might slice her face in half.

"Oh, Nancy, Edie, I'm so glad you arrived just in time to see a real Christmas miracle," she divulges, enthusiastically hopping on the balls of her feet.

"A miracle? Really?" Mom asks, encouraging the nun's ardor further.

"Oh, Nancy, the most generous benefactor arrived out of the blue this morning with toys for the children and winter clothes for the parents, and such a large donation for our kitchen, we will be able to feed ten times as many down-on-their-luck families in the neighborhood! He's even promised to keep up with the generous amount next year as well! Oh, Nancy, isn't this the most incredible news!" Sister Margaret spews, this time truly jumping for joy and hugging my mother in glee.

"It truly is, Sister. A blessing indeed," Mom replies, laughing as well at the news, while patting the nun's back affectionately.

"And that isn't all. He's even staying today to help out with our yearly Christmas lunch. There are no bounds to his generosity," she goes on, and I think I see a little bit of her cheeks darkening a light shade of red.

I do believe Sister Margaret has a little crush on this new benefactor. Hell, I don't blame her. The toys alone for the kids made my heart go gooey, let alone knowing that his donation will put food on the table of many single-wage homes, families on welfare, or worse—people who have lost everything and including all hope. This small offering will give them a little bit of it back. A sparkle, at least.

"Well, how marvelous of him. So, does this generous benefactor have a name? And more importantly, is he single and over forty?" my mom teases, only making the nun blush further.

"I'm not sure of his marital status, Nancy, although I didn't see a wedding ring on his finger," Sister Margaret starts—damn, for a nun, she sure does pay attention to detail, am I right? "But I think he's maybe a handful of years older than your Edie. I've heard some of the other volunteers say he's quite the big deal, a big businessman in the city, but I admit, I've never heard his name until today. Maybe you know of him? Does the name Dean Knox ring any bells?" Sister Margaret queries.

Fuck my life!

Are you freaking kidding me?!

Dean? *My* Dean is Sister Margaret's second coming? New bloody patron saint to St. Mary's?

And he's here? Like now?

Fuck my life!

"Knox… Knox… Wait, doesn't he work for Devina at Royal, sweetheart?" My mom turns to me and asks, and I mentally slap my forehead.

"No, Mom. Mr. Knox works *with* Devina. He's her business partner at Royal," I divulge with a dry simper.

"Oh, that's wonderful! We need help in the kitchen and up front serving all the families, where Mr. Knox will be. Maybe you'd prefer to be in the dining area with him, Edie, and show him around?" Sister Margaret pleads hopeful.

"Umm, Sister, maybe it's best Mom show him the ropes instead of me. I would prefer to keep my professional relationship separate from my personal one if you don't mind," I lie to the nun.

I'm going to hell!

This is the ticket that gets me on the one-way train to hell town, right?

I've lied to a lot of people, but a nun?

I'm so fucking screwed when my time comes to pay the piper.

"Of course, Edie. The kitchen is always swamped, so your help is much appreciated," she asserts, but the previous glee has turned down a notch with my cold-shoulder rebuttal.

"Then I guess this means I'm the lucky lady who gets to help Mr. Knox for the day," Mom announces overly cheerful, coming to my rescue, and bringing back Sister Margaret's upbeat tempo. "Sister, lead the way. Can't wait to meet this mystery man," she goads, not knowing how right she is.

When Dad left, and we moved to Long Island, it was around the holidays. Christmas morning, Mom and I just looked at each other in silence in our living room, still not used to our new surroundings, both of us adrift in our own troubled thoughts by what we had lost. But then my mom got out of her seat, put on her coat, and told me to do the same. We got into our beat-down station wagon and drove until Mom found a decrepit old church with a sign on its lawn. I couldn't read yet, but I saw a line of people with smiles on their faces walking to the back of the aging parish in a single file, so I thought to myself that, where we were going, couldn't be so bad.

Once we got there, Mom talked to a parishioner who put us right to work. Me offering warm rolls to anyone sitting down for a meal, and Mom serving freshly cooked beef stew. Everyone was so cheerful and happy, even though I saw they looked just as beaten and broken as the church's walls. But the energy around me felt oddly comforting. As if I was like one of the old benches we sat on. Yes, it had a bit of wear and tear, but it was still strong enough to hold the weight of eight joyful men and women.

So maybe Dad left, and we had to move to Long Island, so what? It didn't mean I was going to let it break me. I looked over at my mother, and she was laughing. For the first time in months, I heard my mother laughing, and I knew, from that moment on, we would be doing the exact same thing every year.

This year, however, my usual Christmas cheer is replaced with the constant concern that Dean might come into the kitchen at any given minute and see me here. Granted, he still has no clue I'm the woman he's been spending every night with for the past six weeks, but still, this does not bode well for me. If we were back at Royal, I'd be using my *Devina's PA* persona and could hold my own. But here, on common ground, though, wearing nothing but an old navy t-shirt, jeans, and forgone my business-like bun for a high-up ponytail? That spells out trouble to me. I've left myself wide open, with no war gear on to defend myself against Dean's charms. If he looked at me remotely interested, I might blab the whole truth to him. Yeah, I don't think so.

That ain't happening, people!

No way!

No how!

Nuh-uh!

So for the whole day, I stay in the kitchen, keeping myself as busy as I can, not even moving an inch outside to the main hall to see the happy faces around.

"There's always next year," I reassure myself as I send a text to my mom once I've finished up.

I'm not risking going out there to find her either, so I tell her I've come down with a headache and am packing it in for the day. Yes, I know it's another lie, but just add it on to the pile, why don't you? I've lost count anyway, and right now, I'm not entirely sure if I am fibbing, since my head feels it's grown ten times its size with how much overthinking I've been doing. I tell her not to worry and to come home whenever she wants. I'm almost on the church's front doors when hell decides to pull the rug out from under my feet.

"Miss Vanderwalt?"

"Miss Vanderwalt!" I hear Dean call out right behind me.

Shit!

I come to a stop, turn around, and plaster what I hope is a sincere smile, instead of the half-crazed panicked grin that wants to come out.

"I thought that was you I saw earlier this morning," he says, and I see how his eyes discreetly take in my unexpected new look, different from what he's used to seeing me in back at the office. I, of course, am too nervous to do the same to him, focusing solely on his face. The only thing I can see is that he's not in his usual suit and tie either; the v-neck on his dark green sweater being my only clue. I don't dare look lower.

"What a pleasant surprise. I didn't know you lived in Queens?"

I nod and smile, because what else can I do? I'm not going to willingly tell him I live just two blocks over, now am I? He offers me his own relaxed grin, and it startles me how I think this is the first time I've seen Dean smile at me—Edie—not Beauty, but me. I shake the thought away, not wanting to dwell on it for too long and finally ask a question of my own.

"What are you doing here?"

"Athena told me the church in her neighborhood needed some monetary assistance and that they also held a Christmas lunch for the less fortunate in their soup kitchen every year. I thought, why not help out physically as well as financially? So here I am, doing both. Come to think about it, she did say something about one of our employees volunteering , but I have to say, I wasn't expecting to see you here, Miss Vanderwalt," he states, genuine puzzlement marring his features.

"Oh? Well… the same goes for you then, Mr. Knox. I wasn't expecting to see you, either. I mean, shouldn't you be with your family right now?" I ask, thinking of how he told me he would be spending Christmas with Connor and his family. 'Why the hell did you choose Queens over Martha's Vineyard?' is what I really want to ask, but I'm grinding my teeth, preventing the question from leaving my lips.

"Yes, well, a close friend of mine is doing something similar today, so I thought I'd try a hand at being as selfless as she is. I'll meet my family later on for a Christmas dinner. They understand," he continues to grin.

"Oh," I answer, dumbfounded, lowering my head at his heartfelt statement.

"I'm actually relieved she isn't here to see my

foolish attempt. I think she'd be disappointed at how poorly I did," he continues, and I look up again to see a tinge of insecurity strike his strong and usually steadfast jaw.

"Don't beat yourself up. It's your first try. What matters is that you're here." I try to comfort him instead of saying what I really want to, that I'm so proud of him and his good heart.

"Thank you," he replies, genuinely grateful for my feeble attempt to console him. "Miss Vanderwalt? Is it still a selfless act if you do it for entirely selfish reasons?" he adds.

"I don't follow."

"I know I should be content in the knowledge I'm doing something good today, bringing a bit of joy and hope to people who have lost their way in this world. But instead, I'm doing it just so I feel closer to one person. Does my act of charity make the gesture less worthy for it?" he asks, running his fingers through his hair, a sign he's frustrated.

"Mr. Knox, come with me, please," I order, not wanting him to castigate himself any further.

I lead him back into the recreation hall where there are so many joyful faces sharing their meal with loved ones and strangers alike.

"Look around. Do you think anyone cares why you came today to help out? To fill their bellies and donate those toys and clothes so they could have something warm to wear tonight? To see genuine, hopeful smiles on their children's faces that maybe this year they will turn their lives around? They don't. Whatever your reason for doing what you did, the end result is what matters. You gave them a moment of happiness. Why rob yourself of the same?"

"Thank you, Miss Vanderwalt," he hushes.

I nod and start to walk away, because every bone in my body is screaming for me to wrap my arms around him, promising to never let go from this day on. But Beauty isn't here right now.

I am.

Edie.

And Edie has no rights to him, or the intimacy to even touch the vulnerable man behind her. The only thing Edie can do is the following:

Look back;

Offer a kind smile;

And say, "Merry Christmas, Mr. Knox;"

Then leave.

Chapter 21

DEAN

The moment she steps into the room, all eyes are on her, and the need to carve each man's eyes with a blade has never felt more intense. I know it's not their fault. They are red-blooded just like me, and in the presence of such beauty, it's impossible to look away. She looks incredible tonight, in a long, backless red number that has my blood pumping right to my cock.

This woman.

What am I to do with her? She embodies everything I desire, and I still don't know much about her. Nor does she share much willingly, unless I sneakily pry it out of her, which only infuriates me further. She is only my pet for the moment, but at any given time, she can disappear, and I would be powerless to stop her. Impotence, for a man like me, is not a feeling I am accustomed to. I like control, and I like others knowing I hold all of it in a tight grip, daring any to come and take it away from me. It would be pointless in any other scenario, but with her, she has flipped it to her advantage somehow. Unassumingly, she holds all the cards, and it bothers me how she has taken over my thoughts and actions with such ease.

She continues to walk the floor of the spacious club, one step at a time, not making any direct contact with anyone, but still searching for someone. I keep still on my seat, watching her stroll at her leisure. My insides scream to get my ass off the couch and grab her before anyone else does, but my pride will not let me move a muscle—an animalistic craving I can't control, and the desperate need for her to choose me amongst the rest. Especially tonight, when she looks like the devil herself, tempting any desired suitor. Her body might be cool and collected as she ventures to one of the bars to get a drink, but her eyes are restless. I see them examine every crevice of the room, searching, and my body heats when they finally land on me, lighting me up with relief.

Tired of depriving myself of what I want, I place my whiskey glass on the table and make my way to her. It's been a full week without her, and I fear I can't stand a second longer. I see she is not wearing her usual black mask tonight, but instead, the upper part of her face is covered in gold makeup, carefully designed to look like lace. It still camouflages her features well, but I love it when she so confidently walks in here mask-less as if she is naked for all to behold, but none to touch, save for me. I have never been a jealous man, but my need to keep this view all to myself shows just how possessive I am.

"You look beautiful, pet," I say, kissing her cheek softly. Her whole body tremors with the contact, and my ego soars hoping this immediate reaction only occurs within me.

"Thank you, my King," she replies with a breathless sigh, her endearment hardening my cock further.

"Such a shame you won't be wearing that dress ever again," I state, taking the vodka cranberry out of her hands and placing on the counter.

"I won't?" she asks, furrowing her brow. I shake my head and give her a smug grin. I lean in, stroking her hair behind her ear, and whisper in it, making my intentions clear.

"No, pet. By the end of this night, this dress will be ruined on my bedroom floor."

"Your bedroom? We're not staying?" she asks, licking her lips in anticipation of my next words.

"No, Beauty. Tonight this place doesn't deserve you." And maybe I don't either, but I'm too much of a selfish prick to say otherwise. I need her attention solely on me tonight. I missed her too goddamned much.

"Isn't that against the rules? Aren't the rooms provided by the club to prevent sharing our private lives with each other? I believe if you show me your actual bedroom, you are breaking rule number one," she teases, but I sense an underlying hint of uncertainty in her statement.

"Do you trust me, pet?" I ask, feeling vulnerable all of a sudden. She nods, but her hesitation is too palpable for me to ignore. Perhaps she isn't as infatuated with me as I am with her. Maybe the rules of the club are exactly what she wants, always keeping me at arm's length. It seems I might be more invested in this peculiar relationship than she is. Yes, we fuck. We fuck anytime we get our hands on each other. But is that all this is to her? A quick nameless fuck and nothing more?

No.

She knows my name now. And I have hers engraved in my very soul.

"Didn't you miss me at all, pet?" I ask, running my thumb on her lower lip.

"You know I did," she whispers back, looking at me with such undying devotion in her eyes.

Against my better judgment, I find myself saying what I don't mean, but do it nonetheless, for her benefit and my sanity.

"Beauty, I will enjoy you either way. If you prefer we take this downstairs, I'll follow your lead," I state, and the words seem to come out as cold as I feel inside. Beauty's eyes, still fixed on mine, gain new life as she places her hands on both my cheeks, urging me down enough, so she can pillow her lips on mine. The kiss is too sweet. Too decadent, even in its innocence.

"I will follow you wherever you want to take me," she replies, and her eyes seem to hold a promise bigger than the one she's making now.

"Did you bring a car?" I ask, already making up my mind for the both of us, taking full advantage of her willingness to leave with me. She shakes her head and tells me she came by taxi. I text my driver to meet us up front and grab her hand before she has time to change her mind.

Tonight I will see this vixen spread wide on my bed. I will memorize every curve and brand it to my cold heart. Beauty might still be apprehensive in sharing her life with me—her secrets—but I am done with this game. I want her for myself, and before the dawn rises, she will know my intentions. It's a gamble, a risk I'm taking, and I might regret my impulsiveness in the morning. But the idea that Beauty is out there without me, living a life I'm clueless about, is no longer acceptable for my reality. This week without her—not even having a damn telephone number to call her on, unable to hear her voice, see her, touch her in any way—was excruciating and maddening. I will not go through that hell again. I'm done with this. She needs to know I want to rule her in every way. Rule her thoughts, her feelings, and reign over her body from this day on.

As we walk outside the building, and we are both attacked by the light snow drizzle, I put my arm over her, protectively, but immediately feel her current tensed state. Her apprehension still prickles in the back of my mind, but I reassure myself, this is all new territory for her as well. Jitters are natural, although the trace of uncertainty in her features brings a suffocating spotlight, pointing out my own insecurities.

Fuck!

She is mine, goddamn it!

My pet!

My Queen!

And I am her King!

It's about time she is clued into this, too.

Once we enter the car, I instruct the driver to take us to my penthouse before raising the partition to give us some privacy. My mood has shifted, and I'm unable to enjoy the light touch on my thigh by the woman who has me bewildered and under her complete control.

"I've upset you," she affirms, rather than ask.

I turn to her, wanting to ease her concern, yet I'm unable to hide my feelings as well as she wants to hide hers.

"You could never upset me, my pet," I tell her, leaving a chaste kiss on her lips. She's so velvety soft, her warmth alone feels so right here, pressed to my side, it's a wonder how I was able to survive without her this past week.

"Yet, I have," she states, her eyes just as troubled as my inner thoughts.

"It will pass, Beauty. Just give me some time," I confess, not wanting my own self-doubts to ruin the night ahead. She gives me a meek smile, and I hate the mood I'm creating. This was not what I had in mind when I ventured to steal her away from that place for our reunion. She looks intently at me, searching for answers I don't have, and I feel her light touch move closer to the only part of my body that still registers that I'm in a car alone with the only woman who has tempted me to the point of madness. I grow bold with her feathered touch to my groin and grab the nape of her neck to me.

"Am I your King, pet?"

"Yes," she pants, already feeling the effects my dominant grip has on her.

"Are you my faithful servant?" I continue, my heart already beating a mile a minute.

"Yes," she confesses, looking deep into my eyes. My watchful stare sees her breath hitch and her nipples pebble harder with the force I'm inflicting on her neck.

"Show me, pet. Serve your King," I order, and in a second, she is out of my grip, on hands and knees, springing my dick free. The look of hunger in her eyes never gets old, and the way she bites her lower lip in anticipation is enough for me to blow my load. I lean my head back, closing my eyes to enjoy the exact moment her plump lips wrap themselves around my hard length. The minute I feel her warm mouth open up to me, wet and slippery like I know her pussy must be, my eyes roll to the back of my head, relishing the sensation.

"I could fuck this mouth all night," I admit, getting harder with every slow stroke of her tongue.

This sweet torture is what she is good at. She might be servicing me as her King, but I'm the one who is, in reality, kneeling at her altar. The deity in her has converted me in ways I didn't think possible. Her mouth moves up and down in leisurely strokes, enjoying it just as much as I am, and when she starts moaning onto my aching shaft, the vibration alone makes me see flashes of light. I grip the leather of the seat with both hands beside me, holding steady, not to fuck her face mercilessly, but the devil in red has other plans. No longer satisfied with taking it slow, she plunges excitedly on my cock, gripping her lips tighter, so much that I feel the pressure in my balls screaming for release.

She is relentless in her pursuit, so I grab her hair in a fist, giving her exactly what she wishes. My ten inches find the back of her throat, and small tears start to break free from the sides of her eyes, although the sounds she is making tells me she is loving every minute of my attack. I can't take my eyes off of her. She looks beautiful with her mouth full of me, taking every inch like it's her mission in life. I'm too close to my limit, and I tell her so, but this only fuels her drive, and I see her feathered lashes bat like butterfly wings in contentment. I'm certain this woman will be the death of me. I'm still a gentleman, so I give her my last warning since I won't have it in me to give a third.

"I can't hold out any longer, my Queen. Either jump on my cock so I can cum inside that sweet pussy of yours, or continue and take every last drop," I growl, and for a split second, she considers her choices.

I see the mischievous slant in her eyes as she pursues milking me dry. My little pet is loving her power over me and doesn't want to let go just yet. Obediently, I follow through with my promise and cum in her heavenly mouth. Like the good girl she is, she swallows everything I offer and licks me clean, grinning the whole time. I'm too relaxed to even put my cock away, but not spent enough to not grab my pet by the waist and have her straddle me in the back seat. I look to the side and realize we are still far enough from my apartment for what I have in mind. The look of gratification is branded on her face, and I'm sure mine looks as smitten as I feel.

"Is my King satisfied?" she teases, glee in her eyes.

"Not quite yet, pet," I reply, and her grin falters.

Not wanting that look to stay fixed on her face for too long, I rip one side of her dress, right up to her thigh so I can have full access to the dripping bare pussy that is resting on my already wakening cock.

But his turn will just have to wait. I need to see my Queen cum on my fingers at least once before we make it home—that's the only way I can even be remotely satisfied. I plunge two fingers in her at once, and her surprise is quickly replaced with the pleasure I intend to instigate. My thumb finds her quivering clit, and I start my knowledgeable ministration with care.

"You swallowed my cock to perfection, pet. But now show me how well you can ride my hand," I say, biting her hard nipple over her dress.

Her moans are just as loud and violent as my thrusts into her tight, wet pussy. There is no need for foreplay since she is already too hot and bothered from sucking my dick alone. This will be too quick for me to revel in, but it will have to do for now. I intend to have all night to make this woman cum on my demand, and this is just a small preview of what's to come. I'm not two minutes into my torment when my pet arches her back, going over the cliff, falling back onto my chest and settling her head on the crook of my neck.

"Now I'm satisfied," I explain while brushing her hair back.

The sated smile she offers me in reply warms my insides, and the feeling of uncertainty has flown away into the scenery behind us. My driver has had an earful tonight, but I pay him well to be discreet. I'm not sure that my purring kitten even gave him much thought.

A couple of minutes pass by, and the car stops right at my building's entrance. My pet is still enjoying her afterglow, so when we exit the car, I don't let her take a step by lifting her off her feet and into my arms. She doesn't object and wraps her arms around my neck.

"The chariot ride was delightful, pet. But rest while you can. I have big plans for your stay at my castle."

Chapter 22

EDIE

The sun is still not up yet, but after many nights spent at our usual haunt, my internal clock tells me my fairytale night has come to an end. It was a bold move on my part coming to Dean's apartment last night, but after a week away from him, he could have suggested going the moon, and I would have followed.

But today is a new day. A new year, in fact, and certain decisions need to be made. I thought long and hard while I was back home in Jersey, on what I was going to do. Should I call it quits after last night, or should I use Devina's charitable gift to buy me one more month with my King? If I had any doubts that I could stay away, given a chance, last night made it abundantly clear I could not. If I can keep Dean for one more month, live this love just one more month, then I'm all in.

C'mon, guys—can you really blame me?

How can I let go of him if I don't have to just yet? If I can postpone the pain coming my way, living without his touch, his caress, his kiss, and his love, in exchange for actually having all of it instead, then yeah, I'm pressing pause on my impending sorrow and keep milking every second I have with him for all it's worth.

I'll probably have to talk to Bash, though. I'm not sure he'll be totally kosher with the idea, but maybe if I explain it to him, he'll understand.

No?

Yeah, I didn't think so either. I don't have to be at work for two more days, so I'll think of something by then. But right now, I have more pressing matters to attend to, like finding my clothes. We were so ravenous yesterday that I have no idea where my dress ended up, even though I'm pretty sure Dean ruined it beyond repair. Not sure how I'm going to explain how that happened when I bring it back to Royal and the Wardrobe Department. But I still have to find it and see if it can be salvaged in any way. I think Dean tore it off me somewhere in the living room.

I gently remove Dean's arm from my belly, leaving one small kiss on his lips before slipping off the bed. I see a white t-shirt and black boxers neatly placed on his leather ottoman. I pick up the t-shirt and pull it over my head, Dean's cologne immediately intoxicating my senses, making me wish we could turn back the clock and repeat last night all over again.

Focus, Edie!

Get the dress!

Kiss your man and get your booty out of there!

Shit!

Okay!

Living room!

I run to the living room, and of course, I'm blown away by the enormity of it all. Dean is grandiose in everything he does and touches, so why would I be surprised his home is any different? The whole penthouse is sleek and refined, like the man who owns it. Pristine and immaculate, but with enough flair that each decorative piece—including the grand piano with its bench view to Central Park—doesn't come out as cold, but as a chess piece, strategically put in place to make its owner feel like the true King he is. A true castle in the heart of Manhattan.

"JESUS CHRIST!" I yell, elbowing my sudden attacker in his midriff when I feel a shadow suddenly pull me away from my current thought and from the floor beneath me. He quickly sets me back on my feet, still hugging me, chuckling away. I'm still out of breath, my chest threatening to cave in with Dean's unexpected appearance from behind, but he seems right as rain to the abuse I just sprung on him.

"So aggressive this morning, pet," Dean snickers behind me, holding me even closer to him.

"Well, don't sneak up on people then. This is New

York, you know? My first instinct when attacked from behind, is to strike first and ask questions later." I giggle when he starts showering my naked neck with kisses.

"I'll make a note of it, my Queen. But my bed felt awfully cold without you," he coos, making me melt into his embrace. "Whatever possessed you to leave it in the first place?"

"Life, unfortunately, my King. And if I'm honest, a shower, too." I sigh.

"Hmm, a shower. I can definitely go for one of those. I'd love to see this body wet, pushed up against me. On second thought, maybe you getting out of bed wasn't the worst idea at all, pet," he smiles into my neck, giving it one final kiss before taking my hand and leading me back to his bedroom in a mad rush.

"Where are we going?" I ask, slowing my steps, trying to slow him down, too.

"To my en suite, of course. Now that you've planted the idea of me fucking you raw under the shower head, there is no way I'm passing it up." He beams brightly.

"No, my King. When I said I needed a shower, I meant I needed to take one back at my place. That it's time I go home," I explain softly, trying to minimize the sting. However, when his green eyes turn to emerald stone, I know I've done a piss-poor job of it.

"You can take one here." His voice no longer holding the same light it had a second ago.

"No, I can't," I hush, sympathetically.

He lets go of my hand and crosses his arms over his majestic chest. Even only in a pair of designer boxers, he still looks regal. Majestic.

"Why not?" His tone now contains the same chill his glacier stare is providing.

I just point to my makeup, the only thing camouflaging my identity as my reason.

"Because then this will be ruined," I whisper, thinking my painted face is not the only thing I'm referring to if I consent to the King's request.

"So let it. I want to see your face," he replies sternly, and I lower my head instead of giving him what he wants.

The room grows eerily silent, and I can almost hear the drumming of our heartbeats dancing to a different tune, mine in sorrow and panic, his in pain and anger.

"It's late. I should just go home," I finally mutter, breaking the calm before our inevitable storm.

"It's not late. It's early," he counters. "I want to bathe you, fuck you, and fall asleep holding you in my arms, repeating it all over again the whole day through. Why are you being so difficult right now?" He exhales, running his fingers through his hair, showing signs of his utter frustration.

"You know why," I bellow back, my own voice pitching an octave higher than intended.

"What, this?" he asks, pointing to his own discreet black mask, still strategically placed to cover the top half of his face. But before I have time to say another word, Dean's fingers are already at the nape of his skull, untying every string and removing his disguise. My jaw drops the minute his gorgeous face is in my full view, and the man I love is staring at me with nothing to shield his true identity from me. He throws the mask to the ground and looks me square in the eye—mineral green to sky blue.

"Don't use a piece of fabric as an excuse to leave. You know me. With or without a mask, Edwina," he lashes out, his Adam's apple bobbing madly up and down, mimicking my own heartbeat.

"My King—"

"It's Dean, Edwina. You're in my house. I made love to you in my bed. Show me at least the courtesy of calling me by my name," he growls.

How can people still believe a soul doesn't exist, when mine is strangling my very breath from inside me with each angry pronounced word that falls from his lips?

"Please, don't do this," I beg him, my tears already threatening to make an appearance. I could blame it on the discomfort of the lenses, but it's the disdain on my lover's perfect, exposed face that is causing my grief.

"Fuck! You can't even say it, can you?" he snarls, erratically walking back and forth like a caged animal.

"Was it all just about the sex for you, Edwina? Is that it? Was I just a good fuck? The tutor you wanted to learn from until there was nothing I had left to teach you? Huh, Edwina? Is that fucking it?" he shouts, polluting the air we both breathe with such vile lies and misconceptions. It's a miracle we're both still standing with these carcinogenic elements tearing us to shreds. His words, so ugly and hurtful that his whole body shakes in agony at such a realization— that the tears freely falling from me are for his pain as much as mine.

"No, my King. No! Please don't taint the beautiful memories we shared. I will always cherish the time we had together. Whatever transpired between us was pure and perfect. Never think otherwise," I cry, succumbing to my wounds and slumping to the ground; my knees finally giving in to the weight of my despair and his agony.

"I'm not your King right now, Edwina! Damn you! Don't you see, I want more than that? But you don't, do you?"

"You don't understand." I weep into my hands, shaking my head from left to right.

My whole world is crumbling, and there is nothing I can do to stop it. Twenty minutes ago, I was living in a dream, only to be woken to face my worst nightmare. Two strong hands hold mine steady, bringing them down to my lap. Dean, still so volatile, looks just as torn and wrung out as I feel. Yet, he kneels before me, placing his hands on my still-masked face, holding it with the same tenderness as last night.

"Then make me understand," he pleads earnestly, with nothing but love in his eyes.

Oh, God!

"You don't know me, and when you find out who I am, you will not want me anymore," I admit in one rushed sob.

"That's not true," he whispers softly, caressing my cheek with his thumb.

"How can you be sure?" I sob harder, hiccupping.

"Because I am," he replies confidently.

"Well, I'm not. Please, can we just keep things as they are?" It's my turn to beg since he won't see rhyme or reason.

"No. I want you. All of you. I want Edwina," he

states, in a non-negotiable tone.

"Stop saying that, Dean! You don't even know who Edwina is! You wouldn't look twice at her if you did," I yell, pushing him away and standing on my feet.

"Oh, now you say my name!" he growls back, his own attack mode activated by my sudden one.

"You are infatuated with this," I say, pointing to my clever guise. "With the fabrication I created! Don't tell me you want all of me when I know for a fact that a man like you wouldn't ever want anything to do with someone like me," I bark.

"Edwina, stop it! You are one of the most incredible women I have ever met. With or without a mask, you can't hide what's inside of you! Any man in his right mind would do everything in their power to keep you in their orbit, just to have your goodness touch them somehow. But I'm not just any man, Edwina, and I'm also not a fool. I don't want a spectator seat, so front row won't cut it for me anymore. I want to keep you and have you as mine and only mine."

"You want a queen that doesn't exist," I sigh, defeated.

"That's not true. My queen lives, but I want the woman I love more. You," he replies with nothing but true love in each and every word, cutting me further.

"Oh, God, please don't say that. Do you know how many times I've dreamed of hearing you say those words to me?" I lament, turning my back to him, running back to the living room and grabbing my dress from its funeral pyre. I don't even try to put the ravaged thing on, but instead, I search for my shoes and purse that are luckily thrown about the entryway.

"Edwina, stop!" Dean shouts out at my panicked dash.

"You *don't* love me. I wish you did. God, how I wish you did, but you don't," I yell back, putting my high heels on, and my dress under my arm. "This was a mistake. I messed up. I fucking messed up! I wanted you so badly, and now look at us!"

"Edwina… "

"I'm so sorry. I'm so fucking sorry."

I run to the front door, knowing how insane I will look to anyone outside. A girl in gold mask-shaped makeup, wearing nothing else but a men's white t-shirt, Louboutins, and a Yves Saint Laurent clutch.

"Edwina!"

My hand is on the doorknob, but my heartstrings are still being pulled by his voice. I lean my forehead onto the cold door because if I turn to face my love, I'm not sure he won't break my resolve.

"Don't go, pet," he croaks, not hiding what I know will be tears watering perfect green jewels.

Souls do exist.

And they can die, too.

As mine is—when I hear the only man who I will ever love in this life and the next, bleed out in misery behind me, begging me not to leave him.

But I have to.

"You deserve better than me. You deserve a real queen, not an imitation of one."

Chapter 23

EDIE

"E, honey? Tell me what's wrong with you? And don't tell me it's just the flu, because I've been coming to see you every day, and you are suffering from something that has nothing to do with the sniffles. What's wrong?" Devina implores, running her fingers through my hair, trying her best to comfort me.

She's been doing this every day for the last week. Showering me with affection, trying to coerce me into talking. But all I seem to have the energy for is to just lie here in this bed and wallow in my pain.

"You have to let us in, Edie. You can't go on living this way." Lexi appeals to any logic I may have left.

The funny thing is, I think all logic has left the building, folks. I'm nothing but withered bone and raw, mangled flesh. Nothing lives inside me anymore. I yearn for numbness to arrive, pray for it, beg and bargain for it, but instead, my tortured soul is absent of its grace. There is nothing my logical mind can conjure up to lift my spirits. The same intellect, which I was so proud of possessing, fails me since the only organ in my body still responsive has taken control of everything else, and insists on keeping me in my current misery.

I deserve it, after all. I brought this on, so I say bring it. Bring every ounce of agonizing solitude. Bring memories of love that will never be relived. Bring false images of faint touches on my skin, illusions of what I will never feel again. Bring every last memory to torture me into my own insanity. I tell my heart to do its worst and spare nothing because I deserve it—its wrath and its rage. I deserve what it's trying to do to me.

These are my constant companions and thoughts, as my friends sit beside me on my bed, demanding answers this Saturday morning. They too are praying, begging, and bargaining for me to explain why I've become this comatose mess. I know that today, they won't leave me alone. During the week, they had jobs and obligations to attend to. But now, with the impending weekend hanging over my head, they'll camp out on my bedroom floor until they get their answers.

It's probably why I give in. Probably why I open my mouth at all, to speak the very first words I've been able to say in seven days.

"I think I'm dying."

"You're not dying, E. But just an FYI, if Tatiana shows up at your door, don't open it. She might murder you for leaving her alone with me." Dev jokes, trying to brighten my mood, but it's in vain.

Nothing can bring light back into my pathetic existence.

Only him.

"Oh, God!" I sob into my pillow again, a fresh batch of tears wetting it further.

My mother was right.

I am water!

Because this vile stuff keeps leaking out of me like an open faucet, threatening to never close.

"E, please! Please tell us what's wrong? Whatever it is, it must be serious to leave you in so much pain. And it's not about Nan, I've checked on her," Dev discloses.

"You called my mom?" I hiccup.

"Of course! What was I supposed to do? Wait forever to find out why my best friend has locked herself in her room for a full week? Crying every minute of the day. Not eating, not sleeping enough, just withering away as if someone died or something."

"*I* died, Dev! Me!" I howl.

"Babe, don't say that. You're right here with us," Lexi coos, getting misty-eyed, too, holding my hands in hers.

"Fuck this!" Devina roars, rising from the bed and standing menacingly above me.

"Edwina Vanderwalt, you tell me what the fuck is going on right now! Or I swear, I'll go to Jersey myself and get Nan to make you!" Dev shouts, both hands on her hips.

"That's your big plan, Dev? Tattletale on her to her mom?" Lexi shrugs, eyeballing my enraged friend.

But at the absurdity of it all, I let out a small snicker. Here are my two closest friends, my confidantes, so near and dear to me, worried out of their minds and all because of this well-kept secret confined to a small vault in my heart. A secret screaming to be let out and burn whatever remains of me. Might as well light the match now.

"I love you guys, you know that, right?"

Devina's thundering stance immediately softens, and Lexi squeezes my hand, giving me her warm, tender smile.

"You're not going to like most of what I'm going to tell you. You might even resent me a little for keeping it from you as long as I did. But I want you to know, I'd repeat it in a heartbeat. Maybe not the last part—as you can see, I'm pretty messed up since it happened—but every single moment leading up to it, I'd do it again. And maybe I should feel ashamed saying this to you, but if I'm going to be honest, I want to *really* be honest with you, and that may include things which might make you feel uncomfortable—you might even see me in another light you never considered. But I know you love me enough to forgive me, or at least I'm praying you do."

"Edie, honey, just start talking already, yeah?" Lexi exhales, on pins and needles.

So I do what a month ago would have seemed unimaginable to me.

I tell them my whole sordid truth. Beginning to end. Every last ugly lie to each tender loving kiss. All of it. And as the day grows old, and the night sky starts to envelop, decorating my bedroom window pane, I still find more words in me to say. More feelings to explain. More sweet touches to remember and visualize.

The vomiting of my truth to my dear two friends—Devina, who is more like a sister to me since before I mastered my ABC's, and Lexi, who grew with me in those awkward college years of self-discovery—is cathartic in a way. I didn't know how the actual lies had burdened me as much as the loss of my love, but now that they are out in the open, I feel free of their chains. Lighter.

With each tear I shed, my friends share my pain. They bring me water for my thirst so I can continue and bring me food for my hunger when it arises. And they hold my hand, one on each side, showing their undying support and loyalty to a friend who has wronged them in so many ways.

When the moon is high in the sky, the day has passed, I strike it off my mental calendar as another day I've survived without *him*. Only today, it hurt just a little bit less, because I didn't feel alone anymore.

But I've never been alone, have I?

I've always had Dev and Lex. It was my fear of judgment and disappointment that made me falter. It was my own insecurities. I should have never doubted their understanding. I wish I'd had enough faith in myself to realize this sooner.

"Well damn, *chica*. When someone gives you a mic, you sure do hog it!" Lexi teases, handing me a fresh box of Kleenex.

"I wish you would have come to me, E. I would have warned you," Devina says, looking lost and just as wrecked as I feel.

"Warned me about what? There was no way you could have known this would happen, Dev." I squeeze her hand, trying to comfort my overprotective sister.

"Yes, I did. I would have warned you against love. It's nothing but poison, E. It consumes you, and eats you whole. Chews you up until it hears everything break inside just so it can spit you into the ground and trample its heel on you. Beats your face into a bloody pulp, making you unrecognizable, even to yourself, when you catch it laughing at your bloody wounds. I would have warned you against that fucker, Edie. I would have warned you about not falling in love," Dev says, shaken.

"Devina?" I watch her pale face grow ghostly white and feel her hands get clammy. "Lexi, can you please get Dev some sugar water?" I ask, my concern for my sister switching my internal *on* button.

"Sure," Lex replies, confusion marring her expression with an unusually out-of-sorts Devina.

"Dev? You okay?" I ask her, softly stroking her back.

"Uh, yeah. Of course," she replies, still a bit loopy, shaking her head and getting off the bed. She turns her back to me and walks to my bedroom window, looking at the same starless sky I was just admiring.

"You sure? It sounded like you know exactly what I'm going through. Like you were talking about someone. Did anyone hurt you, Dev?" I tenderly grill her to give me an answer.

"No one can ever hurt me. Not again," I hear her murmur, crossing her arms over her chest, to keep still.

"But someone did," I retort. "Who was it, Dev?"

The silence in my room is such that I can actually hear Lexi in our kitchen getting Devina something to drink. Once Lexi comes back, I know Dev won't say anything further. She's too private of a person to open herself up to anyone. Even to me, it seems.

"It's nothing, E. I was talking about my father. Who else could I possibly be referring to?" she replies bitterly.

Their relationship has always been a tumultuous one, and old wounds are hard to heal sometimes. In Devina's case, maybe even irreparable. Of course, she was talking about her father. One of the reasons we bonded in the first place when we were younger was because we had such crappy luck in the daddy department. While my cheating sperm donor left to start a new family far away from me, hers didn't. I saw firsthand what would have happened if my father had stayed. It was the hell Devina had to live in. Yes, she lived in a glorious mansion, with everything money can buy. But a father's love and a husband's loyalty are two things that can't be bought. It needs to be given willingly, and Devina's dad was never the giving type.

"I'm sorry, Dev. Of course, I should have known better. My head is all fuzzy. Please. Sit back down." As I say this, Lexi returns with a tall glass of water and offers it to a recovering Dev.

"So what now?" Lexi asks, looking back and forth from me to Devina, repeatedly.

Dev turns around and offers me a small smirk, and I know she's fully back to herself, or at least trying to be.

"I don't know. Go back to work on Monday, I guess. Take it one day at a time. I'm really not sure," I tell them honestly.

"I think that's best. Routine is your best ally right now. Avoid you-know-who at Royal if you can, but immerse yourself with work. That always cheers me up," Lexi beams, more enthusiastic now that we're thinking of a plan to get me out of this slump.

"Try to avoid Kelley and Walsh if you can, too. I'll try to rearrange the meetings that they're attending so you don't need to be there. I'll take Tatiana instead, feed her some shit about it being good for training purposes. Make her better at dealing with higher-ups."

"You should be doing that with her anyway, since it is good she gains that experience," I chastise.

"Whatever. The sooner you get back, the better. I need my E back in the ring with me," Dev urges on.

"I mean, life does go on, yeah? How long does a broken heart take to mend anyway?" Lexi asks.

Well, it's definitely more than three months.

March has arrived, bringing on its wind the crisp, fresh spring air, but never taking away with it the love I still bear in my heart.

Going back to work had its good aspects and its bad ones. Lexi was right about falling back into my routine. It felt like a comfortable shoe on good days. Devina kept me as busy as possible, never leaving me alone the first couple of weeks, throwing at me task after task. I was so overwhelmed with work, it was hard to think of anything else.

My dynamics with Tatiana also changed. The moment I returned, she was all smiles and nothing but welcoming, like I was the second coming herself. Apparently, one week alone with Dev was a week too many, and she quickly realized I wasn't the one she should be afraid of after all. Natural order was back as it should be.

But then there were the bad days.

I didn't see Dean for ten whole days, but I sure did hear him. His voice traveled all the way to my cubicle with his yelled orders and commands. He was always a perfectionist in everything he did and wanted others to follow suit. But I never once heard him being cruel for the sake of wanting to inflict actual pain on someone just because he could. The howls everyone could hear in the office told a different story of the man I knew. It got so bad that people preferred to seek Devina out first for any work-related issues, instead of Dean, which only added to my workload.

And then there were the meetings not even Devina could get me out of. The ones all staff members were required to attend. Here, not only my ears were witnesses to his pain, but my eyes, too. His disheveled appearance, with dark rings under his eyes, told me I wasn't the only one in constant misery.

Yeah, those were my bad days. Days that would end with me curled in the fetal position, with nothing but guilt for what I had done to us.

I have joked so many times about how I'd end up in hell for the things that I've done, but breaking Dean's heart is my biggest sin yet.

And the devil who wants me to pay up must be Sebastian Kelley.

I've been ditching Bash like the plague just as much as I have Dean. Devina warned me against Connor, but she does it well enough for the both of us. So well that I'm hardly ever presented with the risk of an encounter.

Bash, though, has been harder to escape. He's marked meetings with me through Tatiana, which I have neglected to attend, feigning either sickness or an unavoidable work emergency for Devina. He's even gone as far as to come up to our floor and pass by my cubicle various times in his pursuit to find me. Luckily, I have Tatiana to interject him before he can get to me, and I either run into the ladies' restroom and ask Dev to text me when the coast is clear or leave the office entirely to do errands.

But Bash is nothing if not persistent, and apparently a lucky son of a gun, because one Friday afternoon, while I was distracted texting Lexi, trying to talk her out of dragging me to the Bronx, of all places, for St. Patrick's Day, I got into the elevator after my lunch break, with none other than the man himself—alone and without any witnesses.

Shit!

"Miss Vanderwalt," he greets, standing directly beside me.

"Mr. Kelley," I retort, my eyes focused on the elevator doors.

"You've been avoiding me."

"Trying to. Didn't pan out, now, did it?" I answer sarcastically, straightening my shoulders and stiffening my back.

"You can't avoid the inevitable," he remarks smugly.

"Apparently not," I answer, counting down the floors.

Not wanting to be in this elevator any longer than I have to, I press on the button for the floor where we do most of our photo shoots. It's highly unlikely that he would know there isn't one taking place right now, and it's just five more floors I'll have to endure confined by his disapproving stare.

After we pass two floors, I begin to think Bash is

going to let me get away with escaping without saying a further word.

Of course, I was wrong to ever believe he would.

"He's hurting," he announces, delivering his jagged knife through my already cut-up heart.

"I know," I manage to reply.

"So are you," he asserts matter-of-factly as if he can see, as clear as day, every wound I try to hide.

But I don't respond. I can't. I just have to make it to two more floors, and I'm out of here—away from him and his remarkably accurate speculations.

"But you won't tell him who you are."

"No," I state firmly, making sure he hears the conviction in my voice, stating that I don't want him to disclose my identity, either.

"Can I ask why?"

"Because he deserves better," I answer truthfully, as the ding of the elevator door gives ringsto life—saved by the bell at last.

I walk past Bash, ending this conversation once and for all, but before I can breathe in freedom, he grabs my elbow, halting me in place. Light enough to not cause me discomfort, but with a smidge of force, indicating I'm not going anywhere just yet.

"He won't find it. He loves you too much to even look."

Whatever strength I have, I summon it to look Bash straight in the eye for the first time since I stepped inside this damned box. I thought I would be confronted with a merciless black void, yet what greets me instead is silver moonlight.

"A queen worthy of him will find and fight for him instead, then," I state plainly and remove my arm from his grasp, walking out of this elevator with all the poise I can muster.

"I think she already has," I hear Bash say behind me before the elevator doors close, putting a stop to our little one-to-one.

Chills run down my spine, and I have to hold myself in place for a few minutes before attempting to hit the elevator button again to take me up to my actual floor.

Maybe a couple of drinks at an Irish bar in the Bronx with Lexi tonight isn't the worst idea in the world. After this encounter, I think I'm going to need a couple of shots to erase the last three minutes from my mind. I text her, telling her I'm all in with her idea of celebrating St. Patty's Day.

Six hours later, I regret my kneejerk reaction. If I'd known Lexi's idea of a fun night out was going into a rowdy Irish pub—where most men look like they are extras of The Boondock Saints, minus the yummy Sean Patrick Flannery and Norman Reedus look-alikes—just so she could talk to her snitch, aka source, while I nursed a whole bottle of jack by my lonesome, I'd preferred to have had this pity party at home. I could be in my pajamas and comfy socks, instead of these killer heels she bullied me into wearing tonight. I'm five minutes from bailing when I see Lexi looking at her phone, going red in rage and then shooting me a pitied look across the bar.

That can't be good.

My instincts, on high alert, tell me I should hightail it out of there anyway before she has time to catch up with me.

"Where are you going?" she says, slamming her jacket and purse on the bar.

"Home," I say, already grabbing the attention of the barkeep to settle my tab.

"Nope, you can't go home yet. You need another drink," she says sternly, putting pressure on my shoulders to keep my ass to this bar stool. For a pixie, Lexi sure is strong. Must be all that Pilates and shit.

"Sit your ass down, Edie. I told you, you're not going anywhere. Hey, Danny boy, two tequilas, yeah?" Lexi orders the handsome, strapping redhead behind the bar.

"Name's David, love. Not Danny," he says, giving

her a long appraising look, and then delivering his best panty-melting smile.

"Play your cards right, and I might remember later on tonight," she sasses back. "But for now, the tequilas will do fine."

"I've had enough to drink as it is, Lex. Why can't I go home? And why the hell do I need another drink?" I cock my brow. I'm tired, tipsy, and destitute, so all I want is my bed to end this God-forsaken day.

"Because I'm a big believer in ripping the band-aid," she says as the cute guy brings us the two shots.

"Keep 'em coming, Red. It's going to be a long night," she tells him, downing her liquor then biting the lemon wedge.

"You forgot the salt," I chastise.

"I'll remember on the next round. Here. Your turn," she says pushing the tequila in my face.

"Only if you tell me why you want us to get shitfaced all of a sudden," I insist, not budging.

Lexi's eyes turn to the object she has in her hand, and for a brief second, I see hesitation hit my usually unwavering friend. She nods to herself, mumbling something under her breath, which I can't pick up on since this raucous bar is too fucking loud to hear my thoughts, let alone my best friend's inner ramblings. But it almost sounds like she's apologizing for something.

When she places her phone face up on the bar, and I see her twitter feed blowing up with the latest breaking story, I understand why she had been dawdling and why I'll end this night passed out drunk, in her arms.

Bachelor of the year Dean Knox celebrates St. Paddy's Day with Austrian model girlfriend Aylin Müller in Charity Event.#LuckoftheIrish #TrueLove #SpringWeddingDreams #CoupleGoals

The evil tagline even came with its own photographic proof.

I was wrong before.

This must be what dying feels like.

Chapter 24

DEAN

I'm staring into space when the natural disaster that is Devina Richardson barges into my office, slamming the door behind her hard enough it could have loosened its hinges.

"Why are men such assholes?" she belts, placing both hands spread apart on my desk, looking me straight in the eye with enough hatred that I'm inclined to think that the man she's referring to might actually be me.

"Is that the title of our next feature? Because if it is, I don't think we have enough space in this month's edition to answer that question."

"Then how about why do men not see a good thing when it's right under their fucking nose? Why are they so blind?!" she yells out, and I'm starting to think Devina might be more unhinged than I suspected.

"Devina, whatever Connor did now, do you think you can control yourself long enough for the staff meeting we're having in twenty minutes?"

This woman has got to pull it together. If the staff

sees her acting like a lunatic and talking in code, it won't bode well for her. Devina might be a bitch when she wants to be, but she is extremely good at her job. Maybe even better than me, so there is no way I can take this magazine to its full glorious potential without her by my side. Especially now when I'm a fucking mess and am barely making it through the day as it is. But if she acts like she needs to be locked up in a psych ward, she won't be much use to me, now will she?

"Connor didn't do anything this time. He's an asshole, but at least he owns up to it. The real danger are men who are blind to their dickish ways," she goes on and starts pacing the room from one side to the other, trying to control her temper.

"Are you going to continue to talk to me in riddles, or are you going to tell me what's wrong? We don't have all day, Devina," I groan.

I have enough problems as it is, and a Devina meltdown is not high on my priority list. Another absent blonde is, however, and even though Devina's little rant got me to focus on something besides Edwina for a total of two seconds, I'd prefer to wallow in my own self-pity than fix Devina's issues.

"Care to tell me why I had to find out that my business partner decided to announce his personal affairs to the world over the fucking weekend through social media?" she fumes in utter disgust.

"Jesus, Devina, when have you ever paid attention

to TMZ gossip? For fuck's sake! I've already sent out a statement denying any such allegation. If that's what crawled up your ass this morning, then simmer the fuck down."

For crying out loud! Like I need the added drama in my life. It's already in a sorry state of affairs as it is. I can't handle Devina being pissed at me because some model's arrogant publicist was creative in getting her free exposure. My life is in shambles, and this is what I have to look forward to every day? More of the same bullshit? Depressing isn't even the right word for how I see my future to look like—empty fits perfectly, though.

Ain't karma a bitch? I thought I was empty before *she* came into my life, only to learn what true hollowness feels like without her in it. Let me rectify my previous statement—karma is not only a bitch but has an ironic sense of humor.

"Oh," Devina says, stopping in her tracks.

"Next time, Dev, use the fucking phone and ask me first before coming to my office with shit I have no patience for. It'll make it easier for me to hang up on you," I convey and go back to reading whatever I was before she decided to pay me this little visit.

Not as if I was actually working. I know she's the one who's been carrying my ass for the past three months. I've been short tempered and in too foul a mood to even do the minimal of tasks, Dev has taken over all of Royal's endeavors without even as much as asking me for a reason as to why she was picking up the slack. I've missed board meetings, arrived late to work, sometimes not at all, and still, she never said a thing. Never asked for reason or justification. Of course, she came in here looking for one today. If she thought I had my head on straight enough to get my dick wet, then it should be sufficient for my obligations at Royal as well. I pinch the bridge of my nose, trying to stop my never-ending migraine from increasing further, but the guilt just won't let up.

"I'm sorry, Devina. That was insensitive of me. You don't deserve my abuse. You deserve my gratitude for keeping the ship afloat, while I've been slowly drowning in my own self-pity. I'll try and be more considerate next time," I tell her in earnest.

"Fuck," Devina exhales, slumping down into the couch, defeated. "I guess I'm sorry, too. I am upset. You were right; something did crawl up my ass this morning." She shrugs as if she's trying to lift the whole world off her shoulders. "My best friend just handed me her two weeks' notice."

"You mean Vanderwalt?" I ask, feeling a bit saddened at this new turn of events. "I thought you two were friends."

"We're more than friends, Knox. Edie's my family."

"And she still quit?"

"Yep. She's moving to California. Got a job at a

big-shot movie studio in Hollywood. Not only am I going to lose my right hand at work, but my right hand at life, too," she mumbles.

"Shit. That's a big hit, Devina. Vanderwalt was one of the best PA's I've seen in ages, and that doesn't count for her being able to put up with you every day. She'll be hard to replace." Devina scrunches her eyes at me as if it's taking everything in her power not to get out of her seat and smack me upside the head.

"She's *irreplaceable*, Dean," she spits out.

I get her frustration. If either Bash or Con left me in a blink of an eye like Vanderwalt is doing to Devina, I might be in a piss-poor mood, too. Still, I wasn't bullshitting when I said I thought the demure assistant was invaluable to Dev. She kept her grounded and supported. She is the balance Devina needs at times, and she is a valuable asset, one I would hate to lose.

I look at the platinum blonde sitting on my leather couch, and see in her the second queen in my life; although her blood runs ice-cold, I see how it thaws in sorrow at the impending departure of a dear friend.

"Is there nothing you can do? Any way you can change her mind?" I ask, for purely selfish reasons. Devina without Vanderwalt will be even more of a nightmare.

"There is, but in doing so, I would be betraying her confidence. So my hands are tied. She's my friend, first and foremost. I couldn't, in good conscience, stoop so low and break my word. I want her to be happy. She thinks California might be the way, but I worry she's running away."

"Running from what?" I ask, and Devina looks intently at me, with words that want to break free from her lips but remain trapped between her gritted teeth. Something inside me raises a small alarm—a heightened awareness that whatever Devina is holding back, it's crucial I be made aware of it.

"Devina?" I ask, feeling anxious and restless for her to tell me once and for all. There is a pregnant pause where I think she'll spit up what she's hiding, but then just as quickly as my suspicions arise, she shakes her head dismissively, making the decision not to pursue this conversation any longer.

"It's nothing," she replies, and gets up from her seat, walking straight to the door. "Meet you in twenty," she barks back, but at least this time doesn't slam the door behind her.

Well, what the fuck was that?

Has everyone in a two-mile radius of me lost their damned minds? Or am I the one who no longer deals with a full deck of cards?

Shit is getting tiring. Or maybe I'm the one who's fucking tired. I place my palms on my eyes, pressing them down enough to ease some of the tension I feel building up. These past three months have been shitshow after shitshow. Nothing seems right anymore. Problem after problem, ordeal after ordeal, and me with zero fucking patience to fix any of it. I tell myself that I'm overworked, or juggling too many things at once. But as we've established, Devina's the real one who should be complaining, not me.

It's total bullshit. Work is as it always has been—demanding as hell, which is nothing new. Having too much on my plate is a daily occurrence I used to live for. I used to like my life exactly how it was, with all its trials and tribulations, because I thrived on it.

Then *she* came into my life, and it was as if someone had turned the lights on in a vacant, dark room. Because this was what I was before she made her grand appearance. Nothing but a barren wasteland.

Royal was my life. I ate, drank, and slept the magazine. My happiness was an afterthought, especially when I deluded myself into thinking that Royal's increasing success was the synonym to my happiness. It wasn't, and I was a fool to think so. Happiness was waking up in the middle of the night to summer-sky eyes filled with glistening crystals. Joy was running my fingers through liquid gold hair. I discovered my fucking bliss parting two plump, sweet lips with mine and taking hostage each moan that escaped from her mouth. Royal didn't even come close to the inner peace I felt when Edwina laid safely in my arms, fast asleep.

Once you've seen what your life should always

look like, going back is not an option. The kicker, though, is my Queen flew away from my life much the same way that she entered it. She didn't even give me the option to choose. If she had, I would have always chosen her.

I believed my destiny was entwined with Royal. My one goal in life was to take the reins of this magazine from my father and build it to higher expectations than anyone could even conceive. Shakespeare had it right, 'I am fortune's fool.' Edwina was my destiny, and somehow I had let it slip away.

Nothing held any meaning.

"You ready?" Bash says, knocking on my door, pulling me out of my troubled thoughts.

"What? Oh, right. The staff meeting with Sam," I reply, clearing my throat, so he doesn't pick up how far from ready I am.

"Right. Well, come on, then," he ushers me to get my ass up. Might as well get it over with, since she's been less than pleased with how I've been handling things, too. No doubt more because now she no longer has an ally in weathering Devina's storms.

When we get there, I see the room is still empty, save for Miss Vanderwalt, who is placing memos at each seat.

As I pass by, she lets the papers fall to her feet and puffs out, annoyed that the memos are now decorating the floor, instead of their respective places on top of the table. She hurries along to pick everything up, but at this rate, everyone will have arrived, and Miss Vanderwalt will still be on her hands and knees picking up after herself. I take a breath and kneel down to help.

"Oh, you don't have to," she rushes out, but I'm already gathering everything in front of me.

"It's fine, Miss Vanderwalt. A little crease on my pants won't make me look any less authoritative," I say to ease her awkwardness. The girl is jittery all over, and I don't think I've ever seen her so troubled. Probably has to do with her recent decision in resigning.

"Is everything alright?" I find myself asking, wondering what possessed me to query an employee regarding their welfare, even one as valuable as the modest assistant.

"Hmm, yes. Everything is fine Mr. Knox," she whispers again, and my cock wakes up suddenly from its winter hibernation.

Now I'm the one that's bothered by my body's reaction to her hushed tone. It felt familiar somehow. Only Edwina has ever been able to rise my eager cock from his slumber with just her voice. A pain grips my heart at recalling my sweet pet when I haven't put eyes on her since the day she left a gaping hole in my heart.

Maybe that's why my dick is having this reaction to the conservative girl in front of me. Her demure eyes, behind those thick glasses, remind me so much of my innocent Beauty. Even when she's doing everything in her power to keep her head held low, hurrying to grab each piece of paper off the ground, I can't help but think how uncanny the resemblance between the two is.

The same innocent blue swims in her eyes, the same red flush kisses her cheeks when she's embarrassed, the same creamy soft skin runs down her throat. Before I even realize how inappropriate I'm acting, my eyes trail lower, to the small opening of her blouse. Laced white bra covers ample creamy-skinned soft breasts, and my mouth starts to water.

My hands fall to the side of me in fists as I close my eyes, preventing myself from seeking any other feature of the woman before me. I stand up from the floor and walk out of the room without another look back. The minute I get back to my office, I pour myself a shot of the finest whiskey money can buy and down it like Fiji water.

Why do I feel like I'm being disloyal to Edwina for my body's natural reaction to a beautiful woman? How am I to know she is not doing so much worse? The mere idea some other man is touching what's mine is grabbing my windpipes and suffocating me.

Why did she leave me?

She told me once she was a coward, but I knew in

my heart that was a lie. Could it have been fear that drove her away from my arms? I'm fucking angry, horny, and in desperate need of some answers.

"It's not even ten, Dean. A little early, don't you think?" I hear Bash behind me, closing my office door and blinds, so my employees don't see their boss having a fucking meltdown.

"I'm sure it's happy hour somewhere," I groan, pouring another shot.

"You need to calm down. What happened back there anyway?" Bash asks inquisitively, but if I didn't know any better, I'd swear my best friend could read every dirty thought written on my forehead the minute my cock had come alive.

"Nothing. I wasn't feeling it, that's all," I play off as if my little fit was provoked merely by boredom, and not induced by my own sexual frustration.

Instead of sitting behind my desk, I choose the couch instead, hoping to relax my pent-up rage, as well as the unused muscles that taunt me now.

"So I gather you haven't had any luck with your Beauty, either. Still no word, I presume," Bash queries, leaning against the door, arms crossed against his chest.

"Nothing. Not a fucking trace of her. I have the best detectives in all New York City canvassing for just a clue of who she is and where I can find her, and the incompetent assholes have brought me absolutely nothing in three whole months. I have bullied, manipulated, raised hell on After Hours for them to reveal her true identity to me, yet those fuckers refuse to even to give me the name of her handler. Edwina just disappeared. Vanished into thin air. Poof!" I dramatize, taking another pull of my drink.

"No one just disappears, Dean. When she's ready, she'll come out of hiding, and if she wants to see you, she'll come find you. You said so yourself, she's seen your face and knows where you live, so when she's ready, she'll know how to reach you," Bash says with such conviction in his voice, I almost will myself to believe in his blind faith.

"You weren't there the day she left me," I murmur under my breath, not wanting to remember it myself. But most days it's all I can do—play back that awful day over and over again, hoping it can provide me some clue as to what she was thinking, what was going through her mind. Because to come to the bitter reasoning that I fell in love with someone who didn't love me back is just too painful for me to come to terms with just yet. Maybe one day, when I'm braver, less broken and raw, I might be able to grasp such a notion.

But not today.

And not tomorrow.

Not while my heart still has her name branded on it. Tattooed on my very soul.

Not yet.

"I see today is an *off* day for you. If I wanted a temper tantrum, I'd have gone to see Dev instead. I'll pick you up in a couple of hours so we can head to Luigi's. If you insist on drinking the day away, you'll need some food in you, too." He smirks, knocking on my door frame before opening it.

"Bash, tread lightly with Devina today, alright? She's on the warpath as it is, so don't give her any shit," I tell him, leaning my head against the couch headrest, closing my eyes and praying this day would end already.

I know tomorrow I'll have a repeat of this gray existence, but if I make it just one more day, I know I've survived this one at least. I'll deal with tomorrow when it gets here.

"Oh, yeah? What did Con do now?" Bash turns to ask before he leaves me to my peace—as if I'll ever be able to find that shit again.

"Not Con. Vanderwalt. She quit this morning. Gave Dev her two weeks' notice."

For a minute I think Bash has either already left, or maybe didn't hear me, but when I open my eyes, I see my best friend under the threshold of my office door, standing oddly still.

"That's a tough loss. She was one of a kind," he

finally remarks, lancing another quick look my way before departing for good.

"The good ones always are," I whisper.

Chapter 25

DEAN

I walk past the conference room and see, yet again, a disheartened Edie Vanderwalt on her hands and knees, picking up a fresh batch of documents that she must have spilled on the floor.

Poor thing took the job in California, yet she's obviously miserable in her decision. I should have a word with her and stop her from going. It will make Devina happy, and in the end, it will make her happy; and I, for one, need a bit of that elusive feeling in my life somehow. Might as well start with the young Miss Vanderwalt.

The moment I step into the room, I hear her silent weeping and my chest starts to sting, an oddity which I'm unused to since I'm not exactly the most empathetic of people. I guess her discomfort and sorrow perturb me more than I realize. Maybe it's because the young assistant was kind enough to console me in my own moment of weakness last Christmas, and somehow I've found a soft spot for her now. That must be the reason.

I chide myself for not having done this sooner and spare her this grief. If she's taken this new job because the pay is better, or the job prospects are more appealing, then I'll just double what they're offering and give the woman what she wants. She's earned her stripes anyway, for putting up with Devina as long as she has. I wager her replacement won't last the month anyway.

Still, too inside her head, the blonde beauty doesn't even register me kneeling beside her to help in her endeavor. I lightly grab her elbow to get her attention, when the next thing I see is one small fist smack me right in the eye with all the force it contains, startling me and keeling my ass over right onto the ground.

"JESUS CHRIST!" she yells, and I'm still trying to wrap my head around what the fuck just happened.

"Did you just punch me?" I ask rubbing my soon-to-be-swollen eye.

"Yes! Yes, I did! I told you not to sneak up on me like that!" she continues to shout while grabbing her chest, trying to control the speeding train within.

"I can't believe you hit me. The first time anyone has ever dared, and you're the one to do it." I laugh, thinking about every fight I've ever been in, and not one single opponent, big or small, was ever quick enough to lay a hand on me before I knocked them out cold. And here was this sweet, unassuming woman, with a killer right hook to knock me on my ass.

Will wonders never cease? And what started out as a small chuckle transforms into a deep belly laugh, which I thought I was incapable of ever accomplishing again.

Suddenly a distant memory whispers in my ear of another night that I startled an unsuspecting blonde, and her reaction. I look at the woman before me and blink twice, thinking I must be seeing a mirage, but the soft hue of her cheeks from my constant glare tells me I'm not. My laugh is not the only thing which has been revived this morning in this conference room. Unexpectedly, I feel my broken heart wanting to piece itself together so it can begin to beat and surrender to its true owner.

"Edwina?" I call out, never taking my eyes off her, and she freezes in place, closing her eyes.

"Edie?" I say the diminutive instead, playing her name on my lips, but still too flabbergasted to say anything else. She scrunches her eyelids tight as if in pain, and certainty runs through me.

"Edwina?!" I croak, throat parched and dry. "Edwina? Is it really you?"

She slumps her shoulders, defeated, hugging her ankles together at her side with her hands.

"I really do hate that name, but every time I hear you say it, you make it sound beautiful. Even to me," she whispers, and it's cupid's bow slicing up my still-mending heart.

"That's because it is. It belongs to the woman I

love," I declare without inhibition and restraint.

"Don't," she hushes, her eyes still cast low, and I curse below my breath because I want to see her face.

I've been denied it for too long, and yet I've seen it every single day for the most part of the last two years.

I'm a fool. A damned fool.

I'm about to say as much when other voices interrupt my own. There is banter in the room, and when I look up, I see staff members coming into the conference room, taking their seats, and Devina and my two best friends are amongst them.

"Everyone out," I say softly, still too stunned for my vocal cords to work properly, and my eyes not wanting to let Edwina out of their sight for even a moment.

Edwina continues to sit frozen on the floor, and I see her start to tremble with fear, and maybe embarrassment, for anyone to catch her in this state.

Shit!

That is not what I want, but I'm unable to hold myself back from the earth-shattering growl I make next.

"I said everyone GET THE FUCK OUT!"

"What the fuck?!" Connor yelps.

"Con, Bash, I want everybody out of this room, now! Lock the door on your way out, and under no circumstances are Miss Vanderwalt and I to be disturbed. I don't care if the fucking building is on fire, no interruptions of any kind. If anyone even so much as breathes against that door, I want them fired! Am I clear?" I bellow, now on my feet, trying my best to hide Edwina from the gawking crowd.

"Crystal," Bash says, giving me a nod and starting to usher people along. Connor's face is marred in confusion, while Devina looks like she's about to implode.

"You heard the man, Dev. Let's go," Bash says, giving a gentle nudge to the stubborn, unmoving woman. She tries to have one last look at her shaken friend, but my natural instinct shields Edwina even from her heartfelt gaze. She lifts her sight to me with pure disdain, pointing a menacing finger at my head.

"Knox, if you hurt her in any way, I will end you. It will be the very last thing you ever do. Do *I* make myself clear?" she threatens, and my lip lifts of its own accord.

I have no doubt Devina Richardson would carve my heart out with a blunt knife herself, cut it into tiny little pieces, and feed it to the hounds of hell that she must keep as pets.

"Crystal," I mimic Bash's words.

She doesn't say another word, simply cuts her eyes at me, and pushes her way past Con and Bash like the natural disaster that she is, about to wreak havoc somewhere else with her current rage. Bash places his arm over a puzzled Connor's shoulder, leading him out the door. Once he certifies everyone has left, he lowers the window blinds shut, giving us the privacy we need.

"Thank you," I tell him, before he, too, makes his retreat. He gives me a nod but then looks over his shoulder with a smug grin decorating his face.

"I knew you were going to keep her." He winks and then closes the door.

I almost chuckle at his remark; I would if I didn't feel so insecure about the actual chances of my success. I absolutely intend to keep Edwina, but I just don't know if she'll let me. My eyes fall down to the shrinking woman who holds my heart in her hands, and I vow at this moment to never let her feel she needs to hide herself from me ever again.

I bend down, placing my arm beneath her legs and the other steady at her back, and lift her to sit on top of the conference table. She lets out a small shriek from the unexpected movement but makes no other resistance. Any other time, I'd laugh at her little squeal, but touching her skin again, smelling her jasmine perfume around me, overwhelms me too much for any such laughter to take place. My basic instinct is to part her legs and fit myself in between her, but I fear the move too bold for my skittish love. Instead, I place one finger under her chin, commanding her to raise her head high, like the true queen I know her to be. Her dark-framed glasses are a blurry mess, concealing her star-filled eyes; a grave injustice I rectify immediately. I take them off and start to wipe them clean on my pocket square. Quiet as can be, I feel her eyes transfixed by my every move, cautious about what I'll do next.

Once I make sure her glasses are clear of any tear stains, I take a deep breath and fix my eyes back on her. This time, there are no masks hiding her face. No made-up personas or professional attire to throw me off her scent. Nothing will ever be hidden from me again. Her face is blotchy and tear-stricken, her eyes still watery with unshed tears she's trying hard to contain. Her plump lips are a natural shade of red, and inviting mine to enjoy. Long lashes that have been hiding those bright diamonds in her blue eyes for far too long, and a curious brow that rises every time she's perplexed and needs enlightenment, as it is now.

My beautiful Queen, under my very nose this whole time, was walking the halls amongst peasants and paupers, making us none the wiser. Her true beauty making a mockery of us all, by showing how ignorant we are to identify such a rare thing when it's not blatantly slapped across our faces. Because hers doesn't need to be loud for everyone's eye to behold. Hers is more than skin deep, so only the patient and the strong-willed are privileged to ever see its grace.

"Are you going to give those back?" she finally asks, breaking the silence and my train of thought.

"What?"

"My glasses? I can't see without them," she explains. "I… umm… used lenses at… well, you know," she adds nervously, biting her lower lip. When I see her teeth nibble the piece of flesh, another dart shoots through my heart.

Edwina.

My Edwina.

Fuck, I missed you!

"Of course," I say plainly, trying to control my voice as best I can. I return the glasses back to their rightful home, loving how her soft, silky hair feels over my knuckles, and retreat my unsteady hands behind my back slowly.

The silence between us is deafening, but the words lodged in my throat are just as dangerous. We can't seem to look away from each other, yet both of us are not ready for this dance to begin. But someone needs to take the first step, no matter how frightened we are of how this ballad may play out or the consequences that may follow.

"You're leaving," I deadpan, cutting the first cord.

"I have to." She nods solemnly.

"Why?" I ask incredulously.

"It's too hard to stay." She shrugs.

"You need to do better than that, Edwina. Why is it hard for you to stay? Give me a valid reason why you need to put twenty-five hundred miles between us?" I interject, my tone sounding as bitter as the thought of her even considering such a ridiculous idea.

"What do you want me to say?"

"The truth would be nice, for once," I reply, and regret it the minute her face starts to pale, and the waterfall she so bravely tried to contain begins to rupture, one tear at a time.

"Fuck!" I immediately part her legs open, placing myself at her center and hugging her toward me.

"I'm sorry, pet. I didn't mean it. I'm so sorry," I coo, running my fingers through her lush hair, cradling the small of her back to me tighter, so there is no space between us. She wraps her legs around my waist, her arms hugging my shoulders for dear life, and her face at the crook of my neck. I feel her breath on my sensitive, overheating skin, and her tears cooling it down.

"I don't want to go, but I can't stay, either. It'll kill me," she hiccups.

She's the one who'll murder me if she keeps this up. I can't stand to see her suffering, and she is. My love is fucking bleeding out before me, and I'm not sure if I'm able to stop this wound from festering.

"Tell me why, pet."

"You'll move on. Forget me. Forget *her*. I don't know what hurts more—knowing that maybe it might take you a couple of months to forget Beauty, or when Edie leaves, when *I* leave Royal, you won't think of me ever again."

"Oh fuck, pet!" I grab hold of her tighter.

The misery in her voice is pure torture, and I find myself struggling for air. Still, I fight it because she needs me to be strong, to hold her up when she's at her most volatile, most vulnerable. I let her get all her tears out of the way, my own emotions on edge, but God must take pity on me, and gives me enough strength to keep them at bay.

"I know this doesn't justify it, but you never made it easy for me either, pet, to see you. The real you, I mean. You always hid behind those frumpy clothes and librarian glasses, and I know it's not an excuse, but I guess I just never took the time to give you my full attention, because you didn't seem to want it in the first place," I whisper in her ear.

She shrugs in misery, and I bite my tongue, hating that my words brought her added pain.

"What I mean, Edwina, is you never went out of your way to make yourself known to me, either, aside from Beauty. So I guess, even if you had tried later on, it would have been too late. Love had me blind by then," I try to explain, hoping the second time around I'm able to make my idea clearer.

She pulls back just a little bit, enough for me to see that, while I only suffered these past months from being without her, my Queen had been suffering long before that.

"What does that mean, Dean? Love blinded you?"

"Are you as clueless as I have been, my pet? Don't you know by now that you have my heart, my very fucking soul in your hands? Don't you know I love you, Edie Vanderwalt?"

She scrunches her eyes shut, and I focus on each breath she takes.

"Say it again," she pleads.

"Which part, pet?"

"All of it. I want to hear you say you love me until I believe it," she discloses, and it twists a knife in my gut.

"Is that why you left me, Edwina? Is that the true reason why you were going to leave Royal and move all the way to California—because you don't believe I love you?" I ask, incredulous.

"Yes," the love of my life reveals. "How could Dean Knox ever love someone like me?" she remarks with so much certainty that I'm beginning to think I'm not the only one in this room who's been blind.

I place both hands tenderly on her wet cheeks and lean my temple lovingly to hers.

"How could I not? When you are all I have ever wanted. All I ever dreamed of before I even knew I could wish for such things. Don't leave me now. Not when I just found you," I beg.

Yes—beg.

Because for this woman, I would crawl on hands and knees for her to have me, but for now, all I need is for my words to resonate into her heart.

Please hear me.

Listen to me.

Believe me, Edwina.

She pulls her head back, slicing my insides with her rejection of both my words and my touch. Yet her legs are still wrapped around my waist, so I make no sudden moves to alert her of this fact, in case she decides to take them away from me, too. I do, however, lower my hands from her face and place them palm down on the table at her sides, giving her the space she obviously wants.

"Don't you see? You were right the first time. I have lied to you. *This* is all a lie. You don't love me. You can't! You love the idea of a lie I created," she retorts, putting salt to her open wound, insisting this to be the only conceivable scenario in which I could have fallen in love with her. That I was duped somehow. Tricked into it. I'd laugh if it didn't hurt so much.

"Don't say that."

"But it's true," she retorts, just as empty.

"Okay. Enough of this!" I break, gripping her arms, so she knows I'm up to my limit. "You've said your piece, Edwina. Now you damned well are going to hear mine. I fell in love with the woman who held me at night with all her might, afraid I would disappear. Was she a lie?" I bark.

"No."

"I fell in love with the young woman who looked at me and didn't see dollar bills or a man in an expensive suit, but a man made of flesh and bone, full of fears and doubts. Was that a lie?"

"No," she replies sheepishly.

"And I fell in love with a girl who made me laugh and made me want to do better, be better. Was that a lie, Edwina? Tell me, does that woman exist?"

"Yes, she exists," she replies, and it's the first time I see a small sparkle of light reach her diamond-filled eyes.

"Then don't tell me that I don't love you, because all I do *is* love you, and I can't stop," I tell her, laying it out for her to see there is no going back for me.

I feel her resolve starting to break, and the last burst of its power makes her shake her head in denial.

"You don't want me, Dean. I'm not the woman you should have by your side. You deserve more than me. You deserve it all," she mumbles.

"Now it's your turn to say it again," I order.

She looks at me, perplexed, and I understand why. She thinks her reason is what I want to hear; but far from it.

"My name, pet. Say my name again," I say, pulling the soft strand of unruly hair that has pulled itself free from its confined bun.

"Dean," she whispers, and both my heart and cock make a standing ovation for this moment.

I take her two hands in mine and kiss them softly. I place one of them on my eager cock so she can feel how it wants to worship her.

"Just you saying my name makes me hard all over, pet," I tell her, and the absent blush to her cheeks quickly returns. Then I take her other hand and place it on my heart.

"But the word coming out of your lips has a far more dangerous effect on my heart," I confess, and let her feel how the organ within my chest drums hysterically.

"I'm in love with a woman who knows my name, who knows everything about me, and yet doesn't believe me when I tell her I am lost without her. Do you know how frustrating it is for the love of your life to reject you in such a way?"

She starts to cower her head, but I put an end to that shit fast, by halting the move and gripping her chin lightly.

"No more hiding, Edwina. I need your truth, and I need you to look me in the eye as you say it. Do you love me?" I ask, my panicked heart dreading it won't survive the damage this time around if she doesn't.

"Until my dying day," she replies strongly. "Yes, Dean, I love you with all my heart."

My blood rises, the ringing in my ears so intense, I think I've lost the ability to hear anything else but her sweet melodic words on repeat for a minute. But I can't celebrate yet. Not until we settle this once and for all.

"Are you mine, pet?"

"Yes."

"But do *you* want *me*? I'm offering you all of me, Edwina. Every ugly, shameful, dirty piece of me. You already have my heart, body, and soul. They are yours regardless if you keep them or not. All I want to know is am *I* yours, pet?"

Her tears start to fall again, but this time her smile blossoms, too, accompanied by her nod.

"I want you so much, Dean! I love you so much!" She cries, breaking the reserves of my faint control. Unable to stand being away from her any longer, I kiss her as if my life depended on it to survive.

And it does.

It so fucking does.

We've just made peace with each other, yet our mouths and tongues are at war, seeing who can give more to the other. Grinding together perfectly in tune to each other's needs, as though they, too, were cut from the same cloth.

"Edwina," I sing into her mouth, one grip solidly holding the nape of her neck while the other grabbing her ass cheek to get her closer to me.

"Dean, call me Edie. Only my mom calls Edwina," she moans, biting my lip, devouring me with her killer kiss.

"Then, Edie, that's the name I'll call out when I'm fucking you raw on this table. And you, pet, best call me by my name, so everyone in this office hears who you belong to!"

"Oh, God!" she sighs, as I start rubbing my cock against her swollen clit.

"Wrong name, my love. Let's try that again, shall we?" I retort as I split her blouse in two, buttons flying everywhere.

"Dean!" she screams out, indignant.

"Much better," I smirk, appraising her heaving chest.

"You ruined it. How do you expect me to leave this room?" she rambles, arching an accusing brow.

"I expect you to leave here thoroughly fucked, my love," I shoot back.

"You're incorrigible," she smiles, taking a page from my playbook, tearing the Armani shirt off my body like cotton candy.

"Yes, but I'm also yours," I tell her desperately.

"Yes, Dean. You are," she admits pulling me in for a new divine kiss.

She cages me against her, pulling the zipper from my pants at the same time she entices me with her tongue. My hands are rampantly wanting all of her at once, but one will have to sacrifice itself to keep her safe and steady at all times, while the other enjoys the wonders of her body. The minute I feel soft, gentle fingers stroke my destitute, engorged cock, I almost cum right there.

"Shit, Edie! Fuck, I missed you so much! I'm sorry, my Queen, I promise to make it up to you for the rest of my life if I have to, but if I don't get into you right now, I think I might lose it," I confess.

This desperation is beyond my control, and to anyone else, I would have never admitted such a weakness. This reunion is going to be hard, quick, and dirty. It's been too long for it not to be. But I'll make our second round nice and sweet for my love, and have her cumming on my tongue until she's lost all motor skills. But right now, I need her too much for such diversions. She lifts herself off the desk and hikes up her skirt, just as manic, and I rip her panties apart as the animal in me has finally taken over.

"I actually liked those," she giggles, removing what remains of her blouse, followed by her white lacy bra. I'm greeted with two perky nipples applauding my return, too tempting not to lavish with some affection of my own.

"Dean," she moans, running her fingers through my hair, her wet, glistening core seeking its counterpart. When the two naked parts collide, I freeze motionless.

Shit!

Shit!

"What's wrong?" she asks breathlessly.

I settle my forehead to her chest, kissing her pure heart and praying she forgives my one indiscretion.

"I don't have a condom with me, Edie," I muster, and feel her grow stiff under me.

"That never bothered you before," she utters, confusion and worry tainting each word. I lift my head, putting my chin between my two favorite pillows to look at my black-rimmed, spectacled love.

"I might have a small confession of my own to make. The first night we spent together was the first time I ever slept with a woman without one. I knew After Hours was anal with their birth control policies, and so I knew you were either on the pill or had on a depo shot. . And to get in, you had to pass all their tests, so I knew you were clean. So when you told me you were a virgin, the idea of firsts was too tempting for me not to have one of my own," I confess my own dirty little secret.

"So I was your first, too, that night?" she asks, her body starting to relax.

"You are my only, Edie. I haven't been with anyone since you left me on New Year's Day. The only time I have stepped foot in that club since that night was to threaten to burn it to the ground if they didn't tell me how I could find you."

"What about that Austrian model, Aylin-what's-her-face?" she asks, trying to hide her cute little pout.

"Publicity stunt. The girl was wasted on St. Patty's, grabbing everything she could, not to fall on her ass. Paparazzi caught me holding her up after one nasty spill. I'm sure I wasn't the only one who helped her off the floor that night, but I was probably the most appealing man for her publicist to use and launch a fake headline to boost her career."

"Oh."

"But I understand if you want to take this slow. I'll do anything you want, Edie. I'm burning for you, pet, but this time, you're the one who has to take the lead," I tell her.

She pushes my shoulders up, so I'm now leaning above her. She offers me her hands to pull her up, and I obey dutifully. She keeps her legs wrapped around me and starts gently stroking my chest, admiring my chiseled form, making up for lost time.

"I don't want any more lies between us, Dean," she starts to say, then leans forward, delivering the sweetest of kisses. I abandon all thought and just treasure the sugariness of her lips, but then my bliss increases tenfold when her gentle grip leads me to its home.

"I don't want anything ever between us again," she says with a high-pitched sigh.

"Edie!" I bite her shoulder, leaving my mark on her skin as much as I want to brand her very soul.

"I love you," she moans, kissing my neck, straddling me as if I'm her prized stallion.

"I fucking worship you, Edie Vanderwalt! You're everything to me!" I roar, unable to contain the violent tempo of our love.

For every merciless thrust of the hip I give her, she reciprocates with twice the passion and zeal. I've just barely kissed heaven, and I'm about to keel over like some chump. I blame the vows and the declarations of love this perfect woman—who is just as ravenous to swallow me whole as I am to possess every inch of her—has made.

Who needs foreplay when the one you want most offers her heart willingly and devoutly, for you to protect and nourish? That shit will get you hard and ready to cum the minute you kiss, let alone touch.

"Dean!" she yells, clenching around my pounding cock, her own pussy in agreement with my thoughts.

"Louder, Edie! I want this whole building to hear you claim what's yours because I'm going to make sure every fucker knows that you are mine!" I howl, straining her core, hitting that one wall I know will set her over the edge and release fireworks above us.

She's on the cusp of exploding, with me right behind her. I make sure my next thrusts rub her tender clit just right...

"DEAN!"

"I FUCKING LOVE YOU, EDIE!" I yell, giving her the last remaining pieces of my very being.

Energy is pulsing beneath my skin, my chest against hers, our hearts beating so fast they feel they might leap out altogether just to meet each other halfway. Unwavering love and extreme reverence are all I have left right now, as I fall down on the table above my sweet, sweet Edie. I'm not sure how long we stayed this way, but I'm too content to make a move.

I thought I would die of misery when she left me, but now my heart is so full, I'm afraid it's impossible for one person to carry this much happiness in it and not burst.

What a lovely way to go.

I lift my head to look at my would-be assassin, and her killer smile does me in. When she begins to giggle, I can't help but offer her one of my own.

"Well, I guess the cat's out of the bag now. If we wanted to hide this for a little longer, we just blew our shot," she says, tracing her fingers over my brows.

"I don't care. You've stayed hidden long enough. I'm not hiding my feelings for you," I tell her matter-of-factly.

"How long do you think we should wait before we leave?" she asks.

"I have nowhere else I want to be other than here. Until every square inch of this room has been used by the two of us, I'm not going anywhere."

"Oh." She giggles again.

"There are eighteen chairs in this room, two cabinets, three sofas, and that spectacular view that will look amazing when I'm fucking you from behind. And let's not forget the advantages of that skin rug in the corner. So we're going to be here a while." I tease, kissing her neck, leaving out how I also intend to fuck her standing up against each wall and door of this room. I'll leave that as a surprise.

"Hmm, I see. That's quite the inventory, Mr. Knox."

"Yes, it is. Do you think you're up for the challenge, Miss Vanderwalt, of verifying whether my inventory is accurate?" I goad, feeling my cock and heart ready for anything this woman desires.

"I'm ready for everything, Mr. Knox," she replies lovingly, the underlying meaning clear in her eyes.

"Glad to hear it." I kiss her pure heart one more

time and whisper that I will never let it escape from my hold ever again. I have it under lock and key, just as my love has mine.

I stand up and take a moment to look at my Queen, my Beauty—my Edie, in all her afterglow glory. I've never depended on luck to get what I wanted in life. I worked hard for everything I have. But somehow, luck found me anyway. Because that is exactly how I feel—like the luckiest son-of-a-bitch out there. To have this woman, from this day on, is nothing short of miraculous. And I will keep her and make sure she never finds a fault in me to ever cause her to let me go again.

I pull her by her legs to get her right where I want her to be, and instead of lifting the rest of her skirt up to her waist, I rip that motherfucker off her, too. She just rolls her eyes, but the wide grin on her face hasn't left yet. Not one piece of clothing, aside from the bra, which she took off herself, is intact. I cock my brow and take a knee.

"Now, Miss Vanderwalt, I believe I found you on your knees earlier. We'll have to revisit that scenario in a moment, but first things first. I believe ladies go first, yes?"

Epilogue I

EDIE

I owe you guys an apology.

When we first met, I told you I was no one.

With everything that's happened and all the lies I told, I think this was probably my very first one.

I'm sorry I deceived you, but at the time, I really believed it.

But I was always someone to someone, wasn't I?

A single mother's daughter; her most cherished accomplishment in life.

A protected younger sister, to a fearless woman who would take on the very world to see her smile.

An adored friend, by the most devoted of roommates a girl could ever ask for.

I was all of this long before I ever entered the After Hours club.

But there I became someone, too.

I was a Lady.

A Pet.

A Beauty.

And finally, I became someone's Queen.

I became all of this, yet I've never been so happy in my life in just being me.

Edwina.

Edie.

It took a King to make me feel like a Queen, but it only took the love of a good man to remind me I'm so much more valuable than any crown on my head.

Because I am somebody's someone.

I'm his.

But most importantly, he's mine.

And he's never going to let me forget it.

So I guess my life doesn't suck after all.

My wildest fantasy is now my current reality, and I have to pinch myself to make sure I'm not dreaming.

Life couldn't get any better than this, now could it?

Epilogue II

CONNOR

"I can't believe this is actually happening. He fucking proposed," I utter under my breath as I swipe another champagne flute from the passing waiter. Not even the bubbly drink can wash away the bitter taste in my mouth.

"Believe it, Con, and for fuck's sake, at least pretend you're happy for him. You've been pouting all night. Dean told us he was going to do it two weeks ago. Why the hell are you having a bitch fit now?" Bash castigates with his best scolding look.

Yeah, like that shit scares me.

"I'm just still in shock, that's all. I thought he was just thinking about it. Thinking and actually popping the question are two very distinct things," I grunt, fixing my bow tie.

If I didn't make this tuxedo look good, I'd sue their asses for making this shit too tight. But ties are for work, and bow ties are for play. Only this engagement party is not my idea of a fun time. A threesome with the two brunettes in the corner checking me out like I'm on the menu for tonight's dessert is my idea of fun. My best friend commemorating getting hitched with a woman he's been in a relationship for a fucking New York minute is my idea of a nightmare.

"Well, you're not supposed to be in shock. He didn't say he was dying from an incurable disease, he just said he loved the girl," Bash reprimands, trying to talk some sense of tact and decorum into me. He's known me for ten years, so he should know by now that I don't give a rat's ass.

"Isn't it the same thing?" I taunt my sophisticated, refined sidekick. If anyone had been asked to point out who was the actual blue-blooded of us, anyone in their right mind would choose Bash over me. They'd be wrong, though. While I was being fed with a silver spoon, my best friend probably didn't have much to eat at all. Still, he's the poised one, while I'm the brash and reckless one of our trio.

"You know it's not. Don't be a dick, and just be supportive like he's always been to you," he deadpans, slapping my shoulder with brotherly affection while kicking me in the nuts with that little remark.

Sophisticated, my ass.

Bash is a cool, calculating prick who knows just which buttons to push to get you to do his bidding. If I didn't love him so much, I'd hate him. I guess with me, there is no in-between emotion. It's always either or. Bash was just lucky he fell on my right side of the fence.

"Fine, asshole. But I still don't like it. I mean, can't he have a long engagement at least? Why the sudden rush? *A month?* Who in their right mind organizes a wedding in a month?"

"Thought about this type of stuff, have you, Con?" he teases back with his trademark smug decorating his face.

"Fuck you, asshole! You do remember I have three sisters, right? I know shit," I counter defensively, finishing my drink.

"Whatever," he goads, taking two new flutes for us to enjoy, knowing full well that alcohol will be the only way I'll be able to deal with tonight. Okay, Bash does have his good qualities, and if he keeps me nice and drunk for the whole event, I'll even swear he's a saint.

"Still think this is too soon to be happening," I tell him, not wanting to let it go.

"Well, when you know, you know, I guess." He shrugs as if he just imparted some sort of well-known fact and not a bunch of malarkey.

"That's bullshit," I affirm, offended that Bash would stoop to such a cliché to make his point.

"Is it really, Con?"

"You're spouting pure naïve fictitious gibberish—a made-up line to be used in bad rom-com movies. If all your life experience on the matter is based on crap like that, then you've just proven exactly why I can't trust your judgment on this subject. You've never been in love, so come back to me with a sane answer when you do," I jab.

"Enlighten me, then. What would a sane person say?" he counters, turning to face me head-on, as serious as this onerous, long night.

"A sane person would tell you to take your head out of your ass first, and then second, tell you what I believe to be true. All I know is that hearts can fuck up. You can think you found the person you were meant to spend your life with, only to find out it's a lie later."

When I see Bash's face turn from his annoyed stance to his concerned one, I instantly regret the image I just put in his mind. Fuck, like this night could get any worse. Having an overprotective Bash is a bigger pain in the ass than an annoyed one.

"I mean, I didn't even know Dean was dating her. Last time I checked, he was still banging the blonde back at the club," I whisper under my breath, just in case any one of the three-hundred guests in attendance might be a Curious Cathy or inclined to eavesdrop on other people's conversations. But of course, my real intention is to get Bash to think of something else than what he was currently picturing.

Bash clears his throat beside me as if he just swallowed a damned bug, and I know I've succeeded with a bang because we've switched to a safer topic. I've known Bash long enough to pick up on all his telltale signs, and when he clears his throat like that, out of the blue, it means he's got something to say but either can't, due to mixed company, or won't because he thinks it's best to keep said info to his discreet self.

Yeah, like that's going to happen on my watch.

"What was that now?" I cock my brow, and Bash places his fist to his temple as if he's getting a migraine. "Time of the month there, sweetheart?" I tease him. "Come on, out with it."

"It's the same girl, asshole. Edie is Beauty, idiot. God, you two morons are fucking clueless without me," Bash rebukes, drinking his fill.

"No fucking way!"

"Way, asshole! Now shut your trap, and for heaven's sake at least pretend to be happy for him. He's been through enough shit as it is. He doesn't need to deal with your tantrums."

"It's not a tantrum. It's a valid concern. He's known her for what? A few months? Back home, Momma would say a wedding this fast would mean there's a bun in the oven. Is Edie cooking something? Because she's been drinking champagne all night, too, so I highly doubt it."

"You keeping tabs on her now?" Bash hushes

menacingly.

"Just watching the happy couple enjoy their night, Sebastian. No harm in that, right?" I mock, patting him on the back.

"Con, listen to me. I know you're hard of hearing and all, but just fucking listen for once—Dean is very territorial of Edie right now."

"No shit," I mumble, gesturing from our elegant and standoffish surroundings to the offensive diamond ring on the finger of the bride-to-be. The obnoxious thing can be seen from the moon, screaming out—*she's taken, so fuck off!*

Dean wanted to make a definite statement with the rock and this engagement party. The expression *shout it out from every rooftop* comes to mind. But when that can't be done, well, just put a one-page announcement in the New York Post; it does the trick of letting the whole world know not to mess with Edie Vanderwalt if you do not intend to make Dean Knox your enemy. And trust me, no one is foolish enough to ever want that.

"Don't be starting shit, and don't get caught looking at the future Mrs. Knox for too long, if you know what's good for you," Bash counsels.

"So the term *bros before hos* is completely out the window, is it?" I tease because Bash is just too easy to mess with.

"Open your eyes, Con, and grow the fuck up. Your *King* was lucky enough to find himself a Queen. Take a knee, little *Prince*. She will always overrule us. As she should."

"Bite me," I tell him, grabbing his champagne and downing it before he's able to. "You're a tiresome prick, Bash, when you act all self-righteous. Think I better find someone else to amuse me."

"Yeah, you do that," he snarls back. "I pity your next victim," he goads with a mocking twist.

When I catch a glimpse of platinum hair sway on the dance floor, I laugh at how right he is. I bypass the crowd to get nearer to my favorite plaything, and when the scent of vanilla hits me, I grind my teeth for two seconds before I cut in on this little dance number of hers.

"Mayor Watson, may I cut in? You've been hogging the maid of honor for some time, and as the best man, I think it's fitting I have a dance of my own, no?" I throw on the best politician-like smile my mother taught me even before I knew how to walk.

"Yes, of course, Mr. Walsh. Please have a go at it," he says, placing Devina's hand in mine. "How's your father, by the way? In Washington, I presume? Give him my regards, will you, son?"

"Of course," I nod and smile at the thinning gray-haired man and return to the woman in my arms.

"You haven't talked to your father in years, Connor. Not since you took the job at Royal, and not the one back in DC that would have probably made you a senator by now," Devina hisses under her breath.

"He doesn't know that. And why trouble Mayor Watson with such tedious details? Now he can go back to his wife and say he talked to the vice president's son. Isn't that so much more interesting? And besides, I still see my father, over the holidays and at mandatory social gatherings; we're just not on speaking terms."

"Well, that's extremely healthy," she adds with a snide tone, rolling her eyes, but keeping pace to the beat of the band's music.

"Like you care, either way, about my health, Dev," I snicker, pulling her just a little bit closer, causing her to stiffen her back in retreat. When she does, I put my hand to the small of her back to keep her in line. "Nuh-uh. Smile for the cameras, Dee," I provoke her further.

"God, you're insufferable," she whines, with her long dark lashes hiding her midnight-blue eyes. It's almost the same color as the sequined, backless dress she has on. Such a stunning color wasted on such an evil heart. The devil shouldn't look like a tempting angel, but you know what they say—fool me once, shame on you; fool me twice, have your fucking head examined!

But the Ice Queen, in this killer dress and even more murderous heels, might be of use to me.

"So you going along with this? I thought you didn't believe in marriage?" I start, to see where she lands on this whole Dean and Edie upcoming-nuptial thing.

"I don't. It's a patriarchal institution that I have no interest in. Any practice that has a woman vow to obey a man for the rest of her life is revolting," she spews, looking bored and unaffected by my presence. Such a bad liar, this little devil.

"You know people can write their own vows. Take that pesky word you hate so much out of the whole equation."

She just shrugs, looking around, pretending to see if there is anyone more interesting in the room than her present company. There's not. She's only fooling herself in feigning otherwise. If I'm in the room, then you bet your bottom dollar all eyes are on me anyway. And with Dee by my side, well... Who can ever compare?

"But for someone so against the concept, I don't see you telling your friend Edie over there to get the hell out of dodge or cool her jets," I say, tilting my head to the bride-to-be.

"That's different."

"Why?"

"Edie's happy. All I ever wanted was for her to be happy, and Dean does that," she says, finally meeting my eyes. It's the first time she lets me take in all of her angelic features. Such a clever illusion to behold, and to the untrained eye and inexperienced heart, just as deadly. The only thing that gives a hint of the devil she truly is, it's her sculpted cupid-bow lips, painted with the deepest of reds.

"And anyway, if he ever breaks her heart, I have a 9 mm Sig at home." She smirks, but a chill runs through me since I'm pretty sure she would use it on my best friend in a heartbeat. Devina would have no qualms about killing a man—either by her own hand or other more creative alternatives.

"I don't doubt how lethal you are, Dee. I've known it for quite some time," I reply sternly.

"I told you not to call me that ever again, Connor. It's the second time you've done so tonight. You're testing me, like usual. God, you really should have gone to DC like your father wanted. Why you took the job at Royal, anyway still baffles me," she groans, turning her face to the side, fake smiling to the people around us, even tilting her head the right way so both of us can get into a shot the event photographer is about to take.

Two peas in a pod.

"Baffling? Really? I would have assumed I had made my intentions abundantly clear about why I joined Royal," I tell her, and then give her a nice, long twirl for the crowd, followed by a deep dip. "You thought you'd be rid of me, but instead, all you did was get me pissed. Now I take joy in your misery any way I can get it, even if it means being in your life forever to watch it firsthand," I whisper in her ear.

I pull her back up to her feet, and there is a little applause around us for the small dance act we've just performed.

"I hate you," she spits under her breath, with the same pearly white smile, before turning her back to me and waltzing away.

"Yeah, Dee, I wish I hated you, too. It'd make my life much easier," I hush, and then shake the ugly sentiment out of me just as fast as it came in.

Because when Bash said that stupid moronic remark about finding the one, it was the devil running away from me that came to mind.

Yeah, I knew what it felt like when you found the *one*. But I also knew that finding the one wasn't entirely a good thing like they paint in the movies.

Nope. Not at all.

Dean chose me to be his best man, only I was his best friend long before this request was ever made, so I'm going to do for him what someone should have done for me—spare him a world of hurt.

Love is poison.

I won't let it destroy him like it almost destroyed me.

I'll stop this wedding from ever taking place.

It's the least a Prince can do for his King.

The End

Author Notes

Hi guys. Yep, it's me again. If you're reading this, that means you took the plunge into something different than what I usually write, and I really appreciate you for it. And I'll share with you a little secret. It was freaking hard. Why was it hard? Well, I found myself wanting Edie to keep all three guys. Yep. I truly did.

The only reason I didn't make this a Reverse Harem novel was because I have Connor and Devina's story so well plotted in my head and am already in love with their story. Therefore, I didn't want to rob them of their happy ending. And even if I did make Edie get all three men, I wouldn't believe that she didn't love her King above the other two, which for me is kind of a deal breaker.

So, even though she did get a taste—hehehe— she got her true love in the end like she was destined for and fought so hard to get (even though Con is being a dick about it but that's for the second book! *wink wink*).

She was always a Queen in my eyes. A goofy, awkward, wonderful mess of awesomeness. Just like most of us. The best kind of Royal.

I look forward, as always, in reading your reviews and letting me know if you enjoyed my brand new labor of love. I really hope you do. At the end of the day, my words of love only have meaning because I get to share them with you.

You guys are making my dreams come true every day, so love will always be laced in every word, every page, and in my heart. Because this is what I feel for all of you and all the support you have shown me in this journey of mine. I don't think I'll ever be able to repay all the affection and kindness you have shown me this year, but I will strive to do so, by giving you my very best, my all, one book at a time.

With lots of love and gratitude,

Ivy

xoxo

Ivy Fox Novels

Contemporary Romance

After Hours Series

The King

The Prince – Coming Soon

The Duke – TBA

The Kingdom – TBA

Reverse Harem

Bad Influence Series

Her Secret

Archangels MC

Room for Three – Coming Soon

Hating You – TBA

Savages – TBA

For more news on upcoming projects, get the inside scoop and sneak peeks by joining my FB Author page here

https://www.facebook.com/IvyFoxAuthor/

Or if you're really naughty and daring, join my closed group

Ivy's Sassy Foxes

The Prince (Preview)

Prologue

Do you remember the first time you fell in love?

How you were walking on cloud nine every time you received a text from him, or you caught a glimpse of him without him realizing it? Or even better, caught him looking at you as if you were the only one for him?

Remember that feeling of utter bliss and contentment? Waking up with a smile on your face, so wide, people thought you were auditioning for the role of the Joker?

Remember that feeling?

Well, if you do, then you also remember the first time someone broke your heart and how it shattered something far more precious than you were willing to give up—your innocence, your naiveté.

Because after that heartbreak nothing hurt you quite the same way ever again.

There's a reason why they say the first love is always the worst. Because it sucks ass to fall from way up high smack down on the concrete floor.

So if you remember that feeling, I think my story will be pretty easy to explain.

My name is Devina Richardson.

I was considered one of the top twenty most influential people in all of New York City this year, and I'm not even thirty yet, and trust me, love had nothing to do with it.

So you're probably wondering how did I get here? All the way to the top at such an early age.

The cynical will say "her daddy" of course, and to those I would nod and agree, but I wouldn't let you leave the room without a big 'fuck you too' from me either. I got here with my brains and *balls*. Yeah, I said balls because you have to have double the size of them to make it as a woman in a man's world. I worked my ass off to earn my spot at Royal, the most prominent magazine there is, and don't you dare to give me any other name that would even compare to our savage 'always on the edge of what's new in fashion' magazine.

Royal is what it is now because of me.

Oh yeah, and my business partner Dean Knox. He pulls his own too. Can't argue there.

It's not him I have an issue with. But I'm getting ahead of myself, I was telling you how I rule as queen B to this royal empire. I have my loyal subjects, of course. I'm not a fool. A person's worth is also told by whom she affiliates herself with and I choose to keep my group small.

Well, maybe very small.

Okay, just the one.

I only trust my best friend, Edie, and that's because not only did we grow up together and love each other like sisters, but also because she's loyal. And I value loyalty above all things. Because you can't buy loyalty. Just like love. You either have it, or you don't. And with Edie, I have both. I can't say that of anyone else in my life. Nor do I want to.

So let's go back to why I started this off talking to you about love when it's probably so obvious to you now—to my way of life that word is as foreign as the designer dress I have on.

I talked about love because, surprisingly enough, that's what molded me into the powerful woman I am today. Oh, sorry, my bad, not love really, but the heartbreak did the job nicely. I took stock of what I could control and chose that over a sentiment as futile as love.

Love does not build a career and get you on the cover of Forbes magazine.

It does not show your father that you are ten times the better CEO he ever was, even if he resents you for not being born male.

Love will not show your enemies you have conquered it all and look mighty fine doing it.

No, the only thing love does is to make you weak. It makes you doubt yourself and crave touch and warmth over cold dollar bills in your bank account. I would rather wear a crown on my head than be a jester for love ever again.

Because I was tricked once.

Just the once, since I vowed to never let myself be fooled into falling in love again.

And I would not even be having this conversation with you if it wasn't for one itsy bitsy little snag in my plan for world domination.

The asshole I had given my heart to, the same one who trampled over it with his designer shoes, is the only thorn at my side because I have to look at his smug-perfect face every single day since I work with the shmuck.

And no, I can't fire him.

I already tried that, but if you think of any other brilliant ideas, keep them coming because I'll take anything at this point.

Connor Walsh.

They call him the Prince of New York, but to

me, he's nothing but what his namesake entails—a con.

He's the eyesore in my perfect life. He's my reminder of the one moment of weakness when I was too young to know any better and too foolish to see that his cocky bright smile lit up more than a room. His swagger and charm got into more panties than a woman like me owns.

Sadly, while I'm the queen of my domain, he's the prince who still haunts me.

Acknowledgments

I always get quite emotional when I get to this part. You've probably realized by now I'm pretty touchy-feely as it is by nature, so of course, when I come to the end of a book, my emotions are pretty raw and out there.

When I think of all the extraordinary people who helped me along the way to get me this far, well it's safe to say my heart is pretty full right now.

I started this book dedicating it to My King.

I usually end all my acknowledgments with him and my kiddo in mind. This time around, I wanted to thank them first. Starting with my partner in crime—my husband. The man who believed in me unquestionably before I even dared to believe in myself. He's my biggest supporter and my rock. He didn't know anything about the world we were embarking on, yet it didn't stop him from stepping up and learning whatever he could to help me reach my dreams. From editing to covers and marketing, he does it all now and is my partner in this new journey in every way. It's easy to write about love when I have him in my life.

You will always be my number one muse.

To the second owner of my heart, my son Sean.

This kiddo has been incredible in his support. He knows when his mom is madly writing up a storm not to bother her, or if she's talking to herself, that's it's normal and not to call anyone to lock her up. He makes sure to remind me to eat dinner when I've skipped lunch and demands at least one hour a day of kiddo-and-mommy time, even if it's just to see old reruns of How I Met Your Mother. He'll always make sure to remind me to take care of me, as I've always taken care of him.

You're my first blessing and my reason.

To all my family and friends, thank you from the bottom of my heart for your never-ending support. I know it's not easy being in my life when I'm such a head case. I have crazy hours, go for days without calling or visiting, but I promise I'll try harder to remedy that. When I get into a book it's life consuming but as I said, I'm never happier than when I'm writing. It's my own happy place.

When people say it takes a village to raise a child, well, the same goes for writing a book. This time around I couldn't have done it if I didn't have some extra help with other bits and bobs.

Thank you to my editor Sandy DaBolt for being able to finish The King. This book hit a few snags editing wise one of which was her computer completely crashing. Committed to the task, though, Sandy was able to purchase one the next day, and for that I thank you!

A huge thanks goes out to my extraordinary Beta, the wonderful Heather Clark. This woman has been with me since the beginning, and I could not see any project I have without her touch. I always get giddy when I send my manuscript to her because I know I will always get her honest opinion and when I get her thumbs up, there is no greater feeling! It means my baby is ready to be launch to the world! NEVER LEAVE ME!!! Hahahahaha.

A big hug to my PA Courtney Dunham, who took care of my foxes and gave them all their daily candy when I was submerged in the world of all things King. I can't thank you enough for taking care of my beautiful ladies so I could focus on my writing. I'm so happy you are part of our little Ivy bandwagon now!

A big thank you to my talented "wonder twin" Victoria Schaefer for incredible teasers she was able to create for The King. Not only are they breathtakingly beautiful but they hold the true essence and vibe that depicted The King perfectly. There is a scene in this book where Edie and Lexi go to an Irish pub, and I describe it as it being rowdy and disorderly—going as far as saying it's familiar to McGinty's in The Boondock Saints. This little gem was put in just for my girl Victoria and our shared love of the cult classic. Visually, I'm unable to create such gorgeous scenarios as you are naturally gifted with designing, but I hope my words do your teasers justice. Love you, hun!

This year I have had the good fortune to have met some amazing authors; peers who have taught me so much and have open their arms welcoming me into this great indie community. I have fangirled over some—won't lie, I'm not the coolest girl in the bunch—and their generosity and altruism have humbled me. If I were to name them all, we'd be here all day. But I do want to give a big shout out to one duo in particular—Riley Walker. Kelly Stephens and especially Amy Naylor have shown me so much love and support, that I will never be able to put into words how much their kindness has meant to me. You two gorgeous women now live in my heart so deal with it!

Biscuit you do wonders for my ego and self-doubt and giving you The King to read in its beta stage, was freaking frightening! But I'm so glad that I did it and so blessed to consider your sassy ass a friend!

And last but not least I want to send a huge hug to all my ladies at Ivy's Sassy Foxes! You lovely ladies are what keep me going when I hit a bump in the road. You are the reason I wake up in the middle of the night to get that last minute scene in or add a new chapter to give you more goodies. You lovely foxes are my best cheerleaders, my loyal readers who have been with me since the very start and I sincerely hope I live up to your expectations and keep giving you love stories that get you hot and bothered but also make you fall a little bit in love, too.

I love you all so very much! You ladies are the ones who hold the crown in my court!

Bringing you one foxy romance at a time

About the Author

Lover of books, coffee, and chocolate ice cream!

Ivy lives a blessed life, surrounded by her two most important men, her husband, and son and also the fictional characters in her head that can't seem to shut up. Books and romance are her passion. A strong believer in happy endings and that love will always prevail in the end.

Both in life and in fiction.

Printed in Poland
by Amazon Fulfillment
Poland Sp. z o.o., Wrocław

89773135R00265